A FLAME TREE
BOOK OF HORROR

AFTER
SUNDOWN

An Anthology of New Short Stories

Edited by Mark Morris

This is a **FLAME TREE PRESS** book

FLAME TREE PRESS
6 Melbray Mews, London, SW6 3NS, UK
flametreepress.com

US sales, distribution and warehouse:
Simon & Schuster
simonandschuster.biz

UK distribution and warehouse:
Marston Book Services Ltd
marston.co.uk

Thanks to the Flame Tree Press team, including:
Taylor Bentley, Frances Bodiam, Federica Ciaravella, Don D'Auria,
Chris Herbert, Josie Karani, Molly Rosevear, Will Rough, Mike Spender,
Cat Taylor, Maria Tissot, Nick Wells, Gillian Whitaker.

The cover is created by Flame Tree Studio with
thanks to Nik Keevil and Shutterstock.com.
The font families used are Avenir and Bembo.

Flame Tree Press is an imprint of Flame Tree Publishing Ltd
flametreepublishing.com

A copy of the CIP data for this book is available from the British Library
and the Library of Congress.

HB ISBN: 978-1-78758-457-0
US PB ISBN: 978-1-78758-455-6
UK PB ISBN: 978-1-78758-456-3
ebook ISBN: 978-1-78758-459-4

Printed and bound in Great Britain by Clays Ltd, Elcograf S.p.A.

A FLAME TREE
BOOK OF HORROR

AFTER
SUNDOWN

An Anthology of New Short Stories

Edited by Mark Morris

FLAME TREE PRESS
London & New York

CONTENTS

INTRODUCTION

Welcome to *After Sundown*, the first volume in what will hopefully be an annual, non-themed horror anthology series from Flame Tree Press.

The premise for *After Sundown* is simple. As editor, my brief was to produce an anthology of twenty stories, sixteen of which would be commissioned from some of the top names writing in the genre today, and the other four of which would be selected via a two-week submissions window that would be open to everybody, with the aim being not only to discover new talent, but also to give that talent the opportunity to share anthology space with the genre's best.

As it turned out, the response to the submissions window was phenomenal, and during those two weeks in October literally hundreds of stories poured into the Flame Tree inbox. It was a mammoth job sifting through them all, but as you'll see when you read this collection, the four tales that eventually topped the pile turned out to be absolute gems.

What impressed me about them, and indeed, what is characteristic of all the stories in this book, was their assuredness, their originality, and their ability to grip the reader from the get-go. In my view horror is a genre with extremely wide – indeed, almost limitless – parameters, and as such the tales contained herein vary wildly in theme and subject matter, and thus provide a perfect showcase for the sheer scope and inventiveness that the field has to offer.

There are Victorian tales here; there are contemporary tales; there are near-future tales, in which the very prescient threat of environmental collapse lurks in the background. There are supernatural and non-supernatural stories; there are stories of ancient magic and dark mysticism; there are stories that defy categorisation.

What all of these stories *do* share, though, is a sense of disquiet, of unease; a sense of *the other.* They get under your skin, these twenty little nuggets of dread. And they stay there. And they *itch.*
Oh, how they itch!

Mark Morris
28 February 2020

BUTTERFLY ISLAND

C.J. Tudor

Almost every bad plan is hatched over a few beers in a bar. The end of the world won't finally arrive with a bang or a whimper. It will start with the words: '*Hey – y'know what would be a really great idea?*' slurred over a bottle of Estrella.

I stare at Bill. I like Bill, as much as I like anyone. My affection is undoubtedly heightened by his ready supply of weed and loose attachment to his cash. That's why I don't punch him in the face. I say, "I need to go for a piss."

"No, wait." Bill leans forward. "Hear me out, man."

I don't want to hear Bill out. As I said, I like Bill but he's a fucking moron. He's Australian for a start, which has nothing to do with his intelligence, but does make his stupidity harder to bear. I'd put it down to youth but it's hard to tell Bill's age. His face is so weathered by years of sun and sleeping on beaches that he could be anywhere from twenty-five to fifty-five.

But then, to be fair, we're all a fairly motley crew at this beach bar. At first glance, you might almost mistake us for travellers backpacking our way around the world. That is, if the world still existed in any recognisable form. Look closer and you might notice the ragged, mismatched clothing. The worn rucksacks. The guns and knives people keep quite openly these days.

What we really are is survivors. A rag-tag bunch of nomads who happened to be in the right place at the right time. Or perhaps, more accurately, to *not* be in the wrong place at the wrong time. Killing our days with tequila and Thai noodles. Wondering when *here* will be the wrong place and where the hell there is left to go.

"This is the real deal," Bill says.

"Heard that before."

"You ever read *The Beach*, man?"

"Yeah. Long time ago. From memory, it didn't end so well."

"Yeah, but this is different. Look around. Look at what's happening. What have we got to lose? And what if what the dude says is true?"

"Big if. Huge. Fucking colossal."

"But if?"

He waggles his eyebrows at me. I still don't punch him. My restraint is admirable.

"I heard some mega-rich inventor bought the island years ago and turned it into a nature sanctuary," I say.

"*Butterflies*, man."

"What?"

"A butterfly sanctuary. Hence the name. Butterfly Island."

I stare at him in shock. Bill knows the word 'hence'. Maybe I misjudged him.

"Okay. Butterflies. My point is that I read he went to a lot of trouble to keep people like us away."

"But the dude's dead and who gives a fuck about butterflies now, right?"

"True. But I do give a fuck about armed guards."

"Man, we're on the edge of the fucking apocalypse. Who's gonna waste their time guarding butterflies on an empty fucking island."

He has a point.

"How will we get there?"

"I know a man."

Other famous last words. I know a man. There is always a man. I fully believe that our current apocalypse began because someone knew a man. Who had a really great idea over a bottle of Estrella.

I push my chair back.

"I'll think about it."

I'm halfway to the toilets (a generous description of a lean-to with a hole in the floor) and not thinking about it, when two figures step out of the gloom.

I also know a man. Unfortunately, he is not the sort of man you have beers with. He is the sort of man who smashes a beer bottle on your head and uses the shards of broken glass to scoop out your eyeballs. Actually, that's wrong. He's the sort of man who pays people like these two goons to do the eyeball scooping.

"Well, look who it is." Goon 1 smiles at me.

"I'll get the cash."

"I thought you had it."

"Soon. I promise."

"The sea is full of floaters who made promises."

"I mean it."

"Good."

He nods at Goon 2.

Goon 2 grabs my head and smashes my face into the wall. I taste plaster and feel a tooth crack. Pain shoots up my jaw. Goon 2 yanks my head back and smashes it into the wall again. This time I feel the tooth give and my vision blurs. Goon 2 lets me go and I slide down the wall to the dirty floor.

"No more chances."

A boot connects with my ribs. I scream and curl into a ball.

"Please," I beg. "Please, no more."

"Fucking pathetic," I hear Goon 2 mutter.

I shove my hand into my boot and pull out my gun. I swivel and shoot Goon 2 in the kneecap. He howls and hits the floor next to me. I shoot him in the face. Goon 1 has his gun out but I'm faster. I shoot him twice in the stomach and watch with satisfaction as blood splatters the wall behind him and he crashes heavily down on top of Goon 2.

I push myself to my feet. I still need a piss. I walk into the toilet, relieve myself and splash some water on my face. Then I step over the dead goons and walk back into the bar.

No one has moved, or even looked up in curiosity. That's the way we roll nowadays. Bill is skinning up. He glances at me with mild interest. "What happened to your face?"

I spit the remains of my tooth into the overflowing ashtray.

"So, when do we go to Butterfly Island?"

★　★　★

The sun peers over the horizon. Thirteen of us are spread between two ramshackle-looking boats, not including the drunken locals everyone is over-confidently referring to as 'captains'. A baker's dozen. Unlucky thirteen. I don't believe in fate or superstition. I do believe in drunken morons crashing boats into rocks.

The smaller boat to my right is filled with a group of five men and women in their twenties who already look trashed at just gone 4:00 a.m. Or maybe they're still trashed from the previous night. I wonder where Bill found these people. If this is the best we can do, I think we might as well concede defeat – and superior intelligence – to the cockroaches.

On our boat we have Bill (the man himself) and another Aussie, Olly, a wild-eyed guy with a pelmet of tattoos, a bandana and a hunting knife strapped around his waist, who I keep expecting to say: '*You don't know, man. You weren't there.*' Next to him are a middle-aged couple in matching khaki shorts, black vests and sturdy walking boots, called Harold and Hilda. Probably. I don't actually know their names. They just look like a Harold and Hilda. Opposite them is an older dude with a shorn head and long grey beard who is calmly reading an old paperback of *The Stand*. Less fiction, more like a survival manual these days. Finally, only just embarking, are a muscular black woman with dreadlocks piled on top of her head and...

I turn to Bill. "What the fuck is this?"

"What?"

I point at the young girl, climbing on board with the woman.

"What's a kid doing here?"

"Well, her mum couldn't leave her behind."

"This is not a fucking trip to Legoland."

"Lego what?"

"Fuck's sake."

"You have a problem?"

The dreadlocked woman eyes me coldly.

"I just don't think this is a trip for a kid."

"I'm not a kid," the kid says. "I'm twelve."

"I've got T-shirts older than you."

She looks me up and down. "I can see that."

I address the woman. "Your daughter—"

"She's not my daughter. Her parents are dead. We travel together or not at all."

"Man, we need her," Bill whispers.

"Why?"

"She's a doctor. If anyone gets sick?"

"You did check people out?"

"I don't mean that kind of sick, man. I mean, normal sick."

He does have a point. I glare at the woman and girl and take out my cigarettes.

"I'm Alison," the woman says, smiling faux-politely.

"Good for you."

She crosses her legs. "Well, aren't you a treat."

I ignore her and light a cigarette.

There's a judder as the 'captain' starts the engine. We're off. The crowd in the second boat whoop. I blow out smoke and wonder if having my eyeballs scooped out with shards of glass might actually be preferable. But it's too late now.

It's always too late now.

*   *   *

Forty minutes later and the island draws into view. A jagged dark shape in the distance. It's mountainous, encircled by jungle and wide stretches of white sand. Years ago, back when I was in my late teens, it used to be a popular destination for backpackers. You could catch a skipper from the main island and stop over for a night or two, sleeping on the beach. They tried to keep it unspoilt. But inevitably, it caved to commercialism. A beach bar sprang up. Then, wooden huts were built for those who didn't like roughing it in sleeping bags on the sand.

At some point the crazy billionaire guy bought it and no one was allowed back on. But this was around the time a lot of shit was going on in the world, so my memory is vague, what with all the bombing, chemical weapons and new terrorist groups multiplying faster than the recently revived Ebola virus.

Good times.

I watch as the island grows bigger and more distinct, and the sea, which was a little choppy partway across, begins to calm, becoming more transparent. I can see several dark shapes floating in the water, just beneath the surface. Not corals. Not sea creatures. One of the shapes briefly breaks the water to our right. Round with spiked protuberances. And then I realise. Fuck.

"Cut the engine!" I shout.

El Capitan turns. "Khuṇ phūd xarị?"

"Mines. Cut the fucking engine now and drop the anchor."

His eyes widen. But he quickly does what I say.

"Did you say mines?" Alison says.

"Look in the water," I say, pointing at the round spiky objects all round us.

"Fuck, man," Bill mutters. "They're fucking everywhere."

I glance across at the other boat. Some distance away and a little ahead of us. One of the girls is trailing her hand in the water, centimetres away from one of the mines. I open my mouth to yell a warning.

Too late.

Kaboom! She explodes. Along with the boat and the rest of its passengers. One minute there. The next, gone in a flash of orange and a deafening blast wave. Flesh, limbs and shrapnel fly into the air and rain back down on us.

"Duck!" I scream and throw myself down into the bottom of the hull, grabbing hold of the side as the aftershock hits. The boat rocks violently. Water crashes over the stern. I feel something smack into my head and realise it's someone's shoe, still attached to their foot. I fling it into the water.

Someone is screaming. The boat rises and falls, straining against the anchor. I remain splayed on the wet hull floor. The rocking calms. Water stops slopping over the sides. We're still afloat. Slowly, I sit up. The remains of the other boat and its occupants are spread out over the water, which is murky with blood and fuel; bits of bodies, wood, metal, rucksacks.

I glare at Bill who is curled up next to me.

"*Who's going to waste time guarding a fucking deserted island?*"

He looks shamefaced. "I didn't know, man. I didn't know there would be fucking mines."

I want to punch him until his eyeballs pop out, but I can't afford to waste the time or energy.

"Is everyone okay?" Bearded Dude asks.

"We're fine," Alison says, helping the girl to sit up.

"They exploded. They just exploded," Hilda cries hysterically to her husband. "Why would they do that. Why?"

I'm not quite sure if she's questioning why someone would drop mines, or why people would explode. Either seems a moot point.

Our captain is gabbling in Thai.

"No," I say. "Don't touch the fucking engine."

"How are we going to get to the island?" Alison asks.

"We can't," Hilda says. "We have to go back."

"No," I say.

"No?"

"Look around. There are as many mines behind us as in front. We just got lucky."

"Well, we have to try," Harold says. "What else can we do?"

"We could swim, man." This from Olly.

"Swim?" Harold says. "Are you insane?"

Possibly, I think, but he might be smarter than his bandana and tattoos suggest.

"We could do it," I say. "There's plenty of space between the mines for bodies. Just not boats."

"But what about all of our stuff?" Hilda asks. "Clothes, food, water, phones."

"I doubt there's any electricity on the island, so your phone is going to be dead by dawn anyway."

Plus, who are we going to call, I think. If any of us had friends or family, we wouldn't be here.

"There's supposed to be a stream," Bearded Dude pipes up. "For fresh water. And maybe there's food left in the beach bar."

"If not, we can fish and hunt." Olly grins and I reinstate my previous opinion of him as a survivalist wanker.

"You're all crazy." Harold shakes his head.

"Your call," Bearded Dude says calmly, taking off his flip-flops and sticking his gun into the waistband of his shorts. I follow suit. Bill and Olly chuck off their trainers. Alison looks at the girl.

"You think you can swim it?"

"No problem."

Harold and Hilda exchange glances.

"I can't swim," Hilda says.

Jesus fuck.

"We're going back," Harold says. "He can take us." He turns to El

Capitan and pulls out his wallet.

No, I think. Don't do this.

"We have money. See. Plenty money."

He smiles hopefully, waving notes. El Capitan smiles back, takes them and shoves them in his pocket.

"Khup Kun Krap."

Then he reaches down beneath the wheel and pulls out a semi-automatic gun.

"Get off my boat."

"What? But—"

"Get the fuck off, all of you. Now."

We don't wait to ask about the sudden improvement in his English. One by one we all climb over the side and lower ourselves into the water.

"But I gave you money," Harold protests.

El Capitan jabs him in the chest with the gun. Harold falls back into the water with a splash.

Hilda yelps. "Please. Please. I can't swim. I'll drown. I can't go in there."

El Capitan nods. "Okay. No swimming."

He blasts her with a small spray of bullets. Her body jerks and twitches, spitting red, and then crumples into the boat.

"Linda!" Harold screams.

I was close with the name.

The engine splutters into life and the boat reverses back in a small white wave.

"*Linda!*"

"She's dead," I say. "Swim."

I strike out and follow the others, not waiting to see if he heeds my advice. We all choose a sedate breaststroke, weaving carefully between the mines. Bearded Dude reaches the shore first and walks, dripping, up the beach. Alison and the girl are next. My feet have just touched the sandy seabed when I hear the boom.

I turn. A small mushroom of orange and grey rises up against the horizon.

"Shit." Bill spits out water. "You were right about the mines."

I stare at the smoke.

"Yeah."

I don't say that the explosion is too far out at sea. El Capitan missed the mines.

Something else blew the boat up.

*　　★　　★*

We dry our clothes on logs that line the edge of the beach. I shake water out of my gun and slip it back into the waistband of my shorts. Bearded Dude has taken a battered phone out of his pocket and is pressing buttons and frowning. I haven't had a phone for years. Like I said, no one to call.

We've come ashore on a wide stretch of white sand. To our right, further down the beach, I can see the bar, now boarded up. The huts are further into the jungle.

"So," Alison says. "I suggest our first job should be to check out the bar and see if there are any usable supplies, bottled water, dried food and so on."

"Actually," Bearded Dude says, "our first job should be to introduce ourselves. I'm Ray."

"Alison," she says. "And this is Millie."

"Bill, man," Bill offers.

"Olly," Olly says, sharpening his knife on the log.

Harold is sat on the other end of it, huddled into himself. He hasn't taken his wet clothes off and is shivering, despite the heat of the mid-morning sun. Shock. Trauma. Or in other words, a fucking burden we do not need right now.

I realise people's attention has shifted to me. "The bar, did you say?" I start to walk across the beach.

"Dick," I hear Alison mutter.

Bill jogs to catch up with me. "Man, this is some trip."

"Yeah. I've watched a boatload of people get blown to smithereens and now I'm marooned on a fucking island, possibly facing death by starvation or dehydration. Some trip."

"Man, you really are a dick sometimes."

"I know."

I glance behind us. Alison is walking side by side with Ray and Millie. I can't see Olly.

"Where's Olly?"

"Oh. I think he went to check out the huts."

And pretend he's Rambo.

We reach the bar. A few chairs are still rotting outside. A faded and weather-beaten sign on the front offers a selection of beers and cocktails, crisps, noodles and chocolate.

"Guess this place didn't stay unspoilt for long," Alison says.

"Yeah." I smile thinly. "How d'you like it now?"

She turns and kicks the door in. "I'm reserving judgement."

I stare after her. Ray glances at me and chuckles. "I like her."

It's dim in the shack, sunlight filtering in through gaps in the roof and cracks in the walls. I blink, letting my eyes adjust. My nose is already on the case. Something smells off, rotten. Maybe food gone bad.

Tables and chairs have been piled up on one side of the small room. Directly in front of us is the counter. Glass-fronted refrigerators are lined up behind it, turned off, but still half-full of beer, water and soft drinks. So, we won't die of dehydration right away. And we can also get drunk.

"We should check out back for food," Ray says.

He disappears into the storeroom with Alison. Millie walks over to the fridges and takes out a bottle of water. She checks the date, shrugs and uncaps it, taking a swig.

"Help yourself, why don't you?" I say.

She smiles at me, lifts the bottle again and takes several bigger gulps, almost draining it. She wipes her lips. "Thanks. I will."

I'm almost starting to like the kid. I turn and look around the rest of the room. The smell is still bothering me. I eye the stacked tables and chairs and walk over to them. Something on the wall catches my eye. A motley montage of blues and greens. Some kind of mural, or bits of paper pinned to the wall? I move closer and realise that it's neither. It's butterflies. Huge blue and green coloured butterflies. Dozens of them. Dead. Nailed to the wall by their wings or through their large furry bodies.

"What the fuck is that, man?" Bill is at my shoulder, staring at the wall of crucified butterflies.

"Butterflies."

"I thought this was a sanctuary."

"Looks like someone found another way of saving them."

There's a thud from behind us as Alison and Ray walk out from the storeroom and dump a couple of large boxes on the counter.

"There's packs of crisps, dried noodles, sauces, chocolate. Plus, matches and firelighters. Enough to keep us going for a while," Alison announces.

I sniff again. "Does anyone else smell that?"

Millie walks over and stands next to me. "Smells like when our cat crawled under the porch to die and we didn't find her for two weeks."

I stare at her again. This twelve-year-old is pretty hardcore. And she's right. Something is dead here and not just the butterflies.

I reach for the chairs and start unstacking them and moving them to one side.

"What are you doing?" Alison asks.

"I'm expecting a busy day with customers."

"Are you ever not a dick?"

"Rarely."

I move more of the chairs and slide aside the tables. There's another door behind them. What used to be a toilet, I would guess. The smell is stronger here. I yank it open.

"Fuck!" Bill turns and retches.

"Shit," Millie whispers.

Alison rushes over and pulls the girl back.

A body, or what remains of it, has been nailed to the door. Just like the butterflies nailed to the wall. It's been here a while. The skin has mostly rotted away, just a few stringy tendrils of muscle stubbornly clinging to bone. Straggly clumps of dark hair sprout from a yellowed skull. The figure is dressed in a shirt and shorts, also rotted and ragged. I'd hazard a guess and say it's a man.

"What d'you think happened to him?" Ray asks.

"Well, he didn't nail himself to a door."

"So, there's someone else on the island?"

"And he, or she, is a killer."

He frowns. "We should check on the others."

★　　★　　★

Harold is not on his log. I glance towards the sea, half-hoping to see his lifeless body floating on the waves. But no. Damn.

"We need to go check the huts."

The jungle is dense, the undergrowth beneath our bare feet littered with sharp bits of twig and thorns, and I'm only too aware of the potential for spiders or snakes. Above us, I spot the occasional flutter of bluey-green wings. Butterflies. I think again about the insects nailed to the wall. Weird shit.

The huts are set in a small clearing. Half a dozen of them. Arranged around a central fire pit that must have once been used for barbeques.

Whatever has been cooking on it more recently certainly isn't sausages or burgers.

"Well, this just gets better and better," Alison says.

"Are those *skulls*?" Millie asks.

They are. Five or six, along with an assortment of jumbled blackened bones. We walk closer. I peer down into the pit. Then I pick up a stick and poke at the charred bones.

"Looks like our killer has been busy," Ray remarks.

I shake my head. "A lone killer couldn't possibly kill so many people at once."

"Depends on how big his gun is."

Alison crouches down and squints at the bones. "It looks like these bodies have been burned at different times."

"So, he kills everyone, then burns them one by one."

It still feels wrong to me. I'm pondering on it when Bill shouts, "Olly! Man. What happened?"

We all turn. Olly staggers down the steps from one of the huts. His right arm is bandaged with his torn-up vest but it's still bleeding profusely.

"Someone shot at me," he says. "Missed. No biggie."

No biggie. Ray and I snatch our own weapons out of our waistbands and point them at the surrounding jungle suspiciously. None of us heard a gunshot. A silencer, maybe?

"You think they're still out there?" Ray asks.

Olly shakes his head. "I don't think so. Or they'd have finished me off, right?"

Rambo makes a good point.

"We should get out of here," I say. "Random shooters and burnt bodies aren't making me feel all homely."

"That's not all," Olly says.

I look at him.

He grins. "You should see what's out back."

*　　*　　*

The cross is staked firmly into the ground, in a small clearing behind the huts. The body lashed to it has been here some time, like the guy in the bar. All the flesh has gone. Stripped right back to the bone, which gleams in the dappled sunlight.

"This dude really pissed someone off," Bill says.

"It's not a dude," Alison says. "It's a woman. A young woman I'd say, from the skeleton."

"You think she was killed and strapped up here?" Ray says. There's a note of hope in his voice and I get it, because the alternative is that she was strapped up here, maybe killed, maybe not. Maybe left to die or be tortured.

"Why would someone do that?" Millie says. "Why would they hang her up like this? For what?"

For what? And suddenly something clicks. I can see it all with absolute clarity.

"A sacrifice," I say.

"A what?"

"They weren't all killed together. They were killed one by one. Chosen. Hung out here."

"Man!" Bill says. "Wild imagination."

"No," Alison says slowly. "I think he's right."

"But a sacrifice to who or what?"

The fluttering in the trees has increased. I glance up. I can see more butterflies flying about now. My neck itches. A feeling of unease. The small patches of blue visible through the trees are starting to disappear. The jungle is darkening.

"I really think we should go."

"Me too," Alison says.

Millie nods. "This place gives me the creeps."

We start to move away.

Olly remains, standing next to the skeleton of the young woman.

"C'mon, it's only butterflies."

I glance back. A couple of butterflies have flown down and alighted on the skeleton. Two more perch on Olly.

"They like me."

It happens quickly. There's a rush like the wind and more blue and green bodies flutter gracefully down from the trees and land on Olly, predominantly on his right side. His injured arm. I see his face change, the smile morphing into a frown.

"Fuck, that's enough. Get off."

He shakes his arm. The fluttering increases.

"Man, they really do like him," Bill mutters.

"Ow, shit. That hurts."

More butterflies flock to him. I can barely see Olly now behind the frenzied fluttering of wings.

"Nooo. Aaagh. Get the fuck off. They're biting. They're fucking eating me. *Help!*"

"What the hell are they doing?" Ray asks.

I think about the staked body. The blood on Olly's arm. The frenzied beating of wings. It's quite simple.

"They're feeding," I say. "Now let's get the fuck out of here."

★   ★   ★

We run, crashing our way through the jungle, paying little attention to direction. Olly's screams seem to follow us, long after his torment is out of earshot. We should have shot him, I think. But then, we only have so many bullets.

Eventually, sweat streaming down our backs, feet scraped raw, the greenery thins. We burst out into open air. Grass. Blue sky. Lots of blue sky. Ahead of us, the land runs out abruptly and drops off into a steep ravine.

We all stop, bending over, gasping, catching our breath.

"Guess we can't go any further."

"Nope."

"What the hell happened back there?"

"Flesh-eating butterflies. The usual."

"But how?"

"Who the fuck knows? Chemicals. Pollution. Experiment gone wrong. When a crazed billionaire buys an island and seals it off, it's not usually to make fluffy toys."

"You sound like you know a lot about it."

"Nah, just watched a lot of James Bond as a kid."

"You don't happen to have a parachute stuffed up your butt to get us out of this?" Ray asks.

We look back at the jungle and then towards the cliff.

"Caught between a drop and a fucked place," Bill says.

Alison walks over to the edge and peers down.

"Maybe not. It's not so steep. I reckon we could—" She breaks off. "What the fuck."

"What?"

"There's something down there."

We all join her at the precipice. The drop makes me sway. And then I spot something, glinting at the bottom of the ravine. Something black and metallic with bent and twisted blades. The crumpled remains of a helicopter.

"Man," Bill hisses. "The dude was right."

"What dude?" Ray asks.

"The dude who said this island would make us rich."

"How is a crashed helicopter going to make us rich?" Millie asks.

"Story goes that a helicopter carrying a new vaccine, one that could immunise against the virus, crashed on some uninhabited island. The dude was sure it was Butterfly Island."

"A vaccine?" Alison says. "That could save millions of lives."

"Yeah." Bill nods. "And imagine how much someone will pay for it. I know a man—"

"What! You can't sell something like that. It needs to be delivered to an impartial health organisation."

"Who asked you, Mother Teresa?"

"We're talking about the future of mankind."

"And I'm talking about *my* future."

"Could you all shut up!" Millie glares at them. "First, we don't know if we can even reach the helicopter. Second, we don't know if the vaccine survived the crash, and third, we're stuck here on this island, remember?"

From the mouths of babes.

"And," I say, "we're stuck here with flesh-eating butterflies and at least one psychotic maniac running around sacrificing people. So perhaps we have more pressing concerns right now."

"Oh, I don't know."

We turn. Ray has taken a step back so that he stands behind our group. He is smiling and pointing his gun at us.

I shake my head. "Really?"

"What can I say? Good guys don't survive the apocalypse."

"Don't tell me – you heard about the helicopter too. You want to sell the vaccine for a load of cash, and you don't want to share?"

"Right and wrong. I heard about it, yeah. But my people don't want to sell the vaccine. They want to keep it for themselves."

"Why?"

"Imagine being immune from a virus killing millions. We'd be the most powerful people in the world. Invincible. Like Gods."

Alison eyes Ray coldly. "So how come 'your' people sent you out here alone. Or are you one of the dispensable Gods?"

He smiles at her. "Play nice. Maybe I'll let you be one of the chosen ones."

"I'd rather die."

"Fine."

He levels the gun at her.

"Wait." I hold my hands up. "Like Millie said, the vaccine is no good to anyone if we can't get off this island. We need to work together or we're all going to die here."

Ray's dark eyes meet mine. He reaches into his pocket and takes out the battered phone.

"I got people waiting. I send this text, they know it's done. They come and get me."

"And get blown up by the mines."

"Already told them to drop anchor further out. Just got to swim to meet them. Home and dry."

"Got it all planned out."

"Damn right."

He grins a crooked yellow grin. I see his thumb press send. There's a roar from behind us. Animalistic. Desperate. Olly charges out of the thicket of trees, arms flailing, still half-covered by butterflies. Most of his flesh has gone, eaten away to the muscle and tendon, one eye has popped out. His stomach cavity gapes. He shouldn't be standing. Yet he keeps going.

Ray shoots. Once, twice. Olly staggers but doesn't stop. I grab Alison and Millie and pull them out of the way. Olly barrels into Ray who clings to him like a desperate lover, but there's nothing he can do. Olly's momentum carries them off the cliff edge and down into the ravine. Ray's scream rises into the air along with the butterflies and then both drift away.

"Christ," Alison stares after them. "Fucking, fucking Christ!"

Millie wraps an arm around her waist, and they hug tightly. Bill looks at me.

"Man," he says, and opens his arms.

"Don't even fucking think about it."

"So, what do we do now?" Alison asks, looking at me.

"Well, we either chance the jungle or try our luck climbing down into the ravine. Either way, we'll probably die."

"Great."

"Plus, if what Ray says is true, there's another boat coming. And if Ray doesn't meet them—"

"You think they'll come ashore?"

"Maybe."

"And try to kill us."

"Probably."

"Oh, good."

"And we still have the problem of butterflies with the human-munchies and a crazed killer roaming the island."

"And Linda's husband is missing."

I'd forgotten about Harold. And I have a feeling that I really shouldn't have.

"So?" Bill asks. "What do we do, man?"

We fall into silence. I could really do with a cold Estrella.

I smile. "I've got a great idea…"

RESEARCH

Tim Lebbon

"This is science," Alan said. "Nothing more. There's no emotion in this. We can't dilute the experiment with feelings. And it's very simple science at that. Non-intrusive observation and data collection. Then at the end, we'll draw conclusions."

Sue was watching me as her husband spoke. Her gaze was analytical. She noted my widened eyes, perspiration levels, and the throbbing pulse at my neck. She waited until Alan had finished before taking a photograph of me. After checking the photo on her tablet she grunted softly and took another, then another, until she was satisfied.

"I'm sure you understand?" Alan asked, as if expecting a response. Even though the gag was tight in my mouth, I could have nodded, or answered with my eyes. I gave them nothing.

Sue tapped a comment into her tablet.

"It probably won't take long," Alan said, checking my bindings. They'd tied me in a small but comfortable armchair, my arms strapped tight against the arms, coils of rope around my chest and legs holding me still. "And we won't keep you this constrained past today. But you need to calm down before we can let you go. Accept what's happening. Maybe you can even play a willing part." He chuckled, glancing sidelong at his wife. She did not respond. "It's almost like a plot out of one of your books, yes?"

No, you stupid fuck, it isn't, and I'll never give you the satisfaction of thinking otherwise.

But as they finished securing me to the chair, and Sue took a few more observations, and Alan checked the small basement room to make sure it was safe for me – and, I assumed, safe for them as well – I realised he was right. This was very much like something I might write.

I wasn't in a very good place to appreciate the irony.

My head was still woolly from whatever they'd dropped into my food or drink. My mouth was dry, my limbs ached, and there was a throbbing pain behind my eyes. I had no idea what the drug might have been. I hated research, so avoided it at all costs. If one of my characters was drugged, I just stated that, without taking the time to Google what the drug might be, its effects, its sources and uses. It had never appeared to be a problem. I'd sold over seven million books worldwide.

One thing that had surprised me was my instant acceptance of the situation. There was no doubting, no belief that maybe I was dreaming. This was real. I'd always thought Alan and Sue were strange.

"We'll leave you to calm down," Alan said. "You need to get used to this. Just for a while, just for..." He trailed off, and I realised they hadn't yet decided how long they were going to hold me down here. *I'll be a good pet*, I thought, and I looked at Sue, her empty gaze as she observed every flutter of my eyes, every slight movement of my body.

She was enjoying this.

Despite their assurances, I feared I might be down here for a very long time.

★   ★   ★

They were watching me. There were two cameras fixed high in opposite corners of the room, cheap mail-order units probably linked by an app to Sue's tablet. People used them to keep watch on their pets while they were at work. I saw the cameras even before they left me alone, and when they went I closed my eyes for a while, breathing deeply, and tried to gather myself. It was difficult not to panic.

If they were going to kill me they'd have done it by now, I thought, but I knew that wasn't necessarily the case. If they killed me straightaway, there'd be no story, no experiment. This was, as Alan had told me, science.

I knew what they were doing.

I looked around the room, avoiding staring directly at the cameras. It was a very small basement, featureless, almost useless. Maybe ten feet square, the walls lined with old tongued and grooved timber boarding, with a few darker areas close to the floor that might have been rot caused by condensation or damp. The floor was rough concrete, and the ceiling was the naked underside of the flooring above, with joists and struts exposed. There was no decoration anywhere; even the timber panelling was unfinished. My chair was the only item of furniture. The steep wooden staircase leading up to the doorway into the house above had no handrail or risers, and I guessed Alan had lined this place and built the staircase himself. There was one light bulb fixed into the side of a floor joist, wire snaking through a hole directly above.

That was all. There was nothing else in this room. Only me. It was perfect for what they wanted, and I started thinking back, trying to locate the time and place when they might have decided to do this.

Doesn't matter. All that matters is that it's happening.

I had a book deadline in six weeks. I'd almost finished the first draft of my fourteenth novel, and I believed it was the best I'd written. I hardly ever left my house this close to the end, writing for ten hours each day, eager to reach the finishing line so I could find out what happened. I remembered telling Sue and Alan about my working methods, and their surprise that I never planned in great detail. The climax was often as much of a surprise to me as I hoped it would be for the readers.

They were obviously intricate planners. They probably found that side of my process confusing, even shocking.

It's Alan's 60th, Sue's text had read. *Come along for a couple of drinks.* She'd guilted me into it. I'd backed out of attending a party they'd thrown at our local pub the previous weekend, claiming that I couldn't afford my concentration on the novel to be disturbed by an evening of drinking and socialising. It hadn't been a lie, but it had been an excuse. I liked their occasional company, but over the past few years I'd been less and less keen on larger groups. Some people called me a loner, like it was a bad thing.

I had maybe five thousand words to write until the book was done. A good three or four days' work. I was itching to reach the end, and now...

Now, maybe I never would.

I closed my eyes again as the panic began to build. There was still time to let me go and call this a prank. Alan had been a travelling musician for some years, and he'd told me about some of his antics on tour as a session guitarist with various bands. Sue was a nurse and something of a free spirit. One drunken evening Alan told me they'd used to swing, but hadn't done so since moving here a few years before. I believed it had been the planting of a seed, if not an actual invitation. He'd not mentioned it since.

They were extroverts, an unusual couple with interesting stories to tell. This could be another of their stories, even now, even after drugging me and tying me up. Nothing more dangerous or deadly. If they were filming this instead of just watching, perhaps they'd play it some nights after too much drink, laugh and joke about the time they made their local novelist friend believe they'd kidnapped him and kept him prisoner in their basement so that they could see...

Sue's eyes, I thought. There had been no humour there. If this was a joke, however ill conceived, I didn't think she'd have been able to make herself seem so serious.

I needed the bathroom. I looked at one of the cameras, then twisted to look at the other. They'd have thought of that, surely? They wouldn't allow me to sit here in my own filth.

I struggled against the bonds. The ropes were expertly tied, with tea towels laid across my arms and legs so they didn't cut into my flesh.

I'd intended coming to their house for three or four hours, then going home and making notes on the final part of my novel. Sometimes alcohol greased the wheels of my imagination, and though I could never actually write while under the influence, ideas often came freer and more fully formed. Maybe it was my body relaxing while my mind was set free. Maybe it was something else. Whatever worked for my writing, I didn't analyse it. I was afraid that thinking about it too much would break it.

Alan and Sue were thinking about it. Perhaps too much. Perhaps enough to break me.

I heard the door open thirty minutes, an hour, or three hours later, and when I saw Sue descending with a bucket in one hand and a roll of toilet paper in the other, I knew this was no sick joke. It was, as Alan had said, science.

★   ★   ★

"We had a dog called Skittle when I was a kid. My dad always liked telling me we had a wolf in the house, as if that would scare me. But I just thought it was cool. Who wouldn't want a wolf living in their house?"

Sue looked at me for so long that I raised my eyebrows and shrugged. Maybe yes, maybe no. Whatever, it seemed to satisfy her. She tapped her tablet and went on.

"I used to think my dad was cruel, but I've come to see that he was just curious. He wanted to know things. Maybe some of what he did to discover those things was cruel, but he never saw it that way, and I don't either." She was sitting on the floor in front of my armchair, back against the wall. By my estimation I'd been down here for three days. There was no daylight, no clock, but they'd turned the light off for three long periods, and during the day I could hear sounds from upstairs – a radio playing when Alan and Sue rose, cooking noises from the kitchen, the distant sounds of traffic. Later, a TV.

Three days. *I should have finished the novel by now.* They kept my hands tied to the chair's arms, except when they released me so I could use the toilet. They both stepped back for this, holding broom handles with carving knives taped to the ends. They never said anything, but the threat was implied. *Try anything stupid and we'll stab you.*

Three days.

"One day he tied up Skittle and kept her like that for six days. Didn't feed her, only gave her a little bit of water. He wanted to see what she'd do. She barked for a while, then whined a lot, but she still slept through the nights in our back garden. When he finally let her go he dashed back indoors and closed the door, because Skittle was a big dog and he was worried she might attack him, maybe try to eat him. But she didn't. She could hardly walk by then, but she made it over to our bird feeder, knocked one of the nut cages down, and started chewing at the metal to get to the nuts inside. When my father went out, Skittle came up to him and curled herself around his legs, whining. She even went onto her back for a tummy tickle. Isn't that odd?"

I waited for Sue to finish the story. I wanted to know what had happened to Skittle, partly because I liked dogs and found the whole tale unbearably cruel, but mainly because I didn't like a story without an ending.

Like my novel, I thought. *A hundred thousand words without an ending, and I should have written it by now. If only they'd give me a pen. Some paper. Half an hour untied.*

Sue did not finish the story. She tapped some more information into her tablet, then stood and left. As the door closed behind her the light above me flickered out.

Maybe it was night, and time to sleep.

I knew where I was in the novel, but I could not finish it in my head. Ideas swirled and collided, scenes coalesced, but the telling of my story required writing. Once written, it was told. Otherwise it was just building in my head, scenes and ideas backed up awaiting release. It wasn't about the long period of taking notes and planning, or the stretch of time from publication onwards. For me, letting a story out of my head and getting it down on paper, or onto my screen, was the purest form of storytelling. Before that it was an idea, and after that it belonged to someone else. At the moment of telling, the story was mine.

This was one I needed to finish telling.

I drifted towards uncomfortable sleep, and as I did so I remembered with startling clarity the moment when this situation was seeded. My eyes snapped open again in the darkness, and I realised it wasn't quite pitch black. A weak light bled under the door from above. That would be their kitchen, and that was where we'd been standing.

"But you seem so *grounded*," Sue had said. This was maybe a year before. We'd been casual friends for a while, sometimes meeting in the local pub for a few Friday night drinks, occasionally going to each other's houses. Alan had gone to the bathroom, and she was pouring us all a glass of wine. "I mean, so normal. And yet, all those things in your head."

"So did you ever read anything?" I asked. I'd given them a couple of my books which Alan had consumed. For some reason I'd never found out whether Sue had read them.

"Not my bag, baby," she said, chuckling. "I prefer non-fiction." She handed me a glass, and we stood against opposite worktops, smiling. It was a moment of comfortable silence. I heard the flush from upstairs, and Sue glanced at the open door out into the hallway. I thought at that moment, *She's going to suggest something awkward.* Alan had already told me about their swinging habits in the previous town they'd lived in. My wife had left me four years before, and they both knew that.

I honestly hadn't known what my response might be. But what she said next was something very different.

"All those sick ideas. All that nastiness and crime, gory murder and mutilation. All in your head."

"Actually, *out* of my head," I said. "I get it all out on the page. I guess that's why I'm pretty laid back and level headed." I laughed, and she laughed along with me.

"I wonder what you'd be like if you weren't able to let it all out?"

"Something I hope I'll never have to discover," I said, and then Alan had entered the room, and we took the wine through to their lounge, and I remembered little else from that evening.

That was it, I thought. *That single moment. That one comment.* And now Alan and Sue – but mainly, I thought, Sue – were going to find out just what would happen if I wasn't able to write. All that nastiness. All that murder and horror.

I blinked at the shadows and tried to assess how much of my writing was more than just storytelling. How much of it was essential? How much was the venting of pressure, the bleeding away of a darkness seeded in my soul?

Bullshit, I thought. *It's work, that's all. It's what I do.*

But I had never believed that, and it wasn't the discomfort that kept me awake for hours that night, staring into shadows and listening to the silence.

★   ★   ★

On day four or five they let me get up from the chair. Alan had to help me stand, and Sue leaned over the back of the chair and pushed against my shoulders. My legs felt tingly and numb. They'd let me slide off the chair to use the bucket, but until now I'd been put straight back into position, tied and gagged.

I was readying a plan to escape. Being good, letting them do this without striking out at them, was a big part of it.

"You're standing okay?" Alan said. "Not going to fall over?"

I shook my head.

"Okay, then." He caught Sue's eye over my shoulder. "Sue's got you some food. Same rule with the gag, yes?"

I nodded. Sue untied the gag and Alan pulled it from my mouth.

"New one next time," I said. "That one stinks and tastes bad."

"Of course," Alan said, throwing the piece of material at the stairs. It fell through into the shadows beyond. I heard it slither to the concrete. I hoped he'd forget about it.

Sue fed me while I was standing, and then I used the bucket. It was strange how fast I'd become used to going to the toilet while one or both of them watched.

"How are you feeling?" Sue asked.

"Are you joking?"

Neither of them responded. Alan held one of the broom spears, standing at the foot of the steep timber stairs. I thought if I could knock it aside and go at him, I might be able to push him into the wall. But Alan was bigger than me, and much fitter, and I hadn't been in a fight since I was thirteen. Considering everything I wrote about, it was almost comical that I didn't have the first clue about how to look after myself. *I let it all out on the page*, I thought, and my heart stuttered as I thought about the unfinished book sitting on my computer.

"We'll leave you untied for a while," Sue said. "We can see you on the cameras, and the door is always locked."

"It's still not too late," I said. "Let me out, we'll forget about it. Just a joke, right? Just one of those things." And I meant it. I was so desperate to get home that right then I would have happily welcomed freedom if it meant never talking about what had happened here. There were only a couple of people who might be missing me. My agent, perhaps, although she wasn't expecting the book for another few weeks. A friend in France I emailed once a week.

"You know this is no joke," Alan said. "You're sick. Filled with twisted ideas."

"You get it out on the page," Sue said, and smiled.

Who's sick? I was going to ask. *Who's twisted?* I kept quiet. Though I did little research, I knew that truly mad people rarely understood that they were mad. Antagonising them would ensure I ended up tied to the chair again. At least now I could walk, stretch, keep my muscles limber.

After only four or five days, I already felt like an old man.

★   ★   ★

On day seven or eight, I lost count. On day fourteen or sixteen, I started scratching lines on the timber staircase to count days and they tied me up again, switching the light on and off for random lengths of time to confuse me. Sometimes they left music on in the kitchen above, turned up loud so I couldn't sleep. They masked traffic noise from outside, and filled silence with sound and light so that I could not assess the time.

On day twenty, or maybe thirty, I started to cry and beg them to release me. They exchanged a knowing glance and left me alone, tied up and gagged, and sitting in my own filth.

More ways to drive me mad. This was science.

Tucked down the side of the seat cushion I kept the old gag that I'd retrieved, painstakingly, from beneath the staircase. I'd taken a risk, waiting for a moment when I believed one or both of them were out of the house, hoping that even if the cameras did record rather than observe, they'd not have time to watch all the footage.

The gag was a small hand towel. It was long enough to wrap around someone's neck. When the time came.

★   ★   ★

I wonder what you'd be like if you weren't able to let it all out?

I remembered Sue saying that, and as every lit or darkened stretch of time passed me by, I dwelled on the idea more and more. It was painful to do so because it was what they wanted, but it also bit at me, like a single invisible piranha darting in to nip away chunks of my skin and flesh. The idea began eating me whole. I'd always regarded myself as grounded and reasonable, fair and nice, but I'd never seriously attributed that level-headedness to the fact that I purged my demons on the page. That was a fanciful notion about writers, the same as going hungry in a garret feeding your creative muse. I'd been poor before my writing became successful, and I knew that being cold and hungry only went to fuck the muse over, not nurture it. Similarly, I'd always believed that I lived life as me whether I wrote or not. It was a hobby turned into a job, not a necessity. It was a form of therapy, perhaps. But it wasn't essential.

I'm going to bite her face off, I thought. *When she next leans in to wash my face with a damp flannel, I'll lurch up and chew off her nose.*

That wasn't me, before or after writing.

I'll choke him with the gag. Squeeze so tight that he turns blue and his eyeballs bulge and he pisses himself as he dies.

The unfinished book didn't matter.

Night and day swapped places, fast and slow, and with darkness and light I planned, and became disgusted and delighted with my daydreams of violent escape.

There was some routine, though it was irregular, and it didn't help me count the hours and days. They always came down together. Alan held the spear, Sue released my bonds and fed me. They both stepped back against the wall at the bottom of the staircase while I stretched and used the bucket. Sometimes they let me walk back and forth a little, but there was very little talking. Perhaps they thought that conversation might help me defuse whatever they thought was building inside me. *This is science*, Alan had said, and they treated it as such. I was an experiment. I wondered when they thought the results might begin to show themselves. After forty days? Sixty? A year?

People would be missing me by now. I had a few friends, but we rarely socialised at each other's houses. I saw some of them for a hike every few weeks up the local mountain, and it would probably take them some time before they even realised I wasn't there. It was my agent who'd be most concerned at unreturned phone calls and emails. I suspected it would be her who ended up calling the authorities. A search of my house. No signs of forced entry or struggle, no notes, my car still parked in the driveway. Mail piled behind the door. It was all so cliched. If I wrote it as a book, my agent would wrinkle her nose and say, *But it all feels so familiar.*

Only I could change the plot.

*   *   *

In the end, they failed. Part of me thinks they really wanted an explosive ending, one in which I escaped and beat them, maybe even murdered one of them, and then they could revel in their freaky, insane experiment. *Now we know what you're like when you can't let it all out on the page*, Sue would say, and they'd have their story. I could not see past such an ending. What happens next?

It didn't go that way. In the end it was all very mundane, an anticlimax that left them with their eyes wide open, surprise soaking in like water into dry wood.

Sue untied me. Alan stood back with the spear, but it had been sixty days, or eighty, and he wasn't expecting any trouble from me. He was on guard, but in reality his guard was down. Maybe he was thinking about what they'd be having for dinner, or musing on how they'd get rid of me when the time came. Part of me couldn't believe they hadn't planned for that, but there was an impulsiveness to them, too. They swing. They move. They kidnap a casual friend and keep him in their basement.

I turned to the corner where Sue had placed the bucket, then turned back and flicked the gag at Alan's eyes. I'd kept it clasped in my right hand for the past couple of hours, and it was damp and heavy with sweat. Its end snapped across his right eye, and in that moment of shock I stepped inside the stabbing radius of his spear, grabbed it with one hand, and slammed his head back against the wall. It wasn't a hard impact, but it was enough to stun him. I pushed past him to the first step, then turned to face them with the spear raised before me.

My legs were shaking. I was weak, dizzy from the rapid burst of energy and adrenaline, but this was my moment, and I could hardly believe how easy it had been.

Sue's eyes sparkled. She glanced at Alan. His right eye was closed, but his left was wide and staring at me, not with fear or surprise, but expectation.

"You're idiots," I said. I prodded forward with the spear and Alan flinched back, but Sue only watched the blade jab towards her husband. "Idiots. What you did to me, so unfair. So... inhumane."

"It's been seventy-eight days," Sue said. "How do you feel?"

I want to stab you in the eye, I thought. *I want to watch your brains leak from your skull.* But I smiled. "I feel free." I started backing up the steep stairs, very slowly because I didn't trust my strength. It was shocking how weak I'd become, but I was also driven by the sense of outside, the idea of an open space larger than ten feet square and seven feet high. I wanted distance and sky.

Alan took a step towards the bottom of the stairs and I paused, pressing myself against the side wall. If he came at me I'd have to be firm and ready to stab him. The idea was abhorrent, and rather than make me angry or determined, it just made me sad.

"There's a GoPro on the kitchen table," Alan said. "Will you wear it? When you go outside?"

I laughed. It was little more than a cackle in my pained throat, and it set me into a coughing fit that almost doubled me up. I panicked, afraid that they'd overpower me and imprison me again, and that would be the last chance I'd have to escape.

But they *wanted* me to escape. It was part of the experiment.

How come they're not afraid for themselves? I wondered. *I could just kill them now.* Perhaps that was a risk they'd been willing to take, or maybe they had intended to release me in a controlled way. Aim me, like a missile. Or a rabid dog.

I coughed another laugh.

"Sure," I said. "I'll put on the GoPro. Want me to email any footage to you?"

Alan blinked at me, communicating nothing. *Linked live to their fucking iPad*, I thought. My thoughts were mixed, confused, hysterical from my confinement and my sudden chance at freedom. I hoped that fresh air would blow away the collected cobwebs of over two months and sort my thoughts into some order.

I backed up the staircase until I pressed against the kitchen door. I'd watched them open and close it enough times to be able to locate the handle by touch, set among a mess of heavy locks and bolts. I'd always wondered why it was built to be locked from the inside, as well as from without. It didn't matter now.

The door drifted open and I backed out of that wretched basement for the first time in over two months. The air felt different – lighter, redolent of cooking and cleaning smells, and no longer heavy with hopelessness.

I'm out, I thought. As I kicked the door shut I heard the thud-thud of Alan or Sue running up the stairs, and I crouched, heart hammering, spear ready to jab out. *I'll just get them in the leg. Enough to stop them.*

The door was tugged shut from the other side, and I heard the hasty clank of two bolts slamming home, and the ker-clunk of the mortice lock turning. They'd locked themselves in the basement. Away from me. They were afraid of *me*.

I laughed again, and this time it sounded more genuine, less desperate and mad. It was a laugh of freedom, but also an understanding of how ridiculous this all was. How crazy.

I felt changed from my incarceration, but not in the way they thought. I felt level and fine. They'd fed me and watered me, and though weak in body, my mind was once again flowing and functioning.

I looked around the kitchen. There was a toolbox tucked under the small two-person table. I dragged it out and opened it, found a handful of nails and screws, and went about fixing the door into its frame from the outside. I turned the table on its side and screwed it across the doorway. Then I hauled the kitchen dresser across and pushed it in front of the door and table. Plates fell from the dresser and smashed on the floor. I liked the sounds of destruction. I'd heard little but my breathing and loud music for weeks.

"I'm going now!" I shouted. No reply from beyond the doorway. I imagined them listening, excited and nervous.

I plucked a chisel from the toolbox, knelt, and used it to make a coin-sized hole between two floorboards. Then I sat back, thinking.

They haven't changed me.

I found what I wanted just outside the back door and brought it inside.

I'm the same person I was two months ago, only…

More experienced.

I attached the hose to the cold tap in the kitchen sink and cut off a short length. The cut end I wedged between floorboards, aimed at the hole so that it couldn't be prodded away from below. Even if it was, I would take out some insurance.

I turned on both taps. Water from the hose splashed down into the basement, and I heard a startled cry. With the sink plugged and the overflow blocked with a chunk of soap, it soon spilled over the worktop and floor. The water flowed between floorboards and down into the basement.

I raided the fridge and sat at the kitchen table. I made sure the Go-Pro was aimed at me while I ate, hoping they were watching. Hoping they could see how normal I still was, and how in control. How nothing they'd done had changed me at all.

I ate for some time, and found a bottle of beer which I raised to the camera before drinking. There were a few thuds from below, a series of bangs against the door, and then a shout that was quickly stifled. Nothing else. Calculating how long it would take for the water to fill the basement was beyond me, so I simply sat and listened. I'd always loved the sound of running water, and I had plenty of time.

I decided that I was not going to finish the book I'd left behind. After all this, I had a new one to write.

There was no science in what I was doing. No emotion.

This was research.

SWANSKIN

Alison Littlewood

Later, it is not so much the attack that I see, again and again, in my mind, but what came after it.

The two of them were walking along the shore at evening, a distance ahead of me. The sky and sea were as grey as each other, and the air still had winter's cold nip, carrying now and then a scouring of sand into my face. The town was behind me, a pretty little spill of houses built into the side of a cliff, nothing but the sea in front of it and miles of flat brown land behind. Across the dunes, just ahead of the couple, was a quiet little river mouth, where swans gathered and dabbled for pondweed, no doubt dreaming their strange avian dreams of the north.

I could not make out their features, but I knew who they were. Horrocks, his very name meaning 'part of a ship', owned the largest fishing boat in the fleet; and Syl, his young wife, who walked a little straighter than he and stood a little taller. If I had not recognised her form I would have known her by her hair, which was more golden than the evening sun and rippled finer than the sea.

Horrocks was hunch-shouldered under the weight of a pack, his head turned to the sand, while Syl gazed upward, into the sky. And yet both of them stopped when a riotous clamour arose, seemingly from nowhere, a sound I could not place. It echoed from the dunes and at first I thought of machinery, coming from the town perhaps, though I had never heard such a thing before; and then the wings appeared, as if from out of the ground.

Suddenly they were everywhere, surrounding the two of them, flocking above their heads. The birds were dark against the sky, yet I knew them to be white, for I recognised their cruciform shapes, their chiselled heads, the long, graceful arch of their necks.

Horrocks stumbled. He raised one arm to fend them off as they fell upon him, beating and stabbing. Each one of them was wider than Syl was tall. I rubbed at my eyes, wondering if it was some illusion formed of the sand – swans, I knew, did not attack men, not like this, not all together. One at a time perhaps, if he strayed too close to its nest, and even then, I was certain the stories must be lies: that a swan's wing could break a man's leg; that they had once drowned a man at the edge of the sea.

Horrocks fell to his knees. The birds were shrieking in a kind of blood lust, the beating of their wings a tumult. I couldn't tell if Horrocks cried out; I couldn't see his face. He had blundered into the sea, I realised, though was now hidden by the chaos of feathers and flight.

I began to run towards them, even as I realised that his wife had not moved at all. Syl stood by, no doubt shocked into stillness, horrified; fear-frozen.

Horrocks pushed himself up from the water, roaring and choking the salt from his lungs. One moment the air was thick with plumage; and in the next the swans were gone, beating and creaking their way back towards the river.

All was suddenly quiet. I slowed a little, the sand making hard work of it, but they hadn't seen me; they didn't look at me all the time it was happening. I am uncertain if they ever knew I was there.

After the attack, Horrocks got to his knees and then his feet. His trousers were darkened with seawater, but he did not trouble about that. He did not pause to retrieve his pack from the waves. He half walked, half stumbled to where his wife still stood, tall and motionless. He stepped in front of her, straightening before striking her, hard, across her lips.

*   *   *

Unnatural, they say later, ensconced in their booths, pints frothing across the upturned barrels that pass for tables in the Anchor. *Uncanny. A freak.*

It is the same every night, at least when they are not at sea. The men of the town sail and fish and go home to hot meals and warm beds, but before they sleep they retire to the alehouse, spinning their yarns about the women who are trying to trap them. And yet tonight it is not the same, not quite. There is unease in their words and in their sidelong glances, which meet and slide away from each other.

Their words are cutting. They speak of the chatter of women, meaningless as the gabble of geese. They speak of the one thing they *are* good for, and spurt laughter before falling silent again, staring into their tankards.

They haven't yet said the word *witch*, but it isn't far behind *unnatural*. The air is thick with it, the echo of a thought that is louder than their obscenities, their laughter.

Soon I will go to sea. I shall be one of them – sitting at their table, talking as they do, flushed with drink and laughter. I was intended for a farmer, but the death of my parents ended that; now I live with a distant and ancient relative, a dry husk of a woman, in a tiny cottage nestled halfway up the cliff. The soft ploughed land of my childhood has become rock; the air I breathe has turned to salt.

I leave them, ducking out of the tavern in time to see a bevy of the town's women walking by, arm in arm. I stop and watch them go. Syl is at their centre, the tallest, though I can see little of her face; it is almost concealed by a dark hood. When she sees me, she passes a hand across her mouth, as if to conceal her swollen lips.

Contrary to the men's talk, they do not gabble. Indeed, they do not say a word. One of Syl's companions looks at me sidelong. She is softer made than Syl, though still tall, still elegant. I think I make out, as she goes, a single white feather caught in the soft curls of her hair.

★　　★　　★

At evening, we sit before the fire, my aging relative and I. She rocks in her chair, staring into the flames while my gaze is drawn, over and over, to the window. There is nothing out there but the dark. It is parcelled into tiny squares by the leaded glass.

"You begin to see, then," she says.

I turn to her. Each crease on her face bears its own deep shadow. Her eyes look rheumy, as if damp with tears.

"See what, Aunt?" I call her Aunt, but she is more distant than that in relation. Still, she has never blamed me for burdening her; she never reminds me of the thinness of our bond, that I am a stranger here.

She takes the pipe from between her lips, freeing a skein of mist scented of sandalwood and cloves.

"You'll know the truth soon enough." She gestures towards the window with the pipe's stem, just as a pale shape passes across the sky.

"The swans," she says. "They winter here. But here is not their home. That is what you sense, boy, when you look at them." She silences me with another wave of her pipe.

"Sometimes, a swan may shed her feathery skin. She casts it off and becomes a lovely maiden. And if a man should steal her skin – why, then she will stay, and keep her human shape, and be his wife, as long as her skin is kept from her. But sometimes, a whole flight of her sisters will come. They will try to free their sister and her swanskin."

Her eyes reflect the fire's gleam. "You should beware," she says. "Find a nice girl. A good girl. Not—" She spits, mutters something about *unnatural forms*.

I do not answer, am not certain how, and she takes to gazing once more before nodding in her chair. I do not wake her; I wish to keep to my own thoughts. Somehow, I never once doubt the truth of her words. I half close my eyes, picturing the massing of the swans, the way they swooped on Horrocks as he walked with his wife along the shore. I remember the way he struck her; I see again her grace as she touched her fingers to her lips.

Unnatural forms, my aunt had said, echoing the gossip at the Anchor. But she never did tell me which of their forms was unnatural: whether it was their human or bird shape that was to be feared.

*　　*　　*

The fishermen have sailed, the town left to the women, and to me. I wander the little streets between tall white houses, each set on their own angle, and try not to stare in at the windows. When I reach the largest, though, I cannot resist. I pass by it often and see Syl pacing the rooms, back and forth, restless, and I wonder: is she searching for her skin?

All know it when the boats return. The streets fill with boot steps and chatter, and I too throw on my coat and head down to the dock to help offload the catch. They have been absent, this time, four days. One more sailing and the eldest sea dog from Horrocks's boat, a fellow with half closed eyes and leathern skin, will be done; I am promised his place.

I heft crate after crate of still-squirming silver to the quayside, where the women wait with their curved knives, their trestle tables set out ready. Gulls circle overhead, wailing, ready to snatch whatever they can with bladed beaks. Most of the town is here, I realise: the grizzled men, the soft-skinned maids, though few children, unless it is only that I do not see them.

The women's movements are quick and sure as they grasp the slippery fish. Syl is among the rest. She guts them one by one, her hands gored and shining, and she cuts slivers from the edge of their flesh and swallows them whole. She catches me watching, freezes for a moment, gives a small nod in return for my smile.

Unnatural, they had said. My cheeks colour with shame at the memory of their words; the way they condemned her, forgetting, as perhaps her husband had himself, how he must have stolen her skin, kept it from her, made her what she is.

When the catch is done, the menfolk head up the narrow cobbled lane to the Anchor, but the women walk away, down to the shore. After a moment, I follow them. The sea has by now retreated, smudging the line where the earth meets the sky, and the beach seems a vast stretch of mud. They do not walk towards the brine, however, but to where the river meets the sea. They do not turn and I stand behind them as they look at the swans out on the water, gliding, their necks bent into hooks.

I cannot see the women's faces. I do not know if they are remembering or dreaming, or perhaps both.

After a time the swans beat their wings and skim along the surface, forming a noisy trailing procession before they lift from the water. Their flight is hard-won and the sound of their wings is like applause, as if they are glad to be in the air, rejoicing at their freedom. I wonder if they tell their own tales to each other – stories without words, warning of the wiles of man.

The swans circle around once more. The women exchange not a word, only watching them, tilting back their heads; then they hold out their hands. As I watch, the swans let fall their feathers: gifts for their skinless sisters.

★   ★   ★

The Anchor smells of burning. The air is acrid and dense and I almost don't go inside, but through the haze I hear the rumble of the men. I step across the threshold, blinking against the sting of it. I collect a tankard and the ale is mercifully cold at the back of my throat, though I still want to cough. No one else does, however, and I swallow it down. They are seated in their accustomed places, Horrocks at the centre, his eyes already glazed with liquor – or perhaps that too is from the smoke, which rises in front of him, obscuring his features. He tips a little of his ale onto the table, which extinguishes something with a hiss. He holds up what remains – a blackened quill, the filaments burned away, not a trace of white left.

They all laugh, turning to look at me, this newcomer in their midst, not yet certain if I will be a subject for further laughter or if I will swell its volume. I force a grin, wave my tankard in their direction.

"Sit, boy." Horrocks surprises me with his words, which fly from his mouth in a cloud of spittle. They move aside for me, scraping their stools across the floor. I sit between their bulky warm bodies.

"See this?" he throws down the quill onto the upturned barrel between us. Other burned feathers are scattered there, scarcely recognisable, the source of the stink. "Know what that means, boy?"

I don't know what I'm expected to say, so I simply shrug, then nod.

"You will." Horrocks grasps his crotch and makes a thrusting motion, and guffaws rise into the air.

I gulp at my drink. Then, buoyed by the ale or their sudden silence, I say, 'Where is it you keep the skins?"

Horrocks is suddenly motionless. All traces of humour are gone; his eyes are tiny points of light. They pierce the gloom – pierce me. "Be careful, boy."

The quiet stretches out. I'm not certain what it will become, but then the fellow at my side nudges me in the ribs. "I take mine to sea," he says. "Use it to line my hammock. Keeps me warm."

Glances flit around the group. They still aren't sure, but Horrocks's shoulders relax and amusement ripples between them.

"Feel this, lad." Another offers the edge of his jerkin to my fingers. I notice that its surface is pocked with little dimples. "Plucked and tanned," he says, and they roar. Strike their tankards against each other. Drink spills across the table.

"Buried," another mutters.

"Burned."

My smile fades. I sit in the midst of their noise, their movement. I have no words. I think of them sullying the pure white skins, the things they must have craved, once; loving and yet fearing them, coveting them even as they tear them to pieces. I stare down at the scorched feathers, abandoned now; in them the wrecked hopes of the women who had stood on the shore and snatched them from the sky.

Horrocks suddenly leans across the table, grasps my arm. His grip is hardened by years of working the wet ropes, hauling in the nets, the constant scrape of salt. "We saves 'em, boy," he says. "Never forget that. Not if you want to stay."

The others watch, intent on his words.

"We save them from the spell," he says. "Enchantment. The trap they're in. It's against nature. Remember that."

He waits for my nod before he releases me. I refrain from rubbing at my arm. I can still feel the bone beneath the skin, as if his fingers remain wrapped around it. Does he really believe he has freed them — saved them from what they are — from magic? Does he think he has remade them, shaped them as they could and should have been? And yet how he must value the memory of that magic: the grace of her, the sinuous form, her loveliness beneath the skin.

My thoughts are lost in their mirth, released once more in gulps of amber and guffaws. The volume of it gathers, a rising tide that carries everything with it, so that I only dimly hear it as he says, "A feather bed. I had it stitched inside, right at the centre. We sleep on it every night."

★   ★   ★

They are gathered in the street, just back from the quay, not far from where the Anchor hangs its old painted sign. It is not the day for market, or for sailing, or even for church, which anyway, few here trouble about. They are bending over an object made of wood. I cannot see or guess what it is but a great rustling and struggling comes from within, and they step back, snorting with laughter or mockery.

At last, I can see. The object is a wooden cage made of old crates and lobster pots, and inside is a folded, cramped, crushed creature. A golden beak, tipped with black, stabs at the bars. Momentarily it opens its mouth, revealing a long thin tongue as it hisses. Its feathers no longer appear white. They are damp, soiled, stained. I cannot make out its eyes against the dark sides of its skull.

Another ripple runs through the gathering as someone pokes a stick into the cage. The action is that of a child, but it is Horrocks; he turns, scans the crowd, and I see that Syl is standing there, at the back, looking on; seeing everything.

He nods, as if with satisfaction. Then he calls out, loud, so that everyone can hear.

"A witch." The word, spoken at last, cannot be contained. It runs about the street, touching all, lingering on their lips as they echo it.

"This creature would have beguiled a man. Inflamed his senses. Trapped him." He slaps his hand down on the top of the cage. "But we trapped it first, hey?"

They cheer. Fists assault the air. Someone kicks the cage. They are grinning, slapping backs, congratulating each other. The women stand by, watching, silent. They are cowled in their hoods, perhaps to cover their dangerous forms, their sinuous curves, lest they inflame a man; lest they bewitch him.

The swan in the cage does not make a sound. I do not know what they will do to her, but I cannot help her now; no one can. At least it will soon end, I think, and then Horrocks's voice rises again.

"A cull."

Now they have purpose. Now they know what to do. They gather behind him. Some are carrying guns, I realise, or sticks, or cudgels. They were ready for this. Primed. Someone releases the door of the cage and the swan stumbles out, clumsy on land, its webbed feet sliding on the cobblestones.

"A head start," Horrocks jokes, and they give chase. The swan never did have a chance. It vainly spreads its wings but there is no room for it to take flight. It goes to the ground and one of the men sets his boot on its long and shapely neck.

They begin to chant, others taking it up so that the words become something different and strange. "A cull, a cull."

I try to interject, grasping shoulders, calling out that such a thing is not lawful, that they cannot take it upon themselves. It is no use; my words are lost. They brandish their weapons, pounding the ground with their sticks as they go, stamping their feet. A *cull* – as if it is something scientific they do, something necessary.

They march away towards the river. The women follow, able to do nothing else. Will they fight? They have nothing but the clothes they wear. They trail behind, their gaze fixed not upon the sky but the earth the men have trodden; upon their duty; their destination. Will they watch as their sisters are torn and trampled, their feathers broken and ruined? Will they witness the snapped necks of their sons and daughters? Perhaps it would be worse, after all, to turn their faces away.

Still, as Syl passes me at the back of the crowd, I reach out and grasp her hand.

★   ★   ★

We run, away from the others, unseen, towards her house. She unlocks it using a key kept on a string about her neck and we go inside. I stride ahead of her, as if it is my own. I pass through the living space, not cramped and crammed with knick-knacks and scrimshaw like my aunt's cottage, but airy and neat. I go to the stair. Syl does not protest at this intrusion in her home, only watches, her dark eyes the only brightness.

"A knife," I say, and run up the stairs, not worrying about the noise I make. He will be gone a while yet; there is time. There *must* be time. I wonder for a moment if his boasting words at the Anchor were really the truth as I pull back the embroidered sheet of their bed, wondering if she made it by her own hand. I wonder if the knife she passes to me is the one I saw her wielding by the quay, sliding in and out of the belly of a fish. It is slender and sharp and I plunge it into the mattress.

Feathers: white feathers, downy and soft and choking. They fly into the air, floating down once more, and at first she grabs at them – whether to conceal them or take them back I do not know, but I do not think these are a swan's. I thrust my hand into the rip I have made and feel inward to the centre, trying not to imagine Horrocks on this bed, sweating on top of her.

Then I touch something that does not give, does not slip through my fingers like the other feathers: something that is as soft as they, yet supple, pliant as the finest leather.

I grasp hold of it and pull it towards me. She gives a harsh, choking cry – the first sound she has made – and snatches it from me. It is almost liquid, that brush of feathers against my skin; then it is gone, though I turn and see the glow of it, pure and shining, spilling from her hands.

I almost expect her to throw it over her shoulders at once, but she does not; she turns and runs for the stairs. But of course, there would be no room for her here to fly. The space she leaves behind feels cold and empty and the thought rises: I had imagined she might have spared a word for me.

When I step out of the door she is standing there, staring down the steep little street towards the glimmer of the sea. The swanskin is still in her hands. A muscle twitches in her cheek – it is as if she is tasting the air, a savour she had almost forgotten. She half closes her eyes, then whirls the feathers around her and she runs.

She moves away from me, fast, faster – and I see the stretch and curve of her wings, spreading wide, finding the air, finding their rhythm, feathertips spreading as she casts it all behind her. She is flying, I realise, her feet lifting from the ground, and still she does not look behind her, and still she has no word for me. An image: all the beautiful swans, her sisters, gliding upon the water, and yet separate from it; their feathers, with a simple flick, always remaining entirely dry.

But her transformation is not complete. Beneath the white is the merest suggestion of an arm, a hand, of weight, of darkness. Then a single shot rings out.

At first, her movement does not change. Then she begins to fall.

I cannot do what she would have done; I cannot watch, though I hear her bones shatter on the stone, the sound of her body breaking. Then they are there, the men, blooded and blood-hungry, the red light of it in their eyes, and it is not enough, will never be enough. They are all around and still they do not stop but raise and lower their cudgels and their sticks and they go on and on stamping with their feet.

Then they turn to me.

★   ★   ★

When the boats have sailed, there is time to mend. My arm is still in a sling, and I walk with a limp that I suspect will always be with me. I shall not now go to sea. No one has told me this; they do not have to. The knowledge does not lie in the way they look at me, but in the way they do not.

The women say nothing of what has passed. They clean and they cook and they wait for their men. They sit by the shore, dutifully mending nets and sails, always busy with their needles.

I stay with my aunt, doing whatever tasks she requires of me. Mostly she requires nothing; she sits in her rocking chair, smoking her pipe, staring into space and saying nothing of my failure.

After she fell, the thing that Syl had become was given to the fire. No one wished to look upon it too closely, that mangled and twisted form: fingers, beak, feathers, hair.

★   ★   ★

Outside the window, I hear the pattering of steps. I look out to see hooded shapes hurrying by, heading down the hillside towards the quay. This time there is little conversation, no excited calls ringing into the air, but still I know what it means.

The men have returned from the sea.

At a glance from my aunt, I don my coat and slip out of the door. The cold air in my lungs feels like a relief after the closed rooms and I limp along in the wake of the women, scarcely knowing why.

The tables are set out along the quay, shining knives waiting there like smiles. Waves gently tap the hulls of the boats, lined up against the harbour wall. There is a stink of bladderwrack and brine; the sky is not grey but a fresh clear blue scudded with white, and a firm breeze is blowing from the north. I realise something strange. There are no gulls, not today; no wailing cries ringing across the water.

The women are not seated at their tables, are not waiting for the catch. They stand a short distance away, together, still wearing their hoods. I can barely see their faces beneath them; I cannot see their hands. Then, as one, they cast off their capes.

Beneath, they are naked. They do not wear the clothes their men have given them. Their hair is loose, rippling down their backs. They stand tall. They are unashamed of their bodies, of their bruises, the useless stubs of their wings.

Each is holding a mass of white feathers. They have made new skins, I realise, though not of swan feathers; the men have burned or broken too many for that. I peer into the air once more, cold suddenly, searching again for the gulls, listening for their rapacious cries. The sky is empty.

The women's faces are solemn. I cannot tell by their expressions what they are thinking. It only strikes me then that swans do not cry. They keep the brine inside them; the salt permeates their bones, their blood. It changes them. They, too, can adapt; after all, the river always has flowed into the sea.

The women are ready. And when they take their new forms, red of eye, sharp of beak, gulls sinuous and quick, feathers slick and shining, it is plain for anyone to see that they are very, very hungry.

THAT'S THE SPIRIT

Sarah Lotz

Brendan made a show of breathing out, and opened his eyes. "Spirit is letting me know Percy's here, Mrs. Wilson. Right here in this room with us. I'm getting... I can sense his *essence*."

Mrs. Wilson let out a yip of joy. "I knew he wouldn't let me down. Can you tell him I haven't moved any of his things? His toys are still where he left them."

"He can hear you."

"And he's still happy? He was always so *happy*."

Brendan surreptitiously checked his watch. Ten minutes to go. *Christ.* Mrs. Wilson's consultations always felt like they lasted for days. And where the hell was Helen? It wasn't like her to leave him up to his own devices. "I'm getting..." He frowned slightly, then touched his gut, which, he had to admit, was larger than he'd like. "I'm getting... I'm sensing there's a slight blockage of some sort. Did Percy ever have stomach issues, Mrs. Wilson?"

"Brendan, *no*," Helen's voice hissed through the earpiece, backtracked by the wet wheeze of her battered lungs. "Stick to the bloody script."

He hid a smirk. *Bingo.* He knew that would draw her out.

Mrs. Wilson sighed. "Not that I recall. Well... he did get an icky tummy once when I gave him too much bacon."

Brendan leaned forward conspiratorially. "I think they might be spoiling him on the other side."

"For the love of God, man." Helen was getting really irate now. "She's one of our few remaining regulars. Do you want us to be out on the streets?"

But Helen needn't have worried. Mrs. Wilson was lapping it up. "Poor Percy."

"Don't let it bother you. It's not causing him any undue distress. He's having a grand old time." And maybe he was. No one could *prove* that Percy the recently deceased poodle wasn't cheerfully shitting up the afterlife while Jesus followed him around with the celestial version of a biodegradable poop bag.

"You're sure? And he'll still be waiting for me?"

"Of course. He's a loyal dog. Loyal as they come. There is no death, Mrs. Wilson. The bond between you and your beloved transcends physical limitations." Five minutes left, but fuck it. "I'm afraid that's all we have time for."

"Thank you. You're such a comfort." Mrs. Wilson pressed an extra tenner into his hand, which made him feel a little guilty, but not enough to refuse it. He saw her out and then made for the drinks trolley. He'd earned one. Or several.

As expected, Helen came wheeling out of her room as soon as the coast was clear, bringing with her the scent of *eau de* fag smoke. "Happy with that, were you?"

"Mrs. Wilson was happy. Percy, too."

"Taking the piss out of the poor woman. You're supposed to be easing the pain of her loss, not winding her up."

"She didn't have a clue." He slugged an extra inch of Tesco own brand whisky into his glass and waggled it at her. "Dead pets tell no tales."

"You should have more respect."

"Yeah, well. I had to say something. You weren't much help. Where were you, anyway? Bidding on a broomstick on eBay?"

She eyed his glass. "It's not even lunchtime."

"Everyone has to have a hobby."

"It's clouding your head, making you sloppy. We've got bills to pay, Brendan."

"Ah, give it a rest, woman."

"I'll be resting forever soon. Then you'll be sorry."

"The fuck I will. I could make a fortune renting out your room on Airbnb."

She let out a cackle, which turned into a lung-bashing coughing fit. Emphysema, the gift that kept on giving – how many years had she had it now? He was buggered if he knew. It felt like decades. And God knows how old she was. At least seventy. Half a century of smoking had leathered her skin – her small head resembled a pickled walnut. "And check the email. Had a couple of inquiries that need following up."

"Why can't you do it?"

She flapped a hand at him and then wheeled herself back to her room, slamming the door behind her. She rarely came out of her lair these days. Christ knows what she got up to in there. Which reminded him, he'd forgotten to extract the earpiece, the removal of which always made him feel lighter, somehow. But as usual, he'd mislaid the slender magnet that was the only way of removing the small device. No matter. He knocked back the drink and poured another. A bad idea, as booze always made him maudlin and opened the door to self-pity. And who could blame him? This was his lot: trapped in an unhealthy, co-dependent relationship with his septuagenarian enabler-stroke-flatmate while scraping a living 'reconnecting' delusional old women with their dead pets. The glory days of headlining psychic cruises, filling auditoriums and well-paid newspaper gigs – 'Ask Brendan! Your Hotline to the Psychic Realm!' – were long gone. And he had no one to blame but himself. He'd got sloppy; fell right into the trap laid for him by a sceptic who'd debunked him all over YouTube. If it weren't for Helen, he'd have thrown in the towel years ago. She'd stood by him when the shit had hit the fan, convinced him to carry on, became his manager of sorts. They may gripe at each other all day, but she was loyal, he had to give the old cow that. It was she, after all, who'd suggested they purchase the earpiece so that she could help him in his work.

"The secret service use them," she'd said, when the package arrived. "It connects via Bluetooth. Long as I'm close by and there's a signal, I can hear what you say, and you can hear me. Let's test it."

Helen had trundled into the spare room (the room that eventually, as if by osmosis, became hers), while he stayed in the lounge that doubled as the 'reading' room. Feeling faintly ridiculous, he'd slotted the device, which resembled a large maggot, into his ear canal. It was remarkably comfortable; he often forgot it was even there. A hiss of static, then: "Can you hear me?"

"*Christ*, can I." He could hear the *hiss-puff* of every mucus-heavy breath. She was inside him, a thought that genuinely made him feel like gagging. But it enabled her to feed him reminders (he was always forgetting clients' names, or worse, the names of their deceased loved ones), as well as little nuggets of info she gleaned off punters' social media accounts. Despite her age, she was as adept at mining Facebook as your average teenage stalker.

He'd given up asking why she enabled him. Because here was the rub: Helen still professed herself a believer in what she called 'Spirit', making her a paradox of sorts. Her answer was always the same: "People need comforting, Brendan. You're good at that. Spirit will return to you one day, you'll see. You've just lost your way, is all. And until it does, you'll have me."

Despite all the evidence to the contrary, she refused to accept he was a sham. Because if he didn't have the gift, then the years she'd spent with him were a waste. He'd never had the heart to put her right.

Three drinks in, he did as Helen instructed and checked the bookings. More dead pets, a suicide (no thanks), and then a name caught his eye. *Jesus.*

"Helen! *Helen!*"

He was about to go and bang on her door when she came gliding in. The curtains were drawn to create atmosphere, and in the dim light she looked more like a wheelchaired wraith than ever. "What is it, man?"

"We've caught a big fish." He paused for dramatic effect. "Cheryl Ann Palmer's mother." Everyone knew that name. Back in the mid-nineties, nineteen-year-old Cheryl had gone missing in broad daylight en route to a job interview. She was never found, and her disappearance became one of the UK's most notorious cold cases. It was just the kind of high-profile gig he'd have jumped at in his heyday.

"Why did she reach out to you of all people?"

"She read my book."

"Which one?"

"*Spirited.*" His 'biography'. The heart-rending tale of an Irish lad who'd realised that the voice he was hearing in his head was actually his spirit guide, sent from the other realm to help him develop his psychic gift. A gift that would enable him to escape his abusive, poverty-stricken home life. All bollocks, of course, and more than a little inspired by *Angela's Ashes*, which was big at the time. There was no one left in Ireland who could be bothered to refute that part of the story, and he'd glossed over the next chapter in his life: the escape to London, a career as a small-time con artist, a couple of minor convictions. He'd got into the game when a girlfriend had dragged him along to an 'evening with the psychic stars!' As he'd watched the line-up cold reading audience member after audience member, he knew he'd found his calling – it took a con to know a con. He had the charisma (back then, anyway), and the gift of the gab to pull it off.

"When does she want to come?" Helen asked.

"This afternoon, but that's not enough time to prepare, is it?" Cheryl had gone missing before everyone splashed their lives all over social media. But hopefully there would be a website and/or a Facebook page where Helen could dig up some useful nuggets.

"We'll have to wing it," Helen said. "Now go and brush your teeth, you stink like a brewery."

"We don't even know if Cheryl Palmer is dead. How am I going to handle that?"

"Crossed over," Helen said, piously. "There is no death, remember? We'll be fine."

Still the doubt niggled. The face-to-face consultations he did these days were with pre-vetted safe clientele. But it wasn't just that. Cheryl may have gone missing decades ago, but she was still someone's kid. Dead spouses or parents – fine. Dead pets – even better. But losing a child was a whole other level of pain. Even he had *some* morals.

Helen tapped her ear. "You'll be fine, Brendan. I'll be with you." For once, she sounded almost kind. "Your job is to give people comfort. You gave *me* comfort when I needed it, remember? Why else would I have stuck with you all these years?"

It was rare, these days, for her to bring that up. Sometimes he even forgot that she'd started off as a client. Her son (also named Brendan – maybe that was the attraction) had died of a drug overdose, and she'd come to him a broken woman, hollowed out by grief. He'd taken her money and dispensed vague platitudes, rightly guessing that she felt guilty for not 'doing more' to save her son.

"This is big," Helen continued. "If you don't mess it up, who knows where it might take you?"

She was right. A big-ticket client could help mend his reputation. For the first time in years he felt a flicker of excitement. A flicker of *hope.* This could be a route back to the big time. And, God, how he missed those days. The cash, the attention, and the rush of addressing an audience of acolytes.

★ ★ ★

Mrs. Palmer, who looked exactly as he expected – a fragile soul battered by decades of grief – arrived bang on time, but she wasn't alone. With her was a middle-aged, bullet-headed man who she introduced as her son, Patrick.

"Great to meet you, Patrick."

Patrick ignored Brendan's outstretched hand. He had the flat, black eyes of a psychopath (or a shark). "You don't look like a psychic."

"Well, I only wear the hoop earrings on Thursdays."

No one laughed. "Cut the crap, Brendan," Helen hissed. "This is serious."

He invited them to make themselves comfortable, then dredged up the last vestiges of the charm that used to be his stock in trade. He softened his voice, upped the Irish lilt factor. "And what is it you're hoping to achieve here today?"

"What do you think we bloody hope to achieve?" Patrick sneered. "Answers. Is Cheryl dead? Is she alive? Where is she?"

"Have you been to other practitioners before?"

"Yeah. Frauds, all of them. I told Mum not to come to you either, but she wouldn't listen."

"Most of them said she was dead," Mrs. Palmer said in a soft voice Brendan had to strain to hear. "They said she'd be found near water, or a wood."

Course they did. The majority of the UK was reasonably close to either water or trees, so percentage wise, it was a safe bet. He would have said the same thing.

"Give them the spiel," Helen whispered.

"Before I begin, you should know there are no guarantees with this. I can't know for sure when Spirit will appear and guide me. Nor do I have any control over what I'll be shown, or told."

"Very fucking convenient," Patrick muttered under his breath.

"Tell them you know how difficult this is for them," Helen huffed.

"I know how difficult this is for you."

"No you bloody don't. How many of *your* kids have gone missing?"

"Patrick," Mrs. Palmer whispered. "Shush now. Let the man work."

"Have you brought along something of Cheryl's, Mrs. Palmer?"

She dug in her cavernous bag and removed an electric blue scarf. Brendan didn't want to touch it. Not just because it was a symbol of decades of pain and uncertainty, but also because it was grubby and leaking threads.

He gathered it up, took a deep breath and closed his eyes. "I'm getting... I'm getting... something's coming through. Something..." *For fuck's sake, Helen.* This was her cue to feed him info. The *hiss-puff* in his ear seemed to recede, there was a second of pure silence, and then a voice, oddly absent of Helen's phlegmy signature, whispered, "Chips and rice."

He parroted it out without thinking. Mrs. Palmer and Patrick froze as if they'd literally been put on pause.

"What?" Mrs. Palmer gasped. "What did you just say?"

"Chips and rice. Does that mean something to you?" Of course it did. Mrs. Palmer was tearing up, and even Patrick was looking shell-shocked. *Good old Helen.*

"That was her favourite meal," Mrs. Palmer said, voice trembling. "When she was a kiddie, like. Chips and rice. Nothing else. No sauce, nothing. We used to joke about it, didn't we, Patrick?"

"We did." Patrick had recovered from the shock, and was back to eyeing Brendan with distrust. "Did you put that up anywhere online, Mum?"

"No. Not that I remember."

Brendan touched his ear. Now would be the perfect moment for Helen to follow up with another whammy. But there was no wet wheeze. Had the signal died? That happened sometimes. He was on his own. "I'm getting... I'm getting that she's at peace. A happy spirit." Lame, but it would have to do.

"But where is she?" Mrs. Palmer asked.

He needed to hedge his bets. Not do a Sylvia Browne, who was notorious for telling grieving parents their missing kids were dead only for them to show up alive – and vice versa. "That I can't say for sure. This feeling I get about her... it comes via my guide. Via Spirit. I get a sense of the person, but there is no death. In a metaphysical sense, I mean."

Mrs. Palmer seemed to accept this unfiltered bullshit. "Tell her that her mum's here. Tell her that her Nan's still holding on."

"She can hear you."

"How can she hear us if she isn't here and she isn't dead?" Patrick sniped.

Oh fuck off. He needed to wrap it up before he said something he couldn't cover. Fortunately Mrs. Palmer had had enough. "I think... I think I want to go home now."

Mrs. Palmer whispered a heartfelt 'thank you' as he walked them to the door. Patrick didn't say a word.

"Helen?" he called. "Helen! They've gone."

She emerged and joined him in the lounge. "They were only here a few minutes. What did you say to them, Brendan?"

"What did *I* say? What did you say, more like. Chips and rice? Where did you dredge that up from?"

"What are you talking about? I lost contact. The signal died. Did you forget to top up the Wi-Fi again?"

"Don't give me that. Chips and rice. I heard it in the earpiece, clear as day. And it made a real impression on them. What was it, one of your little nuggets you dug up from an old MySpace page or something?"

"Brendan... I'm not messing with you. I genuinely didn't say that."

Helen could be sneaky; she'd managed to con her way into living in his flat, after all ('best I'm close if we get any walk-ins, Brendan'). But. *But.* She looked genuinely flummoxed. And why would she deny she'd said the deadly phrase? She'd love to take the credit for that. Maybe the old bag was going senile, forgot she said it. "So who was it then?"

"Interference? A radio signal?"

"A radio signal? It's not the nineteen-forties. And anyway, say it *was* something like that, what are the chances it would say that exact, very pertinent phrase?"

Helen wheeled closer. "It wasn't me, Brendan. But I know what it is."

"Just... *don't.*"

"It's Spirit, Brendan. The spirit that came to you when you were a boy. It's *back*."

He bit his tongue. Now wasn't the time.

★   ★   ★

Mrs. Palmer returned the next day, alone, thank God. Hungover, hoarse from arguing with Helen, he could barely dredge up the energy for the pleasantries.

"Mrs. Palmer, before I start, I want you to know that sometimes, we get things coming through that... that may be confusing."

"What you said last time wasn't confusing. That was her way of saying to me that she was all right, wherever she is. And whatever Patrick says." She gave him a watery smile. "He doesn't know I'm here."

"I don't want you to get your hopes up. What I do... it's..." *It's bollocks.*

"Tell her again that Cheryl's at peace," Helen whispered.

"I'll do my best for you, but—" A thump came from within the apartment. Helen dropping something again, no doubt. She could be a clumsy old cow. "It'll be the cat," he said, before Mrs. Palmer could question him. To be fair, she barely seemed to register it. "You have the scarf?"

She laid it on the table, and he closed his eyes and buried his fingers in the scratchy wool.

Helen was AWOL again; probably picking up whatever old lady ornament she'd dropped. *Get a move on, woman.* "I'm getting..." Irritation and anxiety building, he waited, and waited. Nothing but empty air, then, clear as a bell: "Chim chim cheroot." He jumped. Once again, the voice was absent of Helen's Cork accent. Another nonsensical phrase, a play on a line from that old musical, what was it called? *Mary Poppins*, that was it.

"Is she there, Brendan?" Mrs. Palmer was waiting.

He should ignore it. Not play Helen's game. But fuck it. He had to say something.

Mrs. Palmer's hands jumped to her mouth the second he parroted it out. "Patrick... when he was little, he always got the words to that song wrong. Cheroot instead of cheree. It used to make Cheryl laugh. We never put him right."

Brendan had to give it to Helen. The details she was digging up were far more on the nose than the vague crap she usually came up with. And once again, she was doing her disappearing act, leaving him to wrap things up.

When Mrs. Palmer was safely on her way, he gave the drink a swerve and headed straight for Helen's room. "Helen? Helen."

A low moan came from within. The door was locked – always was in case a punter accidentally wandered in there. "Helen?" Another moan. *Christ*. Had the old bag had a stroke in there? Fingers trembling, he fumbled in the drawer for the spare key, and pushed his way in. Helen was lying on the carpet, trying to haul herself up into her chair.

"What happened?"

"Fell out of my wheelchair."

Relief, mixed with irritation. "You daft old cow. Are you hurt?"

"No. Help me up."

She was lighter than she looked, as if her bones were hollow. "You should be in a care home, being abused by minimum wage immigrants, not doing all this."

Her breathing was even more laboured than usual. "I'll call the doctor."

A cackle. "No you bloody won't. Stop fussing, man. I'm fine. Nothing broken. Now what happened?"

"You know what happened. Nice touch changing your accent, by the way. And how did you stop yourself from wheezing like a dray horse?"

"What did it say?"

"You know bloody well what it said."

"Brendan, I've been on the floor for the last half an hour." He glanced at the desk. The microphone she used to relay the messages was lying out of reach. If that thump he'd heard *had* been the sound of Helen tipping out of her wheelchair, then she couldn't have been responsible for the voice.

"I told you. Spirit. Spirit's come back to you, Brendan. After all these years, it's come back."

Mad. He'd met scores of psychics over the years who were convinced they were a hotline to the other side. He'd always assumed their so-called spirit guides were a symptom of fragmenting mental health issues. Perhaps he'd judged them too harshly. *Hello spirit, it's me, Brendan.* Nah.

She was messing with him. Had to be. "Is this some kind of elaborate scheme to make me think I'm going mental?" In a weird way it would make sense. He'd convinced her all those years ago that her son was safe and happy on the other side; and now, with her health fading fast, she needed to convince *him* that he wasn't a fat Irish fraud.

Helen was watching him with the unblinking gaze of a fundamentalist proselytiser. "It's Spirit, Brendan. You know I'm right. And you're scared."

"Only thing I'm scared of is spending the rest of my days locked in here with you." Christ, he needed a drink. And he needed to flee this room, which stank of stale smoke and a darker, unidentifiable odour that he suspected may be encroaching death.

Helen wheeled after him. "Shitting yourself, you are."

"Stop following me around. It's like being hounded by a fucking Irish Davros."

"You know I'm right, Brendan. You know it."

Drinking straight out of the bottle, he rooted around for the magnet pen. Aha. There it was, trapped under the wheel of the drinks trolley. He should pluck the earpiece out and throw it at her. "If Spirit has 'come back', then what do I need you for?"

"You turn your back on this gift you've been given, you'll regret it for the rest of your days."

He'd had it. He rounded on her. "There is no gift, woman. There never fucking was, and you playing mind games with me won't change that."

There. It was done. He should have rammed this home years ago. He waited for one of her follow-up barbs, but none came. She merely smiled sadly, and then trundled off back to her room.

★   ★   ★

It was gone noon when he lurched awake on the couch, his head pulsing from dehydration. Desperate to prove that Helen was messing with him, he'd been up till the wee hours drinking and trawling through 'Find Cheryl' sites for any mention of those on-the-nose snippets. There was nothing. His phone was buzzing on the table, and it took him a while to muster up the co-ordination to reach for it. The number was withheld.

It was either a bailiff or a potential client. He havered for a second, and then answered.

"Mr. Kelly?"

He didn't recognise the voice. "Yes?"

"This is Jonathan Golding from the *Daily Mirror*. The family of Cheryl Palmer has contacted me. They said you've been helping them?"

Jesus. He wasn't sure how to respond, settled on, "I see."

"They've invited me to come along and experience for myself how you operate. Would that be a problem?"

Yes it bloody would be. He'd been down that road before and it hadn't gone well. "My schedule is quite packed, Mr. Golding. When were you thinking?"

"Now. We're right outside."

Shite. Brendan staggered to the window and peered out. Gathered on the porch were Mrs. Palmer, Patrick the dead-eyed wonder son, and a skinny man who looked up and waved before Brendan had time to duck out of sight. Fair play – taking him by surprise was smart. He could tell the journo to sling his hook, but how would that look? He'd only be opening the door to '*Psychic Brendan runs Scared from Scrutiny*'.

"Give me a minute." He hung up, drained the last smidgen of whisky to quell the panic, and made for Helen's door. Whether she was stringing him along or not, what did it matter? He needed her. He didn't dare do this alone. "Helen." No answer. "We're in trouble, Helen. I need you. *Helen.*" Still nothing. What if she'd died in there? No, he couldn't think like that. She was just punishing him.

A knock came on his own front door, followed by, "Mr. Kelly?" Someone must have buzzed the gang into the building.

"Helen. *Please.* I didn't mean what I said last night. I need you. And Spirit."

"Mr. Kelly?"

Shite. He couldn't put it off any longer. Hopefully she'd come to her senses. Wait – what about the earpiece? Hadn't he removed it last night? He pushed his little finger inside his left ear. There was a lump deep in there, which he hoped was the device and not a clump of earwax.

He smoothed his hair, crunched a mint, and then let them in. Mrs. Palmer gave him an apologetic smile, Patrick was his usual charming self, and the journo launched into the type of smarm offensive Brendan used to excel at: "So kind of you to find the time, Mr. Kelly. Call me Johnny."

Mrs. Palmer perched on the edge of the couch, and her son flumped down next to her, radiating passive aggression. Johnny's eyes darted around the lounge-cum-reading room, gathering details he'd no doubt regurgitate later for his readership. And he'd have a field day with that. With its velvet curtains, old lamps, and cloths draped on every surface, the room could easily double as a set for a mini-series about a psychic. Helen's work, of course.

"Mind if I record this?" Johnny asked.

"Be my guest. I have nothing to hide." *Except for the septuagenarian in the spare room.* He automatically touched his ear. *Come on, Helen.*

"I have some questions," Johnny smarmed. "But those can wait. How about we launch straight into it?"

Without being asked, Mrs. Palmer handed Brendan the blue scarf. He closed his eyes. *Come on, Helen.* "Spirit. Spirit? Are you there, Spirit?"

As the seconds dragged into minutes, his shirt collar seemed to tighten around his throat. He was beginning to sweat. "I'm getting... a sense of warmth."

No one reacted to this. Too vague. Could mean anything. "There's something else... something else..." *Come on, Helen.* He found himself praying to hear that voice, whatever that might mean. But there was nothing. Of course there was nothing.

Then, into his ear came the familiar, *hiss-puff, hiss-puff.* He almost cried out in relief. He knew she wouldn't let him down. She'd come up with something.

"Spirit? Do you have something to say to me? Please, Spirit. I'm open to whatever you have to show or tell me."

Hiss-puff. Hiss-puff. Dead air, then: "Fish-fingers on pizza."

Another quirky phrase delivered by that smooth toned voice. Spirit or Helen, what did it matter? He opened his eyes. "I'm getting... do the words, 'fish-finger pizza' mean anything to you?"

Mrs. Palmer looked confused. Not the reaction he was looking for.

"Does that mean something to you, Mrs. Palmer?" *Come on, woman.* She shook her head. "No. Not that I can recall. Patrick?"

"Nope," Patrick said, gleefully.

"It means something to me," Johnny said. "Here."

He held out his phone, and Brendan, who could now feel sweat dribbling down his sides, automatically took it. On it was a comment left under the Find Cheryl Facebook page: 'OMG, remember how Cheryl used to looooove fish-fingers on pizza????'

"I put that up last night under a proxy account. Among others. It's what we call a false fact."

Shite, shite, shite. Almost exactly how he'd been taken down last time.

Mrs. Palmer was looking bewildered. "Johnny laid a trap for him, Mum," Patrick said, with a triumphant smirk. "And he fell for it. I told you he was a faker."

Helen was doing her disappearing act again. *Think.* "I can't explain how that slipped through. Spirit can be... sometimes it can be... Hang on, what about the other things Spirit told me? Chips and rice, and... the other one." He'd gone blank. Worse than blank. He was heading for a full-on panic attack. "Those weren't online. You said so yourself, Mrs. Palmer."

"Both phrases are mentioned in cached pages," Johnny said. "Cheryl's late uncle mentioned her penchant for chips and rice, and one of Patrick's ex-girlfriends put the *Mary Poppins* reference on her blog in the early two thousands."

Bloody Helen. Bloody, bloody Helen. So it *was* she after all. He'd almost believed that Spirit nonsense for a second. What was it, some sort of elaborate revenge scenario? Had she been biding her time until a press-worthy client eventually pitched up in order to nudge him towards another public shaming? If so, he had to admit, she'd played a blinder.

He was going to fucking kill her.

"People like you are vultures," Patrick spat. "You need to be stopped."

Mrs. Palmer gave him a look of such eloquent disappointment and pain he almost felt it physically.

Say something. "Mrs. Palmer, you were the one who came to *me*, remember?"

"Don't fucking talk to her," the son roared. "Don't you fucking dare."

Mrs. Palmer fixed her eyes on the carpet.

"I bring comfort," Brendan said, aiming this at Johnny, and unable to mask the desperation. "I bring comfort to the grieving. That's all I've ever offered."

"Were you bringing comfort to the woman who took her own life after she found out you were a fraud, Mr. Kelly?" Johnny asked, not bothering to hide the smirk.

The sweat coating Brendan's sides turned to ice.

"She'd lost her only son, I believe."

The journo was saying something else, but Brendan wasn't listening. Mrs. Palmer was leaning forward, frowning at something on the carpet. Next to the heel of her sensible shoe sat a familiar white, maggoty shape, complete with a sliver of yellow earwax.

GAVE

Michael Bailey

"Without individuals we see only numbers: a thousand dead, a hundred thousand dead, 'casualties may rise to a million.' With individual stories, the statistics become people – but even that is a lie, for the people continue to suffer, in the numbers that themselves are numbing and meaningless."

Neil Gaiman, *American Gods*

87

Michael Shoe could no longer give, although he tried once more. A pint. Eight weeks prior he had tried for his second to last time, and eight weeks prior to that was his third to last. Perhaps the counts would be high enough this time, he hoped. Three pints of blood wasted. Twenty-four weeks' worth. He gave, but no one *took* anymore.

"What about platelets?"

The nurse blinked and pressed her lips until she made a flat line out of her mouth with small brackets on either side.

"Not today, but in eight weeks you can try again."

"It takes two days for platelets to recover," he told her. "*Whole* takes eight weeks."

Her new look told him she knew this. She was the nurse. She was the one educated in medicine, not the patient. She understood blood. She was also the one who had argued with him the last time he gave. Her name was Stacy, according to the badge.

"The US Food and Drug Administration allows donations of whole blood only *once* every fifty-six days," he told her, because he already knew the regulations and had had similar arguments with nurses like Stacy over the years, "but with every pint of whole blood, a donation of platelets can also be made within that same fifty-six-day window. Or six platelet donations."

If his blood was bad, or low in red cell counts, or whatever the condition may be, at least he had his platelets. He could stop taking his blood pressure medication, and the aspirin; perhaps that would help. Statistically, he only had a few years left that he *could* donate.

Michael returned a generous smile.

"Yes," she said, "but *State* regulations prohibit simultaneous whole blood *and* platelet donations, and at your age—"

"What does my age have to do with anything? I'm eighty-seven and healthy."

"Look, Mr... Shoe," she said, reading the form in front of her, "if you must give, you can return in two days for platelets. Snacks and orange juice are down the hall."

"I'll see you in two days," he told her.

The brackets around her lips disappeared. "You're a generous man, Mr. Shoe. If more people were so giving, the world wouldn't be how it is today." Her words broke at the end.

She was thinking about her mother, he knew, or her daughter or son or husband or whoever had been taken from her. Someone close, he could tell.

"You give and give and give," Michael said, "but the world keeps shrivelling."

She turned, and so did he.

There were millions of people like her, like Stacy, *only* millions, with loved ones falling like dead autumn leaves. Falling by the millions.

The media, what was left of it, recently put world population below a billion.

The world covered in fallen corpses, he imagined.

Soon the tree of life would bare all.

86

He gave because the world needed blood. Lots of it. Every fifty-six days the date on his calendar was circled like a red ensō symbol, like the outline of a blood cell. That's how long it took to fully recover the pint lost with each donation. In between the circled days, he'd throw in a day for platelets. The 'clear blood gravy', someone once told him.

Every eight weeks for whole blood, every eight weeks for platelets, staggered for optimal donating.

Michael first gave at sixteen, although at the time it had required a signed slip of paper from his parents. That was seventy years ago, back when world population was moving in the opposite direction. Now, at eighty-six, he could still remember witnessing that drastic *flip* from acceleration to deceleration.

He knew the exact number, then, the way every boy and girl knew the number: 17,989,101,196... the highest population of people ever recorded – *nearly eighteen billion*. They taught the number in schools, more so when the number drastically plummeted.

Michael ate his snacks and drank his orange juice and noted the new count displayed on the screen in the lobby: 2,472,499,606 – fewer than two and a half billion people remaining on the planet. One could find the current number anywhere, and watch it dwindle in real-time. 605, the last three digits clicked. 604, 603, 594, 589. In those few seconds, twenty-six people died.

A countdown to the end of mankind.

One was supposed to wait between ten and fifteen minutes after donating blood to let the dizziness settle, for a chance to rehydrate. Four glasses of liquids, he'd read a long time ago.

Michael drank, and took this time to calculate numbers. The world loved numbers.

The last three numbers were now 570.

He jotted the math into his notebook. For seventy years he'd given blood religiously. Every fifty-six days, nearly *on* the day.

70 x 365.25 = 25,567.5, or the number of days in seventy years (including leap years).

25,567.5 ÷ 56 = 457 (rounded up), or the number of times he'd given whole blood in those seventy years, and the number of times he'd given platelets... also the number of pints.

457 x 16 = 7,312. The blood he'd donated, in liquid ounces.

7,312 ÷ 128 = 57.125. That same number converted to gallons. *57 gallons.*

And that was *whole* blood, not counting platelets.

How many people were affected by his blood, how many had it gone to? He was a universal donor, for platelets anyway, so it must have gone to some use. His red blood had only gone to those with AB blood types, he knew, but AB was in high demand for both study and to keep those with AB healthy. How much became wasted over the years? How much utilised? How much could he give before he, too, died with the masses?

Others in the waiting room watched the reverse death counter on the screen the way children used to watch cartoons; rarely did they blink.

80

Michael gave platelets because his red cells were still in recovery mode. He glanced long enough at the world population counter to summon a memory. At eighty, he was still capable of remembering the past.

"History repeats itself," his father had said. Michael was ten, then. The phrase had stuck with him for seventy years, hiding until now, hibernating. The counter had awoken the memory at this precise moment because history had in fact repeated itself.

A bicycle accident had sent him head-over-handlebars and crashing into the street gutter, a broken bottle slicing his wrist from palm to elbow. He'd lost a lot of blood in what appeared to be a botched suicide attempt, and staggered his way home, pale and shivering, holding the wound. World population was on the rise then, somewhere around seventeen billion. "I remember the number," his father had said, sitting next to his hospital bed as they watched a small screen, "the population when I was *your* age. The biggest number I'd ever heard of: *four billion!* The world only had four billion people. Can you imagine?" At ten, Michael couldn't imagine, and had nearly decreased the population by one.

"How big's four billion?" Michael had later asked his mother.

"A *very* big number."

Michael remembered counting – there was nothing else to do but watch the blood bag sending its slow red current to his catheter — to see how long it would take to get to four billion. When he had gotten to a thousand he'd looked at his wristwatch. Fifteen minutes had passed. When you're ten, you don': think much about the size of numbers or how many people live on the planet because at ten your world is the *entire* world. Something small.

"What are you doing?" his mother had asked, hearing him count aloud: one thousand ten, one thousand eleven...

"Counting to four billion."

"That might take you a while," she had said.

By the time he'd reached *three* thousand, he'd gotten bored and tried calculating how long it would take to count to four billion. If each number took a second to say aloud, the answer was about 130 years, and that was if he counted nonstop, 24/7. Four billion was *huge*!

Now, at eighty, the number haunted him again, albeit for the opposite reason, for sounding so small. He watched the number on the screen drop to four billion, exactly, and in seconds it was in the high threes.

For that moment, Michael Shoe was ten again.

The hourglass of time had flipped, the sand falling like people.

"Hi again, Mr. Shoe," a woman behind the counter said. "Platelets?"

"Yes. According to my calendar, I'm able."

"I wish there were more people like you, more people so generous. Can you believe there are less than four billion left?"

"*Fewer*," Michael said, correcting her grammar. "And *remaining*."

The doomsday clock clicked rapidly in reverse, and he thought once again how long it would take for a person to do the counting instead of a machine, to count backwards from four billion, until there was no one remaining to count... mankind extinct.

Even if a person devoted half their life, twelve hours per day, it would take more than two hundred and sixty years to reach zero, two hundred if they counted quickly. But mankind didn't have so long if the parabolic pattern of death continued. Nearly four billion people had died in the last twenty years alone.

So Michael Shoe gave.

70

He drank his free glass of orange juice and looked around the room at the others donating that morning, wondering about their blood, wondering about their motives. Were they as dedicated? Had they donated their entire lives? For how many was it their first visit? These questions filled his head. He was seventy, the oldest in the room.

60

"Good to see you again, Mr. Shoe. Blood this time?"

"AB negative," he said, even though he'd seen her countless times before.

AB negative was the rarest blood type, Michael's blood having both A and B antigens on red cells, but neither A nor B antibodies in the plasma, which meant his red cells could go to only those with AB blood types, never to those with O, A, or B; although, since his Rh factor was negative, this meant his blood went to Rh negative patients. He shared blood with less than half a percent of the world's population, which is why he donated plasma as well.

Whatever was happening in the world, or *to* the world, whether an undiscovered blood disease, something worse than blood cancer, or perhaps caused by some stellar anomaly, blood was the key. Those with O blood types, whether Rh- or Rh+, it didn't much matter, were dying at a more progressive rate than those with A or B, and those with AB remained relatively stable, this lowest of populations nearly unfazed.

It was good to be AB, if only for survival's sake; otherwise, donating AB red blood this late in the depopulation game didn't serve much purpose other than to help those with similar blood types, to keep the last of humankind healthy while the rest of the world and their dying blood types fizzled out like stars at dawn.

On the flipside, having an AB blood type made him a universal *plasma* donor. He had his parents to thank for that. With his mother A and his father B, he had thus inherited a blood type per the genetic code of possibilities:

Parent 1	AB	AB	AB	AB	B	**A**	A	O	O	O
Parent 2	AB	B	A	O	B	**B**	A	B	A	O
O	–	–	–	–	X	X	X	X	X	X
A	X	X	X	X	–	X	X	–	X	–
B	X	X	X	X	X	X	–	X	–	–
AB	X	X	X	–	–	**X**	–	–	–	–

"We're short-staffed today, so the wait's about twenty minutes," the woman behind the counter said. She took his paperwork, the same form he'd filled out with the same information, each and every time. *After more than forty years of world depopulation and blood donating, there should be an easier procedure*, Michael mused. *Forty-four years*, to be exact. He'd given blood so many times he could do it himself, but that was against regulations. *They track births and deaths across the entire world, all of us watching that blasted ever-dwindling number in real-time, yet the process of donating blood's still so archaic.*

The population counter on the screen mounted in the waiting area ticked down steadily: 7,938,110,345. More than ten billion people had died in the last forty-four years. Gone. A few blinks and the 345 at the end fell below 300.

Cremation of bodies had become mandatory, the ground unable to take so much expired life. It was illegal in most countries to bury the dead, and so Michael imagined Cemetery Police all over the world struggling to enforce such crazy laws. Larger cities had erected skyscrapers with floors designed like libraries – some called them *Libraries of the Dead* – wherein, for a price, a loved one could be entombed within a book-like urn and be placed on 'bookshelves'. Modernised mausoleums for the deceased. A place called *Chapel of the Chimes* in California had started the tradition, and now they could be found all over the world.

People still got away with burials, whether illegally sticking to tradition or because of religious belief, yet graveyards, much like the human race, were fading out of existence.

As the counter counted in reverse – the numbers a blur – Michael couldn't help but wonder how there could be so many funerals, all at once. So many people crying: enough fallen tears to fill reservoirs. *Or were funerals, too, illegal?* He couldn't remember, although he'd attended more funerals than he *could* remember, lost friends and lost relatives so easily forgotten because their deaths had become so regular. How many had he attended these last few years?

What's the weight of ten billion dead? he wondered. *What about the ashes?*

Michael had read once that the average cremains of an adult male weighed somewhere around 1.6 pounds, and the average female around 1.4. But what about adolescents, toddlers, infants? Even if you lowballed an estimate of one pound per person, over ten billion pounds of ash had been generated over the last forty years.

Imagine the libraries!

Ten years had passed since he'd visited his father's book.

50

"Hey, Dad," he said to the shelf.

His father's book/urn was brown with gold trim and lettering, and matched his mother's next to it, which was similar but had a golden rose etched on the spine where a book publisher's logo would normally go. The Shoes had an entire shelf dedicated to the family name, something his father had wanted in terms of a plot.

The family library, he'd called it. *A collection of shoeboxes.*

"In case you're wondering, today's my birthday. I turned the big five-oh, the same age as grandpa when he died."

His grandfather, Christopher Gordon Shoe, was one of the last generations to be buried in the ground. His body had been unearthed, eventually, the entire cemetery excavated to make room for a hospital. His ashes resided next to grandma Sharon's somewhere in Oregon. Perhaps he could get them moved.

"Ten-point-four billion," he told his father. "That's about how many people were on this planet when you died, that's about how many died in the last forty-four years, and that's about how many are on this planet right now. You were always concerned about world population, and now I'm concerned with world *de*population. How funny is that?"

Michael touched the glass separating him from his parents.

Not so funny, his father would say.

"From the time I was forty until now, the world's lost over three and a half billion, from whatever's killing us. The most lost in a single decade since this started back when I was a teen. I remember when the numbers changed direction. We've lost as many people in the last ten years as how many had lived on the planet when you were that age. I remember thinking how large four billion sounded. *Four billion!* Do you remember? Now it doesn't seem so significant. It seems small. Thirteen billion dead. Imagine the libraries, Dad."

Someday Michael would have his own book on these shelves.

Will anyone be around to pay me a visit? Will anyone be around to pay any of these books a visit, the mausoleums as empty as the libraries – for real books – of my youth?

He remembered going to the library with his father, back when they still existed, and how empty the building had seemed, how wasted. So many books full of magic and wonder and no one wanting to read them. He'd wanted to take his own children there some day, to encourage them to read, to open their minds as his own father had encouraged.

The first book he'd ever checked out was *Stardust* by Neil Gaiman. He and his father had read it aloud together, every night before bed.

Michael never had kids, never wanted any. *Who could have children in a dying world such as this?* he'd always thought.

"We are all made of stardust," he said to his father, as if reading from its pages.

And we all become ash, in the end, his father would say.

You should find someone, his mother would say.

"So that I don't die alone?"

Even if he'd managed to hold onto a relationship with a woman having an A, B, or an AB blood type – which would have given future children the greatest chance of survival – the odds of those children dying were far too great. The ratio of having a child with either an A or a B was around 2:3, with 1:3 having a child with AB. And *only* with a partner having an A, B, or AB blood type. O's were out entirely, as their children would die as so many O's had.

Could he have fallen in love with an O? Those with O had unfairly become humanity's cast-offs, nature's invalids. This late in the depopulation game, were there any O's remaining, or had that blood type become extinct, evolutionarily phased out... the world full of A's and B's but predominantly AB's?

He had witnessed far too many child deaths to play the odds of falling in love and having children, which is how he'd lost Amber; she'd wanted kids, to at least *try*.

All you can do is try, his mother would say.

He touched the glass again, as if she were touching the glass from the opposite side. It was cold, but comforting. Someday he'd be there with them, in his own book, behind the glass, name etched in metallic red, perhaps, like blood.

"I should have tried harder," Michael told them. "I've done everything I can to help those in need, but is it doing any good? The world is dying, and I'm only one man. I've given my *blood*, my *platelets*. I should have given something *more*. I should have tried with Amber, should have listened to you, Mom. Shouldn't have been so selfish. I thought I was being *selfless*, but I was wrong. And now it's too late. Now all I can do is continue to give my blood."

It's all you can do, son, his father would say.

40

"The world needs more *people*," Amber screamed. "More *children*. How can you not *try?*"

"We've tried," Michael said, "and we've lost two already. How can you even *think* of losing a third?"

Taylor was stillborn, B negative.

Dylan died from cardiac arrest two weeks after he was born, A positive.

"Odds are in our favour," she'd pleaded. "The next one will have a chance. The next one will be born with AB and she will have a *chance*."

"I can't go through it again!"

"You're *afraid* to go through it again, Michael. Every eight weeks you give blood, and then platelets. The world doesn't *need* blood. It needs *children!*"

She'd slammed the door and walked out. Never saw her again.

The death counter dropped to 13,929, 503, 071.

30

Michael Shoe never thought he'd make it to thirty. Most friends his age had died. He'd donated blood and the 'clear gravy' for nearly half his life, but for what purpose? He thought of taking his life, of cutting his wrists and letting his blood kill him the only way it seemingly could, and then he met Amber.

Michael was a regular at BloodSource, but she was something new. After the second time he saw her there, she asked him out over paper cups of orange juice.

She was AB positive. He was AB negative. For some reason this attracted them.

"Is this your first time?" she'd asked.

"I've been doing this a while."

"Yeah? How long."

"Since I *could*. I've been coming here since I turned sixteen."

Amber had admired the dedication, the desire to help.

"Down to fifteen-point-eight billion this morning. Can you believe it?"

He could, and by the time the counter hit point-seven, he and Amber had lost their first child together, Taylor. Lost her in the womb. Amber in pain one morning – what she thought were contractions – and their daughter dead shortly thereafter, the ultrasound revealing a pulseless floating baby. And by the time the counter had dropped below fifteen billion, Amber had given birth to Dylan – two months early – and together they'd watched life support keep him alive until it couldn't.

20

He'd been giving blood for four years, every fifty-six days, and platelets in between – his mother and father still alive, his marriage and children still ten years in the future.

The woman behind the counter was new because the prior one had died. Michael knew this one would die, too, because everyone around him had started dying four years earlier.

It had something to do with the blood.

He knew the exact number, the day this hell began, the same way every boy and girl in the world knew the number: 17,989,101,196... the highest population of people ever recorded.

This had happened four years ago, back in high school.

A website was established, everyone mad with numbers and eager to see world population hit fifteen billion. Cell phone apps were created. You could find the counter just about anywhere, everyone waiting for the big day. How this ticker kept track of all death and life was a mystery to Michael, yet every time the number hit a new billion thereafter, people held parties, monitored the counters in schools, on screens, celebrating the explosion of life, despite the maladies created from overpopulation. Michael was in his history class when it happened, his teacher obsessed with watching the number grow. Mr. Laurensen had the counter displayed on a screen at the back of the room, kids craning their necks every so often to look.

"The monitor's stuck," someone had said, maybe Charlie Hanlon, and when his teacher asked what Charlie had said, he said it again. The life counter wasn't stuck, of course, but had tipped the fragile balance between life and death. For a few moments the 196 at the end stayed 196, long enough for everyone to see... and then it had dropped to 195, and then 194.

Never before had the number decreased.

It had always ticked along, growing, numbers too fast to follow, and then forever more the *life* clock had suddenly become the *death* clock.

By the end of class, 1,884 people had died, although Michael knew the number was much larger. People were also born at a surprising rate, so the 1,884 also included *new* life in the world, which meant the number of dead was either significantly higher, or that women all over the world had stopped birthing children.

The woman behind the counter at BloodSource cleared her throat because he'd zoned, thinking about the past. She'd be dead in a few years, he knew, replaced by someone else.

Four years seemed such a long time ago...

16

Michael was nervous because he'd never given blood before, or had never had his blood *taken*, as his mother had said after signing the consent form. It sounded so much worse for blood to be *taken* than to be *given*, and so Michael gave.

The number 17,989,101,196 was stuck in his mind.

"Why do you want to give?" his mother asked.

He shrugged and rolled up his sleeve.

"I heard casualties may rise to the *millions*. Can you imagine?"

10

The last thing Michael remembered was staggering to the front door and ringing the doorbell to his own home, afraid that letting go of his dripping wrist would create a mess if he tried opening the door, and because Mom and Dad would be so mad at what he'd done.

"Michael-oh-my-god!" his mother said, looking from his wrist to the scratch on his forehead to the blood pooling at his feet.

He'd passed out, then, on the porch, and the next thing he remembered was waking in a hospital bed, staring at a blood bag held above him by a skinny metal robot-like arm.

"Where's Dad?" he said.

"He's giving blood. You're AB negative and so is he."

"Is that Dad's blood?" he said, meaning the bag.

She smiled.

"No."

"Then why's he doing it?"

"There are millions of people in the world who need blood, just like you, and there are only so many people like your father willing to share. Someone gave this blood in case a boy like you might need it someday, and some day someone might need yours."

"Can I give blood too?"

"When you're old enough."

87

Millions, Michael mused. *The count's dropped from billions to millions.*

All those years ago he'd been so worried about casualties rising to a number as small as a million, and now that's all the world had remaining: hundreds of millions.

The world needed more donors than ever, as 30 per cent of those capable of donating AB positive or AB negative blood had simply *stopped* donating, their bodies too aged, and those capable of donating A, B, and O were all but extinct. Those like him, who donated AB, had suffered an inevitable decline over the years, 0.09 per cent incapable by age forty, 24 per cent by age fifty, and a whopping 40 per cent by age sixty, and now, at nearly ninety years of age, Michael had become one part of those statistics. Up until a few days ago he had escaped the odds.

What percentage of those his age were even *capable* of donating?

Perhaps he had memorised numbers to avoid becoming one.

Statistically, he thought, *I have 6.4 years left to live, 6.4 years left to help others live.*

"Hello again, Mr. Shoe," the nurse said, lips pressed into an unemotional line.

"It's been two days," Michael said. "You said I could return in two days to donate platelets. I guess my blood's not good enough anymore for red."

"It has been two days, and *yes,* you can donate platelets," she said.

"What's wrong with my blood, anyway?"

"The last few times you've tested anaemic, remember, Mr. Shoe?"

"That's because of my heart, I know. What do you expect? I'm eighty-seven. My doctor put me on pills to bring up my blood pressure… *up,* and so my blood's turned sour. Now he's put me on pills to bring *down* my blood pressure, and suddenly it's too *low.* Taking aspirin and other meds helps the risk of heart attack, he says, and now my blood's too *thin.* And you think I'm too old."

"Blood pressure medication does not disqualify you from donating, Mr. Shoe, nor does your age. There is no upper age limit as long as you are well. What disqualifies you is blood pressure lower than 90-over-50, or higher than 180-over-100, or if you are on blood-thinning medication to—"

"So test me now."

Michael rolled up his sleeve and made a fist.

"I thought you were here to donate platelets."

"I am, and I *will,* but the last three times I've come to donate *whole* blood, I've been denied. I want to see if I still can, is all."

She tested his blood pressure, which he knew was mostly to amuse him, and it was within range: 174-over-94, higher than he'd liked to see, but within the limits for donating blood. And for the third time in the last eight weeks – the last fifty-six days – he'd not *given* blood, but had it *taken* from him... for testing.

"We both know this will come back as anaemic and we'll have this entire argument all over again," she said. "The medication you're on thins your blood—"

"So you admit my medication's to blame!"

He couldn't remember having arguments with this woman.

Stacy, her name badge read.

"Test me again," he said, knowing his blood would be better.

"You can donate platelets today, Mr. Shoe, and if your blood tests well, in eight weeks, you can return to donate *whole* blood."

Perhaps the counts would be higher next time, since he'd stopped the medication, since he went the last fifty-six days *not* taking the damn pills.

And so he gave platelets this time around, and would try for blood again, and again, and again, having cut out the very things keeping his heart regulated – his prescriptions – and he'd continue giving until he gave it all. But would there be anyone left to take?

WHEREVER YOU LOOK

Ramsey Campbell

"Aren't you going to tell everybody about Bretherton, Mr Lavater?"

Maurice is about to read a sample of his latest novel to the Friends of Cheshire Libraries when the voice from the back of the audience accosts him. "Forgive me," he says, "about what?"

"Don't say what, say whom. Simeon Bretherton."

"I'm afraid I'm still not getting you."

"The writer you put in your book you have there."

"They must have crept in when I wasn't looking. I've never heard of them."

"You put their character in."

Maurice has started to feel as bemused as most of the audience look. "Which character?"

"The one you see looking out from behind things." The speaker demonstrates to the extent of an eye, having been concealed by an extravagantly burly man in the row next to the back of the ranks of folding chairs. "And you don't know who they are," he says, "until it's too late."

"I certainly don't know anything about them. Has anybody here heard of Simeon Bretherton?" When this prompts a general shaking of heads Maurice demands "What am I meant to have written?"

"The slanted wide-brimmed hat appeared to have tilted all his features, which might still have been slipping into place. His left eyebrow was lined up with the hat, and his pale blue left eye was higher than its whitish twin. Violence or birth had skewed his long thin nose leftwards. Even his slim black moustache was less than level, canted perhaps by the permanent sneer his pallid lips presented to the world."

All this is spoken in a neutral tone presumably designed to signify quotation. Maurice finds the sentences disconcertingly familiar, which provokes him to retort "Where's that from?"

"Your thirteenth chapter."

Maurice turns the pages of *Bell's Told* so fiercely he almost tears several. It's the scene where Victorian psychic investigator Solomon Bell views portraits of his haunted client's ancestors. Perhaps the subject of the painting is behind the spectral trouble, since he summoned spirits while he was alive, but Maurice never brings him onstage in the novel. Just the same, he's disconcerted not to have recognised the paragraph. "Fair enough, it's here," he has to admit. "It's mine."

"It's Simeon Bretherton, Mr Lavater, and is your hero's name a little tribute too?"

"I'd hardly have done that for somebody I've never heard of. What do you mean, it's him?"

"It's from his story, word for word."

Is the speaker about to claim that he wrote it – perhaps that conspirators blocked its publication? "Which story?" Maurice is less than eager to learn.

"The only one of his they ever published."

"And where can we find it?"

"Wherever you look." Presumably this refers to whichever method Maurice may use to search, since the speaker says "It went out of print before you were born."

"Do you have it with you?"

"I've just brought myself."

"I think we'll have to call any similarity a coincidence, however much of one it is." Maurice is angered to think this could sound more like an admission than scepticism. "Would anybody like to hear a less contentious section?" he hopes aloud.

As he finds the passage he planned to read he's aware that a member of the audience has stood up. A glance shows him a figure in black vanishing around a library bookcase. It's his accuser, who is carrying some item, not a book. "Is that all he came for?" Maurice mutters, not entirely to himself.

He reads the scene where Bell plays bridge with his client and her family and sees faces of her ancestors peering from behind cards as they're laid on the baize. Just now it feels unnecessarily and of course coincidentally like a reference to the tale his interrogator cited. More than one library user eavesdrops on his performance, unless it's the same person who leans around a bookcase and is gone whenever Maurice glances up. He's presenting copies of his novels to the library when the secretary of the Friends brings him an apologetic look. "I've no idea who that person at the back was," she says. "He certainly wasn't with us."

"Maybe just someone else who cares about books."

"So long as we don't get too immersed in them like him."

As Maurice drives home he can't outrun the notion that whatever he told his audience, the passage the intruder quoted seems familiar, not just from Maurice's own work. He hasn't identified it by the time he reaches New Ferry, the Wirral district he has taken to calling No Ferry, not least because he lives so far from the river where there used to be one. Eventually he succeeds in manoeuvring into a space between cars parked half on the pavement in the cul-de-sac shaped like a noose at the end of the rope of a side road, an image he's repeated in so many interviews it feels as though it has tightened on his brain. As he makes for his pebbledashed house, which is no smaller than the other dinky dwellings, front rooms flicker with the light from screens, and he wonders how many of his neighbours ever read a book.

He falls asleep still struggling to disinter the memory he's sure is buried in his brain. In the morning he makes himself ignore the impression while he tries to work on his next novel. Soon he's reduced to gazing at the distant scrap of river that glints between the houses opposite, beneath a feeble sun brought low by October. At least he can swear as loud and as furiously as he likes, since he no longer has the girlfriend who might have been his partner if she hadn't objected to the language his frustration with a first draft always provokes and her rebukes exacerbated. His parents wouldn't approve, and no doubt theirs would have even less. The thought of them reminds him how early he began reading, and then he recalls the first adult book he ever read.

Was he even as old as seven? He and his parents were spending half his summer holidays with his father's parents, whose house Maurice had thought was no more ancient than them, though of course it would have been. In its musty library, where he was allowed to browse unsupervised, he'd found a book of ghostly fiction with a skull embossed on the faded blackish spine. He remembers tales about a sheet that came to life on a bed, and someone who was given a guest room they'd had nightmares about before they'd ever seen it, and two friends who vowed that whoever died first would appear to the other. He can name them and their authors, but might he have forgotten reading a contribution by what was the writer called, Simeon Bretherton?

If he ever knew the title of the book, he doesn't now. An online search for Simeon Bretherton brings just one reference to anybody of that name, the sexton of St Aloysius Parish Church, a position the man held over a century ago. The church is in New Ferry, and the online map places it about a mile away. A glance in that direction shows Maurice the admonitory fingertip of a church spire above a roof across the road.

The information only leaves him feeling more dissatisfied. Even if the sexton wrote the ghostly tale, what help is that? Maurice needs to dismiss all the coincidences so as to work, but they've settled in his mind. Could rereading the passage he's meant to have copied give him back some control? He's searching for it, having put in the description of the hat, when he realises how confused he is. He's looking for the paragraph in the book he's working on.

Of course it can't be in there, and he brings up the file of *Bell's Told*. He pores over the paragraph until the sentences begin to disintegrate into phrases and then into separate words in his skull. He has to reread the paragraph yet again to put its sense together, a process unsettlingly suggestive of reconstructing a presence. Perhaps he did indeed encounter something similar that lodged unnoticed in his head – and then he starts to feel he came upon some form of it more recently than childhood. A more disquieting possibility feels unlikely as a dream, one he wouldn't want to have. Since disbelief fails to shift it, he opens more files onscreen to search for phrases that are lying low in his mind. Soon he makes a sound that can't find a word for his feelings, and before long he releases another. Each of his books contains an image he finds altogether too familiar.

In *Bell, Book and Candle* a sinister punter at a racetrack wears a hat skewed in line with his features, unless it's the other way around. In *Clear as a Bell* the coquettish wearer of an equally wide-brimmed item keeps one eyebrow raised in alignment with it while she describes an apparently spectral encounter. In *Bell Towers* the driver of a hansom cab who takes Bell unbidden into a maze of fogbound London streets looks down at him through the trap with one eye higher than its paler twin. By now Maurice feels as though an unnoticed tenant of his head has been making surreptitious bids for freedom. He very much wants to regard his depiction of the fake medium in *Give Them a Bell* as coincidental – surely many characters in fiction have a dislocated nose – except that Bell can't decide whether birth or violence is responsible for the deformity. Maurice is desperate to find no likeness in *Sound as a Bell*, but then he remembers the pimp who organises vigilantes to protect women of the street from Jack the Ripper – the pimp whose slim black moustache is canted in parallel with his permanent sneer.

Maurice is distracted by a sight across the road. Sunlight between his house and its neighbour lends a streetlamp a reduced shadow like the silhouette of a thin man sporting a hat, a sketch waiting for details to be added. He closes all the files apart from the novel in progress, only to find he can't write another word. His efforts feel like struggling not to repeat any more of the tale his childhood reading buried in his mind, but how will he know if he fails? He has to read the tale.

A new search for Simeon Bretherton only revives the sketchy facts about the sexton. Adding 'story' brings no extra information, and 'ghost story' is unproductive too. Maurice tries patching the entire paragraph from *Bell's Told* into the search box, just as uselessly. He needs to consult someone who might help. In moments he has a list of second-hand booksellers, and he phones the topmost at once. "Boon of Books," a woman says as though she's naming herself.

"I'm hoping you can help me find a book by an author."

"They're mostly by them, aren't they?" When Maurice fails to find much of a sound to make in response she says "Are you looking for romance?"

"Not presently, thank you." Has he somehow contacted quite the wrong kind of service? "Just a book," he says. "I thought that was what you deal in."

"Plenty of romance in those." Rather too much in a counsellor's tone she says "Tell me what you need."

"A book with a story by Simeon Bretherton."

"That doesn't sound like one of ours. We don't do books with stories in."

"Then what do they contain?"

"Love." As Maurice tries not to feel personally addressed by the word, she says "Just one story each."

Maurice does his best to laugh at himself. "Romance novels, you mean."

"That's what Boon's all about. What did you think we were?"

"More than that," Maurice says and feels unreasonable at once.

The shadow on the pavement has grown human in its stature, if less so in its shape, by the time a man answers his next call. "Just For Your Shelf."

"I'm trying to track down a book I once read."

"If it's any good we've got it or we'll get it." He sounds not far from tired of saying so, but adds "What's the name?"

"Mine? Maurice Lavater."

"Not yours. The one you think I ought to know."

"I think perhaps you might know mine. I'm a writer."

"Really." With no increase of enthusiasm the bookseller says "Published?"

"Six novels and a seventh on the way."

"Maurice Lavater." As if he's solved that problem the bookseller says "May I ask your field?"

"My publishers call them supernatural thrillers." In case this sounds defensive Maurice says "So do I."

"That explains my lack of recognition. We wouldn't have you in the shop." Before Maurice can react the bookseller says "Must I assume the book you're seeking is your kind?"

"I believe you could say so."

"I wouldn't, no." More dismissively still the bookseller says "You should consult a specialist."

When he grasps that this is all the help the man intends to offer, Maurice can't resist asking "Do you sell many books?"

"Enough." Although this sounds like a bid to end the conversation, the man says "And yourself?"

"Plenty."

"No doubt you're bound to."

Maurice is in no danger of mistaking this for praise. He terminates the call and searches furiously for names related to his field. Terrific Tomes appears to be, and he calls the number. The supine shadow has vanished. The houses are blocking the sunlight, of course; the silhouette hasn't dodged behind the streetlamp. Just the same, he's squinting at the outline of the metal post to confirm nothing else is there when a woman says "Tomes."

"Terrific, would that be?"

"That's our first name. What can we do for you today?"

"I wonder if you could find me a story by Simeon Bretherton."

"In the wings of the world."

Does this mean she can't? "If that's where you have to look," Maurice tries to hope.

"No," the bookseller says with a delicate giggle. "That's what his only story's called."

"Has it been reprinted, do you know?"

"It was only ever in *Tales of the Ghostly and the Grim*."

As the title goes some way towards rousing a memory Maurice says "Have you any idea where I should look for that?"

"I can see it now across the shop."

"I'll buy it," Maurice says almost before he finds the breath to speak. "How soon can you get it to me?"

"As soon as you've paid. You're looking at fifty-five including postage." When Maurice undertakes to pay at once she says "Let me fetch your book."

As he takes out his credit card he hears sounds suggestive of a distant struggle. The returning footsteps are slower than the ones that went away, and the bookseller says "You'd think it didn't want you reading it."

More nervously than he welcomes Maurice says "How do you mean?"

"My colleague must have wedged too many books in. You'd have thought someone was keeping hold of it on the shelf. Just tell me where I'm sending it." When Maurice gives his name she cries "Not the Bell man."

"I'm glad someone's heard of me."

"We're often asked for your books. Drop in and sign some whenever you're in our part of the country." Having copied his address with a chatter of plastic keys, she says "So there are two of you there."

"Two of whom?"

"You and Bretherton. He was the sexton at one of your local churches." Perhaps she thinks the silence means Maurice needs to be placated, since she says "You're the one people know."

"We know about him."

"I'm afraid we're a dying breed." The phone emits a rustling sound, and the bookseller adds "Well, here he is."

"Who?" Maurice feels further driven to ask "How?"

"My colleague let a draught in, as if it isn't cold enough. Don't pull that face or it'll stay lopsided, Dan." To Lavater she says "It turned up your man."

"His story, you mean."

"I'm looking at his words right now." A thud leaves Maurice unaccountably anxious until she speaks again. "He'll be with you tomorrow."

The thud was her shutting the book, of course. May its imminence let him write? His mind is strewn with fragments of Bretherton's description, and he can't think past them. In the hope of dislodging the obstacles or of coaxing his mind to relax he wanders out of the house. He's about to go for a stroll when he decides to see if anything significant is to be found at the church.

On the far side of the road that divides the district, every second street denies entry to traffic. By the time he finds St Aloysius his mind feels as tangled as the route. As he drives around the outside of the churchyard, pale figures glide from behind others of their species. They're memorials lent movement by the car, but why do some of their discoloured outlines flicker as though uncertain of their shapes? He could think his eyes are growing unreliable, or his mind – and then he sees that the unsteady glare comes from lamps on the roofs of several police vehicles drawn up outside the church.

He's coasting past them and trying to make out the dim interior beyond the porch when he's overwhelmed by an aroma of cannabis so powerful it sets his head swimming. His foot falters on the accelerator, and the car stumbles to a halt. A policeman using a mobile phone stares at him, which makes Maurice stall the engine afresh once he has wrenched a shriek from the starter motor. His mime of comical incompetence brings the officer over to him. More like a warning than an invitation the policeman says "Can I help you, sir?"

"I'm a writer." Since this earns no response, Maurice adds "I was wanting to research the history."

"Too late for that now." Not much less ominously the policeman says "Should we know your name?"

"Maurice Lavater," Maurice says and fumbles out his driving licence.

"Weren't you in the paper recently?" When Maurice confirms this, though he's unsure how accusing the question sounds, the policeman says "This would have been right up your street."

"I don't deal much with drugs. Just opium because I'm writing Victorian."

The policeman gives him a searching look. "How the neighbours found out what was going on would be. The watchman for the gang, he started screaming in the night. That's why someone called us."

"Too much cannabis, do you think?"

"Too much." As Maurice starts to feel admonished the policeman tells him "The watchman said he thought someone kept looking in the windows. Said when he tried to chase them their face came off the inside of the glass."

"There'll be faces in the stained glass, I suppose."

"He said it wasn't one of those, and it kept following him round in the dark. Some of us might say it serves him right." When Maurice finds the notion too disquieting to endorse, the policeman says "What kind of research were you looking to do?"

"Whatever documents there are. Perhaps the parish magazine."

"They'll be well gone somewhere if they're anywhere. The place has been shut down for years, and the priest's house."

Maurice manages to drive away without betraying any further clumsiness. Could breathing in the smell from the cannabis factory have affected him? In that case it should have acted on the policeman as well, and wasn't the man's peaked cap a shade askew? He's out of sight by now, and Maurice sees no way of sneaking back. Instead he drives home so carefully he feels as if he's striving not to wobble his attenuated head.

When at last he finishes inching the car into the only available space near his house, the retired teacher who lives opposite hurries up to him. Her urgency disconcerts him until he realises she's being propelled by a hound large enough to feature in an Edwardian tale. She only just succeeds in tugging it to a temporary halt that lets her greet Maurice.

"Written any books this week?" she says, cocking an eyebrow that's presumably meant to be humorous.

"Ah ha." While this is designed more to acknowledge than to celebrate the joke, does it resemble agreement too much? "Ha ha," Maurice adds without mirth.

When the hound hauls her onwards he makes for his desk, but can't think past the day's events. What's so significant about them? Perhaps the policeman helped him after all, and the church records have indeed been preserved somewhere. Maurice calls the central library in Birkenhead and learns that the archive has a set of the St Aloysius parish magazine. If he requests it now he can view it tomorrow.

First he'll need to wait for the package from Terrific Tomes. He makes himself a pasta dinner before spending time with the television. Vintage films generally help him relax, but all those he tries to watch contain at least one man with a moustache. When this persists in troubling him he retreats to bed. Thoughts that feel like fragments of a tale someone has already told keep him awake, not least because he has an impression that they apply to him. He can't judge how while he's unable to define them. At last he sleeps, only to dream that somebody is pounding on the inside of a lid. The sound pursues him into daylight, and he realises it's at the front door. He stumbles to the window in time to see a uniformed figure heading for a van. "Hello?" Maurice shouts, louder once he has raised the plastic sash.

"On your step."

The man might almost be fleeing the item he brought. He turns no more than momentarily to respond, so that Maurice can't be sure one side of his face is higher than the other. Perhaps it was distorted by a grimace. Maurice hurries downstairs to find a parcel not so much delivered as abandoned, its padded envelope partially unstuffed by a bid to force it through the letterbox. He shakes its greyish innards into the kitchen bin and unpicks the staples with an aching fingernail. The book wrapped in a plastic sheet like a cluster of translucent eggs is indeed *Tales of the Ghostly and the Grim*.

Maurice sprawls in a front-room chair to read Simeon Bretherton's story, which concerns a sexton who rings the church bell most enthusiastically whenever there's a funeral. His gusto appears to offend or else to rouse one of the deceased, who sets about returning piecemeal.

Local villagers the sexton hasn't previously met prove to have features reminiscent of the dead man – one feature each. In preparation for Sunday mass the sexton is struggling to remove hymnals so firmly wedged into a shelf that it feels as if someone is gripping them when they yield all at once, and he almost ends up supine. Did he glimpse a shape behind the books? The shelf is empty, but beside it a mirror reveals the face looming at his back. He swings around to see he's alone in the sacristy, or at least that part of it. The lopsided sneering face is behind the glass, and sidles forth as a long thin greyish arm reaches for his head. When the priest finds the sexton's body, it bears the dead man's face.

Maurice shuts the book and lets it fall beside his chair. Now that he has finished the story, he hopes it has finished with him – hopes it stays trapped in the book. It strikes him as an incoherent piece that could only have impressed him as a child. Surely reading in context the paragraph he hadn't known he quoted will have freed him to write – but when he tries to work on his novel, his mind feels as obstructed as ever. He could fancy Bretherton's description isn't satisfied with its revival, a nonsensical notion he can't dislodge. He still has to visit the library archive, and even if he finds nothing worth the journey, perhaps leaving his desk for a while will shift the hindrance out of his mind.

In twenty minutes he's at the library, where the front entrance huddles under a massive two-storey porch between twin wings full of windows. The stone is grey as twilight beneath the sunless sky. Nobody looks at Maurice until he rests his elbows on the counter in the midst of a multitude of shelves. When a librarian approaches he says "Maurice Lavater."

"Oh yes."

This sounds nowhere close to recognition. Her colleague's glance across a table piled with new books suggests he knows the name, but Maurice finds this less than heartening, since one of the man's eyes appears to be paler than the other. "You have some parish publications for me," Maurice tells the woman.

"If I could just see your card."

Of course she isn't doubting his identity, and he hands over his library card. "Where would you like to start?" she says.

The online paragraph about the sexton gave the date of his death. "I think nineteen hundred may be what I'm after."

She hands Maurice a hefty foolscap box, which he takes to a seat, though not at once. He's wary of sharing a table with a morose man whose nose is spectacularly dislocated, and a fellow sneering so hard at a newspaper that his lips drag his moustache awry seems worth avoiding too. Instead Maurice finds an empty table by a window overlooking a lawn and a wide low shrub, its leaves reduced to blackness by the unforthcoming sky. When he opens the box, the topmost magazine lifts its flimsy cover as though it has been waiting for him.

The cover shows the church as it was more than a century ago. It doesn't mention Simeon Bretherton, but he's lying in wait on page five. The obituary praises his commitment to the church and celebrates how vigorously he used to ring the bell, though the writer stops short of specifying any occasion. Maurice finds he needs to read all this as a distraction from the photograph that accompanies the testimonial. Despite its age, it preserves every detail: the rakish wide-brimmed hat, the eyebrow raised in sympathy with the unaligned and mismatched eye, the sideways nose, the moustache lined up with the sneer.

Surely the sexton wouldn't have chosen this expression for a photograph, and Maurice can only conclude he was permanently deformed by the look. Did he write his appearance into his story in a bid to set it apart from him? Maurice hasn't realised he's clenching his face until he feels it relax. He very much hopes the insight he has gained will let him return to his own tale. He lifts his head as though his mind has raised it and his consciousness, and meets the eyes of the face outside the window.

He could imagine he's still looking at the photograph in the magazine, or at any rate he's desperate to think so. When he wavers to his feet and ventures closer, the face advances too. Was it wearing a hat to begin with? It is now. No, that's the blackened shrub, which he misperceived because his right eye isn't functioning too well. He rubs the eye, an activity the watcher imitates with a finger on a pallid eyeball. Perhaps Maurice is grimacing even though he thought he'd managed to relax, and the watcher is copying him. Maurice leans forward and sees the patch of grass where the tilted shrub stands – sees the grass through the face. Now his viewpoint no longer lets the shrub pose as a hat, but he ducks forward again and again in a wild attempt to rid himself of the appearance on the glass. Before anyone can reach him he has smashed the window with his face, and the opposite as well. He's no further use to me, but now I'm in your book.

SAME TIME NEXT YEAR

Angela Slatter

It's just gone dusk, when the day bruises blue, and Cindy sits on the tomb, one of those big old ones shaped from grey granite into a box, about four feet high by six long by two wide; it's not hers. She's wearing a black leather jacket she got from god-knows-where and she's drinking a beer. It's got the word 'craft' on its label, which is pink, like no beer bottle she'd ever seen in her life. It tastes kinda weird, not like she remembers. Then again, she's not really tasting it, is she?

Hell, it was free, set like an offering on a grave with a bunch of wildflowers that were probably wilting even before they got left, so no complaints. And then again, it's not like the beer does anything but pour through her, what with ghosts lacking in solidity and all. It's just waterfalling from her lips, inside her throat, outside her neck, down her front, through her lap, and pattering onto the slab beneath her spectral butt.

Cindy shrugs off the leather jacket, drapes it on the tomb; it might be here when she gets back, it might not. Things disappear and reappear in the cemetery with surprising regularity. So does she, sometimes. If it was just stuff, just things, she'd suppose *Kids*, like an old lady. Kids daring each other to jump the rusty iron fence and run through, teens trying for the high of making love among the dead ("coming while you're going," someone used to say, yet she cannot remember who for the life or death of her). But who else except her could pick up this thing that's not really made of leather, not anymore, just wishes and cobwebs and bad dreams? Maybe a memory or two, although not ones she can recall. Besides, not many come out here nowadays, none but those who've got no choice.

It's not like she needs it against the cold or anything. Beneath the jacket she's wearing a dress, the dress she woke in, the lavender chiffon whisper of a thing that's almost a nightgown, maybe a prom dress. She wonders, oh yes she does, where she was going and what she was doing when she died, but that seems to have been wiped away with her passing.

Passing.

Stupid word. Dying, gone, rotted, decayed.

Dead.

She's sure as shit she never owned anything like this in life. There are splinters and shards of before she woke here. Cracks and fractures and fragments of a rundown house, small squalling siblings (their number is never fixed), a woman who yelled and a man who yelled louder still. Maybe there was some school, too, but she can't quite lay heavy hold on those thoughts. But there must have been, if she's dressed for a prom, right? Junior or senior? Who knows?

She shivers, a human action remembered, not felt. She looks down, notices some dark spots on the skirt. She waves a hand across them and they disappear: either covered or disintegrated, she doesn't really know. The things she can do she doesn't really understand, but wishes she'd been able to do them in life, might have made living a damned sight easier. Whatever her life was then it doesn't feel easy, not in the broken recollections that float in her head. Whatever comes back to her has no rhyme or reason.

But now, *right now*, she can feel the weight coming upon her – one night, one night a year – she should have waited to drink the beer. How could she forget that? Cindy reaches out and touches the jacket: yes, it feels different now, weighty. The scent of it is dead and dusty, animal and musky. Old, old, old. She pushes herself away from the tomb, takes steps that are at first tiny, then grow longer, grander as she feels her own heft upon the earth. The grass is dry, this time of year, a fire risk, but it's not as if that bothers her or anyone else here. The little chapel by the half-empty pond is painted red and white like a barn; half the roof's caved in. No one tends to anything anymore. The paths are overgrown, the hedges are scrappy, the trees thin-limbed, their leafy cover sparse against the darkening sky; just enough to keep the light of the incipient stars at bay. Clouds cover the moon but she doesn't need light to see by.

The rows of the cemetery aren't especially orderly, and the headstones... many of them have a lean to them, and layers of moss, names and dates worn away. She can't remember where the bones of her lie, not anymore, if she ever knew.

When she begins to *thicken*, some of the memories come back, but not that one, never that one. It makes her think that maybe she wasn't ever properly interred. *Interred*. What a word. Fancy way of saying *planted*.

Cindy.

The last boy called her that. She doesn't know what function she was fulfilling for him, only knows he called her that as he put his hands around her throat, pushed himself into her — there's just one night a year she can be solid. He sounded so angry as he said the name, even angrier when she began to laugh despite the choking pressure of his big hands. Not so angry when she dissolved beneath him, left him with cock rapidly softening, mouth slack and fingers empty.

He got up, though, got up and ran. She just floated along behind, dead breath at his shoulder, a purplish mist. She stayed with him until he ran into an oak tree. He'd put his head down, running like he was heading towards a touchdown, so when he hit the trunk it was at just the right angle to fracture his neck. Not enough to kill him, though; she watched him flop back on the grass and lie still. His gaze shifted — the only thing that could move, she guessed — and he watched her with concentrated terror. How quickly things changed! She watched him in turn for a while, grinning like a loon, then settled on his broad chest, put one hand — suddenly solid, suddenly heavy, this one night — onto his throat and began to squeeze.

He took a while to die. Four minutes, isn't it, to strangulation? She was sure she'd read that somewhere. She'd touched her own throat with her free hand; stroked the non-flesh, felt it give, pushed her fingers through it, just a little — not *entirely* solid, then — and felt creeped out. She'd pulled her fingers away. She wanted to tell him that she was angry too; everybody was angry even if not everyone could recall the why of it, but what was he going to do with that knowledge?

At the end of those four minutes, though, he was gone. Gone. The core of him, the spirit, the equivalent of the whatever-of-Cindy-that-remained-behind: his *went*. She never saw him again, neither hide nor ectoplasmic hair. And Lordy, wasn't that so unfair? That he got to disappear and she had to hang around here like *she'd* done something bad? Stuck forever in detention after school.

Cindy.

She can't even remember her own name, but she remembers that one.

It's as good as any.

They'll be coming soon. It's about time. That's right, she thinks, remembering now, pieces and remnants.

Friday night was always dance night.

They all used to come out here, the kids, drunk and high, brave as crazed 'coons. They didn't think too much at all, just following primal urges, dark desires and yearnings with no consideration of whether getting what they wanted was a good idea. She's pretty sure she didn't get anything good for her, but the memories are still not there, not properly. It's just flickering screens like a ruined film, a flipbook of figures: her, two boys, a case of beer. She doesn't want to look, she decides.

The clouds shift and the moon shows her own face, just a sliver, just a hint.

Cindy shakes her head; doesn't see a lot of folk here nowadays, though. None, really, to be precise. Too far outside of town, there are other places, better places, more comfortable for getting into trouble. Sometimes boys and girls used to come, though − that boy who ran into the tree, and gave her a name, and who she'd have left alone if he'd not behaved so badly, but he'd wandered in that night, that one night, and well... there you go. She didn't encounter too many girls once upon a time, but behaviours changed, oh yes they did, and for a while young women used to hide out, smoke, drink, what-have-you. Cindy listened a lot when they talked, curious and bemused. Apparently equality meant behaving as badly as men, rather than setting an expectation that they behave better. But she'd never bothered the girls; figured they'd got enough shit to deal with on their own without her adding to matters. Cindy shakes her head; the only true equality they've got is death.

Lordy, Lordy, when did she become a philosopher?

About ten years after you died, says a voice in her head, *ten years of sitting alone in a bone orchard talking to yourself.*

"There's no one else around," she says aloud. But even then, she's not quite sure when it was or how long she's been around.

The air's cool on her skin now and Cindy enjoys the sensation. There are no noises in the night, but she's here so seldom, her memory's so thin, that it doesn't really strike her, the lack of owl hoots, possums, foxes, wild cats and the like. Not even an insect, not a katydid singing. Nothing, just her bare feet on dried grass, *crunch, crunch, crunch.*

So the voices come clear through air that's uncontaminated by other sound, though they're low murmurs, that tone boys have before their voices settle proper. Cindy sees them before they see her.

Two boys. Youths. Young men, really, not quite tall and their limbs still gangly like they don't quite know what to do with their bits and pieces. Slicked back hair, one head black, the other blond, both with cigarettes in overly-large hands. Furtive looks beneath beetle-brows, and confused. Uncertain, as if they don't know how they got here. Familiar, familiar, familiar.

Then they see her and stare. Cindy keeps her pace steady, dignified; the pace of a girl going to her prom, so the lavender mist of skirt swirls around her. She clasps her hands in front at first, but it feels wrong, so she swings them, slaps them into the small of her back and suddenly looks like a general on parade. She lifts her chin, too, juts it forward and the moon spills from behind the last cloud to show Cindy's face to the young men.

Whatever they see, they crack.

Cigarettes are tossed to the ground, bounce with tiny red flares on the dry grass, but Cindy walks over the greedy flames, snuffs them before they can get a hold. She feels the burns as a tickle, a lick, and continues on. She doesn't quicken at all, but somehow they can't pull away from her. Maybe it's all the headstones they're dodging around and between, as if they don't want to disrespect the dead by thudding over them. Cindy has no such qualms, she puts her feet down where she will.

"Hello, boys," she calls, but they offer no answer, although she thinks perhaps she hears a whimper. Maybe that's just wishful thinking.

They hurdle the rusty iron fence like track stars. They breach a boundary she cannot, no matter how much she's tried or how often over the years. They slip and slide and tumble down into the dusty ditch by the side of the road that hardly sees any traffic, then scramble up the other incline. Both break onto the asphalt like birds loosed, like they're hitting the tape at the end of a running track: arms up, chests out, heads tipped back.

The car comes out of nowhere.

There's no sound, at least not until the last moment, when the engine roars just before it hits. And it hits them both at the same time. She thinks neither of them have their feet on the ground, they're still in flight, still in motion, still flying through the air with the greatest of ease.

Cindy's hands go to her throat, delighted shock, gleeful awe, awful glee.

Boys and vehicle — a turquoise and white Chevrolet Bel Air with its top up — burst.

One moment, they are themselves. The next they're stardust and particles, strangely wet-looking, a red fleck beneath the moon as the confetti of them drifts down to the road's surface.

"Happy anniversary. Same time next year, assholes," she says, and as soon as the words are out she begins to forget they were ever there. She loses her weight, her density. The dress turns to the consistency of candy floss once again. She can't see the jacket anymore, but maybe she's wandered too far from it. She feels lighter, lighter, lighter, she is moonlight and dust and a bitter breath on the night breeze.

Damn but there was something she wishes she could remember...

MINE SEVEN

Elana Gomel

Black sky, white snow, yellow light.

Lena felt that her vision was being starved of some essential nutrient. She longed for fire-engine red, viridian green, shocking purple. But the electric glow in the Funken Lodge leached brightness out of everything, slashing the entire spectrum down to the uncompromising contrast of arctic winter: darkness and light. It repelled and attracted her in equal measure. She spent most of her time staring out of the curving floor-to-ceiling windows of the lounge, seeing the pale blob of her face surrounded by reflections of the chandeliers like jellyfish swimming in a sea of tar.

Bill, on the other hand, happily mined the darkness for Instagram posts. He would go out with his cameras and come back hours later, stomping his chain-wreathed boots to shake off the snow, removing his multi-layered parka, fur hat and face protector in the side-room the hotel provided for its guests' winter equipment. Then he would bound up the stairs into the lounge to show her his latest pictures. The black sky at midday; the sparkle of fairy lights in downtown Longyearbyen; clumps of ice crystals growing where no plants ever grew. He was gleeful about having caught the Northern Lights on camera. Lena found the greenish smears against the pitch background less than impressive. Tomorrow, though, the Aurora forecast predicted a better display.

Tomorrow was a relative term. In mid-January in Svalbard the sun never rose above the horizon. Darkness was the same whether one was asleep or awake; in the middle of breakfast or having a nightcap. It was like being in a fever dream. The sluggishness of time thickened Lena's blood. She was perpetually cold, her body repelling the generous warmth of the hotel's blazing radiator heaters.

Bill made fun of her. After all, he said, she should feel at home here. Spitsbergen, though a Norwegian territory, had a Russian mining settlement, Barentsburg, and an abandoned Soviet-era ghost town, Pyramiden. Chukchi people were not Russians, she would remind him, but such distinctions were lost on Americans. Most of the time they were lost on Lena herself.

This arctic vacation had been Bill's idea, with Lena tagging along, partly out of curiosity about her heritage but mostly based on the simple 'why not?' They had the money: Bill's startup dividends. Her social-media post about their plans had elicited a flurry of envious likes. But now she felt like a prisoner in the bright lodge surrounded by the encroaching dark, held at bay only by the incandescence of the electric lights that never went out in Longyearbyen.

Until they did.

★   ★   ★

They were as unlike as two women could possibly be: the waitress blonde and thin, with washed-out blue eyes; Lena dark and round-cheeked. But when the waitress, whose name was Irina, took her orders, Lena heard an echo of her mother's liquid vowels and hard consonants in her speech. Irina was overjoyed when addressed in Russian.

They chatted about the hardships and pleasures of living in the northernmost town in the world. One got used to the cold, Irina said. And it was getting warmer too.

"Adventfjorden used to be frozen in winter," Irina continued. "Now it's ice-free all year round. Whales come. Fish too, lots of cod. People go fishing in January."

"Why would they?" Lena asked. "Isn't it too cold?"

Irina shrugged.

"People need jobs," she said. "Mines are gone."

Longyearbyen used to be a mining town. Spitsbergen's greasy coal, dug out of the permafrost, had, once upon a time, been the best in the world. Americans, Norwegians and Russians had competed for the black gold. Lena and Bill had gone to see one of the decommissioned mines, now trying to pass itself off as a tourist attraction. Lena could not imagine anything less attractive than the narrow tunnels flooded with thick darkness and festooned with ice spears, broken machinery frozen into the unyielding ground like sinners in Dante's hell. But men had crawled through these wormholes, hacked blackness out of coal-seams, and coughed their lungs out in the meagre air.

Five of the six mines were closed now. The remaining one provided the electricity that kept Longyearbyen lit and netted the miners a million kroner a year.

"Do you miss Russia?" Lena asked.

A faraway look on Irina's face reminded Lena of her mother's expression on the rare occasions when she spoke of her childhood in the Siberian town of Anadyr. Her mother swore she had nothing to be nostalgic about. But Lena had seen her on more than one occasion furtively go through yellowed pictures of unsmiling men and women in front of deerskin yurts.

Before she could answer, Bill showed up, his face ruddy from his morning photo-excursion. They switched back to English. Lena regretted it, even though her Russian was rusty. As for Chukchi, a native Siberian language spoken by a few thousand in the world, she only knew a hypnotic litany that her Nana had made her learn by heart, telling her it was a powerful spell made up by her shaman grandfather. Lena understood not a word of it but cherished it as a memory of Nana, whose wrinkled-apple face and kind hands presided over her childhood.

Lena picked up Bill's phone, scrolling through the pictures. She paused, staring at a close-up of garishly lit snow piled up against the Falun-red wall of an apartment building. Sharp shadows drew a cartoon sketch of a snarling face on the powdery surface.

Irina refilled their coffee cups.

"My Northern Lights app says we'll have a great display today," Bill declared. "I have arranged for a dogsled ride!"

They had visited a dogs' compound, where big huskies bedded placidly in snowdrifts and puppies who had never been indoors played in the frozen glare of spotlights. Lena looked longingly at the overstuffed armchairs of the library nook.

"All right," she said.

"I went to Svald-bar for coffee," Bill continued (Svald-bar being the cute name of his favourite downtown hangout). "I saw that guy drinking aquavit. I thought I would have some but then I realised it was only 3:00 a.m. Darkness really messes up your biological clock."

He laughed raucously.

"It is Old Sven," Irina said. "He used to be a miner. At Mine Seven."

"What's Mine Seven?" Bill asked. "I thought there were six mines on Spitsbergen."

"It's locked."

"You mean closed," Bill corrected. Irina smiled, tight-lipped, and flitted to the next table. The Funken Lodge had few guests, mostly from Norway and the UK. Svalbard winter tourism was still a niche industry.

Lena reluctantly followed Bill down the stairway that looked magical in the soft glow of the hanging clusters of pearly lights. She would be happy to stay in the Lodge, poring over the old volumes of the history of Spitsbergen and nibbling on a cloudberry jam toast. A dogsled ride would take them outside the perimeter of lights, into the unrelieved darkness of the rest of the island. It felt final.

She took her time, putting on her outer trousers, her padded parka, and fixing the chains to her fur-lined boots, dreading the slap of the frozen air. But when they finally stepped outside, she realised she must have become inured to the brutal cold. She felt numb rather than frozen. Hypothermia setting in? Lena told Bill she wanted a cup of hot chocolate before heading out on the dogsled.

They walked downtown, following the thin setting moon, which was surrounded by a hazy halo. The streets shone like a handful of jewels set in dull black velvet. Longyearbyen had a shopping centre, a library and a museum, all limned in garish electric garlands. The town was positively profligate in its use of lighting. Tall pylons that lined its streets were topped with blinding spotlights, each shedding enough illumination for an average American block. Apartment houses had large windows, defiantly kept un-curtained, that dripped pools of multi-coloured radiance onto the snow. There were fairy lights and bright shop signs everywhere. Electricity was not a problem. The coal was still there.

Nobody was supposed to venture outside the lit zone alone and unarmed. Polar bears lurked there in increasing numbers, spurred on to migration by the melting ice-fields and warming seas. A polar bear had killed a child in the schoolyard a year ago. Since then, more and more people carried guns everywhere. Lena looked at the giant whitish ghosts surrounding the town, leaning into its bright core, and shivered. What good would bullets do against these somnolent monsters?

These were mountains, of course, not enormous beasts. Just mountains where the coal slept.

A man staggered toward them. At first Lena thought he was slipping on the iced pavement, even though most inhabitants of Longyearbyen were surprisingly sure-footed. But then she realised the man was drunk. He swayed and mumbled to himself as he passed by.

"That's the guy I saw in the bar!" Bill said.

The man folded into the snow. They tried to lift him up but he was surprisingly heavy, his parka too tight on his swollen body, bursting at the seams.

Bill frowned.

"He looked smaller in the bar," he muttered. "But it's him."

Two figures materialised out of the gloom, pulled the fallen man up and hustled him away, their wrapped-up heads giving them the appearance of strange insects.

Lena and Bill walked on toward the local bakery. Childishly, she hoped that if she procrastinated enough, the dark day would seamlessly melt into the night and the dogsled ride would be cancelled.

Her hope was realised, though not in the way she had intended.

★　★　★

The owner of the *Fruene* café, a stocky Norwegian named Bjorn, poured two steaming cups of what was advertised as the only gourmet chocolate made beyond the Arctic Circle. Lena swirled the thick liquid in her cup, staring at the stuffed polar bear mounted with its paws waving in the air as if about to slap down a customer. The sign at the entrance said in English: "This bear is already dead. Please leave your gun at the counter."

"Who is Old Sven?" she asked Bjorn.

"Old Sven? A miner. A former miner. He has been in Longyearbyen forever. One of our oldest residents."

"Doesn't he have a family on the mainland? To go somewhere warmer?"

"It's getting warmer here."

"Really?" Bill interjected sceptically.

"Ja. Permafrost is melting."

"Did he work in Mine Seven?" Lena asked.

She caught a grimace of distaste on Bjorn's face as he pondered how to fob her off. But he never had the chance. The lights went out.

* * *

Lena pushed a rolled-up map into the purple maw of the fire and coughed when acrid smoke stung her sinuses. It was fortunate that the Funken Lodge had an actual fireplace in its lounge, even though previously it had been used for decoration only. Now the survivors huddled in front of it, watching the sputtering flame. They had burned all the books and greetings cards in the small hotel shop and started on the fat volumes in the library. The Scandinavian décor had promised a plentiful supply of wood, but it turned out that the glossy blond tables and armchairs were plastic. Somebody tried to burn bedclothes and almost choked the fire.

She was not sure how she had made it back to the hotel. At some point, she had found herself crawling on the frigid pavement without a parka or gloves. Her fingers refused to bend and she thought, distantly, that she might lose them to frostbite. But this did not feel real or urgent enough. She was humming Nana's chant as if it could make the lurkers in the dark acknowledge her as one of their own and let her pass. It was an insane thought and she embraced it because sanity no longer had any place here.

The snow had turned anthracite-black, the town dissolving in the night as thick as treacle. The Funken Lodge was an indistinct smear. Lena's eyelashes hung in broken clumps, the frozen tear-tracks on her cheeks burned like acid. The gaping hole of the entrance was veiled by a swarm of tiny snowflakes, stinging like angry bees. She stumbled over a body on the floor in the changing room. The man was not dead as she had first assumed but in shock, gasping and mumbling. She dragged him into the lounge where Nigel, a British skier who never skied, managed to get a fire going. The man, another tourist, was thawing out while Lena stood on top of the staircase, waiting for more people to come in. 'More people' was a euphemism for Bill, even though she knew he was not coming back. Eventually she gave up and helped the handful of other survivors to barricade the entrance door that was stuck halfway because its electrical mechanism had shorted out.

★   ★   ★

In the café, when the lights had blinked out, Lena was momentarily sure she had gone blind. Even if the wiring had failed there should have been enough illumination coming in from the brightly lit street. But instead she was plunged into the murk ringing with the tinkle of broken glass and Bill's cursing.

"What the hell?"

So, it was not her eyes. Bill's voice was mingling with a whole array of incomprehensible noises that filled the dark: a shuffle; liquid gulping; choking sputter.

"Bjorn?"

The floor under her feet shook as if somebody else had walked into the shop, somebody with a giant's tread. Bill grasped her hand and pulled her to where he assumed the door was.

"We are getting out of here!"

A wave of hot stink assaulted her nose. Mothballs? Wet dog? Blood?

She was bumping into sharp invisible angles. There was a growling and a wallowing in the dark, sounds like a leaky faucet, like a legion of cats, like sobbing, like dying; her brain desperately sorting through a medley of images to put a name to what she was hearing. But the only image that kept coming back was the sign that said: "This bear is already dead."

Bill's hand slid from hers.

She blundered through the writhing shadow and then she brushed something, something shaggy and unclean. A cold spasm doubled her up, and the shaggy mass receded. She slipped on steaming wetness crusted with ice. And then she was outside, hatless and without her parka, crawling through the snow and refusing to look back.

But even if she had, she would have seen nothing.

★   ★   ★

The survivors of the Funken Lodge were few. Besides Nigel who had come to Spitsbergen after a messy divorce with a pair of skis and spent most of his time at the bar, there was a Danish woman who sobbed unceasingly, a Norwegian engineer named Oscar, and several Germans whose limited English seemed to have abandoned them altogether. But no administrative staff were around. Where were the receptionist, the waiters, the shop lady, the cleaners, all the human nuts and bolts that kept the machine of civilisation running? They had gone out together with the lights and had not come back.

Nigel tried his cellphone for the hundredth time. It was useless, all signal having disappeared the moment the darkness came. He turned on the flashlight app and let loose a swarm of bluish afterimages in Lena's field of vision. The glare suddenly felt dangerous.

"Turn it off!" the Danish woman whose name Lena could not remember said venomously. "We need to conserve batteries."

"Much good it'll do!" Nigel muttered, but complied. Perhaps he too felt that bright light could attract unwelcome attention.

A crash of glass resounded in the restaurant, making everybody jump, but then Oscar emerged, carrying a bottle of wine and a loaf of rye bread. They were in no danger of starvation with the fully stocked kitchen, but they had to eat cold food – 'cold' as in 'frozen'.

The man plunked down by the dwindling fire and slurped wine out of the bottle. The rest cast irritated glances in his direction but nobody said anything. It was strange, Lena reflected, how in all post-apocalyptic movies and books the survivors either banded together or turned against each other in a Battle Royale. Neither was happening here; they were just a handful of shell-shocked individuals rather than an emerging tribe or an arena of gladiators.

From outside came a crunching noise.

It was the sound fresh snow makes when it is crushed underfoot. It had become familiar to Lena and for a moment she was glad because it meant somebody was walking outside, somebody was coming in, perhaps Bill, miraculously returning... and then it hit her. It must have hit the rest of them at the same time because the Danish woman whimpered, and Oscar paused with the bottle lifted to his mouth, the black wine trickling down his chin.

They should not have been able to hear the footsteps through the triple-glazed windows of the Lodge. Not unless the walker was large and heavy – *very* large and heavy.

Lena knew she should be screaming or hiding under a chair – but all she felt was a glacial numbness. It was as if Bill's absence (*death*) had spelled an end to the American Lena, cracked her identity open like a shell, and whatever was emerging was as unfamiliar to herself as it would have been to him.

She found herself with her face pressed to the window. Darkness had restored transparency to the glass walls of the lounge, which used to reflect back the shine of the multiple light fixtures. But now she could see outside, into the thick murk diluted by white swirls of snow. And something moved in the murk, a core of deeper darkness trailing wisps of rotten black. The shapeless shape blundered through the drifts and was gone.

Oscar swore. The Danish woman clapped her hand to her mouth.

"A polar bear...?" Nigel suggested uncertainly.

"Come on, man!" Oscar spat. "Even after Brexit you should know that polar bears are white!"

Something shifted in the sky, filmy green streaks of Northern Lights crossing the starless vault. The snow grew brighter, reflecting the scattered glow.

"Look!" Lena pointed to the drifts under the window.

The snow was deeply dented by oval footprints, large enough to have been left by one of those famous Svalbard bears whose images decorated every mug and T-shirt in the shop. But these footprints bore the unmistakable crisscross pattern of snow chains.

★   ★   ★

The Northern Lights winked out and then came back.

Lena regretted that Bill could not see them. Her thoughts moved slowly, wrapped up in the insulation of the hotel's excellent Chablis. At least she had not drunk straight from the bottle like Oscar, she told herself with maudlin self-pride. She had found a glass. Alcohol *really* was fire-water, just like Nana had said. A momentary return of warmth was worth a hangover.

The rest had made a similar discovery because they were all dozing in drunken stupor in front of the dying fire, buried under their piled-up parkas and blankets as the windows bloomed with rime on the inside. But the Northern Lights were bright enough to call her to the glass wall again and gape at the greenish arc that pulsed in irregular gasps of ghostly fire.

Nana had told her that the Chukchi called Aurora Borealis 'the eyes of the dead'. She had told her about other things as well: the persecution under Stalin; the scattering of tribal encampments and the confiscation of their reindeer; death from alcoholism, poverty and despair. Lena had not listened. The American Lena had not wanted to know. And when Nana told her about the shamanic power of her grandfather Sergei who had died in the post-Soviet turmoil, she chalked it up to an immigrant's pathetic pride, clinging to the useless heritage she could not wait to be rid of.

But history has a way of catching up with you, she thought. *History is etched in every cell of your body.*

Nana had told her Sergei could call blizzards upon his enemies, could freeze blood in their veins, could make their bones shatter like icicles. She had thought it was as useless a superpower as they come. What was the need for ice magic in the ice-bound land? Why call the curse of cold upon your foes if nature did it for you?

But what if the curse was lifting and another, bigger, curse was following in its footsteps?

The giant had not come back. A short snowstorm had erased the footprints and the rest of the survivors had agreed that it was a polar bear, after all. Lena did not argue with this conclusion. The book she had rescued from the fuel pile and hidden under a pillow, the book in Russian, remained her secret. They would not believe her, in any case. And even if they did, what good would that do?

The book, with the fading logo of the USSR state publishing company "Young Guard", was called *Arctic Labour Heroes: Coalmining on Spitsbergen.*

★   ★   ★

The knock on the door came at 5:15 p.m.

Lena knew it because this was the last time she looked at her cellphone. The battery was down to one per cent. She scrolled through the album Bill had shared with her, looking at the faces in the snow, the toothed maws of dark houses, the indistinct figure crawling among the dogs' shelters. Why had he refused to see what was in his photographs?

The tiny screen blinked out, echoing the darkness outside. The fire in the fireplace was still alive, but only just, anaemically licking the wooden planks Nigel had found in the storage closet. Besides Lena, he was the only one awake; the rest were hibernating, as if sliding down the evolutionary scale, adapting to winter-sleep.

The lounge was above the entryway. When the lights had been on, one could see all the way down. Now darkness lapped at the landing like stagnant water.

Lena and Nigel exchanged glances. The Brit pulled out his own cellphone which still had enough battery to produce a flickering yellow beam.

"Don't go," Lena said.

The barricaded entrance door drummed under a rain of blows. Nigel started down the stairs, carrying his pathetic puddle of light with him. And then a voice.

"Lena!"

Nigel paused, his upturned face a playground of skittering shadows.

"Your husband?" he asked and afterwards Lena recalled a hesitation in his voice as if he knew the answer and did not want to say it. And so did she but she hesitated too, unwilling to put it into words because if she did it would all be over, and her world – the normal ordinary world of suburban California, work, marriage, exotic vacations – would be gone, flooded, submerged.

Her hesitation lasted only a couple of heartbeats, but it cost Nigel his life. He was down in the entryway when the door burst open in an explosion of glass fragments and an arm reached for him. It was an arm, not a paw, wrapped up in tatters of padded parka fabric. It was as thick as Lena's waist and its rough skin was peppered with black hair and dotted with crudely done tattoos: blue hearts, and vodka bottles, and crossed shovels, and red stars. The black-rimmed fingernails, each the size of a postal envelope, tore into Nigel's throat as he choked on his own blood, and pulled him through the hole in the door, his screams dying into a liquid gurgle.

Lena did not remember running down but here she was, the icy blast from the outside lacerating her face, as she picked up Nigel's cellphone and focused its light on the figure that still waited outside, standing there silently as if it wanted to be seen by her – as perhaps it did.

The creature – the *kelet*, the forgotten name of the Siberian evil spirit popping up in her head uninvited – was so tall that its head disappeared into the gloom and she could not see its face. But she could see the faces that grew out of its broad chest like clusters of grapes: faces of men, hard and frostbitten, ravaged by weather and smoke; men who had laboured in the black bowels of the island for the hidden light. Men who had been crushed when a coal seam collapsed or suffocated when methane flooded the tunnels. Men of Mine Seven.

And Bill's face was among them, even though he had never worked in a mine, had never put his gym-toned body through the meat grinder of physical labour as these men had. Slack and empty, his face recognised her and grinned idiotically.

Had the *kelet* reached in and dragged her out like live bait from a fisherman's tin she would not have resisted. The enormity of what she was seeing silenced the instinct of self-preservation. But it turned around and walked away, revealing the broad back into which bodies of sled-dogs were frozen like fish into the ice on the surface of a winter lake. The clothes that its human core had worn barely clung to its gnarled contours. Its feet were horny and splayed, the snow-chains ingrown like nails. It trailed a ragged mass of something like torn skins or quasi-human silhouettes, or three-dimensional shadows... but the cellphone blinked out, and Lena was left standing in the numbing stream of black air.

She might have literally frozen in place had not the snow brightened to improbable pink and looking up, she saw the Northern Lights again, purplish lavender this time, undulating in the sky like a cosmic opera curtain. It was rare, such a display, and even now the wonder of it made her move.

She went to the changing room where outer gear was kept. Her own parka was not there anymore but there were plenty of others, belonging to the guests and personnel who would not be coming back. She bundled up and put on fur-lined boots with snow chains. They were too big but it hardly mattered.

The Northern Lights flickered out, then on again, enough illumination to keep her on the track that led away from the sightless corpse of the Funken Lodge up into the mountains. She found that her eyes had adjusted enough that she could see their white humps against the clear jet sky. She was staring at them, trying to remember if there was a moon tonight, when she collided with another bundled-up figure coming down from the heights.

They avoided falling into the snow by clutching at each other. The newcomer's face was hidden under the layers of scarves, but she saw the blue eyes.

Irina dragged her to a barn mantled in white. There was an equally mantled snowmobile parked nearby. Somebody in the hotel had tried a snowmobile after the lights went out but it had not worked. Nothing worked: cars and minibuses in the Lodge's garage were so much useless junk.

They stood in the nook of the doorway. Irina pulled down her face protector.

"Did you see it?" she whispered.

Lena nodded.

"It's because of the melt," Irina went on feverishly. "I heard old people talking… but I thought it was *chepukha*. Nonsense."

"I found a book," Lena said. "Russian. An old one, Soviet times. Mine Seven was theirs, wasn't it?"

"It collapsed. Tunnels were flooded. People killed."

"They called them Heroes of Labour in the book, but the medals were awarded posthumously."

"Old Sven was the only Norwegian there. He worked in the office. He said one of the miners was… Chukchi. From Siberia. A powerful shaman, so he said. He put a spell on the mine. A curse. But it was frozen into the ice. Just like their bodies. They were never recovered. The families got empty coffins and medals."

"And now the ice is melting…" Lena said.

"Yes. The ice is melting."

"Old Sven… they grew on him. Like frost on a tree."

Their eyes met.

"I was in the gallery when it happened," Irina said. "Having coffee with Sveta."

Sveta was another Russian girl who worked in the art gallery shop.

"Anybody alive?" Lena asked.

Irina shook her head.

"What are you going to do?"

"I will go down to the harbour. Maybe…"

Adventfjorden was free of ice; perhaps a ship would come in. Or a plane -- Longyearbyen had an airport, and somebody on the mainland was bound to raise the alarm.

If they did not have bigger things to worry about. Ice was melting everywhere, oceans rising, carrying tides of old diseases and old curses, the mud of the past flooding the present.

"Come with me," Irina said.

Lena stared toward the mountains where the red banner of Northern Lights was unfurling once again.

"Where is Mine Seven?"

"Up there. But you… there is nothing you can do."

"I am from Siberia," Lena said. "My family lived in the Arctic. My grandfather was a Chukchi."

"But… do you know how…?"

She did not. The legend that Grandfather Sergei had been a shaman may have been just that: a family legend. Nana's chant may have been a lullaby, for all she knew. But if magic was melting, could not another kind of magic freeze it back, put it in the permafrost where it belonged?

This was a slender hope. But it was all she had now: the Chukchi Lena emerging from under the melting slush of her American identity. She had to try.

They embraced, kissing each other on frozen cheeks. And Lena climbed the shivering mountain toward the black maw of Mine Seven, where rusting pieces of broken metal lay in puddles of inky water.

IT DOESN'T FEEL RIGHT

Michael Marshall Smith

It was all going so well.

Monday had been a debacle, and so we approached Tuesday morning with dedication, focus, and a willingness to play nice. I leapt out of bed at the first sound of activity, jammed my feet into slippers and wriggled into a sweatshirt, moving swiftly so as to give Helena a chance to keep dozing. I hurried next door and ushered Tim out of his bedroom as quickly and quietly as possible. Once downstairs I engaged our son in cheerful banter – or so it seemed to me – while making him a boiled egg and soldiers. He sat at the table (after only about ten minutes' encouragement) and ate it without making it into *too much* of an issue. I heard the distant sounds of my wife going into the bathroom to shower, and checked my watch. 07:24 – a little ahead of a schedule designed to see wife and child departing for school at 08:15, at the latest.

Good good.

Tim declared himself sufficiently full of egg, asked for and was given permission to get down and go into the family room, where he further requested to be allowed to watch an episode of *Ben 10*. This was denied, as part of a long-standing attempt to avoid TV early in the day, especially a show which – while not entirely pointless – involves too much shouting, posturing and inter-species violence for my liking. Tim made it clear that he found this denial unacceptable. We reached a compromise that saw the TV going on, but for an episode of *Postman Pat: SDS*, a spin-off of *Postman Pat*, which finds our plucky mailperson upgraded to parcel-delivery troubleshooter – solid, wholesome entertainment from the BBC which has no shooting or death in it whatsoever.

I tried to hammer out a further deal in which Tim got dressed in his school uniform before I pressed PLAY, but couldn't get any traction on even the broad outlines of such a proposal. Instead I settled for a good faith verbal agreement that as soon as the show finished – approximately 07:49 – we would jointly tackle the donning of clothes in a spirit of co-operation and cheerfulness.

He watched the show. Helena tromped downstairs and made herself some tea and a piece of toast. I hovered in the background, still pyjama-clad, waiting for the TV programme to finish, like a poorly-dressed junior member of the servant classes held in limbo until the ruling classes were ready to get onto the next thing.

The show finished. "Okay," I said, brightly, in the tone parents use when there's a mountain to scale but they're determined to believe they have a chance of achieving it without heavy casualties. "Let's get dressed! Let's see if we can break our record!"

And that's where it all unravelled.

★　　★　　★

Tim's school attire is simple. It involves pants, a vest, a pair of grey trousers, a greyish shirt, a tie (fastened with a piece of elastic; you don't have to actually tie the damned thing, thank god), a sweater. And socks, of course, and shoes – but I'll come back to those. It's not a complicated outfit. It can be donned (as I know from the handful of times when the process has unfolded without incident), in three minutes flat.

It can also take the whole of your life.

Eventually, after following him around the living room, cheerleading with increasingly leaden politeness, I had him dressed (despite Tim feeling that the collar of the shirt felt "scratchy", and taking it off again, twice). I had his teeth brushed (I wound up doing it for him, which I *know* I shouldn't, but sometimes you just have to get the sodding thing done). And while my tone had become clipped, things were more or less proceeding according to plan or at least along lines of quotidian shittiness. All that remained was the socks and shoes. Or, as it's known privately between Helena and I...

Footwear Vietnam.

I don't know what the problem is. I've investigated every possibility I can think of, including suggesting we have Tim checked out by a doctor to ensure that he genuinely doesn't have some kind of skin disorder or a bizarre neuralgia affecting the skin on his feet.

The bottom line is that socks... *are a problem.*

For three months Tim has complained that they have 'lumps' in them. These 'lumps' were originally only discernible once shoes had been put on over the top. He'd claim the socks felt uncomfortable, 'lumpy' – and would kick off, full bore: shouting, crying, yanking off his shoes and throwing them away. Over time the flashpoint slipped earlier and earlier, until the lumps began to present before the shoes went on, and eventually as soon as the socks were in place. He can now look at a pair of socks before they're even on his feet and tell that they will have lumps when they've been put on.

We can't see or feel any lumps, naturally.

We are inclined, if I'm absolutely honest, to believe they don't exist. We have nonetheless bought three extra pairs of shoes, and *god knows* how many socks, from every outlet we can find. Some, for a time, seemed to have made a difference. There were a couple of sets from Gap which were golden, for a while, lumpless and magical.

But then, just as you're starting to relax and think the problem is fading, one morning those socks just don't work anymore.

"It doesn't *feel* right," he'll say, kicking his legs out with sudden, spastic force. "It *doesn't feel right.*"

Full-blown hysteria is only seconds away by that point, accompanied by crying of such violence that I find it impossible to dismiss the whole thing as bad behaviour or difficulty in transitioning or merely proof of what lousy parents we are. We've tried coaxing. We've tried shouting. We've tried being icily polite. We've tried ignoring bad behaviour and rewarding good. We've tried massaging his feet and warming the socks on the radiator and telling him that every sock on the planet has stitching in it and that's *just the way it is and you have to get used to it.* We've threatened to tell his teachers why he's late every morning. We've actually told them. We've done everything we can think of, basically, and still the mornings work like this: one out of five, not too bad; two out of five, pretty bad; the other two, Total Sock Armageddon, and Footwear Vietnam.

This morning was one of the latter kind.

Screaming, shouting. Socks being pulled back off and thrown down the stairs, four times. In the end the two of us had to hold him down and stuff the socks back on (I don't know if you've tried getting socks on a strong and semi-hysterical five-year-old, but it's really, *really* hard, and can be painful, and it is a depressing and deeply crap way to start the day – especially when you love the little *fucker* very much and hate to see him upset, no matter how firmly you have come to suspect that the whole affair is a way of asserting power and has nothing to do with socks at all).

Eventually I wound up carrying a shouting child out to the car without his shoes on (with me still in my pyjamas, of course, hair sticking up as crazy as you like, a real treat for the neighbours, and not for the first time) and shoving him bad-temperedly into his car seat. He banged his head very slightly on the way in, which made me feel terrible. I put on his seat belt and made sure it was secure, Helena strapped herself in, and they drove away. I stomped furiously back into the house, the time still only 8:32, and went to have a shower.

Parenthood – it's not for everyone.

★   ★   ★

Tim is a lovely child most of the time. Sweet, funny, bright and sometimes even helpful. There are these flashpoints, however, and living with them hanging over you the whole time is like playing an especially ill-advised style of Russian Roulette where instead of a single bullet, there's only one *empty* chamber, and thus a very, very high chance of the whole thing kicking off.

That sounds ludicrous, possibly, but it feels that way sometimes, because there's just *such* a difference in quality of experience between a child deciding to be sweet and tractable and him or her electing to go to the Dark Side. A five-year-old on the warpath – with their total lack of care for (or absence of understanding of) punishment or incentive – can make you understand all too well why our prisons are full. The scariest thing is when incentives don't work, the promise of sweets when they get home or a seven-hour *Ben 10* marathon if they'll just consent to you putting on their fucking shoes. Our lives are based on incentives, often hypothetical, long in coming, frankly hard to put your faith in. If incentives are not going to make you behave then you're going to have terrible problems forging a pleasant life.

The biggest challenge for me is nothing else seems to help. No amount of talking or shoe-buying or sock stretching/warming makes any difference – which you can't help feeling means the whole thing must be at best psychosomatic, and possibly completely made up, a line drawn in the sand over which inter-generational strife has been pre-established and can be returned to at the drop of a hat. I have many faults but I am a fundamentally reasonable man, and a rational one. I can roll with the punches and suck it up, so long as the problems make sense. It is the forces of unreason, and irrational acts, that bring me to my knees.

And these *fucking* socks.

★   ★   ★

Thankfully the whole episode ended on an upswing. After I'd had my shower and stomped back downstairs, I made a cup of tea and took it onto the front step for my ritual first cigarette, the time then being about 8:45. I stopped smoking in the house long before Tim was born, and now try hard not to do it anywhere near him, for any number of reasons (including having recently been sternly informed by Tim, as he observed a stranger with a cigarette in the park, that smoking was bad for the environment). As I stood on the step watching the street, I saw a few parents walking by with their own children, en route to local schools. Some of these little groups were chatting nicely, others passed in affable silence; some wore uniform, others smartish casual clothes.

Then I heard the sound of childish dudgeon from the left, the source initially hidden by the next house.

A small boy, perhaps three and a half, was first to enter the frame – cruising along on a scooter, casting an occasional glance back, as if rubber-necking a traffic accident in which no one had been hurt.

Then his mother appeared, pulling another child reasonably gently along the pavement. This little girl – who looked to my not-very-expert eye to be around five years old, the same age as Tim – was wailing at medium volume and intensity, and hopping along.

"I can't do anything about it now," the children's mother said, a well-dressed but harried-looking blonde in her mid-thirties. "We're *late*. I'll look when we get to school."

The child wailed afresh, hopping with exaggerated discomfort, as though the world were a harsh and insupportable place and her mother a graceless harridan who wanted nothing but for her to suffer.

The group slowly proceeded to the right, disappearing from view a couple of minutes later. *Thank Christ*, I thought. *At least it's not just us.*

The sad truth of it is that many of the better moments you have as a parent boil down to that: the promise or hope that at least it's not just you who is making a total pig's ear of the whole business.

Significantly buoyed by this reassurance, I went back indoors and started my day's work.

At the end of which Tim came home, bursting into my study to tell me about something he'd seen out of the window on the journey home, and I picked him up and we went downstairs and watched a *Ben 10* together. I remembered that a threat/promise he'd never watch the show ever again had been a core part of my attempt to get him dressed that very morning, but while sitting on the sofa, the two of us comfortable and content, I didn't care, and there was nowhere else I wanted to be.

At one point he looked up at me and said, as he sometimes does, "I love you, Daddy."

And that's the point where you know that there's nothing better in the world, and nothing you would not do to protect them, and how very lucky you are.

★   ★   ★

The next morning – Wednesday – followed about the same course. Part of the problem is that once you've had a bad morning you brace yourself for the run to continue, and I'm convinced that this anxiety is audible on some psychic wavelength to which children are finely tuned. They can smell your fear, basically.

On Wednesday it didn't even *start* well.

The boiled egg went largely uneaten. My attempts to get Tim into his clothes – the six articles of which are graven in my mind, like dispiritingly tough levels of a video game that's too hard to be any fun – were immediate failures. My son informed me that school was boring, that he didn't care what his teachers thought if I told them about how he was behaving, and *nur-nur-ne-nur-nur.*

Then he glanced up at me, with the smug look that says 'I know that cultural mores stand against you giving me the sharp cuff around the head I so richly deserve, so let's not even pretend you've got anything in your armoury, dickhead' (or at least, that's what the look says to me) and went running out of the room.

So then it became:

Chase him around the house.

Put each item of clothing on him two or three times.

Eventually have to carry him downstairs under my arm, screaming.

Child deposited in the car without shoes *or* socks this time, strapped into seat, wailing.

Wife drives off with stormy expression.

Stomp back indoors.

Helena and I broadly see eye to eye on all this stuff, including the feeling/hope that it's just a phase, an attempt to establish power in a family where Tim is an only child faced with an army of two adults bent on oppressing him at all times. You can still get on each other's nerves – especially when you're tired. One parent tries to do something out of sync with the other, or accidently undermines something said out of his or her hearing, and suddenly you're being snippy with each other, the child slipping out of your grasp, cunning enough to know that this division in the enemy ranks has given him a chance to escape, to regroup, and to take his *fucking* socks off for the *fifth fucking time*.

I had a furious shower afterwards, then calmed myself down while making the subsequent cup of tea and rolling myself a cigarette. I actually don't like rollies very much. The swap was intended to help me cut down. In fact, of course, it merely means I'm now incredibly good at rolling cigarettes. The extra tar and the desiccating qualities also mean that I seem to have aged more over the last nine months than in the previous three years, but this could be down to parenthood: to being woken too early every day of every week; to all of the sentences you never get to finish through being interrupted by either child, or wife admonishing child; to the swallowed frustrations and the anger that goes unexpressed; to the abused-parent daily routine of being perpetually on edge, and on your best behaviour, in the hope of prolonging an unexpectedly good burst of good humour from the child who (despite your declared intentions, and best efforts) basically rules the household.

"Lumps?" I sometimes want to snarl at Tim, "*Lumps*? You want me to tell you about lumps? Try being a grown-up for a while. Try walking in my socks for a day, sonny, and see how you feel about lumps then."

Yes, I should give up smoking. For the sake of my child. I'll get around to it, probably round about the time the child gets round to giving me a break.

I took the cigarette and the tea out onto the step. I was there about the same time as I had been the day before and so the view was much the same. I did notice some kind of confrontation taking place between a red-haired mother I've seen before, and her boy, on the other side of the road: he stopped walking, shouted something, pointing apparently at the pavement. She kept enviably calm and used everything possible in body language to reassure him that she was on his side in whatever debate or problem he was having with reality.

He thumped her on the arm, and there was a lot of screaming, but she held firm, and eventually he went limping after her down the street and out of sight.

A minute later, I heard shouting from the left – and the group of three that I'd seen yesterday appeared, in eerie déjà vu. The younger child, coasting along on his scooter. The mother, looking even more tired than the day before, again dragging the elder child. She was less gentle this morning, and the girl was making a lot more noise, hobbling along in a ludicrous parody of pain.

"I checked them *three times* before we left the house," the mother snarled. "I'm *not* having you make me late for work *again*. Let's just *go*."

The child whacked her on the back, hard, and tried to pull away. She tightened her grip, pulled to a standstill just outside the gate to our path.

"It doesn't feel right," the child wailed, evidently not for the first time. "It doesn't *feel* right."

The woman opened her mouth. I could feel from fifteen feet away just how much she wanted to shout at her, to tell her daughter to stop making it up, to *stop being such a little shit*. Then she caught sight of me, standing on my step, and her mouth closed like a trap.

I shrugged, with a half-smile, trying to load both actions with as much 'Sister, I've been there and I share your pain' as possible.

She smiled back, but it was a short, sad expression. It's *quite* good when another parent signals that they know the score, but it's not great.

You feel that you should be able to do all this stuff effortlessly. You don't want sympathy, however well meant — you want admiration for how well it's going.

Eventually she dragged her daughter out of sight.

I went indoors. Worked.

The day passed.

★   ★   ★

Thursday was about the same as Wednesday. At one point, having caught him as he tried to dodge past me on the main landing, I sat Tim roughly down on the stair and asked him straight out, "Why are you doing this? Do you enjoy the attention, the drama? Do you think you're winning something?" He shouted back that his socks were lumpy, and it didn't feel right — nebulous but battle-tested weapons for which he knew I had no defence. He wrenched away and ran into my study, where he threw himself on the ground and writhed, yanking his socks off, again.

Fifteen minutes later a wild-haired man in a dressing gown — yes, that would be me — carried his kid out to the car once more, stuffed him into his child seat, and made sure his seat belt was secure. Helena had seen me do everything in my power to keep an even temper, and when she caught my eye through the windshield as she started to drive off there was no tetchiness there. Merely tiredness, sadness and a slight look of fear.

I knew what she was thinking, because the same thought was going through my own head:

Is it always going to be like this? Is this what our lives are now, perpetual skirmishes, this endless trench warfare leavened with unpredictable moments of ineffable love, the battle lines doubtless changing as he gets older, but with no cease-fire ever in sight?

I gave her a smile, and tried to make it a big one. She did the same, and off they went.

We weren't the only ones having those thoughts that morning, I suspect. Red-haired mother was having more trouble than the day before, too. Her child lay down on the pavement for a while, kicking at her, shouting. It took her ten minutes to get him back upright and tug him along the road.

The weird thing was that something almost identical happened with another kid, moments later – another boy ranting about his feet, at a brunette woman I'd never seen (or never noticed) before. She managed to get him past, eventually. I'd finished my cigarette and was turning to head back indoors when I heard the sound of a voice I now recognised.

"Please," it said, the tone more pleading, less authoritative than on the last two mornings, "*Please*, Nadja. Please just come along."

There was an incoherent shout, then a burst of tears. I walked down a couple of steps, looked left – and saw the blonde of the last couple of mornings.

She was gazing down at something, impotently, shoulders bowed. She heard my feet on the path and closed her eyes – feeling the shame of having another adult witnessing her powerlessness and rage. The final straw.

I took a gamble and walked further down the path.

At the gateway I could see that the woman's son stood to one side, with his scooter. The daughter was lying full length on the ground, screaming histrionically while she tugged off one of her shoes. The other had already been thrown into the road.

"Yikes," I said. "You look like you're having exactly the same kind of morning we did."

The woman looked at me gratefully. "Really?"

"Oh yes. I had to carry our kid out to the car. No shoes, no socks. Screaming. Before that, I had to brush his teeth while my wife literally *held him down*."

"I'm sorry."

'Most of the time he's lovely. But the mornings... the clothes, the shoes and socks. It is... *not fun*."

"I worry it's us," the woman said. "Sometimes my husband and I sit staring at each other at the end of the day and wonder what we're doing wrong."

"It's how they keep us on our toes. That, and once in a while being so wonderful that you realise without them your life would now be nothing."

She smiled, a little, and the two of us watched as her daughter took her socks off, and threw them away too.

'My feet are cold!" she wailed, immediately.

"Well, yes," her mother said, patiently. "That would be because you've taken your shoes and socks off."

"They're *cold*," she screamed. "It's *your fault*."

"Well, if you put your socks and shoes back on," her mother said, calmly, pleasantly, sweetly, "maybe they'll warm up. Shall we try that?"

"No!" she shouted. "It doesn't *feel* right."

"So. You're upset that your feet are cold because you took your socks and shoes off, but you won't consider putting them back on again, is that it?"

The kid just wailed.

"Good luck," I said, and retreated back to our pathway. This wasn't due to lack of courage. It's what you do. You can't get involved helping discipline someone else's child. It's not the done thing, and you can't let children see adults appearing to gang up against them (nice though it would be, every now and then, to feel you were part of the superior forces, for a change).

You have to let other parents do their thing: give them the space and privacy to snarl rude words under their breath, to tug their child a little harder than they're supposed to. It's all very well banning physical chastisement, but that's like entering a war zone and disarming yourself on the way in. If one of your fellow grunts occasionally lets off a harsher word than they're supposed to, while under heavy enemy fire, you turn your head and let it go.

She eventually got the girl to her feet, still snuffling, still ranting. She coaxed her off down the street, the mother's back straight, and head held high.

And just before they got to the corner and left my sight, her daughter did something odd.

She turned her head, looked back at me.

And smiled.

★   ★   ★

And then it was Friday.

I had high hopes. Tim had come back from school in a lovely mood the afternoon before. Instead of watching TV we played with Lego and did some drawing together. I made him the pasta dish that he appears to like and he ate a lot of it without having to be constantly reminded to follow one mouthful with another. He went up to his bath fairly promptly, denied himself the traditional splashing spasm which sends water up over the MDF surround and will eventually ruin it completely, and got out after only ten minutes' token resistance. He didn't even shout for us much after I'd read him his stories and turned out the light. In general it was what passes for a textbook evening, and when Helena and I crashed out on the sofa in front of Valium television afterwards, it was with a feeling of a job moderately well done.

But then, Friday.

He wrong-footed me by being extremely good for the first forty minutes. He ate his egg. He didn't ask for a *Ben 10*. He acquiesced – like some pampered Restoration nobleman – to being put into his school uniform, while humming an odd tune to himself.

By 8:10 it was looking like plain sailing, which always, in a pathetic way, makes me want to cry.

And then it span off into the woods.

I approached, smiling, holding his toothbrush – already laden with the toothpaste he prefers. I handed it to him thinking that things were going so swimmingly this morning that he might even wield the implement himself.

He threw it back at me.

"Uh, Tim, no," I said. "We don't throw things at people, do we."

He ran past, heading upstairs. I took a deep breath and decided to leave him to it, hoping the moment would pass (as it does sometimes, to be replaced with eerie calm and helpfulness). Meanwhile I retrieved the toothbrush, wiped the toothpaste off the carpet, and calmed myself down. When I started – oh so very calmly – up the stairs in the direction he'd run, I saw first his sweater, then the tie, then the shirt...

He'd taken it all off.

He was back down to his pants.

It took twenty minutes to corner him and get it all back on. While we were brushing his teeth he pulled Helena's hair hard enough to make her eyes water, and refused to let go. It got so out of hand that in the end I rapped him on the back of his hand, barely a slap, but enough to show things were in danger of going critical.

He stared up at me, eyes suddenly full of tears and dismay. "You didn't warn me," he wailed.

"I don't have to," I said, through teeth that were gritted half in anger, and half with appalled guilt at having struck him. "You *know* you don't pull people's hair, especially Mummy's. It *hurts*. How would you like it if I pulled *your* hair?"

He wailed.

The socks came off again.

It was bad. It was a *really bad one*.

It kept getting later and later and he kept getting louder and louder and closer to hysterical and the worst of it was, as always, that every now and then, through all the crap and the shouting, I kept getting glimpses of my son when he was not like this, when he was sweet and lovable and *my child*, instead of this uncontrollable creature – and all I wanted was the best for him, and for him to be nice enough, for long enough, for me to show him how very much I loved him.

In the end, a full half hour behind schedule – late enough that he was likely to get written up in a book at school, and his parents called to account – I carried him out to the car.

He wasn't shouting anymore, however. Not wailing, nor crying. He was silent. I put him not too roughly into his car seat and stepped back.

"You haven't done my seat belt," he said.

"Do it yourself," I snapped.

It was a mistake.

He's perfectly capable of doing his belt up by himself – just as he's capable of dressing himself, and brushing his teeth, and eating his boiled egg without having to be motivated on every sodding mouthful – but yes, it was a mistake.

I heard Helena saying something irritably, but I'd had enough. I slammed the door (making sure, of course, that his fingers were nowhere near; you get used to taking that kind of care even when the red mist is descending), and stomped away up the path.

★   ★   ★

By the time I'd got to the front door I'd realised it had been a stupid thing to do. In his current mood Tim simply wouldn't do the seat belt up. Helena would have to get out of the car and come around to do it, which was the last thing she needed. I was turning round to go back and set things right when I stopped in my tracks.

We were so far behind schedule that it was around the time I'd normally be having my cup of tea and a cigarette, and I saw both the red-haired and the brown-haired mothers on the other side of the road.

Both their little boys were shouting, one lying on his back on the pavement, kicking his feet, pulling off his shoes.

Then I heard a voice.

The blonde woman's voice.

She sounded desperate, near tears.

I walked quickly back down the path, my mind on going to put Tim's seatbelt on, but then saw the blonde woman's daughter was lying on her back on the pavement too. Her feet were bare. She was silent, staring up at her mother with an expression that was hard to interpret.

"Please," her mother said, kneeling next to her to try to help, to be loving, to do whatever it took to break this deadlock. "Please, darling. I've got to get to work. Please just put your socks back on. Please."

Still the girl looked up at her.

And then a shape came running from behind me.

Tim had leapt onto the woman's back before I even realised it was my son I was watching. His weight was enough to knock her forward so that her face smacked into the cold pavement, very hard.

Her daughter was immediately in movement, grabbing her mother's face in both hands and pulling it towards her, or her face towards her mother's, I couldn't be sure.

Tim looped his arm around the woman's neck and started beating at the back of her head with his other fist. The woman's little boy stood neatly beside his scooter and watched – as his sister lunged forward and took a bite out of their mother's cheek.

I shouted something incoherent.

Then I saw that on the other side of the street the brunette woman was sprawled face-down in the gutter, three children on top of her, beating, biting.

The red-haired mother was trying to run, but a crowd of five children had appeared from around the corner and were after her. None of them wore any shoes or socks.

All were running very fast.

I started towards the blonde woman, who was screaming, a ragged strip of cheek hanging down off her face, her daughter and my son pulling at her hair and gnawing at her throat.

But then I saw the windscreen of our car, and the blood splatter across the inside, and the shape of Helena's head slumped over the steering wheel.

I shouted. Something. I don't know what.

The three kids on the other side of the road raised their heads from the body of the brown-haired woman, and looked at me.

I backed away up the path. Then turned and ran.

I got the door shut behind me, put on the chain, drew the bolt.

Their bodies hit the door half a second later.

★   ★   ★

You know the rest.

Or if you don't, you soon will.

It is dark now. The sound of sirens has died away for the moment. If the experience of the last fourteen hours is anything to go by, it will get louder again soon. I'm still in my dressing gown. I'm smoking, inside the house. I don't know what I'm waiting for, or what I'm going to do. I do know what I'm hearing, however, beyond the windows, and I know whose small, dark shape is moving restlessly out there, crawling around the house, trying to find a way in.

I love that shape. I have nurtured it, tried to do the right thing by it, for five long years. I'd know that shape even if it didn't keep saying the same thing.

"I love you, Daddy," it says, in a voice that is not cracked with hysteria now, just low and hard and cold. "But it doesn't feel right."

CREEPING IVY

Laura Purcell

6th June 1892
My dear Professor Cooper,

I believe I told you when last we met that I would shortly be undertaking excavation work on the abandoned and dilapidated Hindhead Manor. It is a project that has proved challenging, to say the least, particularly owing to the fact that the vegetation has been allowed to grow unchecked for years. Among our many discoveries was the enclosed volume, which we unearthed in an area believed to have once been the greenhouse. Although we found it tangled and constricted among a variety of weeds, you will see that the binding is mainly intact with only superficial damage. The pages have fared rather worse. Aside from mould and dirt smears, the ink itself is partially washed away. It appears to be a journal of some sort. To my untrained eye, the handwriting is not legible even at the commencement, but you will observe that it becomes increasingly erratic and scrawled as the pages progress. However, if you can decipher the contents even in part, it would prove a matter of great interest to us as we seek to establish the social history of the house.

Yours with thanks

E.F. Owens

27th October
It is done.

It is *done!*

See how my pen skitters across the page! Relief has made me giddy. No one can share in this tempest of joy, no one must ever know, but if I do not express these thoughts I fear they will burst from my head. This book shall be my confidant, securely locked away inside my desk – although I am not so wary of discovery now. The servants have all been dismissed and she is firmly below ground.

She ought to be happy, there.

I played the role of dutiful husband until the end, standing trussed up beside her grave in my black gloves and weeper hatband. I daresay my expression was ideal: frozen, although not in grief, but in a kind of superstitious dread. I fancied that the corpse might bleed when I came near; I envisaged red tides gushing from the cracks in the coffin and floating it like a boat; I saw her push the lid back and sit up, pointing a long, gnarly finger at me. Of course, none of that happened. She was lowered in the usual fashion and her coffin hit the earth with a satisfying *thud*.

I had let her maid go to town on the funeral arrangements – although the hag always begrudged *me* money, I would not be mean-spirited and give tit for tat. It really was embarrassing to see the excess her loyal servant deemed necessary: profusions of lilies sprawled over the freshly packed dirt. Their sickly, waxy scent overpowered me. I was obliged to put my handkerchief to my mouth; it resembled sorrow as the clergyman approached.

"It is a hard blow for you, Mr. Blackwood," he commiserated.

I lowered my eyes, afraid that my agitated nerves might spill over into a laugh. "Yes. A blow indeed. Still, my wife attained a good age, and led a full life, which is a comfort to me."

Wind soughed through the gravestones and set the flower heads bobbing.

"That she did, sir. We must be thankful for the many joyful years. Yet somehow, such a loss always comes too soon."

Then I *did* give a gasp, but fortunately it passed for a sob.

Too soon! The thankless aeons I have spent chained to that woman... The age difference was severe, I was never blind to *that*, yet during courtship she gave the impression that she would be a sweet old lady, readily coaxed into giving up the fortune her first spouse had left, not the imperious harridan that she truly was: a woman with no affection save for her precious plants.

Well, she will feed the grass now, and I wish her joy of it.

My eyes skimmed over the marble slab, read the engraving 'Ivy Blackwood'. Although the erection was brand new, it seemed to me that lichen had already begun to spot the edges. Mud had worked its way into the chiselled numbers of the dates – if one glanced too quickly, they might mistake it for dried blood.

"Mrs. Blackwood would be pleased with all these tributes," the clergyman went on, indicating the floral explosion. "They are just to her taste. And of course we can find succour in the fact that she died doing what she loved best. It was in the greenhouse, I believe, that they found her?"

"Yes." He did not notice the way my fingers clenched at the handkerchief. "She *would* insist on pottering around in there. The physician could not tell us if it was simply a fall, or an apoplexy that caused her to swoon, yet either way, her poor head…"

I saw it again, cracked open, the juices flowing out like wine. Then the fragment of a shattered earthenware pot, trembling in my hand.

"Quite, quite," the clergyman smoothed over, clearly uncomfortable with the direction we were taking. "Her passing would have been instant. Painless."

I knew that it was not.

On the way back to the house, I noticed her maid watching me intently below the dark brim of her hat. Does she suspect the truth? Perhaps she does, but she can prove nothing. Nobody saw the altercation, and no one would take the word of a recently dismissed servant over that of a gentleman.

As I write, she is packing her things in the attic. Come morning, they will all be gone: the butler, the housemaids, even the footmen.

I have stripped myself of the hypocritical necktie and hatband to sit here comfortably before the fire in the study, with my journal and a glass of brandy. It is like Christmas. I cannot remember a day when I felt so happy.

Tomorrow I will be alone. Free. I am lord of Hindhead Manor at last.

28th October

A wild, holiday spirit has overtaken me. I am a child again. The home that has resembled a prison in recent years has assumed new colours and shapes. I do not even mind raking the ashes from the hearths or preparing my own food — it is worth any inconvenience to be at complete liberty.

Today I smoked cigars in the parlour, while I took down her portrait and replaced it with a watercolour of a fine chestnut hunter.

I let the dogs out of their kennels to roam about the chambers and climb up on the furniture as they pleased.

Even the weather has cheered with the force of my mood. The air is crisp and bracing, the sky a bright stretch of pristine blue. I walked outside with my hands thrust into my pockets and surveyed the grounds as if for the first time. They were strangely beautiful: hills rolling wild and free in the distance; the old, venerable oaks hosting a treasury of golden leaves. The great curtain of ivy that climbs the south side of the house is starting to blush a deep red, from the bottom to the top, as though lit by a flame.

The only eyesores, so far as I could see, were her formal, rigid parterres – for she could not let even flowers grow without restraint – and the glasshouse where she... died.

Its panes were steamed. I pictured a vengeful creature, breathing within.

But that was nonsense and I knew it. I was not about to let the place become fearful to me. Defying the ache at the pit of my stomach, I opened the door and strolled in as casually as I could manage.

Inside reminded me of a chapel: all was still, yet strangely charged. A green, earthy scent weighted the air, while heat panted against my cold cheeks and caused them to prickle.

There must have been a time when I appreciated a lush spread of verdure as much as the next man, but I cannot recall it. To my eyes the herbs seemed grouped together in dark communion. The grape vines and the melon runners were grasping snares, just waiting to entangle their prey. Even the geraniums were splatters of blood.

I stood there for a long time, listening to the hush, my gaze fixed on the tiles where she fell.

Then I began to smash.

First one pot, then another. Dirt exploded across the tiles. I laughed, pushed two more plants from their perches. Leaves tore like paper in my hands. I grappled with the peppers, plucked the tomatoes from their stalks and hurled them against the windows. It was joyous, mad. The fetid air rang with the sound of shattered pottery and broken glass.

Finally I stopped my destruction, placed my hands on my knees and panted. Sweat was pouring from my forehead.

As my heartbeat calmed, an inner voice whispered that my actions were childish, but I could not regret them. The hothouse plants looked wild once more. Even the spot where she fell and bled was covered in a wash of earth.

Returning to the house, I realised that I wore the aspect of a savage: my trousers were torn, there were twigs caught in my hair and my boots were caked in mud. It is fortunate there were no servants to see me thus.

They would think I had run mad.

Evening

I washed my hands under the pump twice, but to little avail. Even as I write, I am aware of dirt pushed underneath my fingernails and a green, juicy stain upon my skin.

Perhaps I should retire to bed. It is not late, yet it does grow exceedingly dark. The ivy that climbs outside the window seems to be blotting out more of the light than usual. It cannot last. An autumnal wind howls, tapping the leaves against the glass, and soon it will strip them from the branches altogether.

What a merry time this winter will be, when both she and all the foliage turn to rot.

29th October

I did not sleep well. Most likely I over-exerted myself wreaking havoc in the greenhouse. I could not find a comfortable position in my bed. My back itched and prickled.

Last night's wind really was fierce. It caused the ivy to rattle not just against my study window, but the casement in my bedchamber too; an infernal *tap, tap* that grated upon my nerves. I was not aware, until now, that the creeper actually stretched as far as the bedroom window.

I have never noticed it scratching before.

31st October

Little improvement in my rest. I fear that I may be growing unwell. It is hardly surprising, given the constant strain my nerves were under following her death. A lesser constitution would have succumbed completely.

For the moment my only symptoms are a cough – which could have been brought on by inhaling spores in that wretched glasshouse – and a feverish rash upon my skin.

It would be absurd to call the doctor out to diagnose such a trifle. Moreover, I do not possess the wherewithal to conceal what happened in the greenhouse quickly. I should not like him to see the evidence of my frenzy. It might sow the seeds of suspicion within his mind.

No, no, it is far better that I stay indoors with the dogs and my books and weather it out. I *do* rather wish there was a lackey still about me to tend the fires and fetch some soup for my poor scratching throat, but it cannot be helped. If the price of my freedom is a stint of convalescence, I am willing to pay it.

Evening

The house is so dark! Only on the south side, where the ivy spreads.

It is a weed. It should have been destroyed long ago.

Both my study and bedchamber face south – it is most vexing, to be obliged to change rooms when I want to read or write. I have an aversion to the other chambers. Their interiors are still redolent of *her*.

2nd November

My cough grows worse. I must confess, I feel sorry for myself. I can almost fancy that I am the last person left in the world – especially late at night, when I am tossing on my bed, listening to that damnable *tap* against the glass.

I did try sleeping in a different chamber, but somehow I could still hear it: a regular rhythm, maddeningly persistent.

In normal circumstances, a line or two would bring a friend to my side, but I am wary of reaching out to others just now. It would not be seemly for a man in mourning to entertain guests.

Besides, who would carry the letter for me? I did not think of that. I have strength enough to amble about the house, but a ride to the nearest village would knock me up.

The dogs have no sympathy for my plight. They have started to avoid me.

3rd November

This deuced *itch*! Whatever can it be? Did I touch a toxic plant when I destroyed her greenhouse? I do not believe so. My wife never grew poison; she had venom enough inside her own heart.

But stop – why does my hand smudge brown across the page? What is this filth, ground into my skin?

I am too ill to recall how it got there. All I can conjecture is that I have walked, feverish in the night, to the scene of my crime.

Good God. I cannot summon a doctor if *that* is the case! What might I tell him in a delirium? What would I do if he should come across this book?

No, no. I can endure a few more days yet.

6th November

My chest scrapes when I breathe. Nothing but sleep and peace will restore my health, but I can have neither while that blasted ivy pats at the windows, hour after hour, night after night. I am resolved. There is just strength enough within me. Tomorrow I will cut it down.

7th November

The tools were not hard to find: a ladder, a saw and some secateurs lay discarded in one of the outbuildings. More challenging was the task of hauling them over to the side of the house through the raging wind. Dead leaves were caught in the blast; they clung to my coat and flew into my face. Somehow, I prevailed, finally managing to hoist my ladder up against the wall.

The ivy rustled and hissed. A tremor seemed to run through it, a repulsion at my proximity.

Shakily, I began to climb.

The rungs of the ladder trembled beneath my feet. I could not hold steady; something tickled at the back of my throat.

I scrambled higher. Higher still. With every step up, my need to cough intensified. Hardly able to see, I snatched at one of the ivy tendrils and began to pull. There was a moment of resistance, then it peeled away with a crackling snap.

It felt wonderful. Glorious. I grabbed another handful and another.

Mortar crumbled as I yanked, but I did not stop. I did not care if I pulled the whole house down, so long as the deuced ivy was gone.

The vines left scars upon the wall: thin, yellow tracks. They marked my hands too, scratching the flesh to ribbons.

The ladder creaked in the wind and I pulled harder; kept pulling beyond my strength.

At last, I could not help it: the hateful spicy scent of the leaves crept into my throat and I choked.

The ladder moved.

My fingers caught on something – a vine – which I clung to with all my might as the coughs wracked my body.

I heard a dry crunch.

Leaves were everywhere, all around me, falling in great cascades. I could not see them clearly, for water filled my eyes, yet I had the wildest notion that they were *not* dropping from the ivy I grasped in my hand.

It seemed – absurd to think of it now! – as if the wash of dead leaves were falling from *me*.

From my very own mouth.

Evening
I pulled it down. I swear upon my life that I pulled the godforsaken plant away from the windows, but hark! The tap!

Darkness has made me a coward. I dare not draw the curtains aside to see what is out there, still scratching away. I am convinced that if I peered outside I would see *her*, tapping, tapping at the glass.

8th November
I dreamt that I visited her grave. Not as a mourner. I was dressed as I am now, in a sweat-stained nightshirt, and the skin that showed on my legs was a furious red.

It was a windy night. Rags of black cloud scudded fast across a full moon. My uncombed hair flew about me and I held some kind of tool in my hand. It was only when I raised my arm, and the moonlight glinted off metal, that I recognised it as a spade.

Strange, how acutely the mind can recreate sensations. I swear that I felt the wooden handle in my grasp, smelt the earth as it flew past my shoulder and landed like a patter of rain. I dug. I dug through worms, through clay and roots, driven by an itch deep in my bones.

That is with me, still.

There was no rain in the dream, yet somehow the soil was wet and claggy, sucking at my boots, squelching beneath my fingers as I dropped the spade and began to burrow like a dog. Her coffin emerged from the filth. A few days beneath the earth had done little damage to the wood, but the brass name plate was tarnished.

From inside the coffin, there came a steady *tap, tap.*

I cracked open the lid, my nostrils braced for the reek of the grave, but it was not rot or decay that spilled out. It was ivy.

We had buried only mounds of ivy.

?? November

Weaker than ever. Even my legs feel weighted, as if something were wound tight about them, binding me to the floor. Have I left it too late to fetch medical attention? How shall I alert anyone to my plight?

Perhaps I could crawl – I *will* crawl down the stairs.

This from her writing desk in the parlour. I did it: I dragged my poor, aching body to the ground floor. One of the spaniels was dawdling at the bottom of the staircase; when I whistled to him, he whined and ran away.

It is truly desolate here. Wind gusts down the chimneys and blows skeletal leaves rattling across the floor.

I must fetch help, but my voice seems dried up and strangled out; all I can do is cough. Perhaps I will take this pen and paper with me. Perhaps I will meet someone on the road.

But I cannot plan at present. The exertion of crawling downstairs has half-killed me and the itch is like ants, scuttling over my bones.

I must rest here on the sofa, if only for a while.

Rest! Ha! Did I write *rest?*

She does not rest!

I know now what it has been, clawing me at night, running its long nails down my spine.

I took the pen-knife, I cut the sofa open, and it was not horsehair I found there.

The cushions, the pillows – they are full of ivy!

Horror of horror!
There is no way out.
Ivy swathes every window. Vines are pushing through the fireplace, through the cracks in the walls.

It could not all have grown while I slept!

I keep trying the door, but it will not budge. Some infernal force holds it fast. Are the creepers *there*, too? Are they stretched taut across the threshold?

I saw a forest wrapped in ivy once: the vines twisting round and round the trunks like snakes. They constricted and squeezed until you could no longer see the bark below. You did not know what manner of tree it was, trapped within.

Merciful heaven, what am I to do?

Who will help me?

[Undated]
This will be my last entry. Let it serve as my confession, if nothing else.

I killed her.

I killed her, but she is not dead.

My wife is everywhere – even in me.

There are little track marks on my skin that cannot be erased; when I stop writing to inspect my fingernails I see shoots, sprouting up beneath. It seems to me that whenever I open my eyes from a coughing fit, the pile of leaves at my feet has grown.

I am going the way of the dogs.

Not that I know for *sure* what became of my pets. All I can say is that there are no longer any animals in this house; instead there are topiary shapes that resemble hounds.

Soon, I will be potted and contained like one of her precious plants, but I doubt she will be satisfied, not even then. My wife is as fastidious in death as she ever was alive.

She is the weed that is plucked and returns each year; she is the root too deep to pull out.

I cut her down. I did.

Yet her hate springs, evergreen.

LAST RITES FOR THE FOURTH WORLD

Rick Cross

David Opuni sits easy, waiting for his wave.

His neoprene-swaddled legs dangle in the chilly surf. The waters of Kawela Bay lap hypnotically at his board. It's a Takayama, and he emptied his savings to buy it, igniting the final blow-up with his old man. He's been crashing with friends ever since, and working maintenance double-shifts at Turtle Bay Resort, trying to claw together enough scratch to put first-and-last on a place with some old high school buddies.

Water slaps his board. His fingers rest on its deck, idly tracing runic patterns there. He's unaware he's doing this. He's attached to the surfboard by a length of frayed hemp knotted loosely at one honey-brown ankle. He likes the way the leash chafes, an itch like a healing burn. The back of his neck itched like that as he withstood his dad's fury, told him in an unwavering voice to go fuck himself, and walked out. *About time*, he thinks. He supposes if he repeats it often enough, he may even begin to believe it.

His eyes scan the rolling waters, watching for the telltale white lip, that sensation of gathering power. Sun's almost down, but he isn't in any rush. He knows the wave will come.

There are a dozen others seated around him, most Oahu natives, surf diehards. None are talking. Carly is among them. She's twenty-one, same as David. Her mom, a divorced Navy officer, moved them here when Carly was fourteen. She was a fish out of water then, the whitest kid in their 8th grade class, but within a couple years she was golden-brown, her blonde hair bleached white by sun and salt, and by graduation she could longboard with the island's best. She staffs the front desk at Turtle Bay where, David has observed, at least three guys a week ask for her number. David's been in love with Carly Desoto since 8th grade, and despairs that she might ever prefer a fiscally challenged native boy like him.

He can't help glancing her way from time to time, though. She ties her hair back when she surfs. Today a single long dread, threaded with tiny shells and twists of old fabric, has escaped her hairband to lay damp across her collarbone, above the indigo wetsuit. She's shielding her eyes with one hand, watching for waves. Her beauty makes his head swim.

He frowns. *She's not watching for waves*, he thinks. *She's—*

Carly is looking down, leaning to her right, tracking something under the water. She puts a hand flat on her board, rising a little.

Oh no, David thinks. *Shark?*

"Hey," he calls. "You okay, Car? Spot something?"

She turns to look at him. "I don't know," she replies, her voice carrying clearly across the water. "Thought it was seaweed tangled on driftwood, but..."

Her words trail off. David is already paddling toward her, navigating around Buzz and Bernadette Kahale, sixty-something marrieds who cleaned up on Wall Street a decade ago and retired to the island. Bernie smiles as David passes. He likes the Kahales. They give him hope.

He pulls alongside Carly's board and leans over, following the angle of her gaze to peer into the blue-green water. It's not deep here, maybe eight or ten feet to the sand, and in the summer it's like sitting atop a rippling glass window, the whole floor visible from the surface. It's murkier now, the powerful winter waves creating more chop, the undertow churning up the sandscape, but these are still the clearest waters in the world, or so the resort brochures claim.

Carly points. "What the hell is it, David?"

He looks again, and now he sees the thing. It *does* look like seaweed snared on a big piece of wood, but the stuff's way too uniform to be random tangles of kelp. As he watches, the current tumbles the big shape, and David sees at once that it's not seaweed at all, but hair.

Hair obscuring arms. Legs. It's a body.

"Oh, shit!" he gasps. "Ikaika! Buzz! There's somebody down here!"

He hears the others beginning to turn their way as he slips off his board, pops his leash and dives. It takes just one hard kick to reach the shape bumping along the sandy floor, and even before he gets there he

knows there's no chance this is a snorkeller's prank. This is a dead body.
And it's not human.

A bear? he thinks, not wanting to touch the drift of weirdly thick brown hair. *Some kind of big shaggy cat?*

Muted splashes around him, and others appear in his peripheral vision: Buzz, an economist named Shep, and Ikaika, a big, cheerful Hawaiian dude a couple years older than David and Carly. Others swim or paddle around beyond and above them.

Ikaika jabs a thumb at the shape, then points upward. All of them seek lifting points on the limbs and torso – *Christ, he's eight feet tall,* David thinks – and push off the bottom.

They surface together. Bernadette's got her waterproof phone out to dial 911. Carly reaches for David as he breaks the surface – until she sees the hairy shape bob up between the men. She pulls back, shocked.

"Get him on a board!" Buzz barks. But they can barely keep the hulking shape afloat, and besides, David observes, even Ikaika's Phantom XL and his own big gun – which Carly's hanging onto from astride her sleek Nusa Indah – look fairly puny next to the waterlogged thing.

"Shore!" Bernie calls, pointing to the beach. "Get him to shore!"

She's thinking about CPR, David supposes. But he doubts she's gotten a good look at the body, or she might think twice about locking lips with...

What the hell is this?

"She's right," he gasps. "Let's get him out."

Hauling the body, the four men kick toward the beach. The others collect boards and paddle in around them. It's no easier even when they can stand. The lolling shape is sodden, impossibly heavy. Carly leaves Bernie to handle the phone and a couple of the others to watch the boards and splashes toward them to help. In the end, it takes six of them to shove and drag the body clear of the water. David, Buzz and Ikaika roll it onto its back as everyone draws near.

"Jesus."

"Is it a gorilla, Dave?"

"It stinks like fucking dogshit, *palāla*."

"You said it, *mijo*."

David says nothing. He's looking at the strange, simian face of the brute, its prognathous jaw and shelf-like forehead smeared with sand, its dark hair hanging in a limp tangle. Both eyes are open and intact, and *that* is both amazing and unsettling; most dead things in the sea quickly become a grazing table for every little nibbler around. They'd chosen not to chew on this thing.

He feels Carly's hand slip into his own, but as his gaze shifts to her, he catches sight of the brute's feet. His grip tightens, and Carly gasps at the sudden pressure. David doesn't notice.

Its feet are bare, and they are *colossal*. Underwater, he'd estimated the creature's height at eight feet. He's not far off – and it has feet to match. Surely not even Shaquille O'Neal or Yao Ming could offer up kicks big enough for this thing to wrestle into. Each foot must be 26-28 inches from heel to big toe. More dark hair sprouts from its instep and from the top of each toe.

Ikaika leans over him, hands on meaty thighs, curly black hair dripping salt water onto the sand, the body, David's shoulder. "Look at those *dogs*, brah!" he says. "And you guys say *I'm* big." His smile is still there, like always, but to David it has never looked so forced, so fake.

And that's when he knows.

He squeezes Carly's hand more gently this time. When she looks into his face, she sees a strange mix of awe and grief there. "What?" she asks him. "What is it, David?"

"Sasquatch," he answers hollowly. "It's fucking *Bigfoot*."

⋆   ⋆   ⋆

It's almost midnight when Jack 'Torch' Torstenson, strike leader for Greater Cali Smokejumper Crew 4, understands that they're going to lose most of the national forest – and probably Ojai and Goleta as well – to the Los Padres wildfire.

"Shoulda called it Los *Madres*," he husks, his throat seared raw. "This is the mother of all blazes, for sure." He hawks and spits.

Torstenson is standing on a blackened ridge a mile north of Ojai, just west of Route 33, which his team has backburned for the past ten hours, trying to stifle the runaway conflagration. The sky itself appears to be ablaze, the clouds lit a nightmarish red by the firelight. He takes off a glove, jams the thumb of that hand first against the left side of his nose, then the right, and blows black snot from each nostril. Not bothering to wipe his lip – he's flinders and ash from scalp to jaw anyway – he lifts his radio and toggles the go-button.

"AirTac-One, this is Strike-One, Crew Four, come back."

Swede and Big John, both knocking away cinders, their axes and boots smouldering, appear out of the smoke which obscures the road and the rest of their team. Jack waves his glove at the stumbling, exhausted duo and they hustle to his position, keeping quiet, knowing he's on the horn with an Air Tactical Supervisor in the big radio plane somewhere high overhead.

Jack tries again, keeping his voice even for the guys' sake: "AirTac-One, come back."

The radio crackles. "Strike-One-Four, Tac-One here. What's it looking like, Torch?"

"Like Dante didn't know shit," Jack says brusquely. "No-go on the backburn. Wind's gonna blow it right across the road, even with thirty yards cleared on the hot side for ten miles, north to south. Wheeler Springs is gone. Ojala too. Over."

Silence from the radio. He trades grim looks with Swede and Big John.

Finally: "Copy, Strike-One-Four. Over."

Jack continues. "I see lights on the road to Ojai, Tac. We set to hold it there? Over."

"Every water tanker and hose-roller within eighty miles is here. Hotshot crews are holding the southeast flank. Forestry Office in Goleta was evac'ed with everybody else south and west of the blaze, but they're staging in Santa Barbara, directing air and ground support from Kern, Ventura, San Luis Obispo and San-Bar Counties. We'll stop her cold. Over."

Swede is shaking his head. "They using their eyes?" he mutters. It comes out *Dey usink dere eyes?* Before he came to the States, first to teach firefighting tactics, then to stay – mad for California girls is Sven-Oli Persson – he was a smokejumper in Scandinavia. His accent has lessened a bit, but when he's tired or upset it comes back strong.

Jack rolls his eyes. "Copy last, Tac," he rasps. "Where do you want us? Over."

"Gather your boys, Torch. Run west two miles, then cut south. We'll have relief units pick you up at Casitas Pass. Strike-Six will step in and widen the firebreak at 150 and 192 all the way to Carpenteria. I'd say you guys have earned a wash and a nosh. Copy?"

Fire's not out, you glib prick, Jack wants to snap back. *You don't drop your gear til the dragon's dead.* Instead, he nods to Swede, who goes to alert the troops. "I copy, Tac," he radios. "We're moving. Strike-One-Four out." He drops the mic, lets it bob and spin at his waist. Spits.

"Christ, boss," Big John rumbles tiredly. "These goddamn kids..."

Swede's rally whistle begins to shrill. Jack glances his way, watching Swede blow for all he's worth. He's maybe twenty yards east, right on the lip of the ridge, looking into the burning valley below for the rest of their guys. He goes on blowing the whistle, and a moment later Jack hears Kilkenny's whistle answer, distant but unmistakable. He sighs, looking around at the burnt trees, the firefly swirl of cinders gusting by on the rising wind.

He properly holsters the radio. "Twenty years defueling wildfires," he snorts. "Chopping breaks, digging trenches... Just *once*, Johnny, you'd think the honchos would—"

Kilkenny's whistle wavers to a stop, and Jack breaks off. There's a booming crash as something – a big valley oak, maybe – topples to the forest floor. Fresh sparks gush skyward, the wind snatching them away. A second crash. Big John turns, takes two steps toward Swede, just as his whistle cuts out too, and—

Christ, was that a scream?

Jack lifts the mic again. "AirTac-One, Strike-One-Four, can you see my team?" He is waiting for a reply when a volley of booming crashes rips open the glowing red night.

No, not crashes. Footfalls. *Massive* footfalls. Coming on the run.

Swede, looking into the valley, stumbles back and turns to look for Jack and Big John. His eyes are saucers. Behind him, something massive looms out of the smoke. It towers over him, closing the distance fast. A gigantic, red-eyed wolf.

"*SWEDE!*" Big John screams, lunging toward his friend.

It's at least eighteen feet tall at the shoulder, and it is fully engulfed in fire, running mad from the flames devouring its fur. Its flesh. The world.

Jack toggles the mic again and roars, "*Tac! Crew Four is in serious fucking trouble!*"

"*Mormor,*" Swede gasps in shock. "*Förlåt mig, Mormor.*"

The gargantuan wolf opens its blazing maw and howls, its voice that of all the demons in Dante's hell and a hundred more unnamed. Jack can see the agonised creature has no idea Swede is directly in its path. Its eyes aren't red at all; the holes where they should be are gushing flame. It's blind. It closes the distance in two titanic leaps, still howling—

And then Big John, running full-out himself, tackles Swede, knocking him to one side. One trunk-like flaming paw grazes the back of John's fireproof jacket and he and Swede are spun further into the bracken. Whether the glancing blow throws off the wolf's stride or it simply submits to the fire's insatiable hunger, the burning animal suddenly stumbles and falls, sliding twenty yards or so before coming to rest in a crumpled, nearly immolated heap. Thick, greasy smoke boils up from its head and hide.

Big John climbs slowly to his feet, breathing hard. Beside him, Swede is on his knees. He has wrenched off his gloves, and his fingers claw weakly at his face. He's weeping.

"Oh, *Mormor*, I should have listened to your stories," he chokes. "Forgive me, Grandmother. Förlåt mig."

"*What!*" Big John barks, eyes watering from the stinking smoke. Behind them, he can hear Kilkenny and the rest shouting as they draw near. "What the hell *is* it, Swede?" he croaks.

Swede puts his face in his hands. "It's Fenrir," he says at last. "The Great Wolf *Fenrisúlfr* is dead."

But John is no longer listening. He has realised they're alone. "Torch?" he calls. He rushes forward, shielding his face against the dead thing's heat. "*Jack!*"

There's something at his feet. John stoops, picks up Jack Torstenson's dropped glove.

He realises where the runaway monster's path has taken it, where it has fetched up. He begins to shout his boss's name, over and over, knowing there will be no answer.

By the time the other smokejumpers top the ridge, the smell of burning flesh is nauseating, and Big John has no voice left to scream with.

★   ★   ★

Seated behind stacked sandbags on a high dune overlooking the town of Mahmudli, twenty-three-year-old Hassan al-Attia shifts his rifle from one shoulder to the other and curses himself for forgetting his second waterskin. He's clothed in a loose, dark-coloured *didashah* and sandals, his red-and-white checkered *shumaq* held in place by its black-banded *ogal*. It's cinched tight to keep the relentless desert sun off his prematurely balding scalp, *in shaa Allah*.

It's Hassan's job to keep watch over the north road to Raqqa and radio the *Quwwāt Sūriyă al-Dīmuqrăṭīya* – the Syrian Democratic Forces – should ISIL fundamentalists come spilling out of the desert like jackals. His friend Amraz, a Kurd who lives in Mahmudli, is supposed to spell him at midday. So far, though, there is no sign of him, the wretched dog.

Hassan has decided to sling his rifle – a Hungarian AK-63, which he hasn't fired since the Battle of Raqqa in 2017, Allah be praised – and go to town himself, when there is a sound like a thunderclap. The sky fills with the cries of frightened beasts, and a long shadow races across the ground below him. He whirls round just in time to see something disappear, smoking, over the next rise. There is a grinding crash of wood and metal and meat, echoing off the dunes.

Anti-aircraft missiles took down an enemy jet, he thinks. *Allahu akbar!*

But now those weird animal cries have turned into agonised shrieks. He's never heard anything like it. Has the downed jet somehow crashed into Mahmudli's camel caravan? He unlimbers his weapon and runs up the dune. His head swims. He realises he has forgotten his radio, but he is too overwhelmed by shock and adrenaline to go back for it.

He clears the top of the dune. Insanity awaits him below.

This is no jet fighter. No recon drone. The sand is chewed up and splashed in all directions, a deepening furrow gouged into the land for forty metres. At the end nearest to Hassan are the first pieces of wreckage.

Silver tinsel glitters in the sun, and it takes him a moment to grasp what he is seeing: hundreds of gaily wrapped packages, some with ornate ribbons and bows. Some are burning. Some have been crushed on impact. They trail along to the far end of the crash site, and there…

The vehicle is smashed, one side buckled on impact, the other blasted apart by whatever SDF Stinger or anti-aircraft missile brought it down. But it's not any kind of plane Hassan has ever heard of. It is tangled in what he first takes to be electrical cables, but then his head clears, and he understands they're traces. Reins. Like those the Mahmudli camel riders handle so deftly.

The boxy vehicle has slid hard into what appears to be a team of shaggy, horned animals, like massive versions of the tiny ibex he saw once in an al-Raqqa marketplace, tied to a post and bleating for its mother. *But these were flying*, his mind objects. *Flying!*

Most of the beasts are dead, necks broken, leg bones snapped and twisted in every direction, but two or three still thrash and bawl in agony. One of these is burning fiercely, and Hassan, shamed and horrified by such suffering, runs forward, raising his AK to put the poor creatures out of their misery—

Then, drawing close enough to discern what else lies in the smoking ruin, he stops.

Hassan al-Attia is twenty-three. He has been the man of his family since his father's murder by ISIL executioners when Hassan was just fourteen. He was at Raqqa when the walls fell in 2014, his father's gun in his hands, and he helped reclaim the city three years later for the Kurds and Assyrians who had lived there in harmony all their lives. Who greeted one another this time of year, whatever their spiritual beliefs, with the words *Milad Majid*. Merry Christmas.

Hassan's rifle slips from his fingers. One hand goes to his mouth.

The downed vehicle's pilot has been ejected from his seat. He hangs suspended over the sand, crucified on the antlers of one of his dead, pinned animals. Blood mats his bone-white hair and beard, and his heavy coat is turning a deeper shade of scarlet. Half his face is blackened, the cheek and eye on that side a crushed ruin. His lips twitch. His one good eye, a piercing blue, fixes on Hassan. He is trying to speak, but only more blood pours from his mouth.

Sobbing, Hassan al-Attia stands in witness to the lonely death of Baba Noel.

★ ★ ★

Within hours, nearly every network and cable channel the world over is reporting on these increasingly strange and terrible miracles, every one thousands of miles from their fabled place of origin. And every one of them dead.

Shaky footage from downtown Tokyo: A dead plesiosaur lies gruesomely splattered atop a flattened city bus, inside which are the remains of some forty people killed instantly when the apparent Loch Ness Monster dropped on them without warning during morning rush hour.

A series of iPhone stills from a family on safari in Africa: A frenzied pack of hyenas tears to pieces a creature that looks like an enormous, bipedal owl. A supplicating hand rises, bloody, fingerless, from the throng of predators, and then the Mothman is no more.

McMurdo Station dispatches a party with portable heaters to warm a massive, icy form enough for teams of twelve men – all of them shocked into silence – to gently unfold and show off to the world the broken wings of the Thunderbird that has crashed and expired in Antarctica.

Grainy video from Wyoming shows the 867-foot-tall Devils Tower slimed with grey mucus, the excreta of the giant, reeking kraken carelessly slopped over the monolith's table-like peak. Tentacles dangle down the Tower's raked sides. The milky eyes are the size of small cars. A CNN crew, recording the hasty human exodus from the area along I-24, catches sight of a shirtless man standing in the bed of a pickup. He appears to be bleeding from his eyes. He does not smile or speak, just holds up a handmade sign: *DEAD CTHULHU LIES DREAMING.*

Anchors bloviate endlessly, filling time until someone can answer questions with no rational answer. Pundits bellow at one another. Anderson Cooper interviews a priest, a rabbi and an imam, then nervously jokes that the four of them are going out for drinks afterward. Nobody laughs. Laura Ingraham throws up on live TV. Alex Jones upstages her by shrieking himself into a stroke on a live webcast. He expires as he is rushed to an Austin, Texas emergency room.

And the unsettling stories keep flooding in.

Osiris, dismembered atop Mount Everest.

Tecuciztecatl, the Aztec 'Lord of Snails', shotgunned to death on a rural road in South Carolina, his body doused in moonshine and set alight.

Hundreds of giant rodents – like hairless mole rats with fangs – floating, drowned, in the Lincoln Reflecting Pool in D.C. It doesn't take long for them to be tagged as *chupacabras.*

★ ★ ★

Swede Persson, Martin Kilkenny and Big John sit at a folding table in one of the relief tents. Kilkenny is mopping at his face with a towel that once was pink and is now mostly black, and John has scrubbed as much soot from his face and neck as it's possible to do without running water and soap. The towel in front of Swede is still immaculate.

Kilkenny's taking pulls off a Löwenbräu, but Swede and Big John are sticking with cups of water. "Anybody got a smoke?" Kilkenny asks for the third or fourth time. No one answers. He sighs, knocks back his Löwenbräu again.

They're off for the next ten hours. Most of Crew Four is already asleep in their racks, or pretending to be, but Swede and John aren't ready to try yet. They both know the Los Padres blaze won't be contained in the next ten hours. Nor in the next twenty. They've also met with Bill Hubscher, head honcho at Greater Cali and an old friend of Jack Torstenson. At one point, Hub called them both goddamned liars, but John showed him the iPhone video someone shot of the giant wolf's carcass. And what they found when they rolled it aside. Hub nodded, wept a bit, then got himself under control and they wrote up the fatality report.

"You guys wanna go find some more beers?" Kilkenny asks. "I'm still all keyed up. Fuck! Whatcha think about that wolf thing, huh? You think—"

"Marty," Swede says. "You don't get the fuck out my sight, I'll knock you down, me."

"Hey now!" Kilkenny sputters indignantly, but Big John puts a hand on his shoulder. The twitchy little cinder monkey sighs and goes in search of another Löwenbräu.

"You okay, Swede?" John asks.

Swede shakes his head. In his sooty face, those piercing blue eyes are haunted. "Not me, John. Not anybody. Not ever again."

John Qoyawayma, a full-blooded Hopi from the rez in Coconino County, Arizona, takes a swallow of water, enjoying how it cools his ragged throat. He wishes Torch was here, cracking his bad jokes to make the big Scandinavian roar with laughter. John doesn't know what to say to ease Swede's pain. *His* pain is also deep, but he is Hopi; pain has walked with his people for generations, like a cruel and greedy cousin they don't much like but cannot send away.

Swede looks at him. "Today I have seen the passing of *Fenrisúlfr*, his mouth open wide, flames burning from his eyes and his nostrils." He says it as if it's self-explanatory, irrefutable. Prophecy and fact rolled into one. The acrid char smell getting stronger all the time seems to validate and reinforce his despair.

John swallows hard and says, as much for his own comfort as for Swede's: "If it is indeed the end, know that a beginning will follow, as a new day follows night." He wants to say more, to find words that won't sound as hollow as everything else does on this terrible night—

Then he stops, looking not at Swede but at something suspended between them: a small black spider, climbing its own silken web.

Big John gasps. He did not see the spider descend from the shadows overhead. It has simply... appeared.

Registering his friend's silence, Swede too spots the spider. He lifts a hand to swat it—

And John catches him by the wrist. Swede blinks in surprise.

"No, brother. Let her be." Big John's gaze never wavers. The spider climbs patiently, unfazed by the enormous beings on either side of her. "There have been four worlds," John continues. "The first three were destroyed by warring and greed. If what you say is true, perhaps we are seeing the end of the Fourth World, and the way will open to the Fifth."

The spider climbs. Its black body appears to be tattooed with runic patterns, some red, some white, all too small to be seen clearly.

Swede almost looks like his old curious self again. "How, John?"

"The *sipapu* will open. Someone will be shown the way."

"What's the... *sipapu*?"

"A tunnel. The World Passage. As the end of one world draws near, the *sipapu* opens to lead humanity into the next. This is the truth of my people. This is the last magic."

They're both watching the spider now. Swede's fingers find Big John's. They clasp hands tightly. "Good night, *Kookyangso'wuuti*," John Qoyawayma says softly. "Remember us."

Swede, his eyes very wide, glances over as John speaks.

When he looks up again, the spider is gone.

★   ★   ★

The sun is coming up over Kawela Bay, and though there's a chill in the air, David Opuni and Carly Desoto are on their boards again, waiting for their wave. They're holding hands.

The two of them stayed long after dark, even after the others drifted away. They told the emergency responders and cops what they could, and watched the coroner's van roll away with the body. Afterward Carly nudged David's hip with her own. "Where ya staying tonight?"

He shrugged. It was embarrassing, how everyone at Turtle Bay knew everyone else's business. "Put our boards in the service shed and meet me out back," she said. He did so, and she snuck him up to the resort's staff suite. It was an ordinary room, one bed, usual amenities. The resort kept it in case a clerk or housekeeper fell ill or a manager needed a shower during a long weekend shift. Looking around the room, David heard the lock click behind him. When he turned, Carly stepped into his arms and kissed him. They fell onto the bed and made love, frantic and fumbling at first, then slower. Better. Later, talking about the dead creature in the bay, Carly cried, and he held her. They fell asleep in each other's arms, and woke before dawn. Dressed. Collected their boards. Ran, giddy and giggling, to the beach and paddled out.

And here they sit.

They're pretty far out. The water is choppy and talkative. High swells. Promising. They wait, enjoying the rising light, the silence, the blended scent of themselves, so very like the sea.

Looking at Carly's hand in his, David wants to speak, to say things to her he's been holding in since junior high, but he's afraid he'll blow it. He finds her looking at him. She leans over and kisses him. "There's time for everything," she says. "Don't worry."

Their boards begin to porpoise in the rolling swells, each higher than the last, and when *their* wave comes they both recognise it a quarter-mile off. That lip of whitish-green foam. That gathering of power. David grins, and Carly claps her hands.

Then they're on their bellies, paddling hard. They turn back *just* at the right moment, as the wave rises up and pitches over, and they pop up at the same time – feet firm on their decks, outstretched hands almost close enough to touch – and take off.

And the wave rolls up, up, *up*. *My god*, David thinks, *it's the mother of all bombs!* It arcs over and around them: a textbook barrel, a tunnel the likes of which neither has ever seen.

Their fingers finally *do* touch as they knife along, and David shouts laughter at the perfect joy of it.

They ride, letting the tube take them wherever it's going to take them.

WE ALL COME HOME

Simon Bestwick

"Do you want me to come in with you?" Lisa asked.

Lennox was badly tempted to say yes, but finally shook his head.

"You sure?" She laid a hand on his arm; warm and soft and very unlike the brittle chill of the October afternoon. "I don't mind."

"No," he said at last. "It's okay. Probably better if I'm on my own. More chance I'll remember something."

Lisa nodded, covered his hand with hers and squeezed lightly. "You can do this. Okay?"

"Yeah. I know."

She touched his cheek, kissed his lips. "I'm proud of you."

He squeezed her hands, then unfastened the seatbelt and unlocked the car door. "You sure you'll be all right here?"

"I'll be fine." She grinned and held up her paperback. "Music and a good book. Can't beat it."

He smiled back and passed her the car keys. "You'll need these, then. I'll see you in a bit."

Lennox turned quickly away so that she wouldn't see the smile fade. He'd managed to conceal the effort of keeping it on his face up till now, but he could feel the gates behind him as though they were pressing against his back. Of course, turning away from Lisa meant that he was now facing them.

A mist was gathering, swirling among the bases of the trees and the tangled ferns and brambles that foamed over the parapet of the low wall that stretched along the opposite side of the road in either direction. Above the level of the railings writhed the trees, thick and old and gnarled, boughs still heavy with their remaining, shrivelled leaves.

How long had he been standing here, looking? If he hesitated for too long, Lisa might worry and insist on going in there with him.

And while God knew – if there was a God, which Lennox hadn't believed for thirty-odd years now – he could have used the comfort, he had to go in alone. Lisa had been right about this. It was his best chance to remember, to gain some peace. How many nights had he woken up screaming from nightmares he could never recall on waking? He'd accepted them as his lot in life, until he'd met Lisa. He owed it to her, at least, to try.

Lennox glanced both ways and set out across the road. He needn't have bothered, as vehicles were few and far between along here and the road was very straight. The site of the New Hall covered a large, almost perfectly rectangular area, and the main gates were sited along one of the longer sides.

They were heavy and built from wrought iron, painted black, and hung from tall granite posts topped with some snarling heraldic beast whose features time had rendered so pitted that the species could no longer be determined. Beyond them a long straight drive led off into the mist. The trees on either side of it seemed to be curling inwards over it, as if to prey on whoever might disregard the KEEP OUT – PRIVATE PROPERTY signs and stray along it.

A chain and padlock secured the gates, at least nominally, but they stood ajar. The chain had been slackly wound through the bars, leaving a gap more than ample enough for Lennox to slip through.

The air felt colder as soon as he'd done so. That was his imagination, nothing more. He was nervous – he refused to use the word 'afraid', even to himself. He looked back. The car was across the road. The light inside was on and he could see Lisa's profile as she studied her book. He willed her to look up but she didn't, and he couldn't just stand here waiting for her to glance at him. He had to press on – even if his nerve didn't fail, the light soon would.

The drive was potholed, and he switched his gaze between the uneven surface and the woods spreading out on either side. The trees that reared above the boundary wall and alongside the path were the oldest; the ones that spread out through the grounds were considerably younger.

"Wardley New Hall was built in the 1890s by the then Lord Cairncross." Facts, history, statistics: they were Lennox's life in the outside world, and they were a comfort to him now. Facts, not feelings: they'd help him through this. "It was intended to replace the existing

Cairncross family seat at Wardley Old Hall, but ironically the New Hall burned down in 1943. The grounds have stood empty ever since."

Empty, at least, except for the trees and other plant life that had sprouted among the ruins. And whatever animals dwelt among them. Lennox heard something crash and flounder away through the undergrowth to his right. A rabbit, he told himself. Or a dog. No, not a dog. A dog on its own could turn feral. An urban deer, perhaps? They'd been sighted in this area.

October dusks were treacherous things. They seemed gradual, which was part of their appeal, the way they slowly drew veils over the landscape, taking colour and definition away by stages while streetlights came on and burnished the drifts of fallen leaves, but in truth they were both insidious and relentless. Every time you turned around there was a little more darkness; the outlines of your surroundings had grown a little hazier.

Lennox could feel panic welling inside him: nonetheless, he pressed on. There was a torch in his pocket, and he had his phone with him. Lisa was no more than a call away, and if he got lost in the woods the police could track him through GPS.

Besides, just for a moment, he'd felt a touch of his old affection for autumn evenings. He hadn't felt that, nothing even close to it, since that night, so perhaps the cure was working.

"Rob?" a small voice said.

Lennox looked around, startled, then tripped over something. He went into a headlong stagger, arms flailing for balance. For a second he was certain he was going to fly forward and crash to the ground, but his staggering slowed down as it ran out of momentum and he didn't trip again. He straightened up, breathing hard, and looked about him. Roots were squirming under the tarmacked drive, and in places it had broken and split. Up ahead, he could see young trees that had forced their way up through the ground.

Lennox felt his chest tighten and his breathing grow a little faster and shallower. This was familiar. He remembered this, the way the demarcation between the path and the woods had begun to break down. When he looked into the trees, he was sure he could see squarer, more regular shapes pushing up out of the earth. The remains of walls. He was certain of that.

He was entering the grounds of the New Hall. That must be why he'd imagined he'd heard someone call his name. It had sounded very like a voice, that of a lad the age he and Doug and Terry had been. But it would have been something else – a bird, maybe, or an animal. Yes, he was sure, almost sure, it hadn't been what he'd thought he'd heard. Well, it couldn't have been, could it?

The New Hall had been a big, rambling place, he remembered that. The young Lord Cairncross had been determined to innovate, to incorporate every new and interesting and clever-sounding idea he could think of into the Hall's design. But Lennox remembered that only from books and old pictures. There was no other way he could, because the Hall had burned down over thirty years before he'd even been born. Eight people had died in the fire, he recalled – another random factoid bobbing up to the surface of his thoughts – including Lord Cairncross himself, by then an elderly recluse considered half-mad by the locals, and his young, heavily-pregnant second wife.

Lennox's chest was tight and his stomach so hollow he thought it might cramp. That would be an ignominious end to his little trip down Memory Lane. He breathed out and went on. It wasn't dark yet, even if his surroundings were several shades darker than they'd been when he entered. Some of that would be down to the tree cover.

He was close to remembering. It was like having a name on the tip of your tongue: nearly, nearly knowing it but not quite. Lennox wasn't sure what was worse – the uncertainty or the prospect of recalling what had for so long been blotted out.

The temptation to turn and run back to the car was suddenly very strong. Lisa would understand, of course she would. They could come back again. How many times had she told him that the impulse to heal had to come from him, that it couldn't be forced? Enough times, both when she'd been his therapist and after she'd become so much more to him.

It wasn't as if he hadn't tried, repeatedly, to recall what had happened that day. Not just with Lisa, either, but at the time, with the police and their psychiatrists. But nothing could crack open the vault. The vault, that was how Lisa had described it: "Sometimes what we do with memories is lock them away where they can't hurt us. Like putting them in a vault. The same way you'd store a loaded gun, if you had one. So that they're safe."

But sometimes, she'd added, you needed to open the safe, because your experiences were who you are. They're what made you the person you become. So when you're bigger and older, when you're strong enough, you have to find a way to open the vault and see what's in there.

The path was almost completely gone now. There were only the dim woods and the humped, irregular shapes of the broken walls. Lennox dug in his pocket for the torch and switched it on.

"All right, Robbo?"

He swung around, slashing the torch-beam through the gathering dusk-haze like a knife. For a second he glimpsed a child's face, but then there was nothing. Nothing. Never had been. His heart was hammering. He took deep breaths.

Doug had called him Robbo. No one else had, or did. And no one had called him Rob in years. Even that day they'd gone into the grounds, Terry had been virtually the only one who still did. Lennox had been the clever one in their group, the one who read books and knew about stuff. That had been why Doug and Terry had used to protect him from the other kids at school; he could always be relied on to know something interesting, or useful.

Why had they gone into the grounds that day? He was close to remembering. And then he did. Yes. A den, that was what they'd been talking about. Because no one came here; all these woods, so many interesting things to discover, and no one came. Parents forbade it. Not that *that* usually stopped kids, especially not round their way, but they'd been, as far as he knew, the first to use the woods as a playground. And the last.

A den, then. All right. Lennox straightened up and shone his torch through the trees. Where might they have gone, then?

Movement. He spun and shone his torch at it, but found only the crumpled remains of some wilted ferns lolling back into the position something had disturbed them from. Rabbits, he reminded himself; a dog, or urban deer. Or a small, hunched figure in a robe made out of sacking.

Why had he thought of that? It couldn't be a memory, even if he *had* pictured it in these exact surroundings, and with such absolute clarity that every detail could be recalled, as if he'd been holding a photograph of it. The figure in his memory's eye – not memory, imagination, it had to be imagination – was small enough to be a child, but too squat and broad And one of its hands was visible, except that it couldn't be called a hand at all. It was something thinner and sharper, bristling with black fur, gleaming and sharp.

No, that was imagination, even though an over-active imagination had never been one of his weaknesses in the past. He had to focus on the details instead. The surroundings. The facts.

The facts, then. He began to recite, as if by rote: "On the evening of the 31st October, 1988, three boys were seen entering the grounds of Wardley New Hall. They often slept over at one another's houses, and so it was not until the following morning that their parents, realising none of them had come home, raised the alarm. The grounds of the New Hall were searched extensively, but no sign of the missing boys was found. One of the children..." He gulped for breath because his throat was so constricted, and a wave of emotion, not only fear this time but grief, threatened to drown all coherent thought. But he forced it down and carried on. Facts. Details. He had to cling to those, not even in the hope of remembering anything now, but simply to anchor himself to reality. He should not have come here. Thirty years was nothing, nothing, not to something like this. But now he was here, and he had to push on.

"One of the children," he repeated, "thirteen-year-old –" he faltered again, but swallowed and continued "– Robert Lennox, was discovered a week later in nearby woodland, alive but badly malnourished and with no memory of the events of the past week. The other two children, Terence Wilson and Douglas Thirley, were never found."

Lennox leant against a tree, then pulled away. More than ever he wanted to run back up the drive to the road, the car, to Lisa. Her warmth, her embrace, her kiss. She understood him, accepted him, cared, whether his memories were complete or not. But no. He wanted her to be proud of him. Then they could go home, back to London, far, far away from where he'd grown up. Back to the University to teach. Facts. Figures. Reality. He could go back to that. But first of all, this. Not even for Lisa, in fact. Just for himself. Just so he knew, so he remembered, and so he could be proud of himself. He'd always been the timid one, nervous and shy. He'd given his knowledge to

Terry and Doug, and they'd given him their confidence and strength in return. Symbiosis.

They would have wanted a den that was like a fort. He would have looked for somewhere hidden but safe. Part of a cellar, perhaps.

A knoll rose up on his left, crowned by broken stubs of wall like jagged rotten teeth. Or the battlements of a mediaeval castle. Yes, that would have caught Terry's eye, and Doug's. Of course, there'd be places like this all over the woods, but... but was it wishful thinking, or did it look familiar?

He climbed up the knoll, shining the torch ahead. This had been the corner of a room, because the wall bent into a right angle. The ground had risen up under it since the Hall's destruction; the wall had broken and cracked into sections. Could this really be the same place his struggling, half-complete memories were trying to convince him it was? The roots would have grown thicker since then, of course – the trees had had another thirty years to change the landscape still further. But even so.

Lennox crouched and studied the wall. The stones were covered with moss. But something was familiar. Something – his hand moved almost of its own volition, to a section of wall that somehow seemed particularly familiar, and his fingers dug into the moss and pulled a chunk of it away. On the stone beneath, three sets of initials had been incised. *DT. TW. RL.*

Again Lennox was forced to gasp for breath with a constricted chest, but this time it was from excitement and not fear. This had been the place. Enough of a fortress for Terry and Doug – but he would have looked for a cellar.

He swept his hand back and forth across the leaf-littered ground, shining the torch. Dead dry leaves, twigs, soil, grass, stones – and then his fingers found something, under the dirt. A flat, regular surface, of the kind that Nature on her own did not provide.

He scraped up the earth and twigs and leaves, found wooden slats and an iron ring-bolt set into them. How could the searchers have missed this? Maybe they hadn't missed it; maybe they'd only found no clues. But they hadn't had what he had. He had the vault and everything locked away in it. Maybe this would unlock it.

Lennox hauled on the ring-bolt. He was afraid it would tear free of the old spongy wood, or that the hatch wouldn't lift, having warped or rotted into place. But then it moved, so suddenly he almost pitched backwards down the side of the knoll. Beyond the hatch was darkness, and a thick, foetid smell that made him draw back and briefly tempted him to close the hatch again. But no; he could feel the memories trembling at the edge of release, like figures about to emerge from the shadows. Like the two small figures who stood among the trees at the foot of the knoll, pallid faces turned up towards him.

Lennox made a noise that was somewhere between a grunt and a strangled cry. He refused to believe what he saw. Whatever had happened to Doug and Terry, and it could have been nothing good, they couldn't be children anymore.

And they weren't. When he looked again, there was no sign of them.. There were some silver birches among the trees. Their pale bark must have looked like faces in the twilight. Even if one of the figures had seemed to have been wearing a red and blue striped V-neck jumper just like the one that had been Doug's favourite. Again he was tempted to leave and come back in the morning. Cold light. Day time. He was close enough to remembering now, wasn't he? It would only take a small push. But what if it didn't work in daylight? What if the vault took advantage of the delay to seal itself all the tighter? No, he was too close now to turn back.

He shone the torch through the open hatch, and to his surprise saw a ladder leading down. It must have been left over from the original cellar, and yet it looked sturdy enough. More than sturdy enough to bear his weight.

He hesitated again; he could imagine the rungs giving way underneath him, pitching him to the floor. Broken bones, unable to move, and then watching the hatch fall shut above him again. Perhaps Doug and Terry were still down there. But did that make sense? If they'd become trapped, what had happened to him? Why had he locked away all memory of that evening?

He extended a leg through the hatch and put a foot on one of the rungs, leant his weight on it. It held. "Sod it," he muttered to himself, then put the torch between his teeth and climbed down.

The odour intensified. He smelt decay, and an ammoniac reek. When his feet touched the floor, things crunched beneath them. He wanted to believe they were twigs or old leaves or dead insects, but he knew they weren't. Any more than the faint sounds he could hear, like kittens mewing, were in his imagination.

He shone the torch around. The space was huge, a vast earthen chamber, and there were holes in the walls – tunnel entrances. He shone his torch down one. It looked ribbed, as if they'd been dug out by hand.

Bones on the floor. Scattered and broken. Too large to be those of animals, surely. Urban deer, he thought again, trying to convince himself. Urban deer. But then he saw a skull on the floor, and it wasn't that of any animal.

Out. Get out. He had to. It was nearly dark, and what if he hadn't imagined the voices in the woods? But his limbs refused to obey him, and he hadn't remembered yet. He hadn't remembered, and yet he was close to it, he knew, closer than he had ever been or might come again, closer than he could bear to come and *not* remember.

At the end of the chamber, a number of long white objects dangled from the ceiling, and as far as he could tell, the mewing came from them. He steeled himself and advanced. The beam of the torch wavered in his shaking hand. What looked like fronds of white lace also hung down from above; when they touched his face they clung stickily to it until he clawed them away, rubbing the strands that stuck to his fingers off on his clothes.

The white objects were large, and of different sizes. Now that he'd reached them he could see there were more than he'd thought, and that the chamber was longer than it had appeared; dozens of the shapes dangled in rows, reaching back. Whenever he shone the torch on one of them, the woven fabric that composed its surface twitched and stirred. Lennox's stomach churned queasily: he thought of the cocoons that insects wove.

They were people-sized, he realised. Some as large as adults, and some the size of children.

He shone his torch at the closest cocoon, and the light probed easily through the gossamer veils of fabric – of cobweb – and found a face.

It was gaunt, wizened, mummified. A skull with leathery skin stretched taut across the bones, with faded, straw-like hair still clinging to its scalp. Its eye sockets gazed upwards, and its mouth yawned open in a soundless cry.

Until it felt the light upon its face, and tilted its head to look at him.

Its eye sockets weren't empty. Something still glistened inside them; something that still saw. The shrunken mouth moved feebly, and that thin, beseeching mew emerged. Lennox backed away; the beam of his torch wavered down to the cobwebs shrouding its chest and picked out the faded blue and red stripes of a V-neck jumper.

"Hiya, Robbo."

Doug dropped through the trapdoor and landed in a crouch in front of him, straightening up to give his old familiar gap-toothed grin. Terence climbed down the ladder, pulling the hatch closed. "Pleased to see us?" he said.

"Too good to talk to the likes of us, are you now?" said Doug.

Soft movements sounded behind Lennox; he turned and saw low, squat figures in sacking robes emerging from the tunnels. Their cowls hid their faces, and Lennox was glad of that as their hands were bad enough; in fact, they didn't really *have* hands at all. Instead, a single curved, chitinous claw, sprouting from a clump of stiff black hairs, emerged from each rough sleeve. The creatures began to make a sound: a low, chittering hum.

"Welcome back," said Doug, and his mouth stretched impossibly wide.

Lennox saw something bristling and black starting to squeeze out into view, and finally he remembered. But if they'd expected it to paralyse him, it didn't.

It was a matter of fight or flight, he realised, and he couldn't flee because he was surrounded and the exits barred. Very well, then: he'd fight. He found himself crouching and picking up one of the long bones on the floor to wield as a club; he was surprised how easily it came to him, along with rage. Now his memory had returned, he was battling to keep it back, to prevent it swamping his awareness. But he remembered enough to feel fury and disgust, and, born out of that, the desire to smash and wound. To kill.

It didn't seem to impress Doug or Terry or the other creatures. A cold hissing laughter came from Doug and the others, gloating and repellent. Terry's laugh was still that of the child he'd been as he came forward. "Ooh," he said. "Look who's a big hard guy now. Reckons he's gonna take us all on. That right, Robbo?"

"Get back," he heard himself say. "I'll fucking twat you." The language of the playground. Lennox hefted the thighbone; Terry opened his mouth and laughed out loud.

They were closing in, all around him. Terry reached out to snatch the bone from his hand. Lennox jerked the weapon back out of his reach, stumbling backwards, then jumping sideways to avoid something that tried to grasp his shoulder. And that just made them laugh louder, and louder, and louder.

His rage flew to a peak at their mockery, but even as he swung the femur, he felt sure that if it didn't shatter into dust on impact, it would have no effect on his attackers. He was resigned to defeat already, to going down with at least a show of defiance, and so he was more astonished than any of them, even than Terry, when the makeshift club connected with his old friend's skull and Lennox felt things break and collapse beneath the blow.

Terry staggered sideways, eyes rolling, and fell to his knees. Lennox brought the thighbone down again, on the top of his head, and Terry pitched to the ground. Dead, stunned: Lennox neither knew nor cared, only that he'd managed to land a blow and make it count. He yelled and whirled about, swinging the bone again; the hooded things retreated. He spun back the way he'd come. Doug was advancing, his mouth now closed and what had been about to emerge from it concealed again, but Lennox ran at him, screaming, and swung another blow. Doug's forehead collapsed beneath the impact, and he too fell.

Some of the creatures scattered as Lennox ran for the ladder; others stood their ground and made for him, but he had even fewer qualms about striking at them than he had at the things that bore the semblance of his friends. He struck and kicked – he stamped and trampled as one of them went down, but then stopped himself. He must escape, that was the priority: there were too many of them here to fight. Brittle though they seemed, they were far from strengthless or without weapons.

With the bone in one hand and the torch in the other he charged for the ladder. The bone was torn from his hands as he smashed it down on a hooded shape; either claws had seized it, or it had embedded itself in its target. Lennox looked back once as he scrambled up the ladder with the torch between his teeth, kicking out at the hands and claws that snagged at his clothes. To his dismay Doug and Terry had risen to their feet again, and the hooded shapes he'd felled were stirring too.

Doug and Terry ran for the ladder and climbed, swift as insects. Lennox heaved himself back outside into the near dark, slammed the hatch down on their pale, laughing faces, and began to run. But the woods were trackless, and as he blundered and stumbled over the uneven ground he heard the chittering sound coming through the trees. There were more of them, and they were swarming.

But then the ground began to level off, and he could see a long gap in the trees ahead – the driveway. He crashed towards it. Thorns and branches cut at his face and brambles dragged at his feet, but he broke through them and the lumpy ground gave way to the tarmac. He could see the streetlights gleaming on the road ahead, nesting among illuminated leaves, and ran faster, refusing to look behind him, willing his thundering heartbeat and rasping breath to drown out the sound that followed him.

He remembered it all now. The three of them climbing down into the cellar, finding the tunnels and the hanging things. The creatures humming as they'd emerged. He and Doug making it out, only to find the woods full of them. The icy, agonising bites, the paralysing venom. Being dragged back to the cellar to join Terry, and woven into their shrouds. The long, immobile days, hanging there, barely able to move, unable to make any noise other than a faint, kittenish mew. More bites, keeping them immobilised as the creatures fed off them.

Realising the venom's effects wore off more quickly for him, that somehow he must have had a greater resistance to it than Terry or Doug. Clawing his way out of his cocoon; fleeing through the seemingly endless tunnels, evading pursuit and reaching the light again by sheer luck. Collapsing, shaking and spent, as his mind shut itself down and locked away the traumatic and impossible events he had endured.

And all this time, the things in the ruins and the woods had been waiting, for the return of the one who'd got away.

Well, they'd get their wish, because he *would* come back again. With help if he could, and if not, alone. Pour petrol into the underground chambers. Burn them all. It was the least he owed Terry and Doug, after leaving them behind.

Tomorrow. In the cold light.

He could see the gates, and beyond them the car. Lisa got out and dashed across the road, squeezing through the gates towards him. He wanted to shout at her to get back, to stay out, to get back to the car and be ready to drive as fast as she could. To get away from the New Hall while he babbled out what he remembered and hoped she believed it. But he saved his breath to run.

She reached out to him; he fell into her arms. "I remembered," he said. "I remembered."

And he opened his mouth to tell her the rest, but she only said, "I know," then pushed him away and slammed the gates behind her.

She advanced on him, her arms outspread. The chittering hum rose behind him. Lisa's mouth stretched wider and wider still. Stiff black fur, long curved chelicerae and eight coal-black eyes squeezed themselves into view, but the creature beneath her skin still spoke in her loved, familiar voice. "Admit it," it said. "It's better this way."

THE IMPORTANCE OF ORAL HYGIENE

Robert Shearman

I have been trying to write to you for some little while now, but every time I do it comes out wrong. But time is of the essence, I fear it may already be too late – and so however this letter turns out, I *will* send it – I shall bite the bullet, let the words fall where they will. And even now I can tell, with all this circuitous preamble, still I am putting off getting to the heart of the matter, and I must push on. I must concentrate, although concentration is such a hard thing for me nowadays. And I had not realised what a fine thing presence of mind can be until I had squandered it forever.

I urge you to read on. I do not presume to offer advice. Not advice, and not judgement neither. I fear you may be in grave danger. And you will understand that in my heart of hearts I truly care not that you are in danger, at times I would rejoice to see all manner of dreadful fates befall you, damn you, I say, damn you. But I think and hope and believe that I am a good Christian woman. In spite of all I have done. In spite of all I have become.

And still I labour the point...! Let me, at last, be blunt.

Point One. I believe that you are in love with my husband. Point Two. Moreover, I believe he is in love with you. Point Three. Moreover still, I believe you have already enjoyed certain carnal pleasures with each other. Point Four (and this may be the most important Point). I know what form these carnal pleasures will have taken, and to what depths they will proceed if left unchecked, and the thought fills me with nausea. For my own jealous sake, naturally, but also, and I hope you can trust me, so very much for yours.

You must not see him again. You must break it off. When you have read this letter, I advise you immediately to pack your things. I advise you to tell your husband, if you have one, that you want to leave this town. Insist on it if you must. Because it is the only way you can be sure to put Crispin behind you. And then burn this letter, so it will never fall into the wrong hands, and cause such scandal to your reputation (and to mine, I suppose, but what of that, really, what of that now?).

I repeat – I do not judge you. I would say, there but for the grace of God go I. But I *have* gone, haven't I? I have been, and I have wallowed in it, and I suspect God had really very little to do with the matter.

The man we love is sweet and even-tempered, for all that he trades in pain. But I fear the consequences of his finding this, and what actions he might be obliged to take against us both. Because I suspect he may be the very dev

★   ★   ★

I apologise for the interruption. Sometimes I lose control. Sometimes I go quite numb, and then I might stare out as if dead, or in a trance. Crispin gives me smelling salts, but they do not always bring me to my senses. He calls these my Deep Moods, and laughs at them as if they are a perfectly normal thing. I do not know for sure how I behave when the Deep Moods set upon me, I think very little at such times. There is a kind of peace to it, a rather melancholy peace but a peace nonetheless. It is taking me more and more frequently, so Crispin says. Crispin may be lying, but I do not think so. For all that he is a deceitful man (as you must already know so well) I do not believe he lies easily.

My fear, of course, was that when the last Mood took me, I was in mid-sentence to you. And that my letter would be discovered by Crispin – really, how could it not have been, as he dosed me from his stock of ammonium carbonate to revive me? When I came to I couldn't see the letter anywhere, and I feared that he must have taken it and read it, and after destroyed it – and the repercussions he would visit on you would be most terrible. That he would have to step up his game. That in trying to warn you, I had only put you at still greater risk. But I found the letter. I found it in my pocket, neatly folded. I can only think that as the Mood descended I still had the presence of mind to protect myself and to protect you.

This letter makes you so vulnerable. It is a curious power I have over you, I realise. The thrill of it. Well.

It is possible, of course, and do not think I have not considered it, that Crispin found the letter, read it, *then* folded it and put it in my pocket. But I am still here. And yes, you are still here. I have seen you arrive at my husband's surgery this very morning. I have suffered the look of ironic amusement you flashed at me as you make your appointment. The contempt you have for me! And I have seen you emerge once more from private consultation, from behind the door I am no longer permitted to open, and you have been all smiles, still quite yourself.

I do not feel such urgency to warn you any longer. I deduce from the ledger this Deep Mood lasted three days. I assume from the number of appointments you have made to see my husband, and so blatantly too, that I am too late, that you are already lost.

Still, I will write. And if I tell you long details of my personal history, and by doing so blunt the urgency of this letter even further, do not believe I am punishing you deliberately. Or, believe it, if you must.

I fell in love with Crispin Watt on the 6th of April, 1844. I did not sentimentalise the date, not even then. But all appointments are recorded within a ledger, and I am now in charge of the ledger, and I can turn back a few pages and see the record of my first visit, so. As you may anticipate, like yourself, I made his acquaintance to employ his professional services, vis-à-vis my aching tooth.

I was not inclined to love a dentist. I confess it, I have a great fear of dentistry. I do not, I should add, have a great fear of pain. I do not enjoy pain, but I understand that a life must inevitably prompt a certain amount of it, and it is an uncomfortable thing but not a frightening thing, and if it is not to be feared then it can be withstood. The birth of my daughter Eloise was especially difficult, and I remember there was a lot of blood, and I was led to believe there was some doubt whether we could both survive the process. I should have died, so my child should live. That would have been the correct form for it. And yet I pulled through – which, I suppose, in retrospect, was a little self-centred of me. I survived because I focused upon the fact there was some objective to it all, the suffering, the pain, the sheer embarrassment of lying there while midwives pulled something breathing from out between my legs – there was a *reason*, and if I could just clamp my jaws tight and ride through it, I would gain a little girl. There would be Consequences. With dentistry, with all the pain there, yes, and all the embarrassment too, what, at the end of the procedure, is the Consequence? A bloodied chunk of enamel to take home, something to stick under the pillow for the tooth fairy. What could I want with that?

And it seems to me that toothache is the most personal and private pain to withstand – because isn't the mouth the most intimate part of the body? When John fondled at my breasts, or put his hand inside my hole, really, it only took the smallest concentration and I could make those parts of the body seem so very far away, they had very little to do with me at all. But my mouth – oh, I didn't want him fixing his lips upon mine – it was mine. And the pain within my mouth was mine too. I would not want a dentist, a stranger, making me open up wide so he could find my pain, to see right into me, to invade myself like that.

When I was a little girl I went to the dentist, and he extracted a tooth. It was probably the work of seconds, and I'm sure he was the best dentist that could be bought – my father would not have stinted in such matters. But it seems in my memory to have lasted a hellishly long time, and I can see that dentist as a giant, a big hulking brute. How I cried. How I tried to fight him off, and my arms had to be pinned behind me. On the way home, after the deed was done, Mother and Father told me that they were ashamed of me. That I should wipe my eyes, and never behave so demonstratively again. And I learned two things from that. I made two vows. That I should never cry. (And I have kept that vow, I didn't shed a tear when either of my parents died.) And that I should never again visit a dentist.

As Baby Eloise was teething I would hold her close and try to will the pain away – but I would refuse to think of my *own* teeth, and how every day my gums would bleed, and how so often (and for so long too) there would be a dull ache when I woke in the morning (John would say I ground my teeth in bed, I think that's what did it), and how I had taken to eating cautiously on only one side of the mouth – this particular side, naturally, varying dependent on which side was the most sensitive that day.

But there came a time when I could ignore the pain no longer. I would pace the house all night waiting for dawn, because it seemed that pain was so much worse in the dark, in the small hours when everyone was abed it turned into a demon and blotted out all thought. And John insisted I must go to a dentist. John was a man who rarely insisted on anything, so I knew it was time to listen. He told me I wasn't running the house efficiently for lack of sleep. That I was snapping at Eloise and at her nanny. That moreover he loved me, and could hardly bear to see me in such discomfort. He told me he would accompany me to the dentist if I so wished, he would take the day off from the bank – and I said that would not be necessary. He told me that he wished he could take my pain from inside my mouth and put it inside his, so he could suffer instead of me. And I rather think he meant it.

I should explain. John is my first husband, some would say my *true* husband. But I don't see how he can be now. I don't see how that is possible. And Crispin and I may have never walked up the aisle together (indeed, we have never together been to *church*!), but he is my husband, he is mine. Just as I fear he may become yours. Just as I fear he may already be.

Of course, I was frightened visiting the dentist. I considered not even entering the establishment – no one could have stopped me – I could have just turned, and fled far away. There would have been Consequences – I would never have seen John again, nor Eloise neither, and my whole life would have changed – and so it seemed like a very drastic option to take, yet still, it *was* an option. But I would still have had the toothache. Believe me, if I could have run from my life and left the toothache behind, I might have done it.

I gave my name to the woman at the desk with the ledger. She was old and ugly, and seemed barely to have any teeth in her head herself, and I remember at the time thinking she was hardly a good advertisement for the firm. The ugly woman wasn't kind, but she wasn't exactly rude, and she told me I should take a seat, and that the dentist would see me soon.

The dentist was not as I expected. You know Crispin, of course. You know what an impression he makes. But to me, with my memory of dentists as being big and brutish, the contrast between my dread expectations and the reality of the man was all the more acute. Bookish, lanky, a gentle face hidden somewhat behind owlish glasses. I looked him over critically.

"Your arms," I remember saying, "hardly seem strong enough to pull a tooth from out of my head."

He smiled. "I assure you, madam, I am equal to the task." And he offered me his hand to shake. I thought that was a peculiar thing for a dentist to do, and then it occurred to me that maybe he was inviting me to inspect the strength of his wrist, so I shook his hand firmly, and was in no especial way reassured.

"Where is the offending tooth?" he asked, and I opened my mouth and showed him. I imagined it was by this stage bright red and pulsating, it should have been easy enough to spot. "I see," he mused, "well, we can have that out in a moment! How long has it been since you last visited a dentist?" And I didn't want to answer that, because to have done so would have suggested my age, and I thought that his asking was rather an impertinence.

"Don't be afraid," he said, and he smiled, and I could see at last his own teeth, and how white they were, and how neat, and how *full* his mouth was. "There'll be no pain. I'm a practitioner in the Arts of Innovative Medicine. There's a new method, straight from the Americas. Tell me," and he leaned forward, as if in confidence, as if he were telling me the biggest, naughtiest secret, "have you ever taken nitrous oxide?"

★　★　★

Another break in the narrative, and I apologise – but even at the mention of that sweet, beautiful gas I give myself up to oblivion. I must be more careful. I *shall* be more careful. I dreamed of Eloise. I think. Sometimes in my Deep Moods I dream of nothing at all, but now there's a memory of Eloise in my head. I'm glad. Most days I can barely remember I even have a daughter.

So even if this letter does you no good – and I worry about you, I see there have been six new appointments made, I fear by now you are as lost as I am – at least writing to you does *me* good, if it brings even briefly my little Eloise back to me.

He'd not told the truth about the nitrous oxide. There was pain, there was a lot of it, and I recall even now with so much else forgotten that awful ripping sensation as he tore the tooth out of my head. But the nitrous oxide meant I didn't care. I knew what was happening was bad, and that every instinct in my body was shrieking at me to protect myself – but I let it all happen anyway.

Isn't that just like love? When you can't stop yourself. Even if you know nothing good can come out of it. Even if you know that all before you is ruin, and shame, the loss of honour and so many more important things besides. But the love makes you woozy.

I get ahead of myself. And besides, you know. You *know*. I can see it in your smiles. I'd like to slap those mocking smiles off your face.

John was waiting for me at home. He was worried for me, he told me he'd taken the day off from the bank anyway, he couldn't concentrate knowing I was undergoing such a fearsome operation. And sometimes when John would say such dear and loving things I'd feel a softening towards him, but now the sensation was numbed, everything he said sounded a bit annoying, and I wondered whether that too was an effect of the gas. I was still in pain. And a rudimentary analysis with my tongue revealed that the dentist hadn't extracted the entire tooth; he'd broken it, and the stump still remained embedded in my gum, sharp now and splintered, and still throbbing away with gusto. John was furious. He told me that he'd go and see the dentist, expose him as a charlatan. He'd find someone more worthy to venture inside my mouth. I told him not to worry. I would go back the next day, see Mr. Watt for myself, and I was sure everything would be put right.

The receptionist didn't look surprised I had returned so soon, and entered my second appointment big and thick into the ledger. I went in to see the dentist. I opened wide, in he peered. "Oh dear," he said, and laughed a little awkwardly. "I do seem to have let you down rather. Let me have another try."

"With more nitrous oxide?" I asked.

"With more nitrous oxide," he agreed, "and lots of it! But this time, if you trust me, I shall have to administer it to you much more carefully. But do you trust me?" I told him I trusted him; I opened my mouth as large as it would go. The day before he had wafted the gas over me every which way with a bit of rubber tube, there'd been no direction or control to it at all. Now he took the tube – he put it in his own mouth – he sucked on it, hard, until his eyes bulged fit to pop.

I was surprised, but I kept my mouth wide open.

And then he clamped his lips upon mine, and blew the gas into my mouth.

As I write it down, I can see that it sounds untoward. But I want to stress that even at this stage this wasn't a kiss, there was nothing informal about it, and as he pressed his mouth against my own, and wiggled about a little to ensure that the gas filled every possible crevice in there, it all seemed very medical and proper. At length he pulled away.

"Are you all right?" he asked.

"Perfectly," I assured him.

"Good," he said, and took another puff. Then he was back at my mouth once more. This time I began to feel light-headed; I determined to enjoy the experience; I closed my eyes, and drifted a bit. I resolved to keep my tongue away from his, but the tongue loved the gas, it danced in it, it *writhed* – and I think it may have brushed against his, it couldn't help it.

I think we forgot about my tooth for a while. Again I told him that his arm was too scrawny to extract a tooth properly, and he laughed, and said maybe I was right; and I said that *my* arm was stronger than his, and he asked if that were a challenge, and I said it was, and we arm wrestled for a time, and I won, although I wonder now whether he let me.

"Oh, your tooth," he said suddenly, maybe half an hour later, and he yanked out the little stump, and presented it to me with all ceremony. He did a little bow. I tried a curtsey in response, but I was lying on a couch, it was hard to do, and I nearly rolled off.

And then suddenly the dentist was holding his head in his hands, turning from me. "Oh, G_d," he said, "oh, G_d."

I asked him what was wrong.

"I think I'm in love with you," he said. "I can't control myself."

I told him that was most unfortunate, because I was a married woman.

"I know," he said, "and I'm a married man, the situation is impossible." He told me he was married to the toothless old crone out in reception. I confess, I admitted some surprise he'd got himself shackled to such a fright. "You mustn't judge her," he said, "she's a good woman, she's kind. And maybe I did all that to her, who knows what horrors we do to each other in the name of love? Oh, G_d!"

He seemed very distraught, and I wanted to reassure him, so I got to my feet. The upright position no longer seemed a natural one to adopt, and I wobbled a bit. And I tried to give him some nitrous oxide of my own, I pressed my lips to his and exhaled deeply, just so he might get some of my last traces.

"I just want to be happy," he said. "Don't I deserve that? I'm not a bad man. In spite of what I do to people. Forgive me!"

I thanked him for his dentistry, gave him one last blast of my gas. Pushed it as far as I could with my tongue, and wiggled it around a bit. And told him I wouldn't see him again.

That night I went back to John. John seemed a very comfortable thing all of a sudden, warm and reassuring, and not a little dull. He asked me if I was all right, and I showed him the tooth stump Crispin had given me, and he winced a bit, and said we need hardly have it as a keepsake, and threw it into the fire.

He said to me in bed, very gently, in the dark, "Darling, I think it's Thursday." And I'd so forgotten which day of the week it was. "But we don't have to," he assured me, "not if you don't want to, not with the awful trial of the last two days." But I told him I was ready. And so he took off his pyjamas, and got up on top of me, and he began to grunt. And I lay there and I thought of the wonders of modern dentistry, that pain could be suppressed so easily, it was really a marvel – and I thought of the dentist too, Crispin Watt, his name was Crispin Watt. I tried the surname on for size, and it sounded naughty, it sounded odd, but it sounded good. "Are you all right?" John asked, and I said I was. And then, and it was the funniest thing, I felt I began to smell the nitrous oxide coming off me. I could breathe it, it was in my lungs, it was in my nostrils as I exhaled, exhaled thick clouds of it, and if I puffed with my mouth I could fancy I was sending out big greasy bubbles of the stuff, bubbles floating over me, floating over John as he pumped away, bubbles that just wouldn't burst. "Are you sure you're all right?" John said, and I said I was, yes, perfectly, yes. I could tell he was wondering why I was panting air at him, so I thought I'd better stop – or, at the very least, pant it out a bit more discreetly. But the gas made me want to laugh, I had to swallow my giggles down, I didn't want John to be alarmed, I didn't want him thinking I was enjoying myself. And then – and then – and then I felt I wasn't quite *me* at all – that I was watching from above, that I was up there floating with the bubbles, and I was looking down on this poor woman being flattened by a tedious old goat, and I was wondering why she'd bothered, why she didn't kick him off and find someone more handsome and more charming and just plain *better* – and then – and then, I swear – it was as if I could feel my skin changing, I could feel it getting looser, puddingy, I could feel my eyes glaze, and I could feel there wasn't a tooth in my mouth – and then there was the pain, the familiar pain, and it pulled me right back into myself, I heard the goat grunt, I grunted too, I couldn't help it – "Are you all right?" said John, as he rolled off. "Tell me you're all right, I need you to be all right, I love you so much," and I said I was all right, of course I was all right, I was always all right, and I said I loved him too.

★ ★ ★

We spoke today. Do you remember? Up you came to the reception desk to make another appointment, and you wanted me to write your name down fat and thick in my ledger. Oh, you *wanted* me to write your name. And I thought this was my chance. I could warn you, right then and there. My tongue is more lively today, I can form actual words – so long as they are simple and don't have too many syllables! Or I'd say nothing at all, just take out the letter written thus far, and thrust it into your hands. Even this incomplete account might be enough to save you.

But I didn't. Because I understood the way you looked at me. I knew. I *know*. The way the mistress looks at the wife. There wasn't a scrap of pity in it, just scorn. You think you're saving him. You think you're saving him from me. The irony of it. I would laugh, but laughter is as hard as talking. You are cruel. Was I cruel to my predecessor at the reception desk? Perhaps. I did not mean to be. I did not help you. I did not save you today. I was not kind, but I was not exactly rude. I told you to take a seat, the dentist would be with you soon.

And I think of Crispin with you, and Crispin on top of you, and Crispin within you – and I wonder, are you enjoying it more than I did? Do you take well to the gas? Are you better at love? At making love, at feeling love, at even knowing what love is? And when will you start turning into me?

★ ★ ★

This time the Deep Mood took me for over a week – nine whole days, in fact! – and when I recovered my senses I still wasn't able to talk for a while. Crispin wheeled me into the back room, and there he fed me tomato soup so hot that it made my throat smart. "What am I going to do with you?" he asked me, though he knew I couldn't reply. "You're getting worse and worse, it breaks my heart. And I need someone working at reception!"

He left me sitting there, facing the *other* Mrs. Watt, my predecessor. And that felt cruel, but maybe it was merely tactless – and it was like staring into a broken mirror. And I doubt the other Mrs. Watt even knew I was there, but once in a while she made a sound that was like laughter, and her eyes would roll, and with no teeth to stop it her tongue would flop out and hang wetly over her lips.

"Do you still love me?" I asked Crispin this morning, and I could see how pleased he was I could talk again. "Of course I love you!" he said, and he gave me a hug. And I dare say he meant it as he said it, but the hug felt awkward to me, it wasn't the hug you gave a wife but a dying grandmother. He said, "I love you very much, how can you doubt it? But I am not *in* love with you. It isn't your fault. It's just what it is. But if I were *in* love with you, this sort of thing wouldn't happen, would it?" And his smile was still kind and reassuring, and his mouth so full of teeth.

So I ask you – how many times has he told you he loves *you*? And how does he do it? Does he tell you, like he told me, that he was lonely? And he needed some tenderness in his life? That his wife couldn't properly satisfy his desires? That he was a good man, really, a good man – and a good man surely deserves a little happiness?

How did he get his hooks into you?

I would go to see his wife at reception when I came for my appointment. Not talkative today – just points a finger at where I should wait. Does she know? She must know. I try to smile at her kindly, but I think it comes out wrong. She doesn't smile back, the sow.

You'll wonder if I didn't feel ashamed. There was certainly shame. Numbed somewhere behind the gas. The wife of John felt guilty, the mother of Eloise felt guilty – but in the soft dentist's chair I was no longer simply wife or mother. I was becoming someone else. Oh, the sweet transformative power of love.

I let him extract three perfectly good teeth before I told him how I felt about him. He was preparing the nitrous oxide, he was sucking it down and was about to blow it into my lungs, and I just came out with it. Said that my front molar wasn't hurting me at all, there was no need for further use of the pliers. I had only wanted the excuse to see him again. And at that he laughed so much, and I don't think it was just the gas. He said I was such a silly. And I'd never felt like a silly before, Mother and Father had wanted me to be a sensible upright girl, and now I *liked* the idea of being silly. We kissed, and it wasn't a medical procedure this time, it was lips and tongues and chewing and gulping, and it's true, there wasn't really a *great* deal of difference, but there was an honesty to it, I think, a relief that our feelings were all out in the open.

"I want to make love to you right now," Crispin then said, and he lifted up my petticoats. I asked him whether we should at least close the door, his wife would be able to see us both at it from the reception desk! But he told me his wife was having one of her Deep Moods, and she'd be dead to the world for hours. She couldn't walk with her thick ulcerous legs. She could barely talk these days.

We made love then on the dentist's chair, and the lights were on, and I had never made love in the brightness before, and it all seemed so different when you could see all the bits flying about. I could see the strain on Crispin's face, and it made him look a little ridiculous, as if he were trying so very hard to do a difficult thing when it was really terribly easy, wasn't it? And I thought of how John's face must have looked all those years, and how mercifully protected I'd been from his facial contortions by the darkness, and I began to laugh. And Crispin laughed too, and then suddenly stopped, and I could see the horror on his face, and he pulled off me, he was staring at me, his eyes wide open, so frightened.

"Oh G_d," he said. "No, G_d, not again, please, not again!"

And I tried to speak, but I couldn't; and I put my hand up to my throat, and my hand was big and meaty and decked in liver spots; and the skin around the throat felt looser, as if breaking into coils; I was becoming looser, softer, I was melting into a fat puddle.

"Not again," he said, and he wasn't looking at me. He was trying not to look at me at all. "It isn't fair! Why does everyone I love end up getting so *broken?*"

I stared into the dull metal of his dental instruments, and the reflection that came back was distorted – but – it was her, it was *her*. It was the woman who sat at reception, the sour-faced fat dumpling of a wife. And I tried to scream, but it hurt, the sound that issued was a low rasp.

"Ssh, ssh, darling," he said. "I know what to do, I've done it before."

He went down on one knee, and he took my hand. "Don't you worry," he said. "You're old and ugly, but you're mine, and I'll never abandon you. Even if I find other lovers, you must know there'll always be room for you in my heart. You're my wife." And I wanted to pull away, but that scrawny wrist of his was stronger than it looked. And besides, his eyes were pricking with tears, I had never seen a man so moved by emotion before. How could I deny the sincerity of his love?

That was the first time he took me to his back room. There sat his other wife, and I stared at her, and properly at last, and I couldn't help it – because I knew now that was what I looked like, and this is what he'd done to *us*.

I couldn't talk for two days. He'd come and feed us both soup. He'd tell us he loved us. He'd give us both hugs. He'd tell us he was sorry.

And two things kept nagging at me. He'd said 'again', this was happening 'again', this 'kept' happening to him. How many other women had he transformed into his fat wife?

And what had he done with them?

He didn't call me by my name anymore. He called me Alice. Just as he called his other wife Alice. And when I could talk again, he moved me into reception. He showed me how to take appointments. What to write in the ledger. And I told him, Crispin, I know. I already know how the ledger works. I've been doing this job for years.

Sometimes I am Alice. And sometimes I fall into my Deep Moods, and I'm really nobody at all, there's nobody home, and I sleep a bit. And sometimes, not very often, but just once in a while – I remember I am a woman who has a daughter named Eloise. And I try to write this letter.

The police looked for me. It was in all the newspapers, I saw it from the ones left in the waiting room. The police even came to the dentists. Nobody could tell them anything. I couldn't tell them anything either, I didn't know anything that day, and when I tried to make my brain work it spluttered and stalled, and my tongue hung heavy in my mouth with the effort.

★ ★ ★

I am writing you a letter.

I am in the back room again. It is very cramped in the back room, just space for me and my other self. That's probably why Crispin doesn't come to visit very often.

I am writing you a letter. That is what I am doing.

I have not been taken out of the back room for some time now. I don't know what that means.

I am writing you a letter. I must remember. A letter, just for you.

It is hard to work out how words fit together. The Moods are really very Deep. But sometimes it all comes back to me in a rush – words, and syntax, and grammar. And meaning! It's so exciting.

I am writing. You a letter.

Yesterday my thoughts returned at such a rush and it was like a sudden burst of sunshine piercing the darkness, and the excitement was too much or my fingers were too thick or maybe I was just too fat and ugly and old and unloved – and I dropped the letter, I dropped the letter, it fell from my hands down, down onto the floor.

I couldn't move. My legs too thick and heavy, even if they weren't so ulcerated, I simply wouldn't have the strength to shift them. All these pages, written over so long, and I couldn't reach them.

I had vowed never to cry. But I had also vowed never to visit a dentist, and look where that had got me. So I cried.

I wasn't shy about it, I think I wailed rather. And perhaps it was the sound of my distress, or maybe the sight of all those tears running down my pudding cheeks. But the Alice opposite me seemed to stiffen. She roused, as if from a long sleep.

If I couldn't move, I knew she couldn't have moved either. Her skin was nothing but ulcers now, it was hard to see the human being underneath. But her hands tensed upon the armrests, I saw old veins bulge and pop with the effort. As she heaved her body out of its chair.

Alice looked at me. Her face was listless. There wasn't enough energy to put expression into it – she was saving all that for sheer physical exertion. She shuffled closer, one foot, then the other, as if forcing them to remember how movement worked. She came right to me.

I am writing you a letter.

And she bent down. I heard bones creak and snap. I saw ulcers burst. She bent down to the scattered pages on the floor.

Slowly, so slowly, she straightened up, and handed them to me.

Our faces so close we could have kissed. She stank of the gas. How much I wanted the gas.

I did not kiss her. I gave her a smile of thanks.

But she hadn't finished. She reached her hands inside her pocket. She took out an envelope, stuffed with a letter of its own. It was almost too much for her. She tossed it onto my lap.

Then she dragged herself back to her chair, almost at a rush, now that the task was done – she collapsed into it.

I opened the envelope. I seemed to recognise the handwriting.

I have been trying to write to you for some little while now, but every time I do it comes out wrong.

I stared.

And my numbed brain began to whirl. The memories I had recorded in the letter, how many had been truly mine? I had lost my body to Crispin's embrace, but I had always believed my mind at least was intact, that the story I told was my own. Was I just parroting Alice's own account – was it Alice who had been afraid of dentists, who had married John, who had destroyed her life? As I told the tale of my affair, was I just narrating hers? (Oh, Eloise! She was my daughter, wasn't she? Tell me she was mine.)

So I refused to read further, I closed my eyes against the words.

When I opened them again, I saw that Alice had more envelopes. Where had she got them from? Why so many? They were strewn across her lap, there must have been a dozen or more.

She managed a smile. I like to think it was a smile of comradeship, or at least of solidarity. But I don't know, I just don't know.

I am writing you a letter.

And I now understand why I am writing you a letter. It is not a warning. It is too late for that. It is a testimony. To be repeated and reinforced, along with all the others.

I can't be sure. But I think. I think that may be more valuable.

Or perhaps you will never read this. Who knows? Perhaps with you it really is true love. You'll be strong enough to love as yourself, and you'll never change. I hope so. I hate you. I hate you with every last fading fibre of my being. But I hope so.

I am writing you a letter, and there is no more left to write. It is a relief to finish. My fingers hurt, and my head pounds from having to squint at the paper. And I know it's impossible, because there is nothing left in my mouth, nothing at all – no teeth, no gums, not even a tongue. But even so, in spite of that, I do seem to have the most dreadful toothache.

BOKEH

Thana Niveau

Vera wasn't eavesdropping, but she couldn't help overhearing. Keeley was talking to someone. The child's high-pitched voice carried from the garden and Vera caught the word 'Rappy'. She smiled. Once Vera had repaired the velociraptor's broken leg, Rappy had become Keeley's favourite toy again. She only talked to her favourites.

There were the usual dinosaur roars and growls, along with pleading from the unlikely victims as Rappy terrorised the miniature landscape by Rhodie Forest. 'Rhododendrons' was as hard for Keeley to pronounce as 'velociraptor', so she had renamed the area. It was only a couple of shrubs, but to a six-year-old they must seem massive.

Vera moved to the open window for a peek. It took her a few moments to locate her daughter. The child's bright green shirt made her blend in with the surrounding plants. But her jet-black hair gave her away: a dark smudge in the garden.

Keeley was crouched with her back to the cottage, one hand on Rappy and the other on a model horse. The horse towered over the little dinosaur, but Rappy was undaunted. Vera had to squint to make out the details. As she watched, the raptor sprang at the horse, going for the throat and thrashing from side to side until the horse fell in the grass, where it kicked and flailed for so long that Vera began to feel uneasy watching it. Even more unsettling were the noises Keeley made to approximate the poor horse's dying screams. Plastic or not, Vera would never have let her toys suffer like that when she was Keeley's age.

But she found herself curiously transfixed. She watched until the horse was finally still, and then Rappy began to feast. The dinosaur ate lustily, all slurps and nom-nom gobbling noises. Vera kept waiting for it to end, but the orgy of violence went on and on, and her blurred vision only made it worse. She could all too easily imagine gouts of blood spraying from the poor beast's wounds and her hand drifted to her mouth as a wave of nausea rose in the back of her throat.

Remember what the therapist said, she reminded herself. *It's just her way of working through the divorce.*

Being abandoned by their father was bound to give any kid dark fantasies, no matter how young. But Vera seemed to remember other peculiar games from before it was just the two of them. Games that had made her feel as though she were standing beneath a dripping icicle. Voices Keeley had claimed to hear in the night, secret 'friends' who seemed just a little *too* secretive.

Rappy finally finished eating. Keeley covered the dead horse with leaves, and Vera wondered how the dinosaur interpreted the giant hand appearing from above. Was Keeley a god in this make-believe world?

Then the little girl did something really odd. She held Rappy in both hands, lifted her up to the rhododendrons, and bowed her head. Vera thought she could see Keeley's lips moving, like someone praying, but maybe that was just her eyes playing tricks. They'd been doing that a lot lately. Possibly her own reaction to the hellish separation.

Rappy lay in the girl's open palms, and Vera half expected to see the creature twitch and start to move on its own. Was a bolt of lightning about to strike and bring it to life?

But her flight of fancy came to an end as Keeley suddenly froze. She dropped her hands and spun her head to look directly at Vera. Her eyes didn't have to rove across the cottage to discover the window at which her mother stood, which made Vera feel even more uneasy.

Keeley didn't move or speak. She didn't do anything but stare, her expression unreadable. Vera arranged her features into a sheepish smile and raised her hand in a little wave, but Keeley didn't return either. She merely continued to stare until Vera was forced to break the uncomfortable impasse and turn away.

She waited a long time before daring to look outside again, and this time she used a different window, the one halfway up the stairs. Keeley was still staring. Right at her.

★   ★   ★

"And when I came back an hour later, she was still there."

Steve laughed. "Aw, kids are just weird. You know that." At his feet, Cosmo barked, as if in agreement. Keeley glanced up from the sandpit at the sound, then returned to her digging.

Steve was Vera's only friend in the village and, like Vera, he had also been dumped by a cheating husband. Fortunately, he had retained sole custody of their golden retriever, Cosmo.

Vera sighed. "Yeah. But mine seems especially weird."

"Trust me," Steve said, shaking his head, "it's nothing compared to what my brother's kid comes up with."

"Oh? Do tell."

"He says there's a foot living in the airing cupboard."

Vera blinked. "A foot. What, just the one?"

"Yup. It hops."

Vera grimaced. "Okay, yeah, that's weird. Jesus, where do kids get these ideas?"

She looked over at the sandpit. Keeley was alone there except for Rappy. If the child ever intended to resurrect the poor horse she'd sacrificed earlier, she hadn't done it yet. Vera had been tempted to dig it up herself, but the idea made her feel anxious. She hadn't been able to rid herself of the idea that she'd be unearthing an actual corpse. In her mind the tiny horse was ripped and gouged from the raptor's claws, with long red furrows revealing exposed bones and viscera.

Something wet touched Vera's fingers and she gasped. But it was only Cosmo, snuffling his nose under her hand. She smiled and scratched him behind the ears and he made a little sound of pleasure, the doggy equivalent of purring. He'd probably sensed her disquiet and come to reassure her.

"You should get a dog," Steve said, not for the first time. "Keeley needs real friends, not just plastic dinosaurs."

Vera lifted her hand from the dog's silky fur and Cosmo immediately pushed closer, demanding more attention. She smiled. "You mean *Cosmo* needs friends."

The dog chuffed softly at the sound of his name.

"Well, maybe that too. *Everybody's* Cosmo's friend. Isn't that right, boy? Who's a good boy?"

Leaves chattered on the ground at the windstorm created by the golden tail as it wagged madly.

"He may be a good boy, but he's a rubbish guard dog," Vera said. "I'd feel safer with a cat."

Steve laughed. He pulled a battered tennis ball from his coat pocket and threw it far across the park. Cosmo went bounding after it. "Can a cat do that?"

As though the talk of a playmate had conjured her, a little girl with ginger hair emerged from the trees. It was hard to see clearly from this distance, but Vera guessed the newcomer was considerably younger than Keeley. She stood for a while on the fringe of the playground before approaching the sandpit, where she crouched a few feet away from Keeley. In her hands she clutched a lavishly dressed Disney princess – Vera had long since lost track of who was who – and she seemed to be trying to work out how to fit the doll into Keeley's prehistoric tableau.

Vera felt herself tensing for the girl's inevitable rejection. Keeley loathed dolls and she wasn't good at sharing.

But the newcomer smiled shyly and Keeley returned a version of the smile. The ginger girl sat down next to her, gazing wide-eyed at the dunes Keeley was sculpting for Rappy to explore. To Vera's surprise, the girls were soon engaged in some sort of game. It mostly seemed to involve Rappy chasing the princess, and Vera secretly hoped the raptor would go hungry this time.

Cosmo returned with the ball and dropped it in Steve's lap. Then he danced on the spot until Steve threw it again.

Something tickled the back of Vera's neck and she reached behind her, slapping at the skin. But there was nothing there. At Steve's puzzled look she said, "Mosquitoes, I guess."

"I haven't seen any. It's a bit late in the year for them. Hey, speaking of 'late', when are we going to do your passport photo?"

Vera groaned. "Oh god, that's right. I keep forgetting! Sure, let's do it before I need glasses and look even older than I feel."

"What are you talking about?"

Vera rubbed her eyes. "Everything just seems out of focus lately. Fuzzy."

"I told you – you're not getting enough sleep. Too much fretting. Too much beating yourself up."

Vera looked down at her hands and sighed.

"Besides, you'll look amazing in glasses!"

Cosmo had been waiting patiently for the conversation to end, posing with the ball between his front paws, but he finally picked it up again, dropping it emphatically. It bounced towards Steve, who took the hint and obliged the dog with another impressive throw.

"Why don't you and Keeley come over this evening? Have dinner with me."

"Oh, I don't want to put you out—"

"It's no trouble, I promise. The food's in the slow cooker as we speak. I'm doing Boeuf Bourguignon."

Vera laughed. "Nobody makes Boeuf Bourguignon anymore."

Cosmo made a triumphant return, this time offering the soggy ball to Vera. Grimacing, she accepted it, but her two-fingered throw did not impress the dog. He was back almost immediately and this time he gave the ball to Steve, who sent it flying into the distance.

"It was my father's favourite dish," Steve said.

"You *hate* your father!"

He shrugged. "It's complicated."

In the sandpit, Keeley's playmate was swiping irritably at the air in front of her. Vera jerked her chin in their direction. "Told you. Mozzies."

"Guess I'm just lucky they don't fancy my blood. But look – please come over. We'll do your passport photo and then I can show you the wedding I shot last weekend."

"The one in the castle?"

"Yeah, the LARP one. It was brilliant."

"Oh! Yes, I do want to see that. Okay, it's a date!"

"Fantastic. And don't worry – I've got chips and ketchup for the less discerning palate."

Vera smiled and turned back to watch her daughter. The ginger girl was stumbling to her feet, waving her hands madly all around her head. Vera tried to focus. That couldn't possibly be a whole *cloud* of bugs surrounding her. Keeley seemed completely unaffected, sitting calmly and watching. When the other girl gave a panicked scream, Vera jumped up and ran towards the sandpit, reaching it in four long strides.

But she wasn't quick enough to reach the little ginger girl, who was now running at full pelt for the edge of the park. Her cries dwindled as she vanished into the trees. Vera was torn between wanting to go after her and staying to protect her own child. But there was nothing to protect her from.

"What happened, Keeley?" she asked breathlessly. "A bee? A wasp?"

Keeley bounced the raptor a few times, making it scale one of the dunes. She turned the dinosaur's head when it reached the top. It was looking in the direction the other girl had fled.

"She didn't like the fairies."

Vera shook her head, confused. "Fairies?"

"Yeah. And they didn't like *her*."

Something prickled her neck again and Vera waved at the back of her head. Keeley noticed and met her eyes with the same cold gaze as before.

"They don't like *you*, either."

The matter-of-fact tone and Keeley's dead expression sent a chill through her. It was a few seconds before she found her voice. "Come on," she said. "We're having dinner with Steve." She didn't like the way her voice cracked as she spoke.

★　★　★

The passport photo took no time at all, and Vera was pleasantly surprised by the result. She didn't look as wretched as she felt. But perhaps Steve had secretly worked a bit of magic with an ultra-flattering lens.

Dinner was lavish and delicious, and it took her mind off Keeley's weirdness for a while, even if it did make her feel a bit guilty. She was mostly a microwave chef, and while Keeley never complained about pizza and Chinese takeaway, it wasn't ideal.

"I need to expand my repertoire. Maybe you can give me a few tips."

Steve beamed with pride. "I'd love to."

Vera noticed with some surprise that Keeley was actually eating the mushrooms. When she discovered them on pizza she picked them off with an exaggerated 'yuck' face.

"Wow," Vera said. "Look at you, eating mushrooms for a change!"

"They're toadstools," Keeley corrected. "Where toads sit."

Vera thought that sounded much less appetising, but she held her tongue.

"Do you like it?" Steve asked.

Keeley nodded without lifting her head from her bowl. She'd eaten the chips first, of course. Then, after some trepidation, she'd tasted the French stew and found it acceptable. Now she was wolfing it down.

"Mummy never makes stuff like this," she mumbled in between mouthfuls.

Vera blushed and looked down at her own empty bowl. "Yeah, well, Mummy's had a lot on her mind. She's trying her best."

Steve covered her hand with his and offered her a sympathetic smile before turning to Keeley. "Maybe you and your mum could make it together sometime."

Vera brightened at the suggestion. "Would you like that, sweetie?"

Keeley shrugged, never taking her eyes off her bowl. "I guess."

It was better than silence. Or veiled threats. "I'll take that as a resounding yes," she said, and refused to allow Keeley's bland stare to dampen her mood.

After dinner, Keeley played with Cosmo while Steve took Vera into his office to show her the pictures. He'd been an enthusiastic amateur photographer all his life, but it was only in the past few years that he'd turned his hobby into a job. That was partly thanks to Vera's encouragement, and she always enjoyed seeing his work.

Steve began scrolling through the images in Photoshop, skipping past what looked like an extravagant wedding.

"Hey, wait. I want to see some of those!"

"Ugh, no you don't. That was a boring gig. I wanted to get some reportage stuff, you know, candid fun shots where they weren't aware of the camera all the time. Only Mother of the Bride said she didn't like 'that frivolous modern style', so everything was posed and staged. Nothing real. Nothing *authentic*. Look at this." Steve opened a thumbnail to show a group of young women in matching mint green dresses. They surrounded a bride who was feigning excitement over the bouquet she was about to throw. "They're like terrible actors in some ghastly play. The phone selfies they took are probably a better record of the day than any of my professional shots. Depressing."

He closed the image and navigated to another folder. "Now this is more like it."

Here was where he could let his talent shine. Vera felt like she was looking through stills from a fantasy movie. She'd been expecting a tourist trap castle with dusty antique furniture sequestered behind velvet ropes. Instead, it was a ruin. A few crumbling walls and arches were all that remained of the once-majestic structure. Vines and lichen were in the process of reclaiming it, creating a magical fairytale effect. The sky was overcast, but that only made it more atmospheric. Best of all, the wedding party were dressed as knights and mediaeval maidens, like characters straight out of Arthurian legend.

"They do roleplay there on the weekends," Steve explained, "which is where the couple met. And they were all in character the whole time. I felt like a time traveller."

"Steve, these are gorgeous!"

He smiled modestly as he continued to page through the pictures. "Yeah, they're not bad."

A sudden gasp made them both jump.

"Fairies!"

Keeley had appeared, as if from nowhere. She pointed at the screen, her expression one of sheer delight. Vera's heart twisted. It seemed like years since she had last seen her daughter smile.

"Where, sweetie?" Steve asked.

And just like that, the moment was gone. Keeley scowled at him before jabbing her finger at the background of the portrait. "There," she said, her voice flat and cold. "Right there."

Guinevere stood at the top of a crumbling staircase that led nowhere but into the sky. The dramatic staging transformed the photo into a Pre-Raphaelite painting.

Steve and Vera shared a look. Then Steve ventured a smile. "Oh, you mean those coloured blurs?"

Keeley's eyes narrowed as she peered at the screen. "Blurs?"

"The camera catches everything, even if it's out of focus – flowers, trees, people. I wanted the bride to be the centre of this picture, so I let everything else get blurred into the background."

Vera was relieved to know it wasn't just her eyes.

"But the blurs are pretty too," Steve continued, "and there's a special name for that effect. It's called 'bokeh'."

"Bouquet?"

"No, BO-kay. It's a Japanese word. You've got a good eye for spotting it!"

But Keeley still looked unconvinced, as though she were being deceived somehow. "But they're not blurry. They're *fairies*."

Vera stared as hard as she could, but all she could see were fuzzy coloured circles. Maybe Keeley's fairies constricted themselves into floating bubbles of light when they weren't expressing their hostility towards those they didn't like.

"Oh yeah," she forced herself to say, as though finally seeing through her daughter's eyes. "I guess they do look like fairies."

Keeley snorted derisively. "They *are* fairies. That's how they look."

Vera's unease was growing. Trust Keeley not to imagine Tinkerbell or butterflies, but some weird amorphous creatures instead, the kind you could mistake for vampiric insects. Vera wasn't sure she wanted to know, but she couldn't stop herself asking. "What are they doing?"

"Watching," Keeley said, her voice matter-of-fact. "Waiting. You've seen them and now it's too late." She pointed at the base of the steps. Thorny brambles and weeds coiled around the rubble and stretched across the stony path like clutching, skeletal fingers. "The rocks are grinning. They can't sing yet but they listen. And they dance. The fairies sing to them and bring them offerings. The rocks dance on them and hold them down in the ground and keep them there."

Offerings. Where the hell was she getting these ideas?

Vera's skin tingled, as if each single hair on her arms were being tugged by tiny invisible hands. She convulsed in an elaborate shudder, but Keeley didn't seem to notice.

"Keeley? Is that what happened to your horse?"

"Uh-huh. It was a ceremony. They were showing me how to make people go under the stones. I can't say the fairy names yet but they let me dance with them." She paused, glancing up at the ceiling. "But I'm not supposed to talk about it. Not to you."

Then she hopped down from the chair without another word and wandered back into the living room.

Vera sagged against Steve. "What. The fuck."

"I told you," he said, "kids are bloody weird." But he sounded less certain now that he'd seen Keeley in action. In fact, he sounded quite apprehensive himself.

Tears welled in Vera's eyes, rendering the bokeh onscreen even blurrier, as if the fairies were now concealing themselves from her. She remembered the little ginger girl at the park, the way she'd frantically waved at her face before running off in terror, the blur Vera had seen swarming around her head. And now she thought she could hear a high-pitched whine just behind her. She flapped a hand at the air, but the noise didn't stop.

"Can you hear that?"

Steve was listening, but not to Vera. His expression went from concern to alarm and he pushed himself away from the desk. Vera followed him into the other room, calling after him. They both froze, staring in horror. Cosmo stood facing Keeley in the middle of the room, his hackles raised, his tail stiff. He was growling.

Steve gave a cry of dismay. "Cosmo? What's wrong, boy? Come on, come to me!" To Vera he murmured, "He's never growled at anyone in his life and he'd never hurt Keeley. Cosmo! Stop it! Come!"

Vera felt horribly uneasy, but not for the obvious reason. Something was very wrong here. Something in the universe had gone askew. And it wasn't the dog. Keeley didn't look even the slightest bit frightened or unnerved by the situation. In fact, she stood tall, glaring down at Cosmo like a bully daring its victim to fight back.

Vera swiped at the air. The whine in her ears was louder and she couldn't keep from pawing and snatching at nothing. She checked her hands again and again, but there was no satisfying smudge of a dead insect. Just the maddening sound and the tiny suggestion of a breeze, like the tickle of moth wings.

Steve was edging towards the dog, crouching low, arms outstretched. "Hey boy, you want a treat? Walkies? Come on, Cosmo!" His voice was all desperation and no authority.

The worst thing of all was the abject terror now in Cosmo's body language. He was shivering, as though freezing. His tail had gone limp and he was slowly tucking it between his legs, backing away from Keeley as he continued to growl. But now the growling was interspersed with pitiful whimpers. Steve took hold of the dog's collar and pulled him back, but Cosmo tore free with a yelp and fled, his claws scrabbling on the hardwood floor of the corridor as he escaped.

Vera and Steve turned as one to look at Keeley, but she was paying no attention to them.

"I didn't mean to tell your secrets," Keeley said, addressing something in the corner of the room.

There was nothing there. Nothing but shadows. And yet Vera sensed movement. She squinted through her tears, trying to see into the darkness, but it was all a blur. In fact, most of the room was. She waved at the air with one hand, wiping her eyes with the other. But everything was out of focus.

"Steve! Can you—"

But he was having the same problem. He was stumbling towards the doorway, flailing his arms madly before him, just like the little girl at the park. "Get away," he gasped. "Get away!" Before Vera could warn him, he collided with the coffee table and cried out as he fell. There was a sickening crack as he hit the floor.

Vera screamed and tried to make her way to him, towards the moaning shape that was all she could see of him. But the air in front of her face was a kaleidoscope of coloured blurs. They darted back and forth in sharp little jerks like angry wasps. She whirled, searching for Keeley, but all she could see were multi-coloured balls of light, blurry and blinding.

The whining had risen to a piercing screech, drowning out Steve's cries. She thought she heard Cosmo in the distance, barking frantically, and from somewhere further still came the crash of breaking glass.

"Keeley, where are you?" Vera wailed, adding her voice to the hideous chorus.

The screaming colours and whirling blurs froze for a moment, enough to allow Vera a glimpse of her surroundings. Keeley was on the coffee table, standing over Steve's prone form, watching calmly as a fuzzy river of black began snaking its way from beneath his head. Then the child laughed in delight and clapped her hands. She began to hop from foot to foot, turning clumsy pirouettes. Dancing.

Vera's stomach lurched and she fell to her knees. She pressed her fist into her mouth to stop herself screaming. If she screamed, she would lose it entirely.

The smudge that was Keeley flung her arms up into the air, her black hair whipping round her face as she danced and spun in the terrible vortex. And laughed. Vera thought the frenzied laughter was the worst sound she had ever heard. Until the wood and stone of the house itself began to clatter and shriek.

Her field of vision dwindled to a single blur as what felt like tiny hands plucked at her, pulling at the threads of her being. In the end it was the singing that finally broke Vera's mind. The voice that came from the stones was vast and harrowing, a single ancient note, endlessly repeating.

MURDER BOARD

Grady Hendrix

"I had childhood dyslexia," Caroline says. "So I don't even know if I can do a ouija board."

"Put your fingers on the planchette," he says.

"Why don't we play Scrabble?"

They'd already played sixteen games of Scrabble, two of chess, six of Rummy. Rain sheets down the massive, two-storey glass wall that covers the entire rear of their house. Caroline looks through the watery ripples, across their saturated back yard, at the dark brown scrubby foothills sealing off their view. They paid a premium not to see any neighbours, but right now she'll take some warm, comforting porch lights. The news says a mudslide has blocked most of Buena Noticia Drive and the rain isn't supposed to stop for two days. She feels completely alone.

She turns back to the board and Bill, staring at her across the table, lines on either side of his mouth cut deep, bristly eyebrows meeting in the middle, lips compressed, breathing through his nose. This is Bill's anger face. More and more, it's the only face he shows.

She insists on meeting hostility with love.

"Let me get candles," she says. "To make the right atmosphere."

Standing, she pecks him on one unshaven cheek. She wants him to know she's glad he's sharing this relic from his past with her.

She finds three Cire Trudon candles (two Moroccan Mint Tea and one Mist Soil) and wishes she could find candles that don't cost $100 each, but she doesn't want to ask David where the candles are. She's fuzzy on what religion they practise in Serbia but David's so square he would see the ouija and assume they're worshipping the Devil, and honestly, they can't afford to lose David.

★　　★　　★

Bill needs her to put her fucking fingers on the fucking ouija board now. This house cost $13 million, he owns over $3 million in guitars, and there's an uncashed royalty cheque for $48,271 lying on his office desk, but the most valuable thing he owns is this ouija board. Calcified masking tape barely holds its box together, there's a gouge through the 'T', and the smiling woodcut moon in the corner has a cigarette burn stabbed in one eye, but if the house caught fire it's the first thing he'd save.

When he was little his old man tried to tell him about money.

"Billy boy," he'd said in that we're-all-pals-here salesman voice he could never turn off. "Do you know what money is? Money makes dreams come true."

His old man didn't know shit about money, but Bill does. And he knows money makes people lie.

Everyone in his life lies. His manager, his lawyer, his agent, his business manager – they all tell him what he wants to hear. He expects that, but the sick, evil, twisted fucking thing is that money even warps ordinary people. Old friends, cousins, his brother, his nieces and nephews, they spin every word because they always need something: a waived licensing fee for one of his songs, a loan, for him to come to their kid's gallery show and spend $12,000 on some shitty metal sculpture that's currently hanging over his front fucking door. They tell him he must be working out but he sees the mirror and knows he's a skeleton wrapped in loose skin. They tell him how great he looks but his face sprouts hairs and brown spots like a mouldy piece of bread.

He trusts David and Miloje because he signs their cheques. They're paid to give a shit. It's an honest relationship. Not like Caroline.

He sees the disgust on her face when she thinks he's not looking. He knows she doesn't breathe through her nose when she gets into bed. She wipes food off his chin like he's his old man. She's always at her yoga and her Peloton and her treatments and with her friends, and they're all gorgeous and young and their husbands take them trekking in Nepal and whale-watching in Alaska, and he's locked her up in this glass and concrete tomb with him, and he strongly suspects she wants to escape. He asks if she's happy and she makes nice noises, but they all lie.

However, something in this board looks out for him. Something in th:s board keeps saving his life. Something in this board tells him the truth.

*   *   *

Caroline smiles at Bill, sparks the lighter, touches it to the three wicks, and a bubble of warmth blooms around them while the rest of the living room sinks deeper into gloom.

"So how do you do this?" she asks.

She's going to make this work. She knows he's still upset about her wiping salad dressing off his chin at lunch, but that one blip won't ruin their day. She's going to make this a positive experience.

"Same way you've always done it," he growls.

Growing up, Caroline only wanted to get out of the LV. Rural Pennsylvania, Lehigh Valley, full of shut-down steel mills and skinheads stabbing each other with screwdrivers at shows. The girls who went to college, and had sleepovers, and pulled out ouija boards, and said 'Bloody Mary' at midnight into mirrors. Those girls didn't invite Caroline over, so whatever they liked, she hated.

But Bill's told her about how the ouija warned him to walk out on that woman the day before she overdosed and the cops raided her apartment, how it told him his first manager was ripping him off, how it clued him in that his second wife was cheating. She assumes this is the same ouija board, and that means he's serious about it, but to her this is silly, it's a Parker Brothers board game, manufactured by the truckload, and shipped out by the millions. There's one in every home. But he's sharing part of his life, so she needs to try.

"Is there some ritual you have?" she asks. "Some way you want me to focus?"

"Put your fingertips on the planchette," Bill sighs.

"Like this?" she asks.

He rolls his eyes and nods.

"Now what?" she asks.

"We wait."

They sit, the two of them, rain occasionally gusting against the big plate glass window with a wet drum roll. The candle flames flicker for a moment then hold steady. Bill closes his eyes. The candlelight softens his lines, bathes his face in a warm glow. He looks like the Bill she remembers.

She knows what people think. He's seventy-one, she's thirty-six, the trophy wife, the gold digger, the woman who pulls on latex gloves and squeezes out a blob of cold lube and gives him handjobs so he'll keep her in his will. That's what his money guy thinks, and his lawyer, and she worries that it's what Bill thinks now, too. He changed after he got his walker last year. He started shutting her out.

She wants to tell him that he's still the rock'n'roll guy to her, still the man with a thousand stories, still the guy she hasn't gotten to the bottom of yet. She wants to tell him how unreal it feels whenever he says Rod, or Phil, or Tom – she grew up listening to those guys, she never thought she'd walk around naked in front of their friend.

In a second she'll gently use the pointer to spell 'love' or 'trust' or something that will restore his faith but before she can do anything it flutters beneath her fingers. "Stop it," Bill snaps.

"I didn't," she says, and feels embarrassed at having to play along because of course he's doing it and pretending he's not.

She's not a dummy. There are no spirits. No invisible angel hovering over the Parker Brothers board. At best, it's the ideomotor effect, meaning they're both making small, unconscious movements that will move the pointer to letters revealing their subconscious thoughts.

But maybe she'll learn something about Bill, so she relaxes her fingers until they barely brush against the pointer. It doesn't move. Her finger tendons tremble, she strains to hold them still, and then the pointer writhes beneath her fingertips and her stomach snaps tight around a frozen pea.

Something invisible whips the pointer back and forth in a tight arc over the blank semicircle between the arch of black letters and the straight row of numbers, gathering force, the one leg missing its felt pad scratching the board.

Then it yanks her arms forward, and her fingers lose contact for a second, and her chest feels full of ice because this feels Not Her. This feels like Black Magic. This feels Unnatural. The pointer hits an invisible patch of thick air and stops on a letter.

"I," Bill reads, then it jerks their arms to the side, pauses on, "W" and shoots off again.

She can barely keep up, and she takes her eyes off the pointer for a second to see what Bill's thinking, and he's smiling in triumph, and it's ugly, and she looks back down because she doesn't want to miss the next letter because it's...

"I," she breathes.

IWI. I witch? I will? Will not?

"L" and then it makes a little circle over L and darts up to the one-eyed moon and back down again.

"I will..." Bill breathes.

The candlelight wobbles as the pointer stops on K, then back to I and then the double L's again and they're both reading out loud, "I... will... kill..." and they both stop reading and it stops moving, resting on the letter U.

Caroline yanks her hands back, Bill doesn't move, and she doesn't want to look at him, so she stares down at the board, wishing it away.

I will kill u.

★ ★ ★

"We need light and positive energy," Caroline says, standing, pulling the pointer out from under Bill's frozen fingers, dropping the board in its disintegrating box. "I know it's special to you but I'm exercising my veto. We don't need this kind of negativity in our marriage."

She walks to the kitchen, snaps on the light and Bill hears her stuff it in the trash. "I'll tell David to leave it there," she says, staying on the other side of the room, far away from him. "I'm going to smudge this space then take a sauna. Days like this you need to practise self-care. Do you want a sauna?"

She doesn't wait for his answer but walks to the other wall where her fingers fly over the controls for the lighting system, tapping it a final time, and the gloomy room blooms with soft lamplight and accent spots. She strides purposefully, youthfully, to the door leading to the hall and stops, so far away her face is just a pink thumbprint. Bill realises she's waiting for an answer. He realises it's been a long pause, the kind of pause people take when they're really turning something over in their minds. He has to make her think it's nothing.

"What'd you say?" he asks. "The rain's fucked up my hearing aid."

"Do you want a sauna?" she asks.

"No," he says, making himself smile. "Thank you. But do you want to open a bottle of wine tonight? It'd be nice to talk."

Even as a blur he can see her posture relax.

"We could use some joy," she says, and comes all the way across the room to kiss him.

He's itching to move but manages to keep his thoughts hidden. The second she leaves he gets up and rescues the ouija from the trash and apologises to it over and over again inside his mind.

★　　★　　★

Caroline gets all the way up to her bathroom, starts the sauna, studies her face in the mirror, reaches past the fluffy towers of spare towels to pull out her spirit box, slides open its wooden lid, and fishes out the bundle of sage between two fingers before she realises what just happened. She stares at the crystals rattling around the box next to a couple of mummified joints, the Buddhist prayer beads, the stiff loop of red string she wore back when she got into Kabbalah, and thinks:

I will kill u.

It's too melodramatic. Too over-the-top. No way did Bill subconsciously project his secret murderous rage onto the pointer because Bill's never been secret about his rage.

Her fingers still feel the pointer squirming beneath their pads, spelling that hateful message, and she stops breathing:

I. Will. Kill. U.

Bill hates emojis, abbreviations, funny misspellings, any word he wasn't taught in school back in the Fifties. His subconscious mind would have perfect spelling. His ideomotor impulse would spell 'you'. But hers? He's always thought of her as a child.

Their marriage, seen through his eyes, flashes through her mind: a young trophy wife after his money, saddled with a fading guitar player who uses a walker after taking a fall. They share no interests. They have zero common friends. They built a house that seemed like an escape but turned into a modern art prison in the foothills.

Her skin prickles hot.

He thinks she wants to kill him.

It's crazy, not even worth mentioning, but shouldn't she reassure him? She walks to the bathroom door, raises her hand to the knob, doesn't know how to bring the subject up, lowers her hand, goes back to the sauna, puts her palm on its door, but she has to make sure he doesn't think she hates him, lowers her hand, then back to the bathroom door, and back, and forth, and back, and forth.

He's rich, he's old, she's young, she grew up poor, he's always in a bad mood — it's got all the ingredients of a true crime podcast. That's ridiculous. You (young, bored) can't just tell your (rich, elderly) husband you're not thinking about killing him out of the blue after a session with a ouija board that he believes has saved his life more than once.

That decides her. She doesn't believe in the ouija, but Bill does.

⋆　　⋆　　⋆

"That's fifty-three thousand dollars," Bill says.

The soft bundles of cash stink like dirt. David doesn't look at them, but both men are very aware of them stacked up on Bill's desk. They're very aware of the open case next to them. Bill took everything out before he called David into his office because he didn't want any confusion over what he wanted.

"You put it all in one of those duffle bags and it belongs to you. But I need an answer right now," Bill says.

David takes care of things Bill can't be bothered with. Housework, errands, that kind of thing. He's used to giving him orders. As long as he pretends this is one more errand, he can do this.

He sees David cock his head to one side and flick his eyes across the desk again, taking in the pile of money and matte black gun box, lid open, showing the matte black .38 lying on matte black foam. For the first time in years, Bill's palms tingle, his chest feels tight, even sitting down his legs shake. Now that he's said it out loud it's too late to go back.

"Okay," David says.

"Okay?" Bill asks, surprised it's so fast, but then again, David is from Eastern Europe someplace. Who knows what the fuck he did over there?

He's probably been in the army, shot some babies, there's no way of knowing what kind of fucked up shit he did before he came to LA.

"Yes," David repeats. "Okay."

"Well," Bill blows out air. "I'm going to say I was in the practice room out back. That's why I didn't hear anything. I can give you three hours. Do it fast, because I'll call the police at—" he checks his Omega, "—7:13 p.m. It'll take them a while to get out here, but every minute you waste is a minute of your head start."

David gets the duffle bag and loads up the money. Relief floods Bill. He knows he picked the right man, and he had to pick someone because the ouija never lies. It told him Roxanne would OD, and he got the fuck out of her house and took the board with him. The second she'd laid it on the table it'd felt like his, so he didn't think of it as stealing. That night she choked to death on her own vomit and the cops were all over her pad and if he'd gotten tangled up with them he'd never have made the audition for Rod's tour, and he would have wound up just another chump, like his dad.

It told him his manager was skimming, and that prick almost choked when Bill dropped the hammer. It told him Gena was putting out for that Greek jazzercise stud and he hid his video camera in their home gym and used the tape to make sure her alimony was as close to zero as you could legally get in California. The ouija had saved his ass again and again. Now it was going to save him from Caroline.

David zips the bag closed and pries the gun out of the gun box. Jesus, Bill thinks, he's just going to strut through the house carrying the thing out in the open.

"Goodbye," David says, already at the door.

Should he say something more formal, Bill wonders? And realises no, there's no time to dick around. If Caroline thought she could slow-poison him, or fuck with his insulin, or put some deadly shit in his vitamins, she's got another thing coming. He's Bill Pfarrer, and he makes fucking decisions and sees them through to the end.

"Goodbye," Bill says.

God, the guy's carrying the gun funny, but then again it's not exactly military hardware. Back in Serbia bullets probably cost too much money. He probably just beat people to death with the fucking thing.

★   ★   ★

Caroline stops on the stairs the instant she detects motion in the living room, then relaxes when she sees David.

"David," she calls. "Have you seen Bill?"

He stops on a dime but doesn't turn and that's not like David who's always so unbearably proper it makes her tense and that's when she sees the gun in his hand and the living room walls feel very, very far away.

"He is in his office, miss," David says, and she doesn't understand why he's carrying a gun.

Then he disappears into the kitchen heading for the suite he shares with Miloje. Did Bill give David his gun? What's going on? She'll ask Bill. She walks so fast she might as well be running down the hall to Bill's man cave.

She taps on the door, pushes it open, and even with the lights out she knows something's wrong. She flicks on the light and immediately sees the empty gun box in the middle of David's desk.

Her head is full of static and she can't put her thoughts together. Why does David have Bill's gun? Did Bill give it to him for protection? Is he scared of her? Does he think she wants to kill u? Then she sees it: the framed poster for the Jamaica World Tour Festival 1982 hanging at an angle. Her gut goes hollow. She knows the code to the safe behind that poster but she doesn't need it because the safe is open and the $53,000 Bill keeps there is gone. They've been robbed and her first instinct is to pick up the house line and call David and then she realises they've been robbed by David.

Immediately, she feels close to Bill. They're victims of a terrible crime. They've both been betrayed. David stole Bill's money. David took his gun. What did David do to Bill? She needs to find her ally. She grabs a Grammy off Bill's bookshelf and hefts it in one hand, holding it like a club. She didn't get out of the LV by dicking around.

★   ★   ★

"What do I do?" David asks Miloje.

They stand at the end of their perfectly made bed with its perfectly smooth duvet. The gun makes a dent in its centre, right next to the unzipped duffle bag of money. It is the most terrifying sight either of them has ever seen.

"You're sure he paid you this money to kill Mrs. Caroline?" Miloje asks, her throat closing tight on the last three words.

Back home, her youngest cousin got killed when he confronted a man for stealing his car. The man was a bodybuilder and ex-con who didn't like the accusation. After it was too late, they learned his brother had borrowed the car and forgotten to say anything. Miloje was eight when she learned that you had to be certain about things.

"He gave me fifty-three thousand dollars and a gun," David says. "What am I supposed to think?"

"Why did you take it?" she wails.

"I panicked," he snaps.

They must calm down. Miloje makes herself sit on the ottoman and presses the palms of her hands together. "You're not going to do it?" she asks.

Her second cousin proposed to his girlfriend without asking anyone first. Her parents liked him very much. She said she loved him very much. But it turned out her parents had already arranged another marriage for her and her brothers burned down her second cousin's barn and killed all his sheep. That's when Miloje learned to never assume anything.

"Of course I'm not going to do it!" David says. "I am a dancer."

This is David's dream. He told her constantly about his seven years at dance academy before his mother sent him to America to avoid the draft.

"Now you have a gun and a lot of money," Miloje says. "And a boss who thinks you are killing the other boss. This is a very dangerous situation."

Miloje came to America to avoid dangerous situations. She does not like what is happening right now.

"I will put it all back," David says. "And pretend nothing happened." Miloje feels her chest tighten.

"You can't," she says. "What if then he does it himself and blames you? Once you touched these things we cannot apologise."

"You want me to kill a human being?" he asks. "It is not like the movies, you know!"

Eighteen months ago, Miloje paid David US $10,000 to marry her so she could get her Green Card. The bosses didn't ask many questions, and David never pressed her for details about her life, but more than him, Miloje knows that killing a person is not like the movies.

"This is already too far," she explains. "We must leave. Right now."

"Yes, we must leave," he says. "But with proper notice. Now I will return these things and tell the boss there has been a misunderstanding because of my poor English. Then we will give two weeks' notice after this is forgotten."

He picks up the duffle bag and the gun and walks to the door. "You watched *60 Minutes* with me," Miloje says, going after him, grabbing his arm. "You know how Americans are with guns. You really think this rich man owns only one? If you say you are not doing this murder, he might shoot you."

David turns from the waist with great dignity.

"We do not know each other well," he says. "But one thing you should know by now is that, as a dancer, I can tell a person's thoughts by their body language. The boss is angry, but it is passing. I will be safe."

Then he stalks through the door as if he's walking onstage.

Over the course of this arrangement, Miloje has come to feel a great deal of affection for this prissy man. If anyone can defuse this mess it is he. But then she thinks about her lawyer cousin, Branko, and the mess he made when he tried to negotiate a lease dispute between their uncles and she twists her hands together, and they are very cold.

★   ★   ★

Shoving his walker across the sodden back yard, rain pounds Bill, soaking him to the bone, and the freezing cold practice room makes him shake. He can't stop. It feels like a seizure. He can't get the heat on. Where are the fucking towels? He makes a mental note to tell David to fix the heat then remembers that if everything goes right he won't see David ever again.

He lowers himself onto the black leather sofa, plastering his ice-cold clothes to his body, and he feels very alone. He'll have to live out here by himself after all this happens. There'll be police everywhere, then Caroline's funeral, all kinds of crap to deal with, and only after it's all done can he start interviewing new housekeepers.

He checks his Omega: it's been twenty-eight minutes. He said he'd wait three hours but he can't. He'll go crazy. He'll freeze to death. He sits, knees jiggling, trying to hear something over the roar of the rain against the French doors.

He looks at the three guitars leaning on their stands and sees thick dust on their bodies and pickups. This is the one part of the house David and Miloje don't clean, and he hasn't been out here in a long time but right now he could stand some blues. He sees himself hunched over his guitar, playing some Leadbelly or some Robert Pete Williams, drowning in their jangling chords until the music makes his fingers start walking by themselves. He imagines doing some kind of stripped down recording, like the Boss on *Nebraska,* or getting Rick Rubin out here to give him the Johnny Cash treatment, releasing a spare, haunting album oozing dark emotions. Something authentic and American, call it *Murder Ballads,* let his feelings really bleed. Caroline would like that.

What is he doing?

What he's set in motion will ruin his life. *Murder Ballads* is a great idea, the best one he's had in a long time, but if this happens it's fucked. But he can turn things back. It's not too late. He can stop this. The only person who knows is David and he can trust David not to say anything. He can't sit here and wait for poor, dumb, sweet Caroline to get shot. He'll never record his album and suddenly more than anything in the world he wants to record this album. He knows Rick's manager. He can call him today. But first.

He opens the door and steps back out into the freezing rain before his clothes have a chance to dry. If anyone dies today it's going to be him, catching his death of cold.

★   ★   ★

Caroline puts the Grammy on the hall carpet to dial 911 because her fingers shake too much to walk and type at the same time. She gets a busy signal. How can 911 be busy? She tries two more times. Still busy. She looks at her texts. Nothing from Bill. She texted him three minutes ago: David is rubbing os. Has gin. Where are you?

She made sure she spelled out 'you'. He hasn't texted back.

She hoists the Grammy and steps into the living room just as a gust of rain cracks across the big glass panel along the back of the house. Through it she sees the blurry outlines of Bill's studio. If he's not in the house, that's where he'll be. They'll hide out there, lock the doors, and wait for David to finish robbing them and leave.

She edges between the sofas and the coffee tables, the lamps giving their comforting golden glow. She wishes she could curl up under a blanket and read a book.

Cold radiates off the huge wall of glass as she approaches. She looks down at the Cire Trudon candles, still burning, and wishes she hadn't wasted them. Behind her, something shrieks and grinds and she jumps, whirls, and sees David pushing one of the Breuer chairs back into place with his knee.

Both of them hold very, very still.

"I cannot hurt you," he says.

"Why are you carrying those?" she asks.

David looks down at first one hand, then the other, like he's surprised to see the gun and the duffle bag there. "Mr. Bill asked me to clean them," he says. "Now I return them to his office."

That makes no sense. How do you clean a duffle bag? Why would Bill suddenly ask him to clean his gun? She hefts the Grammy in one hand.

"You should put them down," she says.

"I will return them to the office," he says. Then he notices the Grammy in her hand. "If you give me that, I will return it also."

He's not pointing the gun at her. He's holding it weird, fingers wrapped around it like a rock. She takes a step backwards and to the right, putting the table between them. David puts the duffle bag down and comes forward, hand outstretched. In his other hand he holds the gun like he's going to club her with it.

"Stay away, David."

"Don't be afraid, I will take everything back to Mr. Bill's office," he says.

David keeps coming. The panel of glass is at her back. She tries to keep as much of the table between them as possible but now he's coming around it.

"Go to his office, David," she orders. "You don't need the Grammy."

David hears the tone in her voice and tries to reassure her because maybe she knows more than he thought.

"I will go," he reassures her. "I will take the music award, and this bag, and this foolish thing," he lifts the gun halfway, "and we will not think about them again, okay?" Why does he keep coming? Why won't he stop?

"David," she says, and her voice is very high pitched. "You're scaring me."

Does she know Mr. Bill's plan, David wonders?

"I am a student of dance," he tries to reassure her. "I will never hurt another human being."

Then David stops and Caroline sees his mouth close hard and his eyes go wide, and she snaps a look over her shoulder and sees a blurry figure pushing his walker through the rain, and it's Bill and she cannot wait for David to have both of them in range and David is still staring out the window, and he shifts his hand around the gun, and she doesn't even think, she hurls the Grammy at him, feeling her shoulder click painfully when she lets go.

It flies at David fast and slams high into his chest with a solid THWUMP and she hears a phantom standing ovation from the bleachers as the right side of his body goes slack, his hand springs open, and he drops the gun.

She hasn't done any warm up, she didn't stretch, her ligaments are tight, but it's the final sprint at Soulcycle and an inner warrior possesses Caroline and one foot is up high, flat on the table, her pelvis shrieks in protest, and she pushes herself up, launching herself at David, knees aimed at his chest, ready to ride him to the ground, his eyes wide as hardboiled eggs, fear scrawled across his face as she comes down at him in a perfect arc, knees like guided missiles. And he steps aside.

Her knees smash into the back of the sofa and she feels her right kneecap break loose and get shoved between the muscle and the skin on top of her thigh and she didn't know her flesh could stretch this much and she lands on the Grammy with the small of her back, and fire rockets up her spine and her side rolls over the gun on the floor and her right kidney erupts with hot liquid and she squirms on the floor, wailing.

There's a crack and a gust of icy wind and Bill shouts, "No!" and David has his hands on her, and she tries to get away, and he tries to hold her down, and she hears Bill shout, "Keep it all!" and David looks at him, and Bill shouts, "I changed my mind. Keep the money. It's okay."

David looks back at Caroline to make sure she is not hurt and that's when she shoots him in the balls.

★   ★   ★

Bill hears the air in the living room go SMACK and the shockwave slaps his face and David's back gets stiff, then hunches, and he takes two steps back before squatting slowly to the floor, hands over his groin. At the last minute he shuffle-steps to the side, uttering a long, agonised groan, so that he does not sit on the carpet.

"My," he says, face white as paint. "Carpet..."

Black blood oozes between his fingers and then it's a torrent, and then it sprays in time with his pulse, a puddle growing on the slates between his legs, and Caroline and David stare at each other, and David's lips turn blue, and he leans forward until his forehead rests in the middle of the puddle.

"I didn't," Caroline gasps, hauling herself up, clutching the back of the couch. "I didn't want to – FUDGE FUDDRUCKER SUGAR – I had to, I had to, he attacked me, he tried to kill you, he was robbing us – FUDGE! SICLE! – He hurt my leg. How's my – I can't look at it." Her face crumbles into agonised tears. "How bad is it? SUGAR! I really, really hurt my leg. I don't know what to do!"

Bill stares at his wife's right leg, already swollen tight beneath her yoga pants, straining the fabric, and David bowed to her, not moving, and what the fuck? Bill needs a minute to think, to reshuffle the fucking pieces.

"Bill, I can't walk," Caroline sobs. "You have to call someone. David needs help. SHIP SHIP SHIP FUDDDGE!"

This can still work. David tried to rob them and Caroline fought back, and no one will know what he almost did, and Jesus fucking Christ she shot him in the dick, where the fuck did Miss Peace, Love and Understanding learn to shoot a gun? "I'll call 911," he says, because okay this isn't plan A but plan B's not so bad, and once this blows over he can focus on *Murder Ballads*. No one knows he had anything to do with this mess, it's a terrible accident but he's still clean.

"Don't move, I'll get you some ice," and even as he says it he knows that's pretty underwhelming. "And Vicodin, and Percocet, I promise. Hang on."

She digs her fingers into the back of the couch, swaying on one leg, staring directly up at the high ceiling, uttering a string of fake profanity.

He shoves his walker into the kitchen, fast, and stops, staring at the ouija board on the counter. *I will kill u.*

You were right, he thinks, only you got the wrong person.

But is David dead? As cold as it sounds, he has to make sure, because if David wakes up in the ambulance then this is for nothing. He needs to be sure.

"Caroline?" he says, taking a bag of frozen peas out of the freezer as an excuse to go back and check on David. "Caroline, put this on your knee." He rolls his walker into the living room and Caroline isn't holding onto the back of the sofa, she's not lying on the floor, she's not hopping around in pain, there's only David, slumped over like a ballerina, thoughtfully bleeding on the slate. Caroline is gone.

★   ★   ★

The minute Bill went into the kitchen the things he said cut through the screaming red fog of pain inside Caroline's head.

I changed my mind.

She has to get to the garage. Her leg hurts so much. It weighs five hundred thousand pounds. It is full of broken glass. Her knee is mush.

Keep it all.

The money. He meant the money. Every light in the hall goes on, screaming bright, turning everything flat and shadowless. Bill. That's what happens when he tries to use the lighting system, he can only turn them all on full.

I changed my mind.

She drags herself along the wall, leaning a shoulder against it, one hand has her purse in it, her purse has her keys in it, and everything is spilling all down the hall behind her, and she's hunched over, hop-stepping on her left leg, trying to protect her right, hearing things fall out of her purse behind her, but she has the gun. She's safe if she has the gun.

I will kill u.

Bill is sick. She's known it for a long time but denied it and tried to fix him with love, but ever since he got the walker he's gotten sicker and sicker and now she's killed David. She's killed a man. Bill made her do it. Bill's sickness forced her to kill David.

He paid poor David to kill her and she had to protect herself and she feels very very very very sorry for what happened but it's not her fault.

Her muscles stop working from the waist down. The garage door is too far. She sinks to the carpet, numb, but she will not let him get her. David's sacrifice will not be for nothing. She rolls herself onto her back. She won't make this easy for Bill.

★　　★　　★

Bill stands in the garage, water running down his legs, listening to make sure no one heard him come in the garage door. He took his walker all the way around the house and he can't feel his skin anymore. It is cold, tight, and hard as marble. He feels fucking dead.

But he has to finish this now. Caroline killed David, now he must kill Caroline. Then he can focus on his album. He never should have started this, but now it's happening so he has to see it all the way through. He'll close his eyes and get it over with and then he can go back to what's important: his album. The only people who win are the people who finish.

Quietly he pushes his walker across the concrete floor. He stops at the door and grips the knob with both hands and uses all his strength to open it slow as shit. Through the crack, he peers down the hall.

Halfway down, Caroline lies on her back, head propped on her purse, arms outstretched, holding the ugly, chunky little gun over her crotch with both hands, pointing it back down the hall. If he had any fucking doubts before, they're gone with the wind: she's pointing it right where he'd be coming if he hadn't gone all the way around the house.

Eight years of trusting her and taking care of her, but the ouija knows the truth.

I will kill u? Not today, sweetie.

He looks down and sees them, forgotten and cobwebbed by the

side of the door: the ten-pound hand weights that were supposed to help him build up muscle in his arms.

*   *   *

The gunshot brought Miloje creeping to the living room. Stomach sloshing with foam, she'd been crouching in the dark hall leading to their suite when she heard the shot and saw the boss go to the kitchen and stroke the devil board tenderly, like it was his baby son. Then she crept after him into the living room and saw him look around, then he let in a howl of wind and left the house. The big glass window strains and flexes over her, two storeys tall, holding back the raging storm. The bright living room is empty, except she sees a hand.

When she sees the hand she knows that this is the end of her job here. It is David's hand, curled up on the floor, sticking out from behind the sofa. She looks at it for a long time, but does not go near. She knows what a dead man's hand looks like. She wishes he had listened to her. She wishes none of this happened. She wishes they never had these bosses.

Then she goes into action. She walks to the suite she shared with David and gets her purse. She keeps all her money inside, just in case. She hurries to the drawer in the kitchen holding the spare car keys. She grips them in one hand.

She has to get out of this house. She will make a plan later, but for now she cannot get hurt if she is not here.

Running fast, before more bad things happen, she rounds the hall leading to the garage and stops, leaning backwards, digging in her heels. Both her bosses stand halfway down the hall, one lying down, one standing over her. Before she can wonder what they are doing—

*   *   *

The shape appears at the end of the hall and Caroline clenches her finger into a fist and even as she does she sees it's Miloje, she wants to scream, why does she keep shooting the wrong people, it's like she's cursed and she makes her hand cramp, and it freezes stiff, and nothing happens.

Over the agony in her swollen, blood-engorged leg she feels a thrill of victory expanding inside her chest, and she knows she needs Miloje's help, because women will help women. She hears her voice echo off the narrow walls.

"Miloje!" she calls, and Miloje stares at her, and then starts to turn away, starts to run, and there is a shadow overhead, rushing down at her, and she looks up and—

★   ★   ★

Bill drops the ten-pound dumbbell from three feet over the bridge of Caroline's nose. The bar slices into her face, right between the eyes. He turns away but he will remember that wet, rawbone crunch for the rest of his life.

He sees Miloje stumbling away into the living room. He thinks it's Miloje. He thinks she is heading towards the front door. He feels exhausted. One more fucking thing to take care of, but he has to finish.

He tries not to look at Caroline's face as he pulls the gun from her spasming fingers, then he puts it in the basket of his walker and wrestles it down the carpeted hall. Miloje is almost at the front door.

★   ★   ★

Miloje can't breathe, she can't get any air, but she makes her body run and sees the front door coming closer, then she looks over her shoulder at the hall and it is empty, then the front door is right there, then she looks and sees the boss at the end of the hall behind her, and the front door knob is in her hand, then he is leaning against the wall pointing the gun and there is nowhere to hide and she closes her eyes.

She hears an enormous noise that's really three noises. The thundersnap of the gun going off, the high-pitched metallic TANG as the bullet hits the large metal wall collage hanging over the front door, and a TAK like a hammer as the ricocheting bullet strikes the plate glass window looming two storeys above them both at the other end of the vast living room.

She sees a shining silver crack split the glass wall like a lightning bolt, running from the top before crazing out in a hundred directions, and then there is a high tea-kettle whistle as the wind streams through the tiny bullet hole, then the wind gets its teeth into the glass, and, with a sound like the end of the world, half the window shears into the room, pulling the other half with it and two storeys of glass are airborne. 300 pounds of silicon shrapnel fire across the room and Miloje covers her face.

★   ★   ★

Bill sees the glass scream roaring for him and he thinks this will be fine, and then as the storm is unleashed in his living room he thinks, at least this will clean all the evidence, and then the album goes through his mind, and the sound of Caroline's nasal bridge shattering, and the sound of the gun popping twice, and he still thinks this will be fine because the ouija would have warned him. The second to last thing that goes through his mind is *I will kill u* and he realises that maybe it wasn't a warning at all. Maybe it was a statement of intent.

The last thing that goes through his mind is a 60-pound triangle of tempered glass that nails him to the wall.

★   ★   ★

Glass flays the backs of Miloje's hands to the bone, then her forehead and chin, and the storm rages through the living room, stripping the walls, shoving the sofas, blowing out the candles, lifting the table. Miloje screams but cannot hear herself over the storm, and everything is so cold and wet and just one hour ago it was nice and warm and she doesn't know what happened, why did this happen, what did they do, how did it all fall apart? Then the table slams into the front door like a battering ram and between the table and the door is Miloje.

★   ★   ★

Weeks later, the ouija board will be put in a dumpster by a cleaning crew in white hazmat suits, hired by realtors handling the sale for the estate. By that time it is a dried husk of cardboard pulp, dotted with black mould. But that's okay. It's a Parker Brothers game. They ship them out by the truckload. There's one in every home.

ALICE'S REBELLION

John Langan

1

Freshly cut, the block of wood sat in the centre of the scaffold, a white box. It was a peculiarity of the Prime Minister to insist on a new block for each of the condemned. Given the number and pace of the executions, there wasn't time to finish the chunks of wood, whose surfaces were rough, covered in splinters, a final indignity. As long as the headsman's blade was sharp, his eye true, it wasn't one Alice would have to endure for long.

He stood to the left of the executioner, the PM, another of his idiosyncrasies. Surely, there was more important business for him to be attending to than this spectacle. Yet so much of his rule was built on exactly such public displays that Alice supposed this was exactly where he was supposed to be. A light breeze tousled his colourless hair, caught his long red tie and made a banner of it. His babyish features wore their usual distracted look, as if he were trying and failing to remember a favourite clever story. Behind him and the headsman, a forest of poles held the heads of those whose feet had preceded Alice's up the stairs to the scaffold. The Mock Turtle's mouth hung open next to the glazed eyes of the Unicorn, whose tongue protruded from between his cracked teeth, black and swollen. The thickness of his strong neck had proved a challenge for the executioner, who had required ten strokes of his weighted sword to sever it completely, and then halted the proceedings to inspect and sharpen his implement. The wind rocked the heads right to left, making them appear restless, impatient for what was to come.

As Alice stepped onto the scaffold, the PM's attention returned from its internal distance, his eyes focusing on her with such intensity they practically bulged in their sockets. He shuffled his feet, gestured at the wood block sheepishly, as if embarrassed by the event the two of them were part of. Alice walked to the block. In front of it, there was a piece of rolled-up carpet for her to kneel on, the fabric sodden with blood. *Of course*, Alice thought. The PM grimaced. With her right foot, Alice slid the carpet to the side. Fear pressed her chest, made each breath an effort. In the far distance, over the ruined red brick walls hemming in the execution grounds, the sea was a grey line. She stared at it as the PM's cough drew her back to the matter at hand. *Or at head.*

The surface of the scaffold was smooth against her knees. She leaned forward until her throat touched the rough top of the block. The odour of pine flooded her nostrils, and underneath it, the mingled pungency of bleach and blood. Out of the corner of her right eye, she watched the headsman pass his over-sized sword to the PM, who took it with none of his usual bumbling, but rather a butcher's practised hold. *I suppose I should be flattered*, Alice thought. He adjusted his grip on it, then swept the blade over his head, tugging the edge of his shirt out of his trousers in the process. Without looking directly at him, Alice said, "I liked you better when you were Tweedle Dee." She saw the executioner flinch.

The sword crashed down, a first time and a second.

2

Though unpleasant, the Caterpillar's attentions were a price Alice told herself she was willing to pay for shelter beneath his great mushroom. Safety from the Red Queen's Numerals was worth the sensation of his fleshy legs crawling over her skin. Honestly, she wasn't clear as to all or even most of what went on when the Caterpillar began to heave his bloated mass in her direction. The vents along his baggy sides released enormous clouds of the violet gas that collected and hung in the air over the mushroom, her head would start to spin (or perhaps it was everything else spinning and her head remaining still), and Alice would lose hold of herself in the resulting maelstrom. Sometimes she would think she had caught hold of herself, only to find she was looking out of six eyes instead of two, her sides rippling with a motion not unlike exhaling, and she would release that self and try for another. Rarely was she successful before the effects of the violet gas had subsided. In the meantime, she might recline in a rowboat drifting on a lazy river under a hot summer sun, her companions a pair of young girls in blue and white dresses, or she might rush burbling through tulgey woods, her wings tucked in close to avoid the branches, her waistcoat tightly buttoned. Afterward, she would lie on her back staring up at the mushroom's underside, the striations like the ribs of a whale, while the Caterpillar struggled to his hookah on top of the mushroom to begin inhaling the dense smoke the engine of his body would refine to purple vapour.

It was during one of those other selves that Alice first encountered the idea of (or for?) mathematical logic. She was a tall man seated at a wooden desk, the pen in her hand scratching row after row of symbols onto the paper before her. For the time she was in the self, her brain was packed full with theorems, each one linked to another, sometimes more, the whole a sort of web whose strands tugged the world into order. Once more herself, Alice could not remember most of the equations she had written, but the idea of things being arranged into systems of cause and effect, with boundaries and limits, remained fixed and burning in her mind. The Caterpillar was no more interested in discussing it with her than he was anything else, but Bill the Lizard proved surprisingly amenable to conversation. Once he was finished brushing out the Caterpillar's vents and inspecting his hookah, he accepted a cup of milky Oolong from Alice and sat with her for the time it took him to drink it.

"I think what I mean," Alice said, "is that the world should not revolve around us, so to speak."

"Ooh, I don't know about that," said Bill, his tail flicking nervously. "If things wasn't to revolve around us, then wouldn't we revolve around them? I'm afraid I should find it awfully dizzying."

"Not exactly," Alice said. "It's more a case of, both we and things would orbit something else, a third thing, a set of... rules."

Bill looked as dubious as a lizard could.

"Or," Alice said, "there wouldn't be any spinning. Things would stay where they were, as they were. When the Red Queen had someone's head chopped off, their blood wouldn't turn into a fresh pack of cards."

"What would it turn into?"

"Nothing. It would remain blood."

"Hmm," Bill said. "That has rather a fatalistical sound."

Alice said, "I suppose it does."

3

"If this plan of yours succeeds," the Dodo said, "I should be extinct."

"It's not my plan, exactly," Alice said. "A great many people have already agreed to it."

"All the same," the Dodo said.

"Well, yes," Alice said.

4

Light clung to the windows of the Jabberwocky's eyes for a long time after its chorus of hearts had ceased to beat.

5

"You know what they say about omelettes," Alice said.

"I'm certain I do not," said Humpty Dumpty.

6

"You mean to turn nonsense on its head," the Mad Hatter said.

"I mean to turn nonsense on itself," Alice said, "and to continue to do so until it becomes nonsensical to itself."

"How odd," said the Hatter. "How would such a thing happen?"

"I'm not exactly sure about all of it," Alice said. "But I think that, if you were to fold nonsense onto nonsense, then onto nonsense again, and so on, you would begin to notice places where the nonsense started to... fall into line with itself. Which would mean it was becoming more sense and less non-sense. If you were to continue folding, the sense would replace the nonsense, until all you were left with was sense.

"Or mostly sense," she added.

"What a fascinating idea," the Hatter said. "However would you accomplish it?"

"It would require frightfully complex equations," Alice said. "And blood: an enormous quantity of blood."

7

The Red Queen shouted, "OFF—"

"Shh," Alice said, placing her index finger against the monarch's fleshy lips. "You don't get to say that anymore."

8

For an instant, Alice felt everything about her become heavy, as heavy as it was possible to imagine, as if she were being pulled down, down underground, down past all the clocks, and the teacups, and the coffee spoons, down past the crust, the upper mantle, the lower mantle, the outer core, all the way to where the inner core spun burning in the darkness, 11,000 degrees Fahrenheit, a measurement in a system she understood, as she understood the haemoglobin in her blood to have a chemical formula of $C_{2952} H_{4664} O_{832} N_{812} S_8 Fe_4$, and $F=ma$ to be an expression of Newton's Second Law, and 1558 to be the year Mary I (aka Bloody Mary, surely a Red Queen if ever there was one) died, and numbers and names, essays and equations, sciences and stories, all the nails necessary to tack down existence, secure it. In that instant, as everything was crystallising but not all the way solid, Alice cast away the Caterpillar and his mushroom sanctuary, the Numerals and their insistent flatness, the Red Queen's scarlet expression, cast away all of it, let words take it, sentences wrap it and bind it between leather covers. She threw away the sun-drenched afternoon, the placid river, the girls in the rowboat, left it to anecdote and rumour.

The world set. She was twenty-four years old, pursuing graduate studies at the London School of Economics. She was renting a nice (if tiny) flat in Wimbledon, and she was seeing a nice veterinarian who had his practice in Croydon.

9

Six good years: not great years, not perfect years, but lit by a quiet glory, a radiance arising from the splash and tumble of water from the faucet as she washed her hands, the sizzle and pop of an egg frying in the pan, the warm weight of the duvet on cold winter nights. There was no shortage of badness: the veterinarian turned out to be married, the chef she took up with after him generally horrible, and she broke her wrist when she tripped running for her train. Even at their worst, though – when she was standing in the doorway to her flat, arms crossed, as Yasmine, Nathan's wife, screamed at her from the hallway, while he hid locked in the bathroom – events unfolded within an underlying framework of order and predictability. Alice finished her degree, found a decent position with the Royal Bank of Scotland, took her holidays in Dubai. She considered moving into a larger flat.

Ironically, BBC 1 gave her the first warning things were unravelling. During one of their roundtable discussions, a pithy older woman described the new prime minister as Tweedle Dee to the American president's Tweedle Dum. Although Alice had the TV on mostly for background noise while she did her yoga, the comparison caught her attention. A number of political cartoonists picked up on the allusion and for the next several days, the print and online editions of a host of newspapers published cartoons illustrating it. Right away, Alice was struck by the almost preternatural accuracy of the journalist's words, and each drawing to appear reinforced her growing conviction that the Tweedles had not only found their way to this new existence essentially intact, but were prospering within it. She did her best to ignore the icy dread rising within her, to put faith in her co-workers' assurances that everything the PM was promising would be splendid. "He'll take things back to the way they used to be," more than one person said to her.

"Yes," Alice said, "that's what worries me."

10

How the Prime Minister (whom she could not stop thinking of as Tweedle Dee, now that she had started) succeeded in picking apart the stitches with which Alice had sewn together this new world, she did not know. Of course, she had been aware not everyone was in favour of her plan to remake their existence, but the Tweedles had not seemed terribly bothered one way or another. And it wasn't as if the PM undid everything. Instead, he and his trans-Atlantic counterpart confused matters sufficiently to throw the world into turmoil. Soon decks of cards were roaming the streets of London and several other large cities, assaulting anyone they thought looked foreign, while flamingos and hedgehogs invaded football and cricket pitches. It was no longer safe to eat oysters, and a knight in battered white armour was reported roaming tube stations, waving his longsword threateningly. It was ever harder to follow the news, which proliferated in the time it took to switch from one channel to the next. A batch of bad tea cakes caused the necks of any who ate them to lengthen a foot and a half. Feral bagpipes were sighted on the Scottish border.

When the mirror war erupted, Alice sighed and submitted to the inevitable. The Dormouse and the Greens were ecstatic, gathering behind her; the Unicorn joined them. Although Alice smiled to see the Unicorn once more, her outlook was grim. There were creatures fighting for the Prime Minister she had not previously encountered, heaps of scrap metal, rusted hulks whose ranks advanced in rigid lock-step. Their thick feet crushed the Dormouse, trampled women and men. For all his ferocity, the Unicorn was hard pressed to defeat their armoured mass, while their crude blades splashed his ruby blood across the floors of the living rooms, churches, and department stores where they battled. What members of Alice's forces survived the Heaps were attacked by drones whose propellers separated hands, arms, and sometimes heads from bodies with brutal efficiency. Once Alice had been steeped in blood, had waded through rivers of it, washed her long hair in it, worn its rich stink as a perfume. Now the copper reek through which she moved kept her every meal burning at the back of her throat. She was still capable of single-minded ruthlessness, but so was the Prime Minister, so was everyone else in this existence.

She had a single conversation with him, a week before what was to be the final battle of her failed war. They met at a coffee stand in Waterloo Station. Alice recognised the nervous proprietor as a former Numeral, a Six of Hearts, she thought. Security was heavy. The PM did not bother sitting at the wobbly table on which had been set a pair of china mugs, sugar bowl, and milk jug. Alice slid out her chair, sat, and prepared her coffee light and sweet. Behind her, she could feel the Unicorn tense as she brought the mug to her lips. She wasn't concerned. Poison was far too sophisticated for the PM. The coffee was better than she would have expected from this sort of establishment. She looked at the proprietor (who had been a Six, yes) and nodded approvingly. He ducked as if she'd thrown something at him.

"I do hope you're going to surrender," the Prime Minister said.

Alice paused. "I was planning to say the same thing to you."

"Whatever can you mean? You're losing. Every time your forces have met mine, we've crushed you, we've slaughtered you. Your supporters are deserting you in droves. If you lay down your weapons now, ask forgiveness, I could pardon you. Perhaps. Anyway, at least no more of you would have to die."

"I mean," Alice said, "that you've done fundamental damage to this existence. You've loosened what was sealed with blood. I don't know if it can be repaired. Even if there's no fixing it, we should be able to prevent it from becoming worse. Yes, *we*. This is why I'm here, to ask you to lay down your arms and join me in finding a way to keep things from coming apart any more than they have."

"But I don't want to," the PM said. "I like what's happened. My friends like what's happened. My followers like what's happened. Why on earth should I want to change it?"

"Because it's not sustainable," Alice said. "Because what you've started is going to harm everyone."

"Oh, I don't know about that."

"I do."

"Look," the PM said, "will you surrender or not?"

"I will not," Alice said.

"The penalty for insurrection is death," the PM said, "I hope you understand."

Alice finished her coffee, stood. "The way things have been going," she said, "I'm not sure death is what it used to be."

11

The final battle began on the streets outside and spilled into the aisles of Harrods. Mannequins that had not picked sides held up plaster hands in protest at this invasion of what was supposed to be neutral ground and were cut down by the weapons of both sides. Display cases were smashed, racks of clothing doused in blood. The fight was over depressingly fast. Through sheer force of numbers, the Heaps overwhelmed Alice's troops, killing those they could not capture. Although she knew he wouldn't be, Alice was hoping the Prime Minister would be there to witness his side triumphant. She entertained a fantasy of fighting her way to him and splitting him down the middle with her blade, Tweedle Dead. But he was nowhere to be seen, unless he was concealed in a back room, watching the battle through the store's security cameras. Failing in her plan for the PM, Alice was hoping for death under the swords of her foes. This did not happen, either. In the end, she was borne to the bloody floor by the combined efforts of a quartet of the largest Heaps.

The inevitable show trial was mercifully brief.

12

The first blow of the heavy sword missed her neck and instead struck the top of Alice's back. Pain blinding white detonated across her shoulders, robbing her of breath. She was able to recover her thoughts sufficiently to think, *Naturally, he'd bollocks this, too*, before the Prime Minister's second attempt cut clean through her neck.

Alice's blood sprayed across and down the sides of the wooden block into which the executioner's blade had lodged. So pleased with himself was the PM (who was still bristling from that Tweedle Dee snipe) that he released the sword and reached for Alice's hair. Her head weighed more than he expected. He lifted it until he was face to face with it. The eyes had rolled under the lids; the mouth hung open. Already, the head looked more like a prop from a movie and less a part of a living person. The PM licked his lips and said, "I've been reading about what happens to you after you're beheaded – to your consciousness. Apparently, there's some evidence it may hang about for a minute or two. Well. In case you're still there, I wanted to let you know, I've decided I'm going to keep your head. I intend to have it mounted on the wall of my personal chambers, together with those of your principal co-conspirators. At the next Guy Fawkes, we'll find a way to work your likenesses into the festivities."

The head did not answer. Had the PM looked down, at the base of the block along whose sides Alice's blood continued to drip, he might have noticed the pools into which it gathered quivering. Had he inspected them more closely, he would have been astonished to see tiny playing cards lifting themselves out of the red liquid and fleeing for the edge of the scaffold, in the direction of the sea.

For Fiona

THE MIRROR HOUSE

Jonathan Robbins Leon

"Did you see the one in the ball gown?" Edgar's face was pink from laughing. Keeping one hand on the steering wheel, he wiped the tears from his eyes.

Stephanie remembered the woman in voluminous lavender satin, her sleeves almost as puffy and unfortunate as her bangs. Yet most of the women had been overdressed. They'd teased their hair and zipped themselves into floor-length taffeta, bows dangling from their shoulders, excited to have tickets to the new Performing Arts Centre.

Having opted for knee-length black satin with Kate Moss spaghetti straps, Stephanie felt acutely out of place. Wives clutched at their husband's arms, thrilled at this access to culture right here in their little town. Stephanie, however, had grown up on museums, opera, and fine cuisine the way others had been raised on meatloaf and *Andy Griffith*. Nothing Durstville could offer impressed her much.

Still, it didn't strike her as fair for Edgar to laugh at the locals.

"I thought the music was wonderful," Stephanie said. "And the chandelier sweeping down like that was something."

"Well, it's not *La bohème*. But it was probably the first time those hicks have ever seen a play that didn't star their dentist." Unable to help himself, Edgar was chuckling again. Stephanie faced the window, not wanting to look at him.

He turned onto their quiet street. Queen Anne castles loomed darkly over large front lawns. Their money stretched further here than in Baltimore, but Stephanie missed their town home. She missed dinner parties and concerts, and she missed her students.

Edgar had begged her to transfer with him to Durstville, where he would be Department Chair at the private college. Stephanie still taught, but instead of lecturing on Gothic Literature, her soul's passion, she dragged Durstville locals through Intro to Lit, a required course. Her new students struggled to understand *The Yellow Wallpaper* and bought CliffsNotes to shortcut *Daisy Miller*. Stephanie handed out C's like Halloween candy. Most of them, she knew, would never pick up a book again after college.

"Edgar!" she screamed. Caught in the headlights, the man had seemed to appear out of nowhere.

Swerving quickly, Edgar just missed hitting him. The car came to a stop, and husband and wife had to catch their breath.

Edgar yanked on the emergency brake and got out. Turning in her seat, Stephanie shouted after him, "Edgar, don't!"

It was the half-wit from across the street. Edgar had called him this so many times that it had become how Stephanie referred to him in her thoughts. Like always, he wore jeans, a white undershirt and boots. Always the same, but never dirty. His arms dangled limp from rounded shoulders, and in the middle of his slack-jawed face were those empty eyes.

Stephanie had gotten used to the sight of him, though his constant staring had unnerved her when they'd first moved in. "He stood out there during the rain," she told her husband once.

"The neighbours say he's harmless," Edgar had said.

"But what is he staring at all the time? Hours, every day, he just stands there, looking in the direction of our house."

"I don't think he's staring at anything." Edgar knocked his knuckles against his forehead. "Empty up there, I bet. A vegetable."

She'd never seen him in the street before. "You fucking retard!" Edgar screamed at the boy now.

Unbuckling, Stephanie got out of the car. The street had been dark a minute before, but a few neighbours had awoken from the commotion, turning on bedroom lights and opening windows to see what had happened. Stephanie approached the pair of men and laid a quieting hand on her husband's elbow. "Let's just go inside."

"We could have all died because of this moron!" Edgar jerked his arm away from her. He came nose-to-nose with the boy. "Can you even understand me?" he said. "Do you hear me?" If he did, the moron gave no sign of it. His eyes were dull as a tarnished mirror.

A porch light snapped on, and a squat woman in a bathrobe came outside, hurrying over. This was the boy's mother, Yolanda. "Please!

Please, I'm sorry," she said, her accent thick, blending the words melodically. She only came up to the boy's shoulder in height, but she threw her arms around him in a protective embrace. "I must have forgot to lock the door. I'm so sorry."

"He was in the street!" Edgar roared.

"I'm sorry," Yolanda said. "Rafael is a good boy. He just likes to be outside."

Stephanie had observed Yolanda and Rafael many times over the seven months she and Edgar had been Durstville residents, but she had never interacted with them. Wedged close to one of the larger homes in the neighbourhood, their house had been built as a separate kitchen in those days when cooking was drudgery and kitchens hot as engine rooms. It was little more than a shack, and the neighbours had informed her that Yolanda was renting. She wore a drab uniform when she left in the mornings, and it was assumed that she cleaned or something. Mother and son lived alone. During the long hours his mother worked, Rafael stood outside, a zombie tethered to the lawn by an invisible chain.

Close for the first time, Stephanie was surprised at his age. She had thought he was a teenager, but he looked closer to twenty-five. His skin was a brilliant copper, and his hair was an untidy ocean of black waves. If a magician's snap could only have brought him out of his trance, he would have been handsome.

"Come, *mijo*," Yolanda said to her son, pulling him away and towards their kitchen house.

"He should be in a home!" Edgar called to her back. Yolanda only repaid his fury with a wounded look before disappearing inside with Rafael.

★   ★   ★

Durstville seemed to have the worst of everything. The mouth-hot heart of summer gave way to the rainy season in late August. Stephanie awoke with a cold. She and Edgar usually rode to the college together, but today she begged off, asking her husband to post a notice on her door that classes were cancelled.

She could have been next to death before she'd have cancelled class at her last post. Those students, however, had been brilliant. Undaunted by the lengthy list of required texts, they showed up to class, their favourite passages of Walpole and Radcliffe highlighted, passionate notes scribbled in the margins. Their questions excited Stephanie. With them, it never felt like teaching, but rather like seducing, drawing them close, teaching them to love.

Today, Stephanie could not face the Durstville disappointments. In her current mood, she'd burn down the college if another student asked her if she'd read *Memoirs of a Geisha* or what she thought of *The Joy Luck Club*. At least once a day she was asked about her lack of accent. "Where are you from?" students loved to inquire. "D.C.," she invariably answered, making her voice frosty as chilled glass.

The grey sky seemed ready to boil into a black storm. Thunder grumbled, and Stephanie decided to brew some Theraflu. After downing it, she trudged upstairs to bed and allowed sleep to drown her.

A crash of lightning woke her hours later. Her head felt heavy as a kettle bell. The room was solid black without the digital display on the VCR player. Outside, wind, rain and thunder played an Antheil symphony. It took repeatedly flicking the light switches on and off for Stephanie to understand that the power was out.

"Edgar?" she called. Fanning her arms, she got ahold of the banister and followed it down the stairs. Again she called for her husband, but there was no answer. She felt her way to the kitchen. There would be candles and matches in the pantry.

On reflex, she pulled the chain to the pantry light, but of course, nothing happened. Emergency supplies were kept somewhere in the back, but she wasn't sure what shelf. She let her hands run over objects, discovering bags of sugar and flour, canned goods, and glass bottles that might be olive oil or liqueurs.

The house was still new to her, so she couldn't recall if there was a shelf along the back wall. Holding her arms in front of her, she walked forward to find out. The pantry was deeper than she remembered. She'd thought it to be little more than a walk-in closet, but after three steps, she'd not yet found the end of it.

Feeling along the shelf to her left, she chanced upon the box of kitchen matches. She opened it and struck one. The pantry was no more than four-feet deep. Had she been taking baby steps? *Theraflu,* she reasoned.

She lit a candle and was turning to leave when the light glinted on something brass set in the back wall. It was a doorknob, and now she saw that the pantry didn't terminate in drywall. There was a door.

It was unsettling to live somewhere seven months and not remember a door. The furnace or something must be behind there, something she'd not taken note of because it wasn't interesting. Still, the jolt of this door appearing out of nowhere had her on edge. She needed to open it.

★   ★   ★

"Please, calm down," Edgar cautioned.

"I'm telling you, there's another part of the house!" Stephanie couldn't get the words out fast enough. "Someone is living in it!" She was pacing Edgar's office, her dripping clothes and shoes soaking his oriental rug.

"Stephanie, sit down."

She did. Trying her best to be still, she said, "You've got to believe me."

Edgar sighed and folded his arms over his chest. "Let's think this through, okay? There's a wall at the end of the pantry."

"It's a door!"

"Stephanie, I'm telling you, it's a wall. And behind that wall is the utility room. You know that."

She was silent. Rationally, she did know that behind the pantry was the utility room. They'd had a new washer and dryer set installed when they moved, and Edgar had hung a bar so that Stephanie could hang-dry her blouses. She spent more time in that room than she would have cared to and knew it to be directly behind the pantry.

But she could not reason away what she had seen. The door had been there, and so had those awful rooms. And the woman too.

"Maybe you got confused. It was dark. You came back into the kitchen, things looked strange to you, and—"

"It wasn't like our house. It was..." How to describe it? The kitchen, with the same tiles as her own, but covered in what looked like ashes. Cobwebs clung to the cabinets, and the counters were coated in a fine veil of dust. What had disturbed her most, however, was that it was her kitchen, only everything was backwards, the fridge on the left instead of the right, the dining room also on the wrong side.

It wasn't just the layout either. She came to the living room and saw her own couch, crusted with mildew. On top of the coffee table was the decorative bowl she'd broken and glued back together. It was all hers, only flipped around and soggy with decay.

She needed to know if there was a door into this place from the outside. She went in search of the foyer and found her waiting.

"There's a woman in there," Stephanie told Edgar. "She was just standing there. I screamed when I saw her, but she didn't turn around."

She'd run then. Having dropped the candle, she had to make her way in the dark, reminding herself to think of the reverse to find her way back. At last in the pantry, she slammed the door to the other house closed. There was no deadbolt, no chain. She couldn't stay here alone with whatever was beyond that door. She grabbed her keys and made a mad run for the car in the driveway. Despite the rain, which fell as if from an open sluice, she drove to the college, bursting in on Edgar.

"What did this woman look like?"

"I couldn't see her face, but she was petite, like me. Long, black hair."

"Like you."

"Yes."

Edgar nodded. "Don't you think it's possible you caught a reflection of yourself in the window?"

"She was facing away from me!"

"Maybe the angle or something? I don't know how to explain it, but darling, what you're describing isn't possible. I think you woke up disoriented. The storm scared you, and your brain got carried away." He reached his hand across the desk to his wife. She had no choice but to accept it, and his explanation.

"It felt very real," she said.

"I'm sure it did."

The storm died down, and Edgar drove them home. The power was back on when they arrived. Stephanie followed timidly as her husband braved the pantry. "No door," he said. She had to agree. There was no door.

★   ★   ★

The following morning, with soggy grass and downed twigs and leaves being all that remained of the storm, it felt obvious to Stephanie that the whole episode had been a hallucination. Perhaps she'd been sleepwalking. Or maybe it was all some fever dream and she'd never gone to the pantry at all. The storm, the cold, the dark, and the sleep-inducing medication had been a potent cocktail, overwhelming her senses, giving flesh to her nightmares.

Still, it had been very convincing. When she came down to the kitchen for breakfast, Stephanie decided against yogurt. She would have cereal. This meant forcing herself to enter the dreaded pantry. She would not allow herself to be controlled by irrational fears.

The pantry was as it should be. Shelves of food and home goods. The bare bulb screwed into the ceiling, its chain dangling. Absolutely no portals to dream houses.

A sharp ringing made Stephanie jump before she realised it was the phone. Closing the pantry behind her, she went to grab the kitchen extension, but the noise stopped mid-ring. Edgar had answered on the portable.

"You old bastard!" she heard him say from the living room. "How long has it been?"

She gathered from the side of the conversation she could hear that an old friend of Edgar's was in town. Because she and Edgar had eloped only a handful of years ago, they'd not gotten through the introduction part of their marriage. Edgar had no family to speak of, but there'd been colleagues, old fraternity brothers and childhood friends. They were all portly, balding, white men. Stephanie's memories of them bled together like boring watercolour reproductions, the sort that might be passed off as art in office building lobbies.

"Wait until you meet her. Don't go planning to steal her from me!" Edgar laughed. "Sure! Bring the wife. The girls can gossip, and you and I will kick back and talk about old times."

Edgar got carryout from Durstville's one decent restaurant, and the scotch flowed over dinner. Short and round, with scrawny legs, Dave was an orange on toothpicks. The front strands of his thinning hair stuck to his sweaty forehead. His wife, Beth, had a body firm from the gym, but her swollen face betrayed her alcoholism. Everyone but Stephanie was blotto before dessert.

Edgar's laugh was louder than she'd ever heard it. He was forty-nine to her thirty-six, but she only ever thought of her husband as older when he brought men his own age around. On these occasions, she could recognise that Edgar too was growing flabby. His dashing salt-and-pepper hair was spiralling into baldness in the back. In ten years' time, he'd be as unappealing as Dave.

"I think I'll make a big pot of coffee to go with the tiramisu," Stephanie said.

Beth rose on wobbly legs, but not a strand of her newscaster hairdo strayed out of place. "I'm coming with you. I want a splash more of that fabulous wine before I call it quits." The boys retired to the living room, and Beth followed Stephanie to the kitchen. "This house is ginormous! No wonder you and Edgar left Baltimore."

Stephanie dumped four hefty scoops of grounds into the coffee filter and closed the lid. She hoped the life-reviving sludge would sober up her guests so they could leave. "Did you and Dave ever live there?"

"No. We're in Philly."

"Is that where Dave met Edgar?"

"I'm not sure. They were friends before we ever married." While the coffee maker gurgled and spat out its bitter molasses, Beth took possession of one of the kitchen chairs. "You're just what I expected, though."

"Oh?"

"Just Edgar's type."

"What do you mean?"

"Oriental." Beth's hand fluttered nervously to her mouth. "Or are we not supposed to say that?"

"Edgar doesn't have a thing about Asians." Stephanie was so sure this was true. Edgar had never treated her like some of the men she'd dated, expecting her to wait and dote on him like a Chinese bastardisation of a geisha. One of her college boyfriends had actually bought her a cheongsam for her birthday. She'd learned to avoid men who asked, pride gleaming in their eyes, if they were the first white guy she'd ever been with.

Beth snorted and kicked off her high heels under the table. "Sure he does! For a while, there was some Vietnamese girl who came here with her Christian parents. Witnesses. Lord, she was a drip! And then there was Katsuko. And Wendy. She was a student, I think? Really young. But then again, you all look young, don't you?" Beth had laid her head on the table, her eyes closing without her consent.

The sputtering of the coffee came to a stop. Loud, manly laughter was heard from the living room. Stephanie had a quick vision of herself going in there and dumping a boiling mug of coffee on her husband's khaki crotch. Instead, she turned off the coffee maker. The boys, wrapped up in their reminiscing, didn't notice her go up the stairs to bed.

★　　★　　★

Edgar had found his way upstairs. Stephanie awoke to find him beside her. His pants were gone, but he hadn't bothered with the shirt. She had not felt drunk at dinner, but now her mouth was dry as the dead. She slipped from under the sheets and went downstairs.

It occurred to her that Beth and Dave might have been too drunk to drive, but checking the driveway, she saw that their car was gone. The neighbour boy was out though. She could just see the white of his T-shirt. Could he see her in the window, parting the curtain to stare at him? Stephanie doubted it, but something told her he sensed her, the same way she'd sensed that he would be there tonight and had known to look for him. He was not brain-dead, she was certain. Only locked up inside himself. She closed the curtain.

In the kitchen, a luminous moon bathed everything in a halogen glow. The swamp coffee was still in the pot. Stephanie emptied it into the sink.

Why had what Beth said upset her so much? She'd stopped revering Edgar long ago. He'd cut an impressive figure when Stephanie, as a new professor, had first met him. He'd been fond of quoting Robert Browning and looked very handsome in his Dr. Indiana Jones tweeds. She had projected all sorts of romantic qualities on him. Marriage, though, had been like the house lights coming up after a film, turning the silver magic of cinema back into a ripped and tattered screen.

It was the jolt, she decided, of learning that her husband had pursued her because she fell into a certain type. What else had she failed to notice? This was the same gut-sinking dawn of knowledge that she'd felt when she found the door in the pantry.

But of course, that wasn't real.

She filled a glass with water from the sink and emptied it down her parched throat. Now she could return to bed.

Yet, having thought about the pantry, she felt drawn to look. It was silly, but she needed to assure herself that nothing was there.

The moonlight failed to penetrate the darkness of that closet, so she had to step inside to reach for the light. She pulled the chain, and her breath stopped. Not three feet in front of her was the door.

She thought of running for Edgar, but suppose the door was gone again when she returned? Oddly, she wasn't afraid. She'd known somehow that it would be here this time, perhaps because it was night and she was alone. What lay beyond the door would reveal itself to her, but to no one else. She grasped the knob and let herself in.

Like her kitchen, this one was awash with moonlight. The place had taken on form, becoming less of a shadow and more of a mirror. Though grime remained at the edges, most of the filth had disappeared from the floor. The cobwebs that had clung like Spanish moss were gone.

The woman was there. "Hello?" Stephanie asked, but the figure did not move. Stephanie circled, keeping a good distance between her and the other. Coming around, she saw the face: it was her own. Even their nightgowns were the same. The eyes, though, were absent, like blown bulbs.

Stephanie had a hand outstretched, ready to touch her doppelganger, but sound came from further in the house. She followed a soft shuffling to the living room. Edgar was pacing there in his shirt and underwear. She said his name, but he did not stop, only kept tracing and doubling back over the same five-foot length of floor. Like the woman, his eyes were extinguished, and Stephanie realised where she'd seen a pair just like them.

"There you are." It was not Edgar who had spoken, but someone behind her who had just entered. Was it Stephanie's imagination, or had the voice made the bowl on the coffee table tremble? She froze, and a pair of arms encircled her. They were brown and taut with youth. A man held her tight against his chest, his nose inhaling the scent of her neck. *He thinks I'm her,* she realised and knew that she must be absolutely still.

He stepped in front of her. Beneath his wavy hair, Rafael's face was vivid with animation. The lights were on in his expression, and as she had expected, he was handsome this way. Stephanie willed herself not to show any sign of recognition, locking her eyes on a point behind him.

Cupping her face in his hands, Rafael said, "You feel cold. Would you like a sweater?" Would the other Stephanie have answered his question? Did she speak? "I'll get you one," he said.

Only as he turned to go, Edgar's path grew wide, and Rafael collided with her catatonic husband. Both men fell, but Rafael got quickly to his feet. His trim body was so alert, so responsive, while Edgar seemed unable to contemplate righting himself.

"You fucking retard!" Rafael thundered, and the whole house shook. Stephanie clamped her lips shut to keep her breath from coming out in frightened gulps. Rafael stepped towards Edgar, and Stephanie was sure he was going to kick him. Instead, he stared for a long moment. A tear slid down his cheek as he said, "You should be in a home."

They were dolls, Stephanie realised. In this world, she and Edgar were Rafael's toys. Here, it was he who had the power to be kind or cruel. She watched as he brought Edgar to his feet and led him to the couch. "Sit here and rest," he said, pressing Edgar down by his shoulders.

He returned to Stephanie, but he seemed deflated, no longer any happier to see her than if she'd been a television. Swallowing, he made an effort to be cheerful. "Are you still cold? Stay there and I'll—"

He broke off, staring behind her. Stephanie didn't dare look, but she could guess by his clouded expression that her other self had come into the room. Which of them was the mirror Stephanie, he would be wondering, and which of them was the real one.

Before he could decide, Stephanie dropped her false stupor like a cloak from around her shoulders and tore off through the kitchen.

"Please!" he called after her, his voice making the dishes in the cabinets rattle. "Please, don't leave me!" But she was in the pantry now, shoving the door securely closed.

★   ★   ★

"The showing went great," the realtor said over the phone. "Nice couple. Seemed like it was a little bit out of their price range, but they had that look. I think they'll make an offer." Stephanie thanked her and snapped the phone shut.

"Well?" Edgar asked.

"She thinks they'll bite."

They'd gone to dinner to be out of the way during the showing. Stephanie's short ribs were smothered in a sickeningly sweet sauce that made them inedible, but Edgar was stuffing the last of his burger into his mouth and had ordered dessert.

In another month, construction would be finished on their new home. Stephanie had decided against telling Edgar why she desperately wanted to move. Instead, she complained to him about the drive to the college and the musty smell of old houses. She wanted a new house, somewhere where the depths of closets and pantries were facts she could check against blueprints before they were ever built. A house without any past or parallels.

On their way home, Edgar orated about how he didn't intend to take any less than the asking price. "Not with the improvements we made. And the appraiser said neighbourhood values have increased by over ten per cent."

Stephanie leaned her head against the window. He'd given this speech before. Ever since her talk with Beth, she saw her marriage more clearly. On the surface, they had a marriage of equals. Edgar didn't expect her to do the laundry or clean the house (after all, they could afford dry cleaning and a weekly housekeeper for those things). But scratch away at the laminate, and you'd hit the particleboard core of their union. Stephanie had fallen in love with Edgar without knowing that the emotion wasn't necessary for her to land the part of his wife. She had the qualifications. She was intelligent, accomplished, attractive, Asian, and willing to put his needs above her own. Had she deviated in any way from the kind of woman Edgar saw for himself, had she been black, or somebody's secretary, or just savvy instead of book-smart, she wouldn't be in this car now. There was so much more to her, but all that Edgar required was that she tick the boxes.

He had not noticed the change in her. She'd stopped engaging in their conversations, but he filled the silence with his own voice, repeating things he'd already told her, talking endlessly about himself. "No less than asking," he said. "And even then, I think we should wait until the last minute to accept. Maybe there'll be another offer. I want to net at least—"

There was a heavy thud, then a metallic thunder as something tumbled over the roof of the car. Edgar slammed on the brakes, and Stephanie jerked hard against the seatbelt before slamming back against the seat. A dark lump lay in the road behind them. It wasn't moving.

Lights appeared like fireflies, and bathrobe-clad neighbours stepped onto their porches or stared from parted curtains. Stephanie was out of the car, walking towards the fallen shadow. Her stomach churned, threatening to spill vomit down her front, and her knees felt fragile and weak as blown sugar. Still, she lurched forward, needing to know what they'd hit. Person or animal?

"Rafael!" Yolanda rushed past Stephanie, reaching the boy's body first. She threw herself on top of him, her hands pawing at the bloody wreck of her son. "*Mijo!*" she sobbed. The wail of sirens sounded from streets away, red lights flashing against the night sky, speeding towards a tragic scene after the last line had already been spoken.

★   ★   ★

Stephanie did not arrive home until quarter-to-three. Because she was hysterical, Yolanda had not been allowed in the ambulance. Stephanie had driven her to the hospital. "Stay with me. Please," the older woman had asked, taking a fierce grip on Stephanie's hand.

They sat together in the waiting room. No nurse came by with a word of intermittent courage, and Yolanda and Stephanie knew better than to ask. It was not a shock when the doctor finally came, tail between his legs, and told Yolanda that Rafael was dead. She nodded and thanked him, but when another man came around with a clipboard and questions about final arrangements, she allowed herself to be overcome, sobbing until he handed Stephanie a form and went away.

"He was such a good boy," Yolanda said in the car. "Nothing behind the eyes, but so much going on upstairs. I could tell. He was my baby. I know."

She had to be helped into her house, the keys taken from her shaking hands to open the door, held by her elbow so that she could be guided to bed. She would not take off the bloody pyjamas she wore. Stephanie pulled the blanket up, tucking it around her trembling mass. "Can I do anything?"

"No. Thank you." Yolanda closed her eyes, and Stephanie returned home.

In their living room, Edgar was asleep on the couch. The television was on, and a half-empty bottle of bourbon sat on the coffee table, its wax-sealed cork beside it. He was curled up into the foetal position, a pillow clutched to his chest. He looked like a pitiful child, but Stephanie remembered his words after the accident. "He was in the street!" he told anyone who would listen. "He came out of nowhere! What was he doing in the street?" No one was accusing him, but he kept asserting aloud that it wasn't his fault.

Stephanie would let him sleep here. She could not stomach having him in her bed. Some remnant of this disgust for him would remain forever, she was sure. Would she be able to continue on with him? Did couples get past evenings like this?

The questions were too great to be answered now with a cloudy brain. Her clothes were still redolent of the hospital. She grabbed the scotch off the table. This would be her dinner and her toothbrush. She would lock the door to the bedroom, take a shower, and drink to oblivion. In the morning she would consider what must come next.

She was mounting the stairs when she saw light from the kitchen. Automatically, she went to turn it off. Expecting to find the stove light on, she was taken aback by the open door of the pantry. But of course, this was where the scotch was kept.

For a long time, she debated whether to turn around and go up the stairs. She had not entered the pantry at night since the last encounter. Instead, she'd resorted to putting food away in the cabinets, cramming tea and cereal boxes next to the plates and glasses, not caring that it annoyed Edgar. Even in the day, she would swoop in, grab what she needed and rush out, never daring to look at the back wall for fear of seeing the door again.

She could choose. She could turn her back on the light, go up to bed, and in the morning abandon this place, with its mysteries, and her marriage, with its frailties.

Instead, she went ahead, towards the pantry. Easing open the door, however, she found only shelves and a back wall. *Of course*, she thought. *He's gone.*

Yet as she went to pull the chain to the naked bulb, the filament burst, plunging her into darkness. She reached for the back wall, no longer sure of what might be there. Her fingers found panels and followed their contours to the doorknob. Trembling, she grasped it firmly, willing herself still and ready.

★   ★   ★

His wife had not come down to breakfast. Her car was in the driveway, but Edgar didn't dare go upstairs to check on her. She had left him in the living room, which meant she blamed him. *That boy was in the road*, he reminded himself, but the excuse rang hollow.

He rolled from the couch into standing. Having slept hunched over a pillow, the fibrocartilage in his back had turned to gravel. Coffee, he decided. Black, in part to wake him, and in part as penance. He did not deserve rich cream or the pleasure of sugar.

Stepping into the kitchen, he was surprised to find his wife. "I didn't hear you come down." He waited for her to face him, but she did not acknowledge his words. "I know you must hate me. But please, look at me."

He stepped around to see her. "Stephanie, please. I'm your—"

Something in her stillness compelled him to stop. "Stephanie?" He squeezed the fleshy part of her arm, but she gave no response. Grabbing her chin, he tilted her head towards him and stared into her eyes, which gleamed with the lifeless lustre of glass.

THE NAUGHTY STEP

Stephen Volk

One voicemail. Could be worse. Could be ten. She listened as she hurried back to her car, started the ignition, phone pressed to her ear. Instantly recognised Comms.

Minor been found at a crime scene. Age about six. Male. Not yet located anyone to look after him. Calling out to EDT to attend scene.

Accelerating, she punched in the postcode of the address, already thinking ahead to finding this one a room and food. Ran through her mental Rolodex of emergency foster homes she could rely on at a moment's notice. The Hendricks. The Garretts. Those people were godsends.

Not in physical danger... at least there was that. Even so, Friday after hours you never knew what was going to hit you. Shoplifting at closing time was classic Morag. She'd been needed as the appropriate adult during the police interview, then to talk her down before delivering her home to mum and stepdad. Morag was just the sort of teenager who'd disappear through the cracks if you let her. She wouldn't.

You have reached your destination.

The street's dark gullet widened ahead. Neighbours like meerkats at their front gates. Coppers telling them to stay indoors, to not film with their phones please. The rectangles of illuminated screens you get at a rock concert.

She parked, got out.

No tape up, so presumably the crime scene was contained. Forensic people drifted in Arctic white. Two ambulances. Two police cars. A van marked PRIVATE AMBULANCE, which she knew to be an undertaker's vehicle for the removal of a body.

Death was present.

She'd known that from the police control room saying there was nobody to look after the child. One or other parent, she was pretty sure, was in that

PRIVATE AMBULANCE. She'd seen it before, too many times. Violent break-up with the kid as piggy-in-the-middle. Wished to God she hadn't.

A female PC – stab vest, tool belt – stood outside the house next to a male with a clipboard making a log. She knew a few, but didn't know her. Afro-Caribbean heritage, which was good. Diversity getting out to the sticks at long last.

"Emergency Duty Team."

The woman in uniform looked over to a skinny man in a suit, who gave her the nod.

Pathetic. Ten years since she started as a social worker and it was still ingrained in the culture. Women deal with the kids. Men deal with the offender. The big, macho guys won't deal with children or domestics. Gay domestics, forget it. Once someone told her about a pair of queens living in a caravan park who used to regularly get into fights. The females were always sent from the station to sort it.

"What happened?"

"Still piecing it together. Neighbours reported shouting. Most likely scenario, a domestic that got out of hand. Woman in her thirties didn't make it."

"Where's the boy?" She peered into the back seat of the parked police car.

"Still inside."

"You're kidding me."

"No, I'm not. We tried to move him, he wouldn't come. Went into a shit fit like you wouldn't believe."

"God."

"We didn't want to push it."

"Good."

Truth was, every cop knew if they laid a hand on him that'd technically be assault in the eyes of the law. The child had done no wrong, they couldn't arrest him, and they couldn't manhandle him. Why risk it and lose your job? Worst case scenario, a public inquiry, tabloids descending like jackals. Pass the buck to Children's Services. Let them be the fall guys.

"Never seen anything like it." The PC shivered in the cold. "Not a word of a lie. He's sitting at the bottom of the stairs. Just staring into space. Won't move an inch. Wouldn't take my hand."

"Was he witness to…?"

"Everything, we think."

"Jesus Christ."

"It wasn't pretty. Still a bit of a mess."

"And you left him in there?"

The PC didn't like that frown of accusation, and tightened defensively.

"CID say you can go in, as long as you limit yourself to the hall and stairs, and put on a suit. DI is understandably keen to interview him as a witness on video as a priority."

"Yeah, well. He needs emergency foster care *as a priority*. Can you imagine what kind of a—?"

"Trauma. We're aware of that."

She could see the officer's taut expression, and felt for her slightly. She had a job to do as well. They were picking up the pieces.

"What state is he in?"

"Unharmed, from what we can see. I've spent the last hour sitting next to him while SOCO do their stuff. Trying to get through to him, without much luck. No reaction. Not a dickie bird. Nothing. Nothing in his eyes."

"What do you mean by that?" She knew what the PC meant. She meant the kid was weird as fuck. She'd heard it all before. *Weird kid. Bad child. Waste of space. Scrapheap fodder.* To her mind, there were no bad kids, just hurt ones.

"I'm just saying. If you ask me, he's not—"

"Thanks." The sarcasm showed on her face.

"Yes, well, you work your magic, if you've got any." The PC moved away.

"Are you going to tell me his name?"

"Sorry. Jared. Jared Simkins. Mother Michelle, deceased."

"Father?"

"Location unknown."

"Anybody got any previous history on the system?"

"Not on ours."

"Grandparents? Uncles? Aunts? Friends of the family?"

"We're working on it."

The PC lifted the flap of the SOCO tent for her. She went in alone, feeling a little guilty, cutting the PC some slack. She'd probably seen the crime scene first-hand. God knows what she'd seen. Or the kid had seen, come to that.

She zipped up the white plastic forensic overalls. Thought of the corpse that had been zipped up in a black body bag hours, perhaps minutes, earlier. Put the little plastic booties over her shoes. They made her think of babies.

Jared. Jared. Jared.

She reminded herself of his name as she walked back to the front door. The male PC stood out of the way, allowing her to enter.

The boy was sitting at the bottom of the stairs. Underpants. Bare legs and feet. No sign of neglect. No dirt. No bruises. Blue pyjama top with rockets and stars on. He wasn't looking at her. He wasn't looking anywhere. If he did look up at her, what would she look like? Some sort of alien. ET in the white body suit.

She took her hood down. Removed her pale blue rubber gloves. She could see the SOCO team moving about in the kitchen, silently measuring, fingerprinting. The flash of a camera strobed, the battery buzzing as it recharged.

She sank to a crouch. Put on a soft voice, aware that, though she was born and bred less than ten miles away, her accent was a bit too posh for some of her families on these kinds of estates. Too "minted peas from Waitrose" as one teenage mother put it.

"Hi. My name's Linda. I've come to look after you for a short while. Just to be with you for a bit, is that all right?"

No reaction.

She dredged up her training from the Tavistock all those years ago. How to deal with an elective mute. Don't ask questions. Don't demand that they talk back to you. Just talk until you earn their trust.

She knelt on the floor. Another strobe. Another buzz. She glimpsed a man in white checking the screen of his digital Pentax. Ridiculous she was avoiding trigger words when this was going on all around them. A firework display.

"You know what? I felt a bit lonely outside. I thought I'd come in. I thought I might come in and, you never know, find a new friend, maybe."

No reaction.

No eye contact at all. Autistic? No. Lord knows, kids could be uncommunicative because people like her represented the system and they shut off. She was the one their mum yelled at because they couldn't get re-housed or benefits. The one who was taking them away from the person they loved, sometimes. But it wasn't that either. It wasn't wilful lack of co-operation. She knew what that looked like. This boy was in a state of shock.

"It's a bit cold in here, isn't it? I'm freezing." She stroked the radiator. Edged her knees closer to him. Palms resting on her thighs.

She found it disturbing because one thing she liked about dealing with kids was their forthrightness, their honesty. Painfully so, sometimes. She was used to telling them there was nothing to worry about, and they didn't believe it, and, most of the time, neither did she. "You know where I'd really, really like to go? Somewhere comfortable." She extended her right hand, hoping he might take it, but he wasn't even looking. Yet his whole body tightened.

She put her hand back on her thigh, pretending she never meant the gesture in the first place.

The boy's chest was rising and falling rapidly. Jaws locked. Knuckles on his own knees bone white.

She blew into her hands. Slid her palms under her armpits as if sheathing weapons. Smiling broadly. Some would say inanely.

Made no difference.

She could see what the female PC meant now. He was having none of it.

Jared. Jared Simkins.

Hunched, almost foetus-like. Rigid.

Slowly she edged closer to him, one knee at a time.

Over her right shoulder, the open door to the living room. She couldn't help giving it a quick glance.

Sofa and cushions. Facing a TV set? Did she watch daytime TV? Was she watching daytime TV when it happened? CD covers on the floor. Left there or dropped there? *Pure Heroine* by Lorde. Rag 'n' Bone Man. Christine and the Queens... One of her own favourite albums of late – how strange was that? Did Michelle dance to it, hand in hand with her little boy? Listen to it on the dashboard stereo as she drove to school? Is that what kind of woman his mother was?

Michelle. Michelle Simkins.

She thought of the wallpaper around her. How had they chosen it? Had they had a big fight? Did he leave it to her or was he the controlling type? A bully? She told herself it wasn't always like that. But, surprisingly often, it was.

"Y'areet, big man?"

The child suddenly gasped and covered his eyes with his hands.

A man, big man, almost filled the doorway to the living room. SOCO white. Monstrous to the boy. Rubber gloves. Plastic evidence bag. Carving knife inside it.

"For fuck's sake."

The Geordie giant shielded it, turning his back to the boy.

"Children's Services," she explained.

"Does Chris Holroyd know about this?"

For fuck's sake. The DI, she presumed. Gave him an incendiary glare. *What do you think?*

"We'll give you some space, then." Backing off. "Give them a DNA swab when you leave. For elimination purposes."

"Yes, go away now, please."

He went, taking the photographer with him, a woman in a baggy forensic suit that un-gendered her almost completely. They left the front door ajar. Darkness outside. Soundless. Frozen. No radio crackle. No chat. Just the wind gently rustling the white plastic of the forensics tent in the middle of the road.

She walked to the door and pushed it shut. The security chain was just like the one she had at home. She didn't need to put it on. How often did Michelle do that, though? Trying to protect herself? Trying to feel safe?

The boy still had his hands over his face.

The idea surged up in her: what the hell had he seen? Had he heard his mum's cries as she was stabbed? Or had it gone chillingly silent? Had he cried out, terrified, and got no reply? No wonder he was in a state of shock. It was incredible he wasn't catatonic. Fight or flight? He couldn't fight, he couldn't fly, so he froze. And to break it, to come out of it, to let reality back in, would be unbearable.

"Sorry. Sorry." She sank down on all fours. "They're gone. They're all gone now. It's all right. Nothing's going to happen. There's nobody here. Just me. Just you. Promise."

Silence.

Then the boy took away his hands tentatively. For a fraction of a second his eyes met hers – then abruptly shot down to the carpet at his feet.

Her eyes fell on a toy car next to the skirting board. Smaller than the Dinky and Corgi toys her brother played with. A red car with fire along the side. Eyes in its windshield.

"This is a nice car. It's not a car, is it? It's a sports car." She turned in a circle, running it along the carpet. "Brooom Brooom." She made a squealing noise of a handbrake turn, taking an imaginary curve on two wheels.

She sensed he was watching her, but as soon as she looked at him directly he looked away.

The length of the hall between them, she pushed hard and made the car run across the floor towards him. Unable to get traction on the carpet, it stopped short, half way. Beyond the reach of his arm. Unless he moved.

He stared at it. Blank, black eyes. So black she couldn't tell where the irises ended and the pupils began.

"You can play if you want."

Nothing.

"You can even get down on the floor like me if you want."

The boy shook his head.

She crawled closer. Flicked the car with her finger.

It hit the step. He leaned over slowly and picked it up.

"Lightning McQueen." He frowned as he saw her blank expression. "He's called Lightning McQueen."

Turning sideways on the step, one knee raised, he ran the car up his thigh, making it do a jump to the wall. Doing so with no sense of distraction or enjoyment a child normally had in play. She could see only a focused, insular, hermetically sealed determination. A force field holding her back.

The bleep of a text. She turned and stood up. Snatched her phone from her pocket, switched it off. Didn't want calls to interrupt her or spook him.

Crouched again, one hand on the bottom step, inches from his bare foot.

"Are you hungry, Jared?"

He shook his head.

"Thirsty, maybe?"

Again. Then a nod.

"Do you want a drink of water?"

"Juice."

She should call out. She knew that. Except she didn't want to use her mobile and didn't want to leave him alone to go outside. Not now.

"Where do I get some juice?"

"In the fridge."

"Okay."

She walked past him, down the two steps to the passage to the kitchen. It was the same layout as the house she was brought up in. She thought of the time her mum left the gas on and caused an explosion, just a big FUFF like the air got sucked away, and it took off her eyebrows. There'd been a different explosion here.

Bright red smears on the stable door leading to the garden, tagged with a SOCO sticker with an L-shaped metric reference scale and photo cross hairs. She tried not to look at the blood on the floor. The claggy smell made her feel sick, but she couldn't be sick, not with the boy there. She had to control herself. Control her stomach. Control her eyes.

In her peripheral vision the windows looked dirty, almost opaque, but she realised they'd been powdered with a Zephyr brush for fingerprints to be lifted.

On the fridge door she read J-A-R-E-D in fridge magnets. A photograph pinned there showed a younger Jared – age two or three – long hair, shining yellow. His mother must've been sad to see it go. Maybe he wanted it off. Maybe he was being teased for looking like a girl. School certificate for Outstanding Schoolmate held by a magnet of the Eiffel Tower. Another photograph of a barbecue chicken sitting on a beer can. Beer can up its arse. So funny. Mum and dad puckering up, snogging (fake-snogging?) for the lens. Were they happy then, her glasses askew, Eric Morecambe-style? On the old Sancerre? Pink stripe of dye in her blonde hair? Sleeve of tattoos, small mouth, doe eyes. Him, the nameless one, grinning at a party in the garden, showing his hairy belly button for the finger she inserts, laughing her head off.

Inside the fridge door – milk, orange juice. The shelves were packed.

Big jar of mayo. Babybels for his lunchbox. Cream cheese dippers. Ready meals for the week. Nobody intended to die today.

She separated one of the apple juice cartons from the six pack, tore the straw off the side, broke the seal to insert it. Hung on the banister, behind and above him. Handed it down.

He slurped eagerly.

"You know I have a favourite place, and sometimes I want to go there and never leave it. It makes me feel really good there."

"I don't have a favourite place."

"It isn't the stairs?"

"The stairs?" Again like she is mad. "Why would the *stairs* be my favourite place?"

"I don't know. I thought you didn't want to leave it."

"I *want* to leave it, but I can't leave it, can I?"

"Why's that?"

"Because!"

"Because what?"

"Because *she* said!" Anger overspilling, he flung the juice carton away down the hall. It tumbled, splashed and lay.

She lowered herself, holding the banisters like prison bars. "What did she say, sweetheart?" He struggled. Sighed. "It's okay." She touched his knee.

He recoiled as if receiving an electric shock. "It's not okay! It's *not* okay!"

"Tell me, Jared love, and maybe I can help."

"You can't! I *know* you can't!"

"How do you know if you don't tell me? You're hurting. I can tell you're hurting inside and I want to do something about it."

"You can't! *Nobody* can!"

Wait. Wait. Wait. Her heart was breaking, but she knew she had to give him time. She had to give him the air to fill with his words. Maybe the space she gave would tug them out of him. Maybe they were ready to come, like a baby tooth that had worked itself loose.

"It wasn't my fault," he said, then it came like a dam burst. "All I was doing was watching *Transformers: Cyberverse*. She *said* I could watch another one, but before it finished she said *come and have your pasta*, and I said, *mum, Transformers hasn't finished yet* and she said *now!* and *Jared!*

and *Jared, listen to me!* and I said *but you promised!* and she said *right, get you-know-where and think about the way you're behaving and don't come back until I...*" He stopped, gasping, trying to catch the words. "And I *did*. I went to the naughty step."

And that's what you're doing. Waiting. Waiting for her to call you. Waiting for her to say it's all right. But she never can call you, can she, sweetheart?

"Jared, what if I said it's okay to leave the naughty step now?"

"It isn't."

"Why?"

"Because *she* has to say. That's the way it works. That's the way it *always* works."

But your mum's not going to say anything now, is she, Jared?

She heard a tap on the front door. Shape outside. She went and opened it.

"Can I have a word, please?"

"Quickly," she said to the female PC, looking back at the boy whose arms now covered his head.

"It would be better if we spoke outside."

The cold hit her as she stepped out. The scene was depleted. Fewer cars, fewer officers. Seemed like that. What she was wearing, foolish. No coat, no stab vest.

"The father's been found dead. Suicide." The PC turned her crackling radio to mute. "Found by the railway tracks. Use your imagination. There was an allegation against him, apparently. Made by her."

Shit.

"Yeah. Look, CID's going mental. We need to get this kid out of there."

"Great. How do you intend doing that? By force? By sedating him? Dragging him kicking and screaming into the back of a police car?"

"Obviously not."

"What then? He's the responsibility of my department now."

"And what are you intending to do?"

"Stay here." She didn't care whether the PC thought she was mad or incompetent or both. She knew what she was doing and CID wasn't her problem. "He's got to start relaxing, the adrenaline can't last forever. The body will eventually level out. You can't deal with fear indefinitely."

"You're the expert. How long?"

"As long as it takes."

"My shift's over soon. Anything I can do?"

"You can go and feed my cat."

She almost got a smile out of her at that. Almost.

"Wait a sec." The PC disappeared into the dark, her equipment giving her pear-like figure a kind of waddle, reappearing a minute later with a plastic bottle of water and a Yorkie. "It'll keep you going. I've got ten more in the glove compartment." She retreated back into the gloom. "Good luck. One for the memoirs, huh?"

Memoirs?

She supposed it was a joke, smiled, left the night to its own devices and shut the door gently after her.

It was a neat seal, like the door of the fridge. She switched the porch light off, kept the hall light on. The fact the PC had gone home weirdly unnerved her. Her cat would be all right, of course. A vet had told her once it was healthy for a cat to miss a meal once in a while. More like in the wild. Didn't stop the thing whining if she did, though.

"Go. Go if you want to." The boy.

"I don't."

"Why?"

"Because I like it here. Right here, with you."

She held out the bar of chocolate. Head shake. Water. The same.

She leaned against the wall and stripped off her crinkly white SOCO suit and the shiny elasticated slippers, to reveal a green M&S pullover and jeans.

The boy looked at her with curiosity, as if seeing her for the first time.

"Are you somebody's mum?"

"No."

"Why not?"

She thought it best to answer him in a way a child would understand. "Nobody loved me enough, I suppose." She unexpectedly felt tears welling, and blinked them away, fighting them off with a smile. A smile she wanted him to see.

"My mum and dad loved each other."

"I know."

"They did."

"I'm sure they did, sweetheart."

Anger again, bedding down into a knotted confusion. "Why do mums get so angry? Why did she have to get angry and shout at him?"

"Maybe she couldn't help it."

"She *could* help it. All she had to do was stop. If she stopped..."

"It wasn't her fault, sweetie."

"I know. I *know*. It was *my* fault. They were arguing about me."

"Don't say that." She sat next to him on the step. Put her arm around him. "Don't think it. Think about nice things."

"What nice things?" A sob escaped. "*What* nice things, though?"

She couldn't say. But felt the soft, almost unnatural warmth of him. The proximity of him like a glow.

Could she scoop him up right now, she thought, when he was upset and vulnerable, less likely to fight back? Could she just hold him to her tightly and make a run for it, get through that door and outside to the police car that was parked in the street?

No. It would feel like the most terrible betrayal. After her earning his trust, it would destroy him. She could imagine him howling in her arms. Trauma heaped on top of trauma. It would destroy *her*. She couldn't... But she needed to do something. Soon.

"My dad loved me."

"They both loved you in different ways. I'm sure they did."

Allegations.

"He wouldn't leave me, would he?"

"No, he wouldn't," she lied. Hand on his back. Ready to urge him to stand up. Leaning forward. "Do you think you can come as far as the front door, can you do that for me?"

He stiffened. Went rigid – his back like an ironing board.

"Sorry. Sorry. Sorry—"

"I can't!"

"I know you can't, sweetheart. I know you can't."

She sat back down, rubbed his spine. The hotness radiated through her palm. She settled, and let him settle. Let his heart slow down. Let hers.

What time was it? She daren't look at her phone. Was it nine now? Ten? Without the porch light on it was really dark, as dark as she could ever remember seeing, and the house felt cold and unloving. She sometimes felt that when she visited. Toxic relationships, you could feel them, you knew something was brewing, you knew it wouldn't end well, there was going to be no saviour, no knight in shining armour.

His breathing was heavy, guttural, his sinuses blocked.

She wondered if she could creep upstairs to the bathroom cabinet and get him some Calpol. Something that would relax him. It was a sedative. If it calmed him down, that would be a good thing. If it got him to sleep, even better.

He leaned against her, his cheek against her chest. His breath against her heart.

"It'll be all right, you'll see." She cradled him. "A lot of people are here to help you. I'm here to help you." She didn't know if there were, but she knew one thing for sure. She'd stay there till he was ready. "You know, if you want to come with me, that's all right. Nobody's going to be angry with you. Your mum wouldn't be angry. She's never been angry with you for very long, has she?"

Nothing. His face snuffled in closer.

"Sleep. That's it. Sleep, if you want to. It doesn't matter. I'm here."

He was quiet for a long while.

She wondered how often the house was this quiet. This still. This cold.

The letterbox lifted, breathed. The wind had become strong. Gusty. Something began banging, clattering out in the garden. Loose corrugated iron on the roof of a shed, she thought. She wondered if the fence he jumped over when he'd escaped, fearing the neighbours would see him if he went out the front way, was broken. Pictured his wet hand on it. Wet with blood. His wife's blood.

"Sometimes we hear foxes." The little voice next to her chest. "Sometimes they make me scared. My mum says there's nothing to be scared of. They just want to get in our bins. She says they're more afraid of us than we are of them. Is that right?"

"Shshshsh. Don't think about things like that. Go to sleep. Just let it all float away, yeah?" She rocked him. "There were ten in the bed and the little one said, roll over, roll over..."

When the song was over, her voice a drone, lulling, she heard a long, warm sigh.

He was drifting away but he wasn't off yet. She didn't envy his dreams, poor mite. Or perhaps they were an escape right now. She hoped so.

Perhaps when she was sure he had dozed off she could carry him to her car without him waking up. But what if he woke when she was driving to the emergency foster care? And she didn't know where that was yet. She should've phoned before she got here. She told herself not to get anxious about things that hadn't happened yet. It would all work out, as long as she didn't panic. And there was a team outside to help her – wasn't there?

She heard a bin blow over. A high-pitched dog, if it was a dog.

They're more afraid of us than we are of them.

"It's all right." The voice below her. "I know it'll be all right because he promised."

"Shsh."

"He's going to take me. He said he would. She said no. She said she had enough of him letting me down, but he didn't, he was busy sometimes and couldn't come on time, that's all. She was *wrong* and he was *nice. He* was the nice one. Why did she have to be so *horrible?*"

"Darling—" She felt her insides tighten. Hands knotting them like rope.

"He said we'd go somewhere special." Squirming. "He's going to come back and take me somewhere special!"

"No, nobody's coming, darling. Don't worry."

"He will though. He comes every Friday. He's *got* to come!"

"I'm sorry. He's gone, darling. Gone a long way away. He can't touch you now. He'll never touch you ever again."

"No! That's not true!"

"It is true."

"It's not! He's *here.* He's here now! I can hear him!"

The wind outside rose to a whistle. Buffeting against the stable door in the kitchen. She could hear it shake. Something had fallen against it. A tree or branch. Something heavy and unrelenting. Something beyond the bloody fingerprints.

"*Dad?*"

The boy sat up. Alert. Eyes wide. Trying to pull her arms off him. She tried to hold him, but he was like a snake, and she heard herself say the worst thing, and she knew it was the worst thing. She simply didn't know what else to say.

"But you can't go, sweetheart. Remember, your mum said you have to stay here. Your mum said!"

Her arms wrapped around him, trying to hold him tight and still and safe.

"Let go of me!"

"No. You don't understand. Jared. He doesn't love you."

"He does! He does!"

Allegations.

"He called it love but he wants to hurt you and I won't let him."

"Let me *go you fucking bitch!*"

She saw the knife go in. A rolling wave of filth seeped from the kitchen, through the air between them, and she knew that he stood there, in the kitchen, nameless and hairy-bellied. Saliva or snot on his lips. Hand on his knife or his cock.

"I won't let you go! He's not going to have you. I won't let him!"

A vow. A prayer.

She crossed her arms over the boy's body. He kicked. He grunted. He screamed.

She shut her eyes.

Her own father once took her to a hawk sanctuary and she'd stood with a baby bird sitting on her finger, a peregrine with its perfect yellow feet, and it was a day they weren't open, but her father asked them to open just for her. Just for his Lindy. And they did, and the owls had a feeding time and they took these dead mice from the freezer and her dad said not to look but she did just a little bit. And one of the teenage girls had a leather glove and put the mouse on it and the owl flew the whole length of the barn and landed on it, and its eyes were what she remembered now, and the rich smell of the dead animals from the freezer and the sawdust. That smell was in her nostrils now.

"Bastard. You bastard."

She wouldn't relent. She would be brave. She would be courageous. She would do her job.

She would save this little soul, even as she felt the breath of the dead thing on the back of her neck.

"You can't have him. You can't."

★   ★   ★

By morning light, the police and paramedics have to prise his body from her. When they examine him, they think his ribs are broken, she held him so tight.

The DI asks them how long it would have taken for the child to stop breathing.

They say the boy probably struggled for some time. They think his face was held against her chest, his mouth and nose pressed against the green sweater probably inhibited his breathing. He suffocated and his little heart gave out.

When they found her, she was stroking the boy's hair. Humming a lullaby. Maybe it was a hymn. Maybe it was Kylie Minogue.

She doesn't answer their questions. She doesn't see them. She's staring. Her arms wrapped around herself now.

They ask her to come with them, but she doesn't move.

Remains sitting on the step.

"Let me talk to her." The female PC crouches level to her face, and finally she speaks.

"I saved him. He's safe now. He won't be hurt any more. I protected him. You see that, don't you?"

"I see that," the other woman says.

Standing aside as men take her.

Watching as she is led into the light, blinking up at a cloudless sky. Put in the police car, smiling, vindicated, content.

And the female PC closes the front door quickly as she leaves, for she felt something looking at her while she stood in the hall, and, whatever it was, invisible, mocking, and wet, it had been holding the small, invisible hand of a little boy.

A HOTEL IN GERMANY

Catriona Ward

The movie star calls Cara at 3:30 a.m.

Cara is dreaming of a night forest. She hears the tattoo of spongy elk hooves on the forest floor, glimpses dark hide through the lacework of foliage. The shrill of the telephone merges with the sounds of her dream, entwines with her breath and beating heart. She emerges slowly, reluctant. Perhaps it is not a dream but a memory, resurfacing. That has been happening, of late. She lifts the phone with mitten hands. "Hello." Her tongue is clumsy with sleep. There is no answer. But Cara recognises the resentful silence that rises between those who love one another. Family.

"Axel," she says, then, with difficulty, "Rose?" Her dead brother is calling, or maybe even her dead daughter, whose name still hurts to think or say, like a wound in her mind.

The receiver crackles with rage. "It won't work, Cara," the movie star says. "It won't be quiet. I've tried everything." She means the TV remote control: her anger is so vast, it can only find tiny outlets, pinhole cracks in a great dam.

"I'm coming," Cara says. Reality settles around her.

She gets out of bed slowly, careful of her limbs, her elbows, her toes. Her body remembers slower than her mind and she hurts herself, sometimes. She puts on clothes at random, plucked from the floor. The hotel corridor is dimmed for the night, with only glowing bars of soft white at floor level.

Cara lets herself into the movie star's suite. The TV plays the news at deafening volume, fighting the radio, tuned to a country station. Cucumber slices spill from a glass dish across the parquet floor. The air is filled with the scent of sandalwood. The movie star engages all her senses, day and night. Cara understands that. If you leave a space you can never predict what will arrive to fill it.

The movie star sits upright at the centre of the bed, sheets whipped up around her like meringue. Gleaming specks of gold and jet and emerald and diamond are scattered across the white. Velvet pouches and silk-lined boxes are piled beside her.

"I've told you not to take your jewellery to bed," Cara says. "Something will get lost."

The movie star holds out the remote control to Cara, appealing. Her anger has melted into sadness. These mercurial shifts of feeling make her mesmerising on the screen. She is a clear pool in which dark fish swim. Cara mutes the news and puts on the shiny chrome kettle, which the movie star never leaves home without. She slices lemon and plucks mint leaves from the plant on the windowsill. As the water heats Cara returns each piece of jewellery gently to its box. Then she puts the boxes back in the safe, listing them as she does it.

"Gold collar set with pearls," she says. "Drop earrings, white gold and yellow diamond. Platinum cuff with sapphires." The movie star nods along and ticks each item off on her fingers. "Gold ring with diamond solitaire," Cara says. "Ruby pendant." The ritual imparts a pleasant sense of order.

When all eight pieces are in the safe, the movie star gets out of bed with a sigh. Cara turns her back while she enters the safe combination and locks it. The kettle begins to emit light wisps of steam. It makes no sound as it boils. Money can buy silence, even from a kettle. Cara pours out two cups and adds the lemon and mint. Their clean scent fills the air.

The movie star holds her cup tightly in both hands like a child. She gestures towards the silent screen which shows a sun-baked village and a thin man picking sticks out of the dust. "Look at this," she says. "The state of everything. It makes me so angry, keeps me up at night." She looks into the large mirror beside the bed, pulls an eyelid up, peers at her clear, white eyeball.

"You should get some sleep," Cara says. Her own eyelids give with the sandy weight of exhaustion.

"I can't," the movie star says. "This room! It faces north and the windows don't open. I can't think in here. *Smothering*. What is your room like?"

"A single," says Cara. "Not a suite like this."

"What direction does it face?"

"West, I think." Cara knows that it faces west. Some muffled instincts remain to her. She still feels the pull of sunrise and sunset like a twist in her belly.

"Let's go to your room," the movie star says.

They pad along the corridor like cats in their bare feet. The movie star leans heavily on Cara's shoulder.

★   ★   ★

Cara moves her discarded pyjamas off the single bed. The movie star gets into it. She pulls the sheets up to her chin. She looks very beautiful. "That's better," she says. "Can't you feel how much better the energy is in this room?" Cara sits in a chair and waits.

The movie star starts to talk in a low voice about her mother, and how she misses her. She talks about how it feels to love someone and fear them at the same time, because they can hurt you so badly. Cara listens. The movie star talks about the producer, who is messing with the script, giving her male co-star the best lines. Cara nods and makes more hot lemon. The little white hotel kettle whistles and roars. "You're lucky to be so small," the movie star says. "My legs are too long for most beds." She wiggles her toes, which peep out pink from beneath the duvet. "This is nice. I like it when it's just the two of us."

At length the movie star's words begin to slur and her head droops. She rests her cheek on the pillow and sleeps.

Cara rises silently. She goes to the bathroom and takes the little green bottle from the cabinet. She paints her sore gums with the brush that comes with the bottle. At first it tickles, then the cold feeling rushes in, making her mouth numb and icy. She takes the pills. Blue, then white, then white and yellow. Her reflection regards her; her small thin face like a serious antelope. Dark hair cropped boy-short like all the other assistants in LA this summer. She looks too young to be taken seriously.

The movie star snores gently. Cara sets the alarm, and then curls up in the armchair by the window. *I am lucky*, she reminds herself, as she does each night before sleep and in the morning on waking. *One of the lucky ones.*

She drifts as the sun comes up, spilling shattered fragments of light on the broad running river below.

★ ★ ★

The shooting day goes well. In the evening, the movie star hums as Cara makes pine needle and calendula tea. The movie star holds each butterscotch candy in her mouth for three seconds before removing it. Then she adds it to a glistening pile on the little silver plate at her side. A piece of steamed salmon sits untouched under its silver lid on the white-clothed table. "I need tomorrow's call sheet," she says.

"I'll go and copy it," Cara says. Each day the call sheet has to be taped to the movie star's mirror, to the back of her bathroom door, placed in a clear folder in her handbag, and another left on the desk. The movie star can't hold times and days in her head. Cara can. Maybe it's because she doesn't own anything. Her life is uncluttered.

"Don't take hours about it like last time." The movie star sounds imperious but Cara sees her fear. When Cara leaves the room there will be a gap in which thoughts may creep in. Cara touches the back of the movie star's slim brown hand and goes. *Don't let it be Greta on reception*, she thinks. She is bad at human conflict. *Be the nice girl with the round pink cheeks*. As the elevator drifts down towards the lobby Cara closes her eyes and whispers, "Not Greta, not Greta, not Greta..." She tries to make a spell of it.

Greta's silver name badge gleams in the low light. Her false eyelashes look like peacock feathers. Her skin is smooth and beautiful. She looks tired. Before Cara can speak she holds up a pointed red nail. Her fingers fly over the nubs of the console.

Greta does not like Cara. Cara is the conduit for all the movie star's needs; three changes of suite, a screened off area in the dining room, so that no one can see her eat, silence in the corridor outside her room from 9:00 pm onwards. The movie star does not like to phone housekeeping. She needs to be seen. She prefers to go down to the lobby, glide past the people waiting at reception and ask for things in her clear voice. Despite the name tag, the movie star calls Greta "you – girl!" "You, girl – I need a bouquet of freesias in each room." Or she talks to Greta through Cara. "Tell the girl I need fresh towels."

Greta gives a final violent tap on the space bar and looks at Cara, black eyebrows raised.

"Could you please print four copies and send them up to her room?"

Cara puts the memory port on the desk. It pulses gentle silver and white, as if it had a secret.

"We don't print," Greta says. "Who uses paper anymore?"

"The other receptionist did it for me yesterday," Cara says.

Greta raises her eyebrows. "And we don't print from memory ports. Hotel policy. Infection, you know."

Cara is beginning to feel a helpless panic. This has taken too long already. The movie star is waiting. "It was ok yesterday."

"Then you are very, very lucky that there was no infection." Greta's voice is filled with quiet triumph. "That member of staff will be disciplined."

Cara goes up to her room, and puts the file on a data stick. She imagines the movie star's anxiety mounting. Her need for Cara seems to creep under the door like mustard gas.

Back at the desk, Greta says, "We charge a dollar a page. In cash. I can't leave reception to take it to the room, so you'll have to wait here."

Cara gives Greta eight dollars, which is all the money she has. The movie star doesn't carry it. Cara feels like explaining, "You are not hurting her by doing this, not at all." But offended dignity needs bloodshed, and Cara is available.

★   ★   ★

"I thought you were dead," says the movie star. The mountain of sucked butterscotch has grown. The steamed salmon fillet has been picked at and turned over to hide the gnawed places. The movie star eats like a dying animal – in secret, lashing out if discovered. "I was just about to report you absconded. Where have you been?"

"Printing the call sheet," says Cara. The movie star is always threatening to report Cara absconded. That doesn't mean she won't do it. She might, and then be very sorry afterwards. Cara smiles to cover the cold fear lancing through her chest. Then she quickly closes her lips. Her gums ache. "It was eight dollars for the printing."

"That's absurd," the movie star says. "I won't pay it. I'll dispute my bill with the manager. I need quiet now, to centre myself. Absolute quiet. You'll be in your room?"

"Of course," Cara says.

As Cara closes the door behind her the movie star is picking up the phone. She is calling the director, to tell him to change the shooting order.

★   ★   ★

Cara cannot leave her room, but she has a window. She can give the implant something pretty to watch. The night river runs by sleek and strong. A group of women walks along the bank, laughing. They are in their twenties perhaps, in the middle of their evening, flowing from one place to another.

One has a clever face like a raccoon. She puts an arm around her friend's waist. As she does, she lifts the back of her friend's gauzy skirt and tucks it into her belt. The raccoon-faced girl laughs, the girls walking behind laugh too. The friend walks on oblivious, long brown legs ending in black panties. Cara wonders when each of the girls will die. In sixty years? Tonight? The certainty of their death, moving through them with every breath they take. Cara can't remember what it felt like.

The implant is a tiny silver node on her brow, hidden just above her hairline. Sometimes Cara thinks this is why the movie star likes her so close. Whenever she is with Cara, the movie star is being watched too.

★   ★   ★

The phone rings at 4:00 a.m., breaking her brittle sleep. "Axel?" Cara says.

"It's happening again." The movie star is crying. "*Now*, Cara."

"Don't move," Cara says. "I'm coming."

She pulls on clothes, fear coming in cold rushes.

★   ★   ★

The night lighting in the lobby is velvet, dusk-like. Early stars are scattered across the distant ceiling. Greta's face is serious, eerily lit by the glowing keyboard. Her fingers move like spiders. Tap, tap, tap. Greta looks up as Cara approaches. Then she turns and vanishes through a black door behind her, leaving the desk glowing and pulsing like an undersea creature.

Cara presses the glowing blue button labelled 'Assistance'. The alarm or bell or whatever it is rings in some distant place, out of sight. Cara presses the button again. The lobby is still. The black door does not open.

"Hello," Cara calls. "She needs a kit," she calls. "Now."

Nothing happens for a minute or so. The door opens slowly. Greta emerges smooth as a wave. "Of course," she says. "Please excuse the brief wait. We're short staffed." She puts the kit on the desk for Cara. It looks like a small black briefcase.

"This is a level ten," Cara says, looking at the label on the leather handle. "I don't want it that strong."

"This is all we have. I can send out. It will take a few hours." Cara sees in Greta's porcelain eyes that she knows what using the kit means for Cara. Cara can almost feel it already, the sick seismic movement of pain.

Cara says, "I'll take it."

"Corpse," Greta says softly, holding Cara's gaze.

"What?" asks Cara, even though she heard.

"I said, of course."

As Cara goes Greta says something else under her breath in German. It means, roughly, *knife-face*. Cara knows all those words. She has heard them many times.

Cara understands, now. Greta hates the movie star, but she hates Cara for different reasons.

★　　★　　★

The movie star is curled up in a corner of the bed, making herself as small as possible in the smooth expanse of white sheet. The TV and radio are silent. She grunts in time with her pulsing pain. When the cancer comes back it moves fast, blazes with unnatural speed through cartilage and bone. Tonight it is in her spine.

Cara does not waste time on words or comfort. She breaks the seal on the kit, takes the green and white pill from its plastic cartridge and swallows it.

She trembles as her body begins to purge itself. Oily, rose-scented sweat oozes from her pores. She grabs a tissue from the silver box beside the bed and coughs up grey, glistening lumps. Cara feels her insides twisting, molten. She runs for the bathroom.

"Don't go," the movie star pleads. "Don't leave m—" Cara slams the door behind her. She reaches the toilet just in time. Red and pink liquid roars out of her throat, hot, both acid and sweet. It seems to go on forever. Then everything goes quiet. Cara lifts her head. Her eyes stop watering. Her stomach settles.

It begins to happen; comes like a beam of sunlight through a deep ocean. The night takes on a velvet touch. Cara hears the fish speaking in the night river, the silent language of fin and tail. The implant is forced out of its lodging in her brow, lands with a tinkle on the marble floor. Cara's body has rejected it. The world becomes a dark flower opening, with Cara at its centre. Everything is alive – she gasps at how alive.

She is almost as she once was, now. Memory and pain wash through her. Also love. There was that, too. She feels the shape of her mouth change as the nubs grow into elegant scythes. Her tongue licks the ivory smoothness of them. She misses these, perhaps most of all.

She opens the bathroom door. She sees each mote of dust spiralling on the cold hotel air. The movie star is still curled up in the corner of the bed. She does not move as Cara approaches. She has passed out. Cara hears the dry sound of the cancer growing in her spine.

It is difficult not to drift, not to lose herself in the music of everything. But she must be fast, before her skin becomes too tough. When Cara takes her arm the movie star comes to, screaming – not with pain but with fear. Her body knows what Cara is. She hits Cara's face weakly with her fist. Cara catches the movie star's wrist with ease and inserts the IV line into her vein. She slides the cannula into the vein in her own neck. She has to stab repeatedly, and hard. In a moment, it would have been too late. Cara releases the valve and the thin plastic tube turns black. Her blood flows into the movie star.

After a few seconds the plastic tube begins to melt. They are designed to be perishable, so that no more than the legal amount of blood can be transferred. The tube disintegrates in saggy drips. It falls in smoking remains on the white sheets. Cara smells the singed sweetness, mingling with the deep earthy scent of her blood. Cara pulls the cannula from her neck. The wound closes faster than even her senses can catch.

The movie star gives a shuddering sigh. Her eyes are filled with black light. "You took so long, Cara," she whispers. "I was afraid you had left me."

Cara takes her in her arms, just as she did when the movie star was a little girl; as she did the movie star's mother, once upon a time. "I am always here," she says. "Rest, now."

The movie star's head nods wearily. "I love you," she says. "You know that, don't you, Cara?"

"I know," Cara says.

"And you love me too."

"Always," Cara says, holding her tightly. But they need each other so much that it's hard to tell.

Cara makes tea and puts it by the bed. The steam spirals, makes silk ribbons on the air. Cara gazes, then shakes herself. She could watch it for hours. Once, she would have done. All she had was time.

"They'll pick you up in an hour for the night shoot," she tells the movie star. "You should try and nap until then." She strokes the movie star's hair. The movie star grunts softly. She is lost in the dreams carried by Cara's blood.

Cara knows she is delaying the moment. She takes the last items from the kit. The pills, the bottle. Too powerful. It is going to hurt. She looks around the room one last time. She has not been this strong for many years. She wants to commemorate it somehow, before she makes herself weak and grey again. But what would be the point?

★　　★　　★

Back in her room Cara lays them out on the nightstand. Blue pill, then white, then white and yellow. Green bottle. This will be bad; nearly as bad as the first time, many years ago. But the thought of pain is nothing compared to Cara's sorrow at losing the world again, its myriad detail, the stark clarity of it, the thousands of warm lives she can feel for miles around, like burning stars in the night.

She fingers the long graceful points in her mouth. She lets their razor edges slice her fingertips, leaving long black bloody lines which vanish instantly. She bids them farewell.

She wonders what would happen if she didn't take the pill. She can make it to the river, she is sure. Once she's underwater the stuff they put in the air can't affect her. *I could live in the ocean*, Cara thinks. *Never surface. Or there must be remote islands, forgotten by people, where the air is clean. I could live there.* She pictures pale sand littered with the white bones of shipwrecked men. The peace of it pulls at her. *I'll do it*, Cara thinks, wild. *What else is there for me?* She had forgotten how deeply it is possible to feel. *Maybe Axel found one of those islands. Maybe Rose—* no. She cuts off the thought. She knows it leads nowhere.

They were in the forest when the mist came. Axel fought. That is why he died. Cara lay still and watched. She was allowed to live because she was useful. The movie star's grandmother, Cara's great, great, great granddaughter, was permitted to keep Cara for medical purposes. Cancer runs in the family. Cara knows that as well as anyone. *Rose.*

If the movie star has children Cara will help to raise them, as she raised the movie star, and the movie star's mother before her. She will hold the children at night when they are scared and feed them balanced diets and help them with their homework. When the movie star dies Cara will belong to them. If the movie star does not have children maybe a distant relative will take her. The immunity will not be as perfect as with Cara's descendants. It is most powerful in the direct line. But someone might still want her. Humans are all related to some degree. The blood always helps, even if only a little.

How many like her are left? Cara doesn't know. She sees them sometimes, back home in California. People walk them on leashes in the parks like dogs. Sometimes they are missing a limb. They move slowly as though through water. Maybe the ones who are left wish they were dead too. If no one wants her when the movie star dies, the state will cull Cara like the others.

The movie star thinks of Cara as family. *I am one of the lucky ones.*

Cara takes the blue and white pills, then the white and yellow one. They go down her throat with plastic ease. She paints the ivory lengths in her mouth with the little brush.

The pain takes her. She is in its molten core. Her limbs are threaded with fire, bones jagged. Pain swills around, finds the cracks in her. Dimly she hears the phone ringing. She cannot answer. She has no hands, no arms, no voice. She is just pain. Time expands and contracts.

Through the tumult she thinks, *I'm a coward who can't bear to be alone.*

★   ★   ★

She breaks the surface slowly. Each limb feels like lead. Cara is surprised to find that the night has passed and a cold dawn hangs over the river. She licks her smooth top gum, her blunt teeth. The grey mantel lies over the world. Everything is dulled once more. She takes a new implant from the box. It is not advisable to stay offline too long. They like to keep track. The sharp legs pierce her flesh and then flip out, fixing the little button in place on her skull. She dabs at the thin trickle of blood that runs down her brow. There is no power in it, now.

The phone rings. "I've been calling and calling," the movie star hisses. "They're gone, Cara."

★   ★   ★

The TV roars, a movie about a kidnapped girl. The movie star cries and eats pistachios from a silver bowl. Pistachio shells litter nearby surfaces. A quiet man in a beautiful suit perches on the arm of a chair. He nods and listens to the movie star, draws no attention to himself. Cara understands that he is important.

"I could have been here, in bed, when they came," the movie star says. "I could have been killed in my sleep."

The hole in the safe gapes like an eye. The combination lock has been neatly cut out. "Tidy," the man says, almost approvingly. "Professional." The thief came during the three hours the movie star was on set. It suggests that they knew her schedule, somehow, knew she wouldn't be in her room in the middle of the night.

★   ★   ★

The movie star moves to a different suite and the hotel stations a security guard outside her door. She tells Cara to stay with her until she falls asleep.

"Could you, you know?" the movie star lifts her lip in a snarl and taps one of her perfect canines, to show what she means.

Cara shakes her head.

"Come on," the movie star says. "You could protect me better than these idiots." Her eyes light up at the thought of Cara shedding blood for her. She doesn't seem to understand or care what would happen to Cara, after that.

Cara feeds the movie star a spoonful of sleeping draught from a gold bottle. "The car will pick you up at 7:00 a.m," she says. The movie star says "Mmmm," not listening. She has found one of her movies on TV. Her head starts to nod. On screen the movie star churns butter and wipes sweat from her brow.

The movie star is young but she has travelled in time and lived many lives. She has farmed wheat in Kansas; raced horses dressed as a boy; fought righteous courtroom battles trembling with conviction; walked home alone at night with footsteps following ever closer behind her; fallen in love many, many times with men and women on bridges, in diners, at parties in New York loft apartments, on buses, on a submarine, in war-torn deserts and once up a tree.

But it is this movie in particular that Cara remembers. There is a moment coming soon where the woman played by the movie star discovers that the harvest is spoiled.

Cara watches. The moment, the discovery of the ruined crops, is coming now. The movie star strides across the stubbled blighted fields, skirts billowing, brave and slender as a wand, face crumpled in grief. The camera slowly, lovingly zooms in on her face. In that moment her expression is Axel's. The eyebrows like dark wings, the hurt and furious gaze, are his. And the expression is hers, Rose's, as she died, battling the disease. Infinite betrayal, high cheekbones. Rose, who has been in the ground so many long years. Her haughty, furious face passed down through the generations. Cara touches the screen, strokes the cheek with a shaking hand.

The movie star rolls over in her sleep, groaning, and Cara starts as if waking. Her hand has left a long smudge on the screen. She rubs it away with her sleeve and goes back to her room.

★　　★　　★

The phone wakes her again at 5:00 a.m., and she holds the receiver sleepily to her ear. "Try to go back to sleep," she says. "You have two hours until the car." Through the receiver she hears light, frightened breathing.

Cara pads along the corridor and lets herself into the movie star's suite. The movie star snores heavily, arms flung out as if in flight. Another of her movies is playing. It must be a marathon. On screen the movie star looks across a crowded bar in astonishment, at a woman who looks exactly like her. It is the one where she plays a pair of long-lost twins. She hated making that one, Cara remembers. So much work. The stand-in who read the other twin's lines was the wrong height so the eyeline was always off. The movie star is caught forever gazing slightly to the left of where her long-lost sister stands, as if she can't bear to look into her face and feel so much.

Cara watches the movie star sleeping deeply for a moment. Then she closes the door silently behind her. Another one. The calls happen several times a night, now. Cara pictures Greta standing like a statue in the dim lobby, receiver pressed to her ear, as the pastel lights move over her frozen smile.

Whatever Greta means by them, the calls have become a strange comfort to Cara. She sits and listens to the silence for minutes on end, stroking the old-fashioned spiral cord. She pretends the dead are calling. Her brother or her daughter. "Rose," she whispers into the vague crackle of the line, "I miss you." And the silence seems to hold an answer.

★　　★　　★

The movie star picks at quartered pieces of grape. She went to a club with some of the other actors last night. She raises her dark glasses to look at Cara. She has startling white compresses under her eyes, snail venom patches to take down the puffiness. "Can we do the touch thing?"

"You're hungover," Cara says. "It will make you sick."

"If you don't do it I'll throw up in your lap." The movie star grins. Not her pretty, public smile, but the rude healthy grin of the girl she once was, who built dams in streams and caught lizards in her quick hands, who stayed out all day and almost wept when it was time to come inside at night. "Please, Mama." She called Cara that when she was little, before she understood the way things were between them.

"Ok," Cara says, "it's your funeral."

Cara thinks for a moment, then goes to the heavy earthenware jar that stops the door to the suite's vast living room. The jar is full of peacock feathers, green and sheeny blue. Cara draws out a single quill.

She concentrates, makes her mind an arrow, points it at the movie star. Slowly, Cara traces the feather over her palm, thrilling at the light touch, barely-there. Across the table, she hears the movie star catch her breath. Cara raises the peacock feather to her face, traces it over her closed eyelids, her earlobes. "Sure you can handle this?" Cara asks.

"Bring it on," the movie star says.

Cara pushes the soft silky end of the feather gently into her own ear. Her ear canal is unbearably full of whispering touch. Ten feet away the movie star shrieks and claws at her ear. "Ok, stop," she begs, almost weeping with laughter.

Cara smiles and grazes the inside of her ear with the feather, again and again, as the movie star screams and rubs furiously at the side of her head. Cara is laughing too, so she doesn't notice for a moment that the movie star has stopped. She looks at Cara with her blank blue gaze.

"You'll be there, won't you?" the movie star says. "You'll probably organise everything perfectly. My funeral."

*　　*　　*

They discovered the game when she was a girl and had not yet become the movie star.

It was a hot spring day and the jacaranda threw frilled shadow on the edges of the softball field. The smell of warm earth rose up from under the bleachers. The movie star's mother sat silent like a ghost. Cara stood beside her. The leash hung silver about her neck, fastened to the bleachers. They both watched as the small figure ran base to base. She was going like the wind. Cara felt her heart swell with pride at her grace, her speed. But the ball was chasing her, and as she slid into third in a cloud of dirt, the kid on base hurled himself towards it.

There was a sound like a carrot broken in two. The girl's face was a mess of blood and dirt. She didn't cry as she got up, knees dusted brown and palms bleeding. She was trying so hard not to. The movie star's mother started as if waking from a dream. She was already deep into the pills by then. She rarely saw anything that was not inside herself. Her face was blank as she walked towards her daughter, too upright, like a puppet with the string drawn tight. The mother put a vague hand on her daughter's shoulder. The girl did cry then, tears mingling with the blood on her chin.

Her mother stood for a moment longer and then walked off the field, not back to the bleachers but into the trees, in the direction of the car. She could only handle so much at a time.

Cara wanted to run out into the field, wanted to take the girl in her arms and soothe her. She knew she couldn't. The leash held her in her place by the bleachers. But she wished for it so hard she could almost feel the shape of the small, familiar silky skull under her hand. *Don't cry*, she thought. *Don't let them see that.* Then Cara saw the yellow-blonde head move, as if leaning into a caress. She looked at Cara, and smiled a little through the blood and tears. Cara caught her breath. She could feel the warmth of the sun in the hair under her palm.

Cara was scared, when they got home, that the girl would tell her mother. But she didn't – not that day, or any day since. She and Cara keep the secret.

She doesn't know if others have it; this connection, this vicarious touch. She has never had it with anyone else, not even with Rose.

★   ★   ★

Cara is crossing the lobby with an armful of freesias when the man arrests Greta. He wears another beautiful suit of herringbone. He does it quietly with a word in Greta's ear. He does not touch her. Greta screams as if he had. Then she whispers, "I didn't do it." Her eyelash paint runs down her face in green and blue streaks.

Cara drifts nearer. She says to Greta, quietly, "I enjoyed my midnight phone calls."

Greta looks at her, mouth a skewed 'O'. "What?" she says. "What phone calls?"

"She's been harassing me," Cara says to the man in the herringbone suit. "Nuisance calls to my room at all hours of the night."

"We'll make sure we go into that in due course," he says smoothly. Cara can tell that they won't. It's not important, what happens to Cara. She is property.

"I didn't call you," Greta pleads, tearful, as if that would mend all. Cara looks at her in surprise. She can see that Greta is telling the truth.

The man holds out his hand. Greta puts her silver nametag into his open palm. He follows her respectfully out of the glass doors, into the street. A black van is waiting.

As expected they find the movie star's jewels in Greta's bag with a copy of the call sheet. That's how she knew the movie star's schedule. There are only seven pieces of jewellery, however; the platinum and sapphire cuff is missing. Greta must have sold it already. "That was my favourite," the movie star says. "These other things are just trash. I'll donate them to charity when we get home." Cara knows that whichever piece was missing, it would have been the movie star's favourite.

Cara packs the recovered jewels into their bags, into their boxes, the travel safe.

"I could have been killed," the movie star says once more, standing before the mirror. She smoothes the dark wing of her eyebrow with a licked finger. Her cheeks are plump, still luminous with the residual effects of the transfer.

★   ★   ★

Shooting is finished. Cara packs the movie star's shoes, encasing each one in an individual silk bag. She will be glad to get back to Los Angeles. There are special parks in the city where they don't lace the air so heavily. Cara can go outside, see the sun. People in California want her to feel she has rights. The old world has no such concerns. Maybe it's more honest that way.

The travel unit is waiting in Cara's room, a long silver cylinder. Its mouth gapes wide. Cara gets in and the lid slides silently closed, sealing her in darkness. There is a brief hiss, and then the synthetic scent of roses. The hormones are designed to smell like flowers. The light mist settles. Her skin absorbs it quickly. Sleep nudges at her. She is alone at last. The implant can't see in the dark.

As she drifts, Cara recalls the tinny bite of the safe as it gave to her teeth. Dreamily she slides up her sleeve, stroking the platinum and sapphire cuff where it is fastened high on her forearm. She found a way to commemorate the moment, after all. For some reason she didn't want to leave this with the rest of the jewellery, in Greta's bag.

The cuff is valuable but that's not why Cara took it. She can't sell it – she can't even look at it in the light, unless she wants the implant to record it. She does not know exactly why she kept it. If she is caught it will be the end of her. Cara fingers the fine mesh of the platinum. She can't give it up. The movie star's voice echoes in her mind: *I love you, Cara.*

Cara thinks, *You can't love someone you own.* But she thinks of the little girl on the softball pitch, her face wet with tears. There are different kinds of bondage.

Sleep begins to take her in its dark folds. She slips into memory. Firelight on a cave wall. Elk blood runs hot between her teeth. Rose, her brother's dead smile. The time before the weak came, with their poison mist and their pills, before they hobbled her limbs and took her teeth. The fear that lived in all their eyes, then – those eyes looked up at her, not down on her as they do now. When the powerful still ruled the earth, from the dark.

Cara hopes the dead will call again; that she will hear their beloved, cold breath through the receiver, through years and time and space; feel them reaching for her with their silence, telling her that she is not forgotten. She hopes and hopes.

BRANCH LINE

Paul Finch

He'd been 'Ricky Gates' when he was at school. Now, he preferred the more adult 'Richard Gates'. Which was understandable. He was fifty-nine, after all.

While they didn't find him as odious as they'd expected, his presence was discomforting. He was a hefty man, expansive around the gut, but with a barrel chest, immense shoulders, big arms and heavy-knuckled hands. He probably only stood about 5'11", but he was seated when they entered, so it was difficult to be sure. His hair was long, lank and grey, his jaw grizzled, his face pale and pockmarked. He was rolling his own at the time, a delicate process, which he worked at carefully, not stopping even when they sat down. He watched them intently though, his eyes deep-set and red-rimmed.

"Let me guess," he finally said. "You want to know about Brian O'Rourke?" He didn't bother waiting for an answer. "I understand. A young boy disappears in curious circumstances... curious but also mundane. An ordinary afternoon during the summer holidays, the sun shining, the sky blue. An everyday location – a little isolated, but not especially far from town. Mysteries of this nature rarely fade, do they? It's only logical that questions will be asked – time and again – of the last person allegedly to see him alive."

He sat back, his rollup dangling between gnarled, nicotine-stained fingers.

One of them leaned forward, offering a light. He accepted, chugging for a few seconds. The cigarette was unfiltered and smelled foul. One of the visitors coughed. This was 2019. Indoor smoking was rarely permitted these days.

Gates smiled.

"Alas," he said. "I can only tell you the same thing again. My statement will be exactly as it was that long-ago summer of 1973. Not one single aspect of it has changed. You know why?" He smiled again, more broadly, showing stubby yellow teeth. "Because, incredible as you'll find it, it's the absolute truth."

★   ★   ★

It begins with a ghost story.

Have you heard this tale? About the old Branch Line that skirted the eastern edge of our borough? You know it vaguely. Then, let me appraise you fully.

First of all, you need to think of the Branch Line as a railway ring road, which allowed coal and other freight bound for Preston and Blackburn to head north and at the same time avoid clogging up the passenger workings in our town centre. But it also functioned as a short-cut from the Manchester line into central Lancashire, so from time to time it transported passengers as well, and that's a crucial point.

It was discontinued in the late 1950s, but by 1973 the rails and sleepers still occupied the old track bed, albeit forgotten and overgrown. It ran along a deep cutting, which was accessible on the east side of town from the spoil-land encircling what was then the defunct Alexandra Pit. From there, it led several miles southeast to northwest, traversing industrial land initially but after that farmland and finally woods that once used to be part of the Hanbury Hall estate but which by the 1970s were owned by the local authority, and therefore were wild and untended. Finally, it crossed Twenty Bridges, as we called it, a disused Victorian viaduct. It wasn't possible to go further along the Branch Line than this as the viaduct was unsafe, and entry to it barricaded with barbed wire.

So far so scenic, but where does the ghost story come in?

Well, I'm getting to that.

We all knew about the Branch Line. We'd grown up with a rumour that sometime in the past, a young bride from Manchester was on her way north to spend her honeymoon in Blackpool when tragedy struck. She was still in her wedding garb when her new husband advised her that this was a marriage of convenience and that his heart lay with another. The bride was so dismayed she threw herself from the train and was instantly killed. No one knew at which point along the Branch Line this was supposed to have happened, but if you check some of our old local newspapers you'll see it was a genuine event dating to 12 April 1894. Julie-Anne Merridale was her name, and she did indeed take her own life by jumping from a train on her wedding day.

All of this is hard fact. Less factual was the story soon circulating that her ghost now haunted that stretch of line, a story which refused to die and in fact spread like wildfire once the Branch Line was abandoned. By the time I was at school, everyone in our town knew about it. Indeed, it had grown more terrifying with each telling. There were rumours that several people who'd attempted to walk the derelict line from its south end to its north had simply disappeared, never to be seen again.

"Well done for adding some background creepiness," you're doubtless thinking. "But every town has a story like this: a genuine tragedy mythologised for the amusement of juveniles. What we really want to know is why you and Brian O'Rourke went up to the Branch Line together on the afternoon of 25 July 1973, and how it was that only you returned."

Well, to get close to understanding this, you need to know what Brian and my relationship was. In 1973, we were at St. Aloysius's High School, a Catholic comprehensive in the heart of our town. We were in our third year, which made us thirteen years old. Most people are already aware of this, of course: that we were schoolboys together. But they make a mistake when they refer to us as schoolmates.

You see, Brian O'Rourke didn't have any mates.

I'd been at primary school with him before middle school, so I'd known him from the beginning. At first glance, everything about him seemed normal. He was average height, lean, inoffensive to look at, and his school uniform was never less than immaculate. But he had pale, angular features, which gave him an odd gaunt appearance, while his mouse-brown hair was severely shorn, which, in the early 1970s, with everyone else having long hair, made him an object of ridicule. Of course, although this invited mockery, the actual *dislike* originated elsewhere.

The first person who ever punched me in the face was Brian O'Rourke. We were in the infants, no more than five years old, and a dispute over a crayon box led him to snatch it off me and throw a right hook. While it wasn't a hard blow, it surprised and upset me; at that age no one else had laid a hand on me but my parents. Hitting people, or threatening to hit them, became Brian O'Rourke's stock-in-trade during those early days, though he never gained the reputation for being a bully because it didn't last. Within a relatively short time, most of the other boys, including me, were at least as tall as he was, and many of them brawnier. But when he was no longer able to enforce his will through brutality, he replaced it with slyness. This was a child who would happily tell tales to the teacher if getting you in trouble suited his purpose, or who'd spread lies about you, accusing you of saying things you hadn't, to try and break up friendships he was jealous of.

However, even this low-level vindictiveness faded as primary school progressed. Because Brian had begun to realise that childish games like these were gaining him nothing and costing him a lot, and that at some point soon he'd actually *need* friends — because the spectre of middle school was approaching and then he'd have a whole new world of hostility to deal with.

The reason for this was simple. Our primary school wasn't the only one that sent pupils to St. Aloysius's. There were several, and at two of these other schools Brian O'Rourke's mother and father were teachers. And even by the standards of the time, they were tyrants. Mr. O'Rourke had his own cane, and he gave people 'the whack' for just about everything. Mrs. O'Rourke was in the habit of hitting wayward pupils across the face with a Bible, usually after quoting some snippet of wisdom from it, which would be meaningless to a youngster so terrorised he could barely think straight. At St. Aloysius's Brian was going to have to answer for this to a procession of children who were older and bigger than he was.

I know what you're thinking. Nothing I'm telling you is allaying your suspicion that I was responsible for Brian's disappearance that July afternoon. Perhaps you're wondering if my own grudges against him had gone deeper than anyone knew?

I can understand why you might think that, but you'd be wrong.

By 1973, our third year at St. Aloysius's, the dynamics had changed again. Brian had been chastised throughout his first two years and was mostly now ignored. Perhaps in this regard people were still punishing him. There is no sadder figure than a solitary kid standing by the schoolyard wall when all the others are running around enjoying themselves. But he'd even adapted to this status in time, becoming studious and developing hobbies — and to an extent this brought him back into acceptability.

We were all now doing what we called our 'options', which meant we'd finally started our O-Level courses, and as part of this, there were after-school sessions for those who were struggling, with some of the more advanced pupils volunteering to stay behind and assist. Brian was one of these, and he helped me with my Maths. I wouldn't say this made us friends, but as we'd never actually been enemies – I hadn't joined in the feeding frenzy when we'd first arrived at St. Aloysius's – it didn't do our relationship any harm. At the same time, one of those hobbies I mentioned was hill-walking and hiking, and Brian got involved in the school Rambling Club, of which I was also a member. I was surprised by this because our trips to North Wales and the Lake District were pretty strenuous, and whereas I'd become a decent rugby player during my time at middle school, Brian had been useless at sport from the start and was still pretty inept when it came to anything physical. But it seemed to be something he was determined to try, mainly I suspect because he was tired of life without company. And as it turned out, his first attempt to get chatting with a bunch of us while we were on such a trip paid immediate dividends.

It was the end of the summer term, the last weekend before our holidays, and about thirty of us had traipsed along Striding Edge and were now descending into Glenridding. I was with the three lads I was closest to in the Rambling Club: Mark Phelps, Andrew Fletcher and John Doogan. We'd all been at primary school together and were still close buddies. Probably for that same reason, the rest of them were just about tolerating Brian O'Rourke, who was hanging about on our periphery.

Our conversation ranged over all the usual subjects, from football to films to rock music... to sex, or rather to men's magazines, or 'mucky books' as we called them, which were the only experience of sex that we'd had. We'd first become aware of these in recent years, and though we only had limited access to them, they'd fast turned into objects of fascination. At this moment Phelpsy was waxing lyrical about a dog-eared magazine he'd discovered under his older brother's bed.

Needless to say, the rest of us were engrossed, our tongues hanging out.

I know it sounds pathetic, but you need to understand how much a contradiction in terms our experience of life in the early 1970s was. We were teenagers, fizzing with hormones, but most of us had been raised in Catholic households so prudish that the mere appearance of a bare bottom on evening TV would see us shouted at and sent from the room as if it was somehow our fault. Yet the world had changed dramatically even during my short lifetime. In 1960 *Playboy*'s centrefolds were so coy they wouldn't even shed their bikinis, but only thirteen years later, the average men's mag could have doubled for a gynaecology manual. And yet the likes of us still only caught glimpses of this: half a minute of *Benny Hill* before our mums switched it off; a fleeting glance past some bloke's shoulder on the bus as he drooled over Page 3; the billboards outside the cinema whenever a *Carry On* film was playing, showing Barbara Windsor's cleavage and Liz Fraser's stockings...

We knew it was out there – it tortured us with its proximity – yet we still couldn't reach it.

"I saw a massive pile of mucky books recently," Brian chimed in.

We glanced around at him, a switch of attention so abrupt that he looked surprised and flustered.

He shrugged awkwardly. "I found them in a bin in the backs near our house. They were in this plastic bag. There were loads of 'em. I've never seen as many."

As our silence persisted his confidence grew, as he realised that for the first time in his life he had an interested audience.

"I think they're imports," he said. "Because they're hardcore."

We didn't know what 'import' or 'hardcore' actually meant, but we had some vague idea that they probably meant *really* mucky.

Inevitably he was asked where the magazines were now and when could the rest of us see them, and though he didn't exactly become evasive, I got the feeling this hadn't been part of his plan.

"I've... erm, hidden them," he replied. "And I'm not saying where because I don't want them to go walkies. But when I get back from my holidays, I'll give you all a call and you can come round."

It was a bit surreal, the thought we'd all be sitting at home, impatiently waiting for Brian O'Rourke to ring us and give us permission to visit him, but if nothing else, he'd known how to sell a mucky book to us.

It turned out he was going on holiday with his parents almost straightaway, and as the following fortnight dragged on and the rest of us got involved in other summer activities, interest faded. I also remembered his evasiveness about where his stash was hidden, and started to suspect he'd been spinning us a line so that he could get in with the crowd.

Either way, I was surprised when on the morning of 25 July, the phone rang in our house and my mother called up to me that it was Brian O'Rourke. I lifted the receiver with mixed feelings. On one hand, I hadn't expected this to happen and felt a resurgence of excitement, but on the other, I hoped it wouldn't become a regular thing – Brian O'Rourke ringing me at home.

"If you're interested, I'm going up to the Branch Line this morning," he said.

I was bewildered. "What're you going up there for?"

"You wanted to look at those mucky books, didn't you?"

"You hid them all the way up there?"

"Well, yeah." He sounded surprised. Despite his reputation for being a liar, he never seemed prepared for the possibility that people might doubt him. "They're... like I say, they're really nasty. I can't risk being caught."

Something about this whole business seemed improbable. But he'd told us he'd let us know when he was available, and the Branch Line was only a couple of miles from where I lived. On top of that, all I'd really planned for that day was to loaf about the house.

"I've rung the others," he added.

That decided it. If nothing else, larking around on the Branch Line would be different.

We arranged to meet at 11 a.m. and headed up to the Alexandra Pit separately because we lived in different parts of town. These days it's common for youngsters to wear backpacks, but it was unusual then. Nevertheless, when I arrived, getting off the bus opposite the old Alexandra Pub, taking a path between two rows of houses and climbing over a gate onto the cindery wasteland beyond, I found Brian waiting there with a pack on his back.

"I assumed you wouldn't have thought to bring any lunch," he said, "so I've made some sandwiches for us both, and brought a bottle of pop we can share."

I was gobsmacked. It was thoughtful of him, I suppose, but it was nannyish too. Plus, that was the kind of preparation you made for hiking trips in the Lakes or Wales, not for checking out a derelict railway line on your home patch.

I made this point, but he shook his head. "You know what the Branch Line's like. We'll have to be ready for anything. We'll be up here quite some time, I expect."

Personally, I *didn't* expect that. The Branch Line was about three miles long; as an energetic thirteen-year-old, I could have covered that distance in an hour. But I now noticed that, while I was wearing a Wrangler jacket, T-shirt, jeans and trainers, he was in the Rambling Club's unofficial uniform of plaid shirt, zipped-up cagoule, corduroy trousers and mountain boots. He clearly intended to drag this thing out. To make it an epic adventure.

"When are the others getting here?" I asked.

"They're not," he replied in the sort of uninterested voice that suggested it wasn't worth mentioning again. "Just said they weren't bothered."

It was this kind of thing that always saw Brian O'Rourke come unstuck. Despite the many harsh lessons he'd learned about his lowly place in our world, he still couldn't help but talk one-to-one as if you were the follower and he was the leader.

"So, what you told me on the phone was a downright lie?" I said.

"No." He tried to stay calm, as if it still didn't matter, but his cheeks had tinged red. "I said I rang them. I didn't say they were coming."

I shook my head with disbelief. Mr. Slippery was at it again.

He tried to turn placatory as we trudged towards the railway cutting. "At least, this way we'll have the mags all to ourselves."

I was too vexed to reply. There was still time to dump him, of course. All I had to do was tell him to shove it and head back. It wouldn't have cost me anything apart from the bus fare. But one of the reasons I hadn't joined in the persecution of Brian O'Rourke when we'd first arrived at St. Aloysius's was that I'd felt sorry for the guy. He'd been ostracised so much during his childhood that it was hard not to feel something. Yes, he'd brought it on himself, but he'd been raised in a household where his sole role-model was a dominant alpha male, and yet his own cack-handed efforts to achieve that status had left him all but blacklisted.

Even by 1973 no one liked him, and he was painfully aware of it. That had to hurt.

We descended a slope of compact clinker dotted with tufts of scrub-thorn, and at the bottom, perhaps thirty feet down, stepped onto the track bed. Initially, the soil here was so barren that the railway lines were fully exposed, the rails broken and dislodged but dwindling away along the flat-floored cutting in a straight line ahead of us. I must admit that, up to this point, I hadn't even considered the Branch Line's eerie reputation. But several hundred yards along it, thick groundcover appeared, and soon the only sound was the swishing of foliage as we kicked our way through. A short time after that, trees and thickets crowded to the tops of either embankment, which indicated we were past the colliery spoil-land and the housing estates adjoining it (and therefore the nearest next bunch of people). It briefly occurred to me that this wasn't perhaps the best idea. Okay, there was going to be a reward for us here, but already it felt as if we were very alone.

We pressed on, the sun beating down. The Branch Line wasn't an obviously scary place, but a couple of times I glanced around as if expecting to see a face peering down from the greenery at the top, or looked behind me... expecting what? I'm not sure.

"What reasons did the others give?" I said, trying to distract myself.

Brian had fallen quiet, still aware of my disapproval. Now he shrugged. "Just said they couldn't be arsed."

"Pull the other one." I glared directly ahead. "Phelpsy would crawl through broken glass to see some tits and fannies. Fletch was up for it too, and Doogie."

His face flushed again as he chewed over what to say.

"The thing is," he finally said, "I didn't get in touch with them."

"I guessed as much. Why not?"

"I don't trust that lot. These books are... well, they're illegal in this country, which makes 'em valuable. They'd have nicked 'em the moment I turned my back."

That had half a ring of truth to it. As I've mentioned, mucky books were a currency back then. And if this guy really *was* sitting on a stockpile, and they really *were* as good as he said, the likes of Phelpsy wouldn't be able to resist helping himself.

But I was still angered by his deception. "The problem is, Brian... what if we meet some gang of dickheads, and there's only two of us?"

"Oh, come on!" he scoffed. "If we *do* meet some dickheads, what use would Phelpsy, Fletch and Doogie have been?"

He had a point there too. None of them had a rep for being fighters. But I was still unsettled by the revelation he hadn't even asked them. Again, it seemed a bit non-laddish, if such a word exists, that he'd rather knock around with me on my own than with the whole crowd. I didn't get a chance to articulate this concern though, because Brian now spoke again, his tone subtly different.

"You know what I think? I think what you're really scared of is that stupid ghost story."

"No, I'm not," I responded quickly.

"Course you are!" he sneered, which I seriously didn't like. That this guy could mock me, when I'd been just about the only person who hadn't beaten the crap out of him over the last few years! The only trouble was that he wasn't completely wrong.

"You don't have to be embarrassed about it," he continued, placating again. "The stories *are* pretty scary. Did you know... about ten years ago, some hippies came up here looking to pitch a camp." His face wrinkled with disgust, no doubt echoing his parents' views about hippies. "There were three blokes and this bird. They wanted somewhere to shag her. That's what they do, hippies. They set camps up, smoke some dope and then gangbang the birds till their tits go red."

I mused on this. After some of the hippy chicks I'd seen around town, that didn't sound like the worst idea.

"Anyway," he said, "everyone told them they shouldn't come up here. The Branch Line doesn't lead anywhere, and it's haunted. But these hippies, they think they know fucking everything. No one hears anything from them for about two days. And then suddenly, the bird turns up at The Fox and Badger... you know, on Vicarage Lane?"

I nodded, intrigued. I wasn't sure there'd been any such thing as hippies ten years earlier, but The Fox and Badger was a real pub, and it was accessible from Loomin Lane, a farm track which ran underneath the Branch Line about a mile ahead of us.

"None of the blokes were ever seen again," Brian added. "But this bird... she was starkers, and her hair had turned snow-white. Her bush too."

"Get out of it!" I snorted.

"It's true!"

"Her bush!"

"Everyone's heard that story. I'm surprised you haven't."

"What did she say had happened?"

"She didn't. She'd gone totally nuts." Brian was po-faced as he recalled the tragedy. "All they got out of her was this baby babble. She finished up in a loony bin, and no one's had a sensible word out of her since."

I decided that this was a pack of lies. I felt certain I'd have heard about it if some hippy chick had turned up naked at a local pub with her hair and pubes bleached white. Even so, it was a disturbing story. Again, I was aware how heavy the summer heat lay on the deep foliage to either side of us. Much of it had now advanced down the embankments, enclosing us even more, creating a green tunnel-like atmosphere.

"I don't know if I believe that one either, if I'm honest," Brian said. "Sounds a bit lurid."

I nodded, unsure what 'lurid' meant, though it sounded like the right kind of word.

"There's another story which comes from a bit further back," he added. "And this one I actually *do* believe because my dad told me."

Must be true, I thought, *if it comes from mad Mr. O'Rourke.*

"Back in the early Fifties, when trains were still coming along here, he knew this bloke who worked in the old signal box."

"I didn't know there was a signal box," I said.

"It's not too far ahead of where we are now. Third of a mile, I'd say."

I squinted forward, that disorienting, straight-as-an-arrow cutting tapering into a distant indistinct haze. Here and there, the rails broke through the vegetation, but you didn't need that to know you were following a railway line, or what remained of one. In that regard, it didn't seem too unlikely there'd be an abandoned signal box.

"Anyway," Brian said, "this bloke worked the night shift. On his own, of course."

"Bet that was bloody boring," I said.

"Spooky, more like. Didn't bother him though... because his wife had recently died, so he was happy to work nights. Until something happened that really put the shits up him."

He let that hang.

"Go on," I said. "What was it?"

"He starts hearing someone calling his name. Outside, on the railway. Whenever he looks out, he sees nothing... just darkness. But it keeps happening. Night after night. And it's like a woman's voice. First couple of nights, he just assumes it's some kids messing about."

"Some kids and a *woman*?" I said dubiously.

"Well, you know... older kids. Some set of dickheads trespassing on the railway. But he can't work out how they know his name. The last night, the night before he quits, he hears it again. This time it's a lot closer, like, whatever it is, it's right outside. Now, he doesn't dare look, because suddenly he doesn't *want* to see what it is. But the next thing, he hears this clattering on the rungs of the ladder leading up to the signal box door..."

Despite his OTT spooky tone, I found my hair creeping.

"Anyway, he rushes to the door and puts the bolt on – and just in time. Immediately, the door starts rattling, the latch going up and down. He hears this voice again, calling his name. And while it sounds female, it's horrible as well... it's like a squawk, like a crow or something."

He lapsed into silence as we plodded along.

"How did he live to tell the tale?" I eventually asked.

Brian's expression became serious, almost reverential. "He dropped to his knees and prayed. First to his dead wife... you know, asking for protection. Then to God himself. And this thing... well, it just went away."

Looking back on it, that was the obvious way a church-going hardman like Mr. O'Rourke would have wrapped up a ghost story. But while I don't dismiss the possibility of a benign deity, even as a child I knew that if it was that simple there'd be no disasters in the world. That said, it didn't seem completely implausible that a prayer could turn away evil. After all, that was how most of the Hammer movies were resolved.

"And he never worked there again?" I said.

"Would *you* have?"

I couldn't answer that, just glanced behind me. We must have come a mile by now, which meant we weren't even halfway along the Branch Line, though we were deep into it. I had no idea where, if we were to cut out of it at this point, we would actually go. Even if we were on the Hanbury Hall estate, it was extensive woodland crisscrossed by a maze of footpaths that could have led us anywhere.

"Just out of interest," he said, "you had your first wank yet?"

If anything could have distracted me from my disquiet, it was a question like that.

I glanced at him, stunned, but Brian was now chirpy and businesslike. "Don't be embarrassed if you haven't. I'll show you how."

Even anticipating the dozens of naked women I was about to feast my eyes upon, this gave me pause for thought. Yes, I was eager. But it had never occurred to me that I was going to be expected to play with myself. Certainly not with Brian O'Rourke offering instructions.

"Anyway, we're here," he said, stopping abruptly.

I glanced around, puzzled. Lush heavy leaf hung to left and right, the cutting still tapering away in front and behind. Nothing looked any different from the last God-knew-how-many-thousands of yards we'd traversed. "You sure?"

"That big stone marks the spot." He pointed down at a heavy piece of squared-off masonry half buried just to the left of the track. "Okay, right..." For some reason now, his posture was stiffer, and he wore a slight frown.

"What's up?" I asked.

"Nothing." He hunkered down and pushed open a dense mass of knotweed, reaching through it and pulling out a raggedy bin-liner that was bulging at its seams. Immediately, I saw splashes of colour through the rents in it and for half a second went a little dizzy. Clearly, there weren't just magazines in there, there were *lots* of magazines, and yet all the way here I'd half assumed he'd been conning me, that I'd been lured to the Branch Line mainly to be Brian's new friend. *This* was a very agreeable surprise.

And yet his body language was strange. He stood rigid, clinging to the bag with both hands. Suddenly, his eyes were roving everywhere; he would not look me in the face.

"Thing is," he said, "you've got to be grown up about this."

"Yeah, sure." I wasn't really listening; I just wanted to get to the girls.

"No, Ricky... we're not kids anymore." His tone intensified, but he still wouldn't look at me. "This is adult material, and we have to behave like adults when we use it."

"Okay..."

"I'm serious. If I'm going to let you look at this stuff, I have to know I can trust you."

"Brian, what the hell are you talking about?"

Now he *did* look at me, his expression grave. "This is *our* secret, Ricky. As far as I'm concerned, it'll only *ever* be our secret. No one else will know about it."

"Just open the fucking bag!"

He gazed at me hard, as if unnerved by my impatience. Finally he flung his arms apart and the bin-liner fell to the ground. It was so tattered that it burst open and maybe thirty magazines spilled out.

I dropped to my haunches, grinning like a chimp.

But it didn't take long for my enthusiasm to flag. I might have been young and immature where sexual matters were concerned, but I was old enough to know that the sight of naked male buttocks did nothing for me, much less the sight of naked male appendages, either flaccid or otherwise (and given that this merchandise clearly *was* imported, the vast majority were otherwise).

"These... these are poofter mags," I said, glancing up.

He watched me nervously.

"Where are the ones with the birds in?" I demanded.

"You sure that's what you want, Ricky?"

"Yeah, I'm sure." I was frustrated and bewildered, but I still tried to laugh as I got back to my feet. "You saying you brought me all the way out here to look at some dicks and balls? What's wrong with you...?"

And then it dawned on me.

My mouth sagged open, my eyes widened in shock.

He came forward urgently, grabbing me by the wrist. "Look, Ricky... you of all people. You must understa..."

"*Me of all people?* What the fuck, Brian!" I yanked my arm free.

"It's not so bad," he said. "It's really not."

A whole rush of understanding came over me.

About why he'd not told the others. About why he'd never dared hide this find anywhere near his own home. A copy of *Penthouse* falling out of the cupboard might have merited a thick ear, but *this*...?

"You're a queer," I stated flatly. "A fucking bender."

"No, I'm *not!*" he insisted, his cheeks blazing. "Don't say that, Ricky."

"Or what... you going to hit me with your pink furry slippers?"

"Look..." He scuttled back and forth like a deranged crab, before swooping on the heap of glossy mags and grabbing two, hanging them open as he offered them to me.

"Just try it, yeah? Just give it a go."

"You've got to be kidding." I backed away along the cutting.

"Ricky, wait!" he pleaded, almost tearful. "Look... it's just sex. It'll turn you on. Look... I just thought we could have a bit of fun together. To see what it's like."

"And you're seriously telling me you're not queer?"

"Where are you going?" He was actually crying now.

"Where do you think?"

"It's not that way."

"The bridge over Loomin Lane is this way. I can still get home."

"Look... just hang on."

I couldn't take any more. The shock revelation, the predatory nature of his bringing me here, how dense I was to have perceived all these warning signs and not read them, and now tears – genuine, honest-to-goodness tears – streaming down his pathetic face.

I turned and walked forcefully away, determined to put distance between us.

"*Ricky, wait!*"

I glanced back and saw him crouched down, frantically trying to shove magazines back into what remained of the bin-liner. Hurriedly he straightened up and slung the sack one-handed into the undergrowth, before running after me.

"Look, I'm not queer!" he insisted.

"Save it for your mum and dad. Maybe they'll believe you... after your dad's knocked your fucking brains out on the shelf over the fireplace."

"You're not going to tell anyone!" He was coming up behind me fast, but there was a plea in his voice rather than a threat.

"Am I not?" I said over my shoulder.

"*You* came up here too."

"Yeah, because you lied to me. And I've got a shedload of witnesses. All the lads heard you say these were proper girlie mags."

"I thought we could at least be mates!"

Sensing that he was right behind me, I spun to face him. He stopped short, only to stand there sniffling, wiping at his tear-begrimed cheeks.

"Look, I've always liked you, Ricky. You're the only lad who's not given me a shit time while I've been at school."

"Brian... treating you like a human being was not inviting you to have sex with me."

"It's not about the sex. Look... that was nothing. It was just supposed to be an ice-breaker."

"An ice-breaker?" I shook my head, before turning and walking again.

"We can still be mates." He hurried to keep up. "I mean close mates. Proper mates."

"Once and for all, Brian, I'm not what you're looking for."

"But I've no one else to talk to about it."

I glanced back one final time, feeling there was no option but to tell him to piss off, that I'd had enough of his weird, over-the-top shite – only to stop in my tracks.

Brian's look of torture briefly faded. And then he realised I was staring past him.

"Someone's here," I said.

He turned fast. Presumably, like me, his first fear was that, whoever it was, they might have been close enough to overhear us.

Half a second later that seemed like a minor concern.

A figure was approaching along the cutting. Initially it was too far away for me to observe any detail, but all the time I'd been here I'd been glancing over my shoulder, trying to suppress an odd feeling that someone might be following us. And each time there'd been no one there. Until now.

"Who is it?" I said, shielding my eyes against the sun.

Brian didn't reply. Although the figure was still a couple of hundred yards away, there seemed to be something not quite right about it.

I presumed it was a woman, because it was wearing a long dress or gown. But although it moved slowly and awkwardly, it appeared to be advancing at pace. In what seemed the blink of an eye it almost halved the distance between us, and now we could see the figure in much more detail: how the dress hung to the floor in ragged folds; how, even from this range, the limbs and body inside it looked emaciated; how a veil hung over the face. And how, like the dress, that veil was an ugly green-grey colour, even though once it had clearly been white.

Slowly we began retreating.

When the figure waved a gloved hand, I half-relaxed, thinking it was Phelpsy or Doogie, playing some stupid game. Except that neither Phelpsy nor Doogie knew we were up here. Nobody did.

Then it called to us.

The voice was gruff, coarse, and the sound it made was more a squawk than a word.

We ran.

Literally turned and went pell-mell along the abandoned railway line. There was no shouting or gasping; we were dumbstruck but suffused with energy. We must have run a hundred metres in record time; Brian, who was no athlete, staying neck-and-neck with me. And yet we barely knew where we were headed for. The bridge over Loomin Lane was somewhere ahead, but I didn't know how far. I glanced back once, an inner voice telling me there'd be no one there, that it had all been a mistake, a misunderstanding.

But that inner voice was wrong.

Not only was the figure still present, it was closer than before despite our headlong charge, maybe less than a hundred yards behind us. And still it wasn't running; it hobbled and stumbled, and yet was visibly gaining on us. Only now did words burst from my throbbing, phlegm-filled chest.

"Run... bloody run!"

We did, and it called to us again. That same raucous, crow-like voice now so close that I could hear what it was saying.

"*Brian.*"

"Jesus!" I shouted. "It wants *you.*"

Brian wasn't listening. He kept abreast with me but was evidently in trouble, froth seeping from his tight-clamped mouth, eyes bugging from a face turned lobster-red.

"*Brian!*" it cried again.

"This way!" Brian shrieked, veering sharply to the right, tripping as he tried to cross the rails, stumbling forward clumsily, just about keeping his feet.

On that side, half hidden amid towering foliage, stood a drab, decayed cabin perched atop the rusted frame of an understructure, its windows covered with plywood hoardings. It was the old signal box, the relic of the ladder still affixed to its right-hand side. At the top I saw a catwalk and an entry door hanging open on rank darkness.

"In there?" I shouted, dismayed.

"It's the only way," he panted. "We can lock the door."

I followed him. It seemed like a lunatic plan, boxing ourselves in, but by now the thing was perhaps only thirty yards behind us.

Brian climbed the ladder first, blundering his way up in useless, knock-kneed fashion, constantly losing his footing. I hung below him, screaming and swearing. Any second I expected my legs or feet to be snatched from beneath me.

But the next thing, we were on the catwalk together. It creaked and tilted down as if about to break loose. Frantic, we barged through the door into the musty interior.

It was dim in there, the only light spearing down through an open skylight in the roof. Brian banged the door closed behind us, swore when he saw there was only one bolt remaining, near the top, and swore again when he found it thick and immobile with rust. I assisted, and together we managed to grind it into place. After that, we backed off, unsure what would happen next, hoping that this would be the end of it.

For several seconds there was no sound. Finally we glanced around. It was hot and stuffy in there, and completely bare, an empty box except for some broken planks and a few piles of leaves. There was certainly nothing we could use as a weapon, though perhaps a weapon wouldn't be needed.

"*Brian.*"

That terrible cawing voice again. Just outside.

Brian turned a sweat-drenched moon-face towards me. But he seemed outraged rather than terrified; as if it was just so damn unfair that this thing – this terrible, unknowable thing – was ready to pick on him before anyone else.

Arthritic timber squeaked as new weight arrived on the catwalk.

We each backed into a different corner, listening to the scrabbling of claws on the other side of the door. I sank to my haunches, eyeing the shadow filling the gap at the bottom. Hugged myself as the door began bowing in its frame, the woodwork shuddering.

"You can't come in here!" Brian bleated. "Go away!"

The weight against the door relaxed. There was a taut, lingering silence. And then a heavy blow. The door shook violently. We screamed. When a second blow followed, Brian screamed even louder. By some miracle the ancient bolt mechanism held.

I felt a brief sense of hope as the shadow disappeared from the gap, only to freeze up again when I heard the scraping and scuffling of some heavy object scaling the side of the signal box. Dust drifted down as it moved across the roof. I peered up through hooked fingers, but it was only when the twisted silhouette appeared in the skylight hatch and halted there, stiff and silent, that I screwed my eyes shut.

I heard it as it clambered in: the rustling of its rancid, ragged clothing; the creaking of its dried, long-dead limbs; the heavy impact as it landed a few yards away. I whimpered and wept and curled into a ball, and imagined it was the same with Brian. I certainly didn't hear any sound of him trying to get away, but just to ensure this didn't happen, I pointed and shouted, "There! Over there! That's him. That's the one you want!"

You look at me with loathing. But what would you have done?

He'd already been marked. His was the name it had called, not mine. But in any case, I doubt it needed further identification. It was *his* corner it lumbered over to. *He* was the one who squealed like a trapped piglet when I presume it laid its hands upon him. After that, I heard him chunnering some verse or other as he was carried up and away, and I realised he was saying the *Our Father*, though it lost all coherence when he was taken out through the skylight, transforming into a series of hoarse, gibbering shrieks, which gradually faded into the summer afternoon.

All I remember after that is how quiet it was in there. And though suffocatingly warm, how at peace I felt. I certainly had no desire to move from my corner.

I knew that I was safe. I knew it was over. I just wasn't taking any chances.

★   ★   ★

"Why did the prayer not work for him, when it had for the signalman?" Gates mused as he rolled himself another cigarette. "I've often wondered if perhaps a degree of genuine belief is required. I mean, Brian professed belief, but, well... raised in a household where Bibles were used as weapons, he must have been confused."

"You must think *we're* confused to believe a story like that," the younger detective said.

Gates smirked. "What you believe is immaterial to me. My die is cast."

"Don't be too sure of that, Mr. Gates," the younger detective replied. "There are only two reasons you weren't charged back in 1973. Firstly, because you were so young and seemed so messed up by it yourself. And secondly, and more importantly, because there was no physical evidence. But times have moved on, and so have forensics."

Gates shrugged. "Present them."

The older detective leaned forward, again offering a light. "You were found sleeping in that derelict signal box. Two whole days after this incident you allege."

"As I said," Gates replied, "I had no desire to move."

"The search parties found no trace of Brian O'Rourke. Only his backpack, which had been dumped in the woods on the Hanbury Hall estate... torn to shreds."

"I can only assume that happened in the fight."

They watched him carefully.

"Fight?" the younger one said.

"The fight he presumably put up before it ended for him."

"Is it possible," the older detective said, "that this... thing, this person who pursued you, could have been an ordinary man wearing a costume?"

"I've considered that over the years," Gates replied. "But no, I don't think so. We all know who it was. Why try to hide from the fact?"

"Because it's not a fact," the younger detective said heatedly.

Gates regarded them as he smoked. Then smiled wryly. "I really don't know why I'm playing this game... attempting to persuade you of something you clearly had no intention to believe. Why would you, when all you're doing here is fishing for a conviction you've never earned? But at the very least, you must admit it all adds up?"

"Nothing adds up," the younger detective said, sounding affronted. "I can't imagine what it is you think you're trying to sell us. That this... *thing* took Brian O'Rourke because he was gay?"

Gates blew out a wad of smoke. "Only a true millennial idiot would think I was trying to sell you that."

"You were found back in 1973," the older detective said, "because when your two pictures appeared on the local news, an old lady recognised you as having travelled up there on the bus. When the search was launched, they didn't just find you and Brian O'Rourke's backpack, they also found the bag of magazines you mentioned."

Gates shrugged.

The older cop leaned forward. "So, we've no reason to doubt anything you told us up to that point."

"It's what you say happened after that that gives us a problem," the younger one added. "You trying to pretend that Brian O'Rourke being gay had nothing to do with it is a give-away in itself. You see, we believe it had *everything* to do with it."

"We think he *did* lure you up to that old railway line under false pretences," the older one said. "He'd developed a crush on you because you were one of the few people who'd tolerated him while he was at school. But by your own admission, this tolerance had its limits. And when you found out what he really wanted you flew into an uncontrollable rage. Which we all know you're more than capable of."

This time Gates looked at them pityingly. "Brian O'Rourke was *not* taken because he was gay."

"You attacked him, didn't you?" the younger one said. "Maybe you didn't intend to kill him, but..."

"Did I attack the signalman in the 1950s? Or those other people, who, if you bother to do any research, you'll notice have also gone missing from the Branch Line? Some as far back as the 1920s?"

"Genuine reports of people who've gone missing up there are countable on one hand," the older detective said. "And we're talking over a period of many decades. It's hardly conclusive."

"Not everyone who walks the Branch Line will be a victim," Gates agreed. "But think about the signalman. He actually existed. His name was Harold Collier, and he'd just lost his wife. Then think about Brian O'Rourke and what he had lost. Gentlemen, it surely can't really be that the brightest thing about you is your buttons. Why else do you think I killed Gaynor Grant in 1981? Why did I kill Jenny Hurst in 1995? And why not any of the other women I've had relationships with over the years?"

"No doubt those two said the wrong thing to you, Mr. Gates." The older detective gathered his papers together. "Just like Brian O'Rourke. Look, we're done here." He stood up. "We've wasted enough time on this."

"Because I was getting close to them, maybe?" Gates said, answering his own question.

The detectives glanced back at him, perhaps partially interested in that, but mainly because he disgusted them. The interview room's barred door closed behind them with a clang.

"You probably don't believe that," Gates called out. "When you see me, you see a madman with a hair-trigger temper. But don't draw comfort from *that*." They walked away down the gunmetal grey passage, his voice echoing after them. "Don't think *that's* all it is. And don't get close to anyone, detectives. Ever. Because if you do, and you lose them – your fault, someone else's fault, it doesn't matter – *she* will know. *You hear me?*"

That final shout was a howl, the other inmates shrieking from their cells in response.

"Don't chance the Branch Line if you've lost the love of your life." He calmed again, the rollup dangling from his fingers. "Because even if no one else hears your tears, *she* will."

BIOGRAPHIES

Michael Bailey is a writer, editor, book designer and a resident of forever-burning California. He is the recipient of the Bram Stoker Award, the Benjamin Franklin Award, over two dozen independent accolades, and a Shirley Jackson Award nominee. Publications include the novels *Palindrome Hannah* and *Phoenix Rose*, the fiction and poetry collections *Scales and Petals*, *Inkblots and Blood Spots* and *Oversight*, and more than sixty published stories, novelettes and poems. Edited anthologies include *The Library of the Dead*, *You Human*, *Adam's Ladder*, four volumes of *Chiral Mad*, and many more. Find him online at nettirw.com.

Simon Bestwick is the author of six horror, dark fantasy and post-apocalyptic novels, the novellas *Breakwater* and *Angels of the Silences* and several short story collections. His short fiction has appeared in *Black Static*, *The Devil and the Deep* and *The London Reader* and has been reprinted in *Best Horror of the Year*. Four times shortlisted for the British Fantasy Award, he is married to long-suffering fellow author Cate Gardner, with whom he lives on the Wirral while striving to avoid reality in general and gainful employment in particular. His latest books are the story collection *And Cannot Come Again*, newly reissued by Horrific Tales, and the novel *Wolf's Hill* (the third in the Black Road series, also due for reissue by Horrific Tales in 2021).

The *Oxford Companion to English Literature* describes **Ramsey Campbell** as 'Britain's most respected living horror writer'. He has been given more awards than any other writer in the field, including the Grand Master Award of the World Horror Convention, the Lifetime Achievement Award of the Horror Writers Association, the Living Legend Award of the International Horror Guild and the World Fantasy Lifetime Achievement Award. In 2015 he was made an Honorary

Fellow of Liverpool John Moores University for outstanding services to literature. Among his novels are *The Face That Must Die, Incarnate, Midnight Sun, The Count of Eleven, Silent Children, The Darkest Part of the Woods, The Overnight, Secret Story, The Grin of the Dark, Thieving Fear, Creatures of the Pool, The Seven Days of Cain, Ghosts Know, The Kind Folk, Think Yourself Lucky, Thirteen Days by Sunset Beach* and *The Wise Friend*. He recently brought out his Brichester Mythos trilogy, consisting of *The Searching Dead, Born to the Dark* and *The Way of the Worm*. *Needing Ghosts, The Last Revelation of Gla'aki, The Pretence* and *The Booking* are novellas. His collections include *Waking Nightmares, Alone with the Horrors, Ghosts and Grisly Things, Told by the Dead, Just Behind You, Holes for Faces, By the Light of My Skull* and a two-volume retrospective roundup (*Phantasmagorical Stories*). His non-fiction is collected as *Ramsey Campbell, Probably* and *Ramsey's Rambles* (video reviews). *Limericks of the Alarming and Phantasmal* is a history of horror fiction in the form of fifty limericks. His novels *The Nameless, Pact of the Fathers* and *The Influence* have been filmed in Spain. He is the President of the Society of Fantastic Films. Ramsey Campbell lives on Merseyside with his wife Jenny. His pleasures include classical music, good food and wine, and whatever's in that pipe. His website is at www.ramseycampbell.com.

Rick Cross is the author of *Lethbridge-Stewart: Times Squared*, co-author of *Lobster Tales* and *Warp: A Speculative Trio*, and a contributor to *Lethbridge-Stewart: The HAVOC Files 2*. He is a founding member of the Loose Lobsters writing collective and for twenty-one years has been the senior media writer at NASA's Marshall Space Flight Center in Huntsville, Alabama, where he lives with his wife Heather, their son Declan and a feisty dog named Lexie who insists she's a panther. Find him on Facebook: facebook.com/rickcrosswriter.

Paul Finch, a former cop and journalist now turned best-selling crime and thriller writer, is the author of the very popular DS Mark 'Heck' Heckenburg and DC Lucy Clayburn novels. Paul first cut his literary teeth penning episodes of the British TV crime drama *The Bill*, and has written extensively in horror, fantasy and science fiction, including for *Doctor Who*. However, he is probably best known for his crime/thriller novels, specifically the Heckenburg police-actioners, of which there are seven to date, and the Clayburn procedurals, of which there are three. The first three books in the Heck line achieved official best-seller status, the second being the fastest pre-ordered title in HarperCollins history, while the first Lucy Clayburn novel made the Sunday Times Top 10 list. The Heck series alone has accrued over 2,000 5-star reviews on Amazon. His first crime thriller from Orion Books, *One Eye Open*, was published in 2019. Paul is a native of Wigan, Lancashire, where he still lives with his wife and business partner, Cathy.

Elana Gomel is an academic and a writer. She has taught and researched English literature and cultural studies at Tel-Aviv University, Princeton, Stanford, Venice International University and the University of Hong Kong. She speaks three languages and has two children. She has published six non-fiction books and numerous articles on posthumanism, science fiction, Victorian literature and serial killers. Her fantasy, horror and science fiction stories have appeared in *Apex Magazine, New Horizons, The Fantasist, Timeless Tales, New Realms, Alien Dimensions*, and others. Her stories have also featured in several award-winning anthologies, including *Zion's Fiction, Apex Book of World Science Fiction* and *People of the Book*. She is the author of three novels, *A Tale of Three Cities* (2013), *The Hungry Ones* (2018) and *The Cryptids* (2019). When not busy writing or teaching, she can be found on a plane, heading for distant countries in search of new monsters.

Grady Hendrix is the Stoker Award-winning author of *Paperbacks From Hell*, and he avoids speaking with demons whenever possible. His novels include *My Best Friend's Exorcism, The Southern Book Club's Guide to Slaying Vampires, We Sold Our Souls* and *Horrorstor*. His movies include *Mohawk* and *Satanic Panic*. You can hear him blather on and on at www.gradyhendrix.com.

John Langan is the author of two novels and three collections of stories. For his work, he has received the Bram Stoker and This Is Horror Awards. His new book *Children of the Fang and Other Genealogies* is his fourth collection. He lives in New York's Mid-Hudson Valley with his wife and younger son.

Tim Lebbon is a New York Times best-selling writer from South Wales. He has had over forty novels published to date, as well as hundreds of novellas and short stories. His latest work is the eco-horror novel *Eden*. Other recent releases include *The Edge*, *The Silence*, *The Family Man*, *The Rage War* trilogy, and *Blood of the Four* with Christopher Golden. He has won four British Fantasy Awards, a Bram Stoker Award, and a Scribe Award, and has been a finalist for World Fantasy, International Horror Guild and Shirley Jackson Awards. His work has appeared in many Year's Best anthologies, as well as Century's Best Horror. The movie of *The Silence*, starring Stanley Tucci and Kiernan Shipka, debuted on Netflix in April 2019, and *Pay the Ghost*, starring Nicolas Cage, was released for Halloween 2015. Several other projects are in development for TV and the big screen, including original screenplays *Playtime* (with Stephen Volk) and *My Haunted House*. Find out more about Tim at his website www.timlebbon.net

Jonathan Robbins Leon describes himself as a queer author of contemporary and speculative fiction. He wrote the screenplay for *Signal Lost*, which recently debuted at the Central Florida Film Festival, and his work has appeared on *A Story Most Queer* and *Tales to Terrify*. He lives in a dusty, historic house with his husband and son only blocks away from the library he haunts in Kissimmee, Florida.

Alison Littlewood's latest novel *Mistletoe* is a seasonal ghost story with glimpses into the Victorian era. Her first book *A Cold Season* was selected for the Richard and Judy Book Club and described as 'perfect reading for a dark winter's night'. Other titles include *A Cold Silence*, *Path of Needles*, *The Unquiet House*, *Zombie Apocalypse! Acapulcalypse Now*, *The Hidden People* and *The Crow Garden*. Alison's short stories have been picked for a number of year's best anthologies and published in her collections *Quieter Paths* and *Five Feathered Tales*. She has won the Shirley Jackson Award for Short Fiction. Alison lives with her partner Fergus in Yorkshire, in a house of creaking doors and crooked walls. She loves exploring the hills and dales with her two hugely enthusiastic Dalmatians and has a penchant for books on folklore and weird history, Earl Grey tea, fountain pens and semicolons. Visit her at www.alisonlittlewood.co.uk.

Sarah Lotz is a novelist and screenwriter with a fondness for the macabre. Her collaborative and solo novels have been translated into over twenty-five languages. Her most recent work includes the novels *The Three*, *Day Four*, *The White Road* and *Missing Person*. She currently lives in the UK with her family and other animals.

Mark Morris (Editor) has written and edited almost forty novels, novellas, short story collections and anthologies. His script work includes audio dramas for *Doctor Who*, *Jago & Litefoot* and the *Hammer Chillers* series. Mark's recent work includes the official movie tie-in novelisations of *The Great Wall* and (co-written with Christopher Golden) *The Predator*, the Obsidian Heart trilogy, and the anthologies *New Fears* (winner of the British Fantasy Award for Best Anthology) and *New Fears 2* as editor. He's also written award-winning audio adaptations of the classic 1971 horror movie *Blood on Satan's Claw* and the M.R. James ghost story 'A View from a Hill'.

Thana Niveau is a horror and science fiction writer. Originally from the States, she now lives in the UK, in a Victorian seaside town between Bristol and Wales. She is the author of the short story collections *Octoberland*, *Unquiet Waters* and *From Hell to Eternity*, as well as the novel *House of Frozen Screams*. Her work has been reprinted in *Best New Horror* and *Best British Horror*. She has been shortlisted three times for the British Fantasy Award – for *Octoberland* and *From Hell to Eternity*, and for her story *Death Walks En Pointe*.

Laura Purcell is a former bookseller, who lives in Colchester with her husband and pet guinea pigs. Her gothic novel *The Silent Companions* was a Radio 2 Book Club pick, appeared on the Zoe Ball ITV Book Club and won the WHSmith Thumping Good Read Award. Her most recent novels are *The Corset* and *Bone China*.

Robert Shearman has written six short story collections, and between them they have won the World Fantasy Award, the Shirley Jackson Award, the Edge Hill Readers Prize and four British Fantasy Awards. He began his career in the theatre, and was resident dramatist at the Northcott Theatre in Exeter and regular writer for

Alan Ayckbourn at the Stephen Joseph Theatre in Scarborough; his plays have won the Sunday Times Playwriting Award, the World Drama Trust Award and the Guinness Award for Ingenuity in association with the Royal National Theatre. A regular writer for BBC Radio, his own interactive drama series *The Chain Gang* has won two Sony Awards. But he is probably best known for his work on *Doctor Who*, bringing back the Daleks for the BAFTA winning first series in an episode nominated for a Hugo Award. His latest books are *We All Hear Stories in the Dark*, an interactive modern spin upon the Arabian Nights, and a novelisation of his *Doctor Who* episode *Dalek* for Target.

Angela Slatter is the author of the Verity Fassbinder supernatural crime series (*Vigil, Corpselight, Restoration*) and nine short story collections, including *The Bitterwood Bible and Other Recountings* and *Winter Children and Other Chilling Tales*. Her gothic fantasy novels, *All These Murmuring Bones* and *Morwood*, will be published by Titan in 2021 and 2022 respectively. She's won a World Fantasy, a British Fantasy, an Australian Shadows and six Aurealis Awards; her debut novel was nominated for the Dublin Literary Award. Her work has been translated into French, Chinese, Spanish, Japanese, Italian, Bulgarian and Russian. You can find her at www.angelaslatter.com, @AngelaSlatter on Twitter, and as angelalslatter on Instagram for photos of food and dogs that belong to someone else (the dogs, not the food).

Michael Marshall Smith is a novelist and screenwriter. Under this name he has published over ninety short stories and five novels – *Only Forward, Spares, One of Us, The Servants* and *Hannah Green and her Unfeasibly Mundane Existence* – winning the Philip K. Dick, International Horror Guild, and August Derleth Awards, along with the Prix Bob Morane in France. He has won the British Fantasy Award for Best Short Fiction four times, more than any other author; and 2020 will see a *Best of Michael Marshall Smith* collection. Writing as Michael Marshall he has written seven internationally-best-selling thrillers including *The Straw Men* series, *The Intruders* – made into a BBCAmerica series starring John Simm and Mira Sorvino – and *Killer Move*. His most recent novel under this name is *We Are Here*. Now additionally writing as Michael Rutger, in 2018 he published the adventure thriller *The Anomaly*. A sequel, *The Possession*, was published in 2019. He is currently co-writing and exec producing development of *The Straw Men* for television. He is also Creative Consultant to The Blank Corporation, Neil Gaiman's production company in Los Angeles, and involved in the development of multiple shows including *Neverwhere* and *American Gods*. He lives in Santa Cruz, California, with his wife, son, and three cats.

Main Site: www.michaelmarshallsmith.com

eBooks: www.ememess.com

Twitter: @ememess

Instagram: @ememess

C.J. Tudor grew up in Nottingham and now lives in Sussex with her husband and young daughter. She left school at sixteen and has had a variety of jobs over the years, including trainee reporter, radio scriptwriter, TV presenter, voiceover artist and dog-walker. Her first novel *The Chalk Man* was a Sunday Times best-seller, sold to over forty countries and won the ITW Award for Best First Novel, The Strand Award for Best Debut and the Barry Award for Best Debut. Her second novel *The Taking of Annie Thorne* was also a Sunday Times best-seller. Her third novel *The Other People* has just been published. All three books have been optioned for TV. Everyone calls her Caz.

Stephen Volk is best known for the BBC's notorious 'Halloween hoax' *Ghostwatch* and the award-winning ITV drama series *Afterlife* starring Andrew Lincoln and Lesley Sharp. His other screenplays include *The Awakening* starring Rebecca Hall, and *Gothic* starring Natasha Richardson as Mary Shelley. He is a Bram Stoker Award and Shirley Jackson Award finalist, a BAFTA winner, and the author of three collections: *Dark Corners, Monsters in the Heart* (which won the British Fantasy Award) and *The Parts We Play*. Arguably his most acclaimed fiction so far is *The Dark Masters* trilogy, consisting of *Whitstable*, which has as its protagonist Peter Cushing; *Leytonstone*, based on the boyhood of Alfred Hitchcock; and *Netherwood*, featuring novelist Dennis Wheatley and occultist Aleister Crowley. His provocative non-fiction is collected in *Coffinmaker's Blues: Collected Writings on Terror.*

Catriona Ward was born in Washington, D.C. and grew up in the United States, Kenya, Madagascar, Yemen and Morocco. She read English at St. Edmund Hall, Oxford and is a graduate of the Creative Writing MA at the University of East Anglia. Her next gothic thriller *The Last House on Needless Street* will be published in March 2021 by Viper, an imprint of Serpents Tail, followed by a further book in 2022. Her last novel *Little Eve* (Weidenfeld & Nicolson, 2018) won the 2019 Shirley Jackson Award and the August Derleth Award for Best Horror Novel at the 2019 British Fantasy Awards, and was a Guardian Best Book of 2018. Her debut *Rawblood* (W&N, 2015) won Best Horror Novel at the 2016 British Fantasy Awards, was shortlisted for the Author's Club Best First Novel Award and a WHSmith Fresh Talent title. Her short stories have appeared in numerous anthologies. She lives in London and Devon.

FLAME TREE PRESS
FICTION WITHOUT FRONTIERS
Award-Winning Authors & Original Voices

Flame Tree Press is the trade fiction imprint of Flame Tree Publishing, focusing on excellent writing in horror and the supernatural, crime and mystery, science fiction and fantasy. Our aim is to explore beyond the boundaries of the everyday, with tales from both award-winning authors and original voices.

•

Other horror and suspense titles available include:
Snowball by Gregory Bastianelli
Thirteen Days by Sunset Beach by Ramsey Campbell
The Hungry Moon by Ramsey Campbell
The Wise Friend by Ramsey Campbell
The Haunting of Henderson Close by Catherine Cavendish
The Garden of Bewitchment by Catherine Cavendish
The House by the Cemetery by John Everson
The Devil's Equinox by John Everson
Voodoo Heart by John Everson
Hellrider by JG Faherty
Sins of the Father by JG Faherty
Boy in the Box by Marc E. Fitch
The Toy Thief by D.W. Gillespie
One By One by D.W. Gillespie
Black Wings by Megan Hart
The Playing Card Killer by Russell James
The Portal by Russell James
The Dark Game by Jonathan Janz
The Raven by Jonathan Janz
Will Haunt You by Brian Kirk
We Are Monsters by Brian Kirk
Greyfriars Reformatory by Frazer Lee
Those Who Came Before by J.H. Moncrieff
Stoker's Wilde by Steven Hopstaken & Melissa Prusi
Stoker's Wilde West by Steven Hopstaken & Melissa Prusi
Creature by Hunter Shea
Slash by Hunter Shea
Misfits by Hunter Shea
The Mouth of the Dark by Tim Waggoner
They Kill by Tim Waggoner

•

Join our mailing list for free short stories, new release details, news about our authors and special promotions:

flametreepress.com